the BOOK CLASH

Legendary Legends
of Legendarious
Achievery
Volume 1

the BOOKS of CLASH

Legendary Legends of Legendarious Achievery

Volume 1

WRITTEN BY GENE LUEN YANG
PENCILS BY LES McCLAINE
INKS BY ALISON ACTON
COLOR BY KARINA EDWARDS & ALEX CAMPBELL

EDITED BY MARK SIEGEL & HEATHER ANTOS
DESIGNED BY KIRK BENSHOFF, ANGELA BOYLE & MOLLY JOHANSON
PRODUCTION EDITING BY DAWN RYAN & AVIA PEREZ
SPECIAL THANKS TO THE SUPERCELL TEAM: PATRICK ALMGREN, MIGUEL DIAZ,
MICHAEL GURMAN, LYLA JEONG, BILL KANG & RACHAEL SLOCUM

First Second
NEW YORK

SUP
ERC
ELL

CHAPTER 1

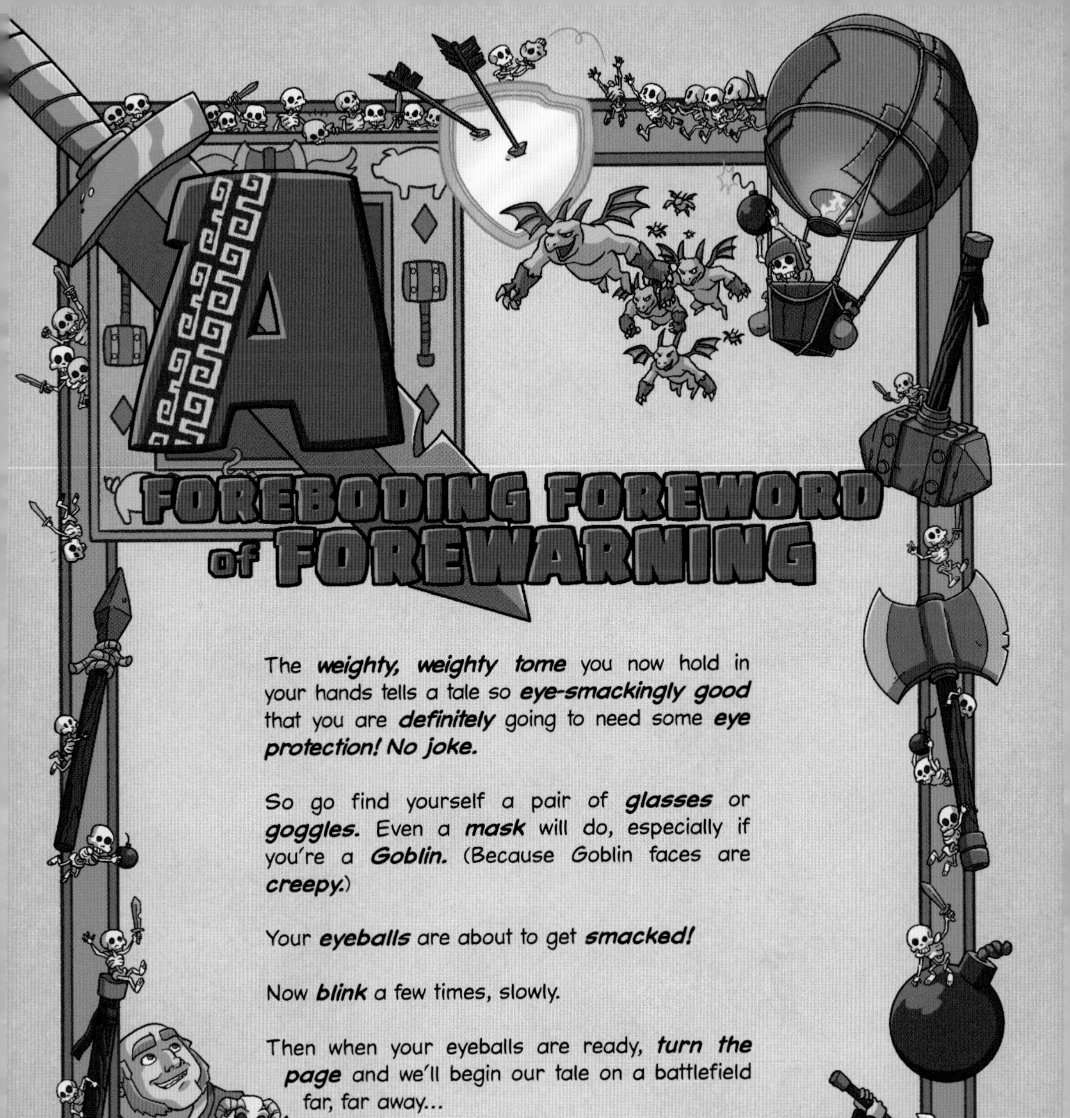

FOREBODING FOREWORD of FOREWARNING

The ***weighty, weighty tome*** you now hold in your hands tells a tale so ***eye-smackingly good*** that you are ***definitely*** going to need some ***eye protection! No joke.***

So go find yourself a pair of ***glasses*** or ***goggles.*** Even a ***mask*** will do, especially if you're a ***Goblin.*** (Because Goblin faces are ***creepy.***)

Your ***eyeballs*** are about to get ***smacked!***

Now ***blink*** a few times, slowly.

Then when your eyeballs are ready, ***turn the page*** and we'll begin our tale on a battlefield far, far away...

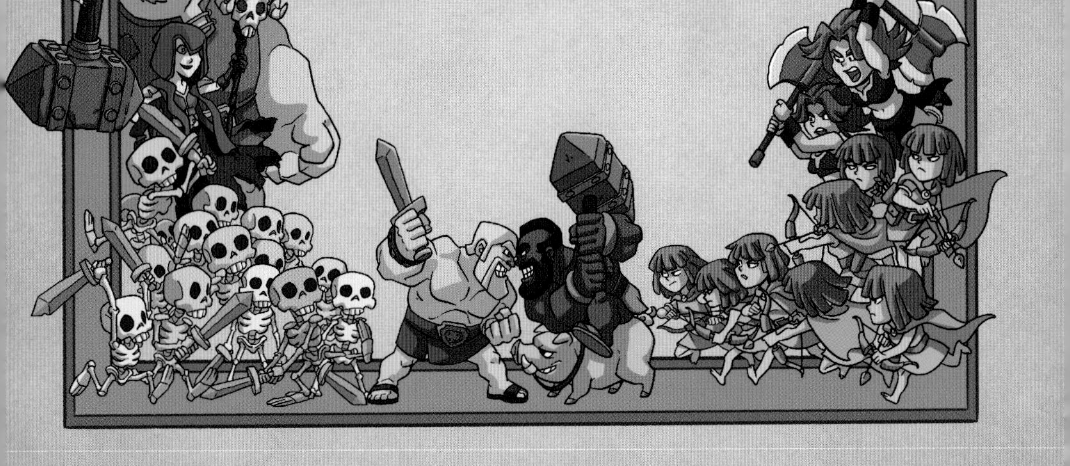

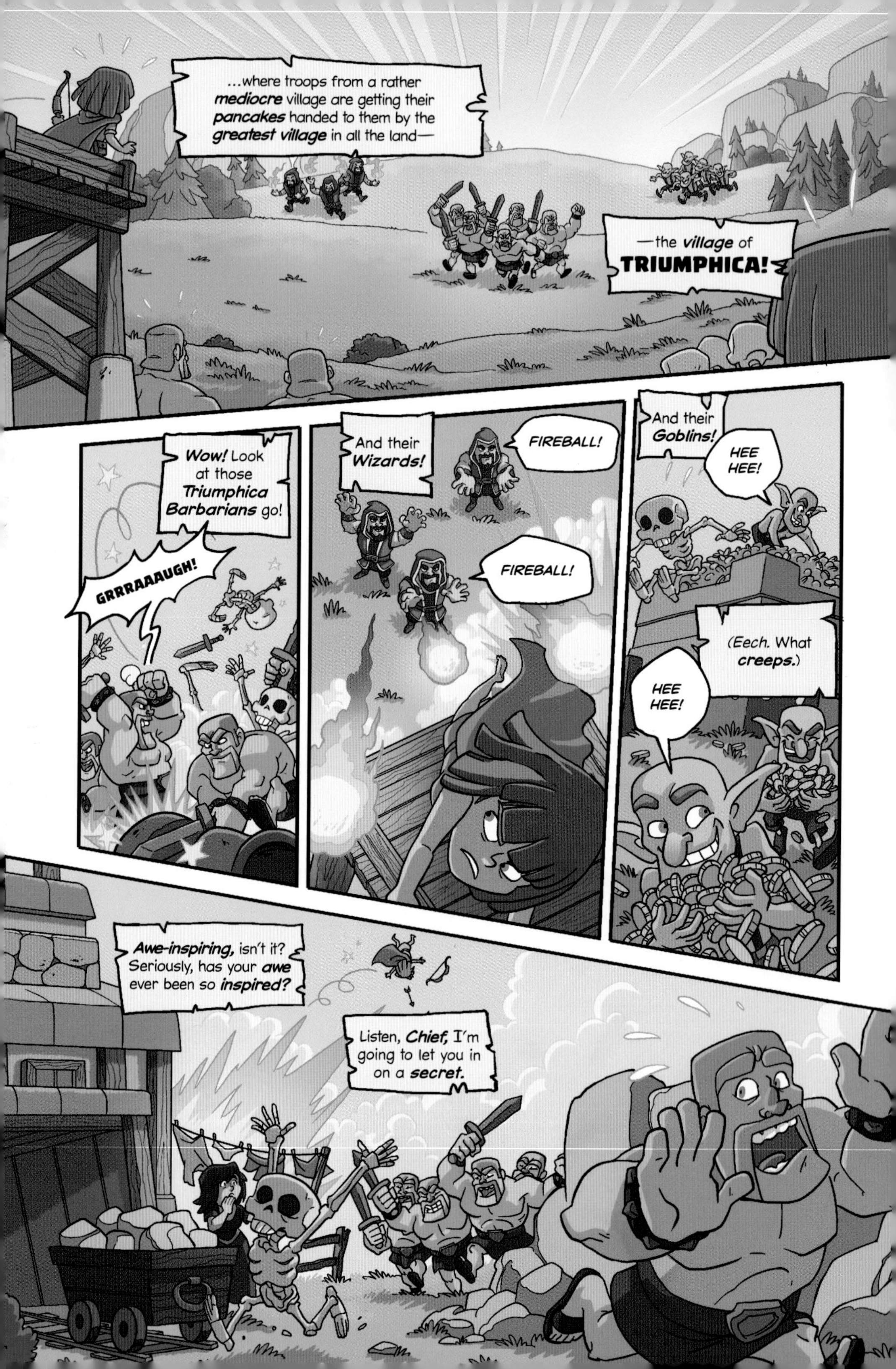

...where troops from a rather mediocre village are getting their pancakes handed to them by the greatest village in all the land—
—the village of TRIUMPHICA!
Wow! Look at those Triumphica Barbarians go!
GRRRAAAUGH!
And their Wizards!
FIREBALL!
FIREBALL!
And their Goblins!
HEE HEE!
(Eech. What creeps.)
HEE HEE!
Awe-inspiring, isn't it? Seriously, has your awe ever been so inspired?
Listen, Chief, I'm going to let you in on a secret.

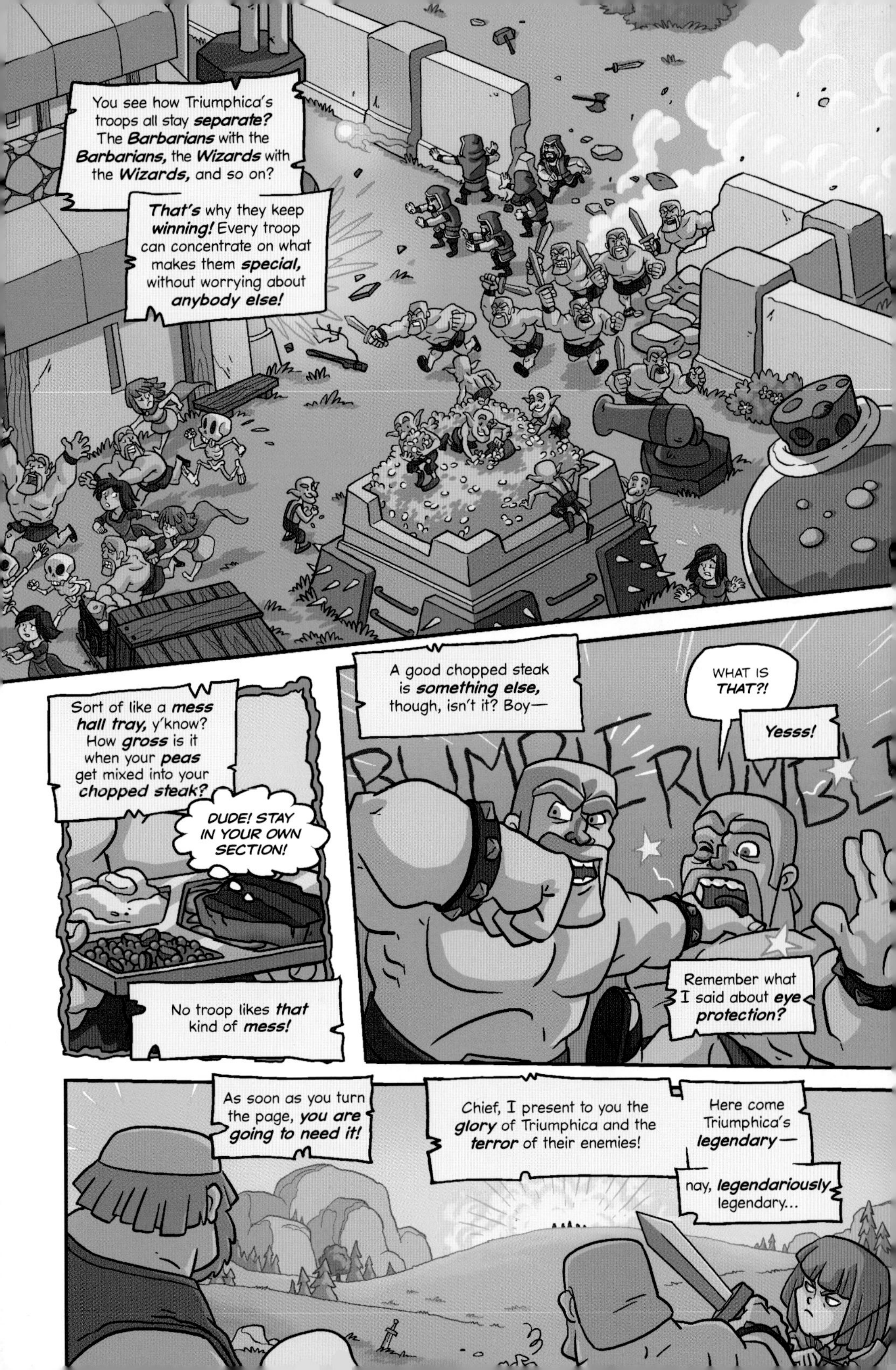
You see how Triumphica's troops all stay *separate?* The *Barbarians* with the *Barbarians,* the *Wizards* with the *Wizards,* and so on?
That's why they keep *winning!* Every troop can concentrate on what makes them *special,* without worrying about *anybody else!*
Sort of like a *mess hall tray,* y'know? How *gross* is it when your *peas* get mixed into your *chopped steak?*
DUDE! STAY IN YOUR OWN SECTION!
No troop likes *that* kind of *mess!*
A good chopped steak is *something else,* though, isn't it? Boy—
WHAT IS *THAT?!*
Yesss!
RUMBLE RUMBLE
Remember what I said about *eye protection?*
As soon as you turn the page, *you are going to need it!*
Chief, I present to you the *glory* of Triumphica and the *terror* of their enemies!
Here come Triumphica's *legendary*—
nay, *legendariously* legendary...

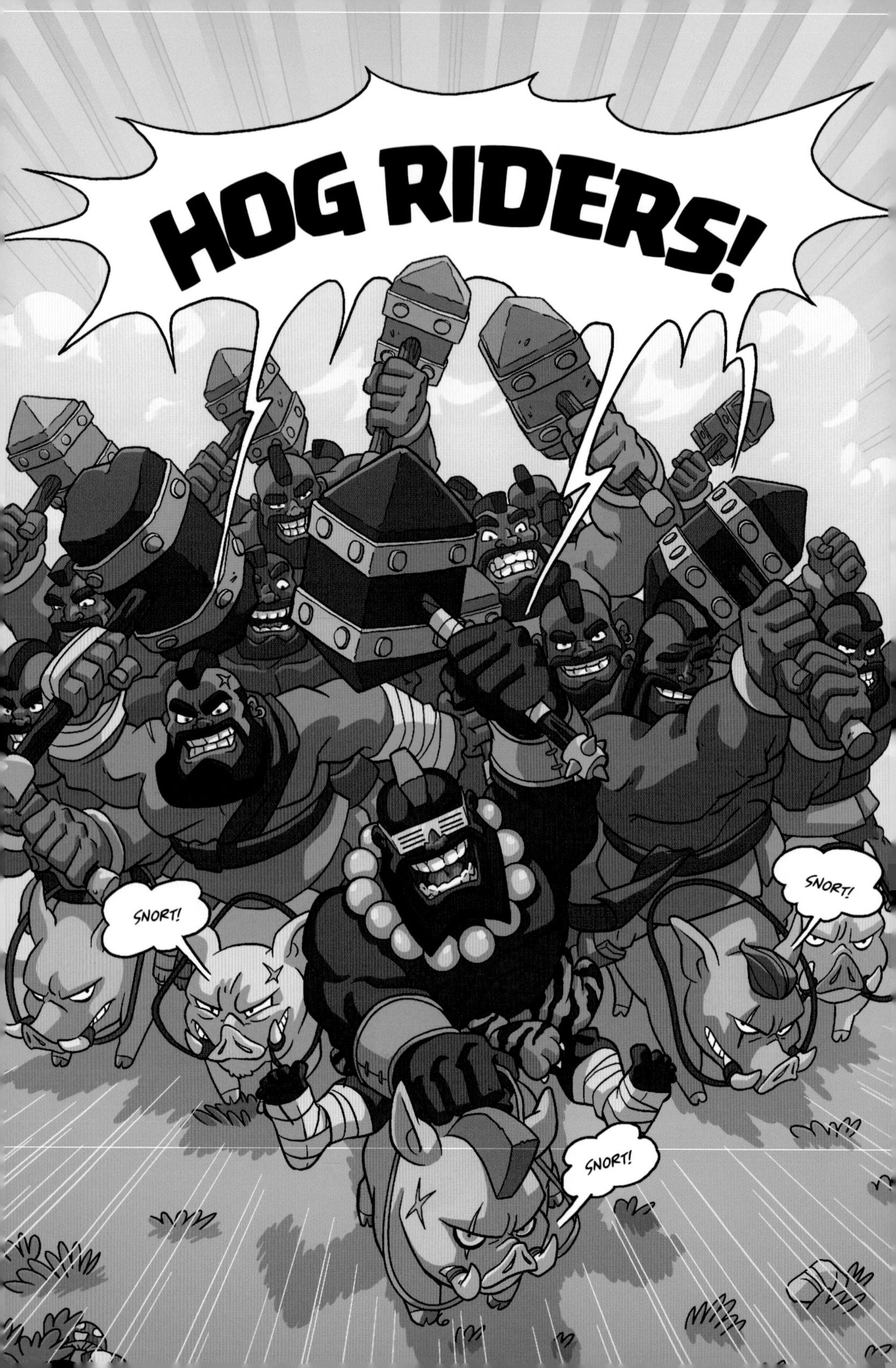
HOG RIDERS!
SNORT!
SNORT!
SNORT!

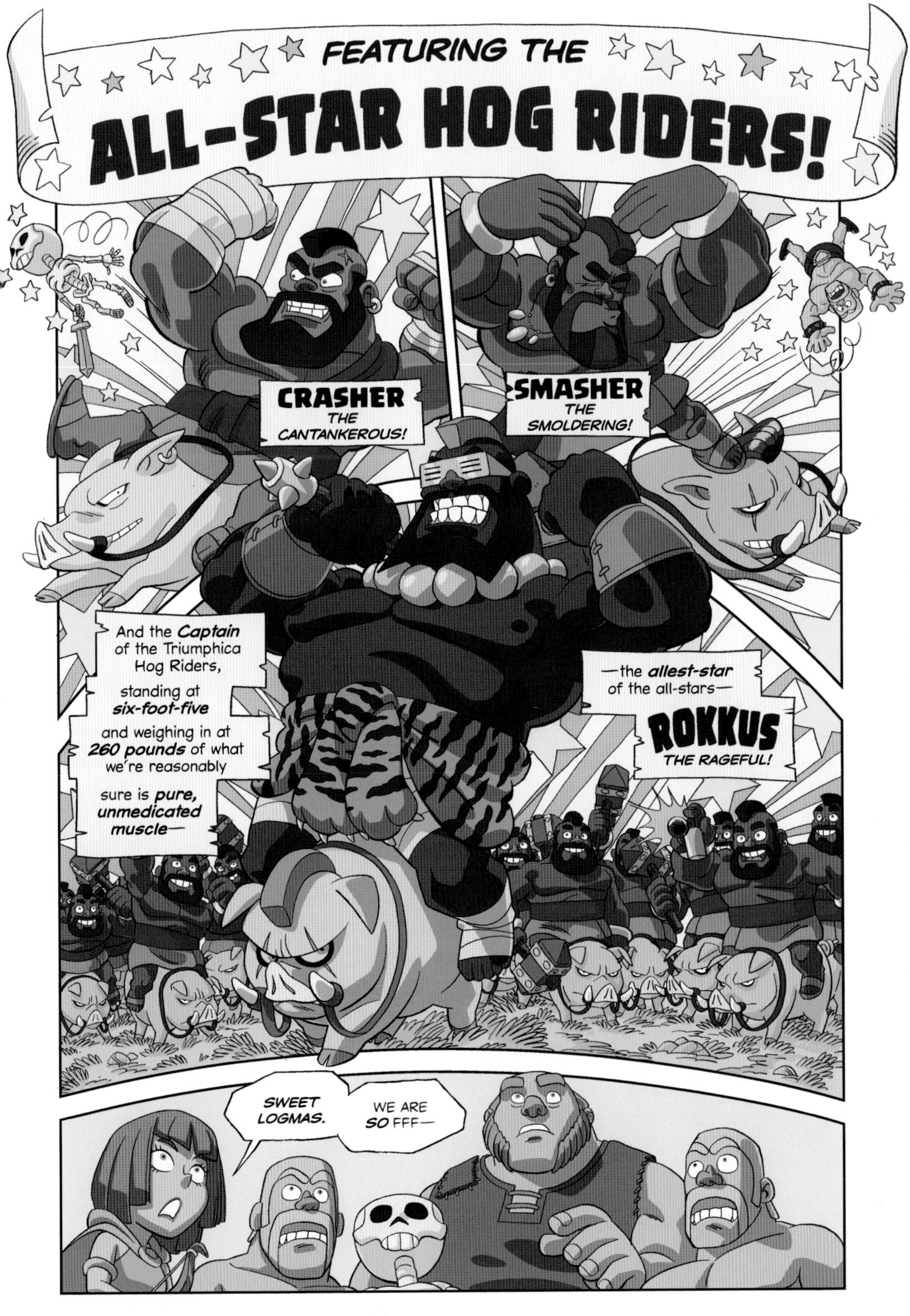
FEATURING THE
ALL-STAR HOG RIDERS!
CRASHER THE CANTANKEROUS!
SMASHER THE SMOLDERING!
And the Captain of the Triumphica Hog Riders,
standing at six-foot-five
and weighing in at 260 pounds of what we're reasonably
sure is pure, unmedicated muscle—
—the allest-star of the all-stars—
ROKKUS THE RAGEFUL!
SWEET LOGMAS.
WE ARE SO FFF—

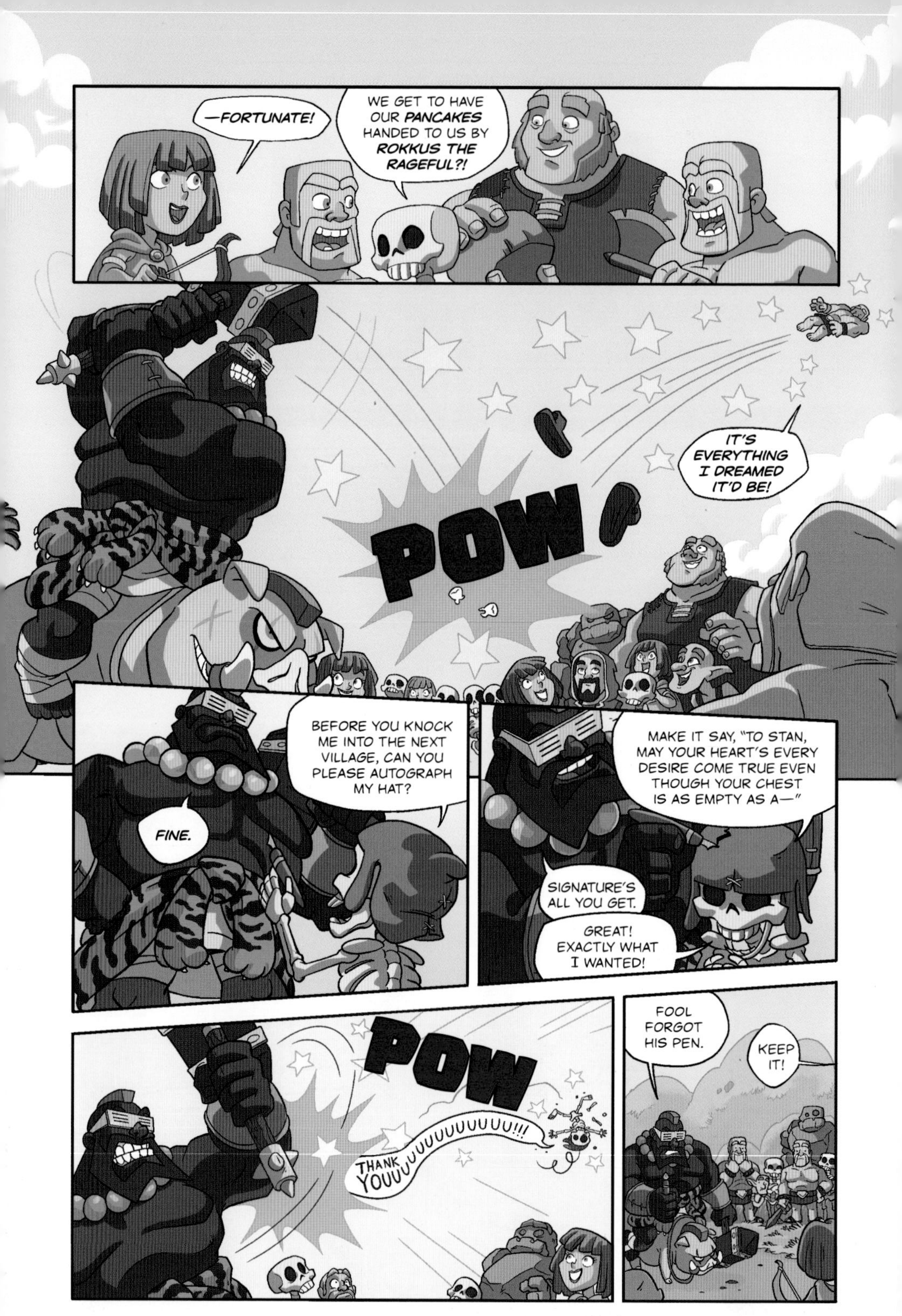
—FORTUNATE!
WE GET TO HAVE OUR PANCAKES HANDED TO US BY ROKKUS THE RAGEFUL?!
IT'S EVERYTHING I DREAMED IT'D BE!
POW
BEFORE YOU KNOCK ME INTO THE NEXT VILLAGE, CAN YOU PLEASE AUTOGRAPH MY HAT?
FINE.
MAKE IT SAY, "TO STAN, MAY YOUR HEART'S EVERY DESIRE COME TRUE EVEN THOUGH YOUR CHEST IS AS EMPTY AS A—"
SIGNATURE'S ALL YOU GET.
GREAT! EXACTLY WHAT I WANTED!
POW
THANK YOUUUUUUUUUUUUUU!!!
FOOL FORGOT HIS PEN.
KEEP IT!

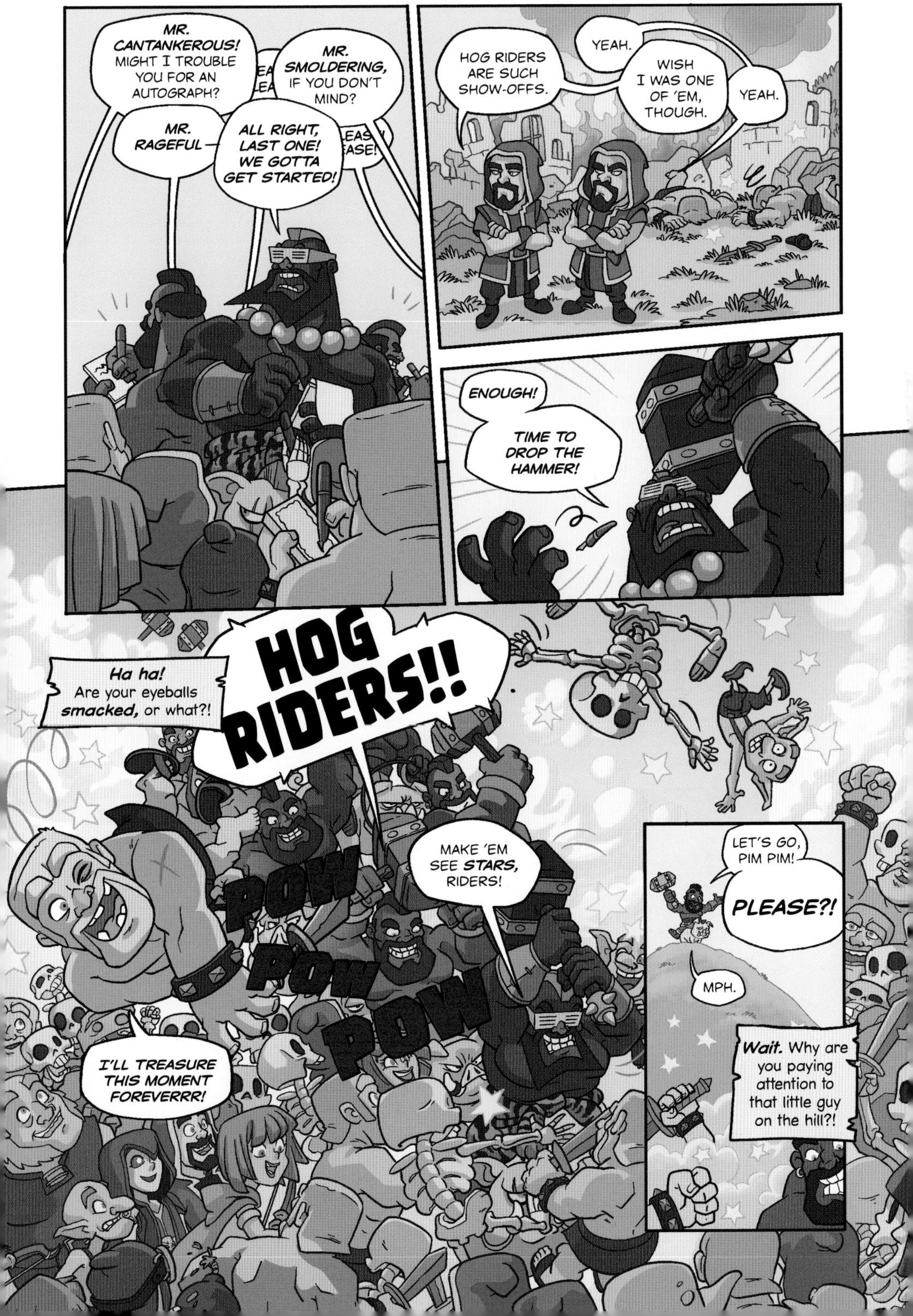
MR. CANTANKEROUS! MIGHT I TROUBLE YOU FOR AN AUTOGRAPH?
MR. RAGEFUL—
MR. SMOLDERING, IF YOU DON'T MIND?
ALL RIGHT, LAST ONE! WE GOTTA GET STARTED!
HOG RIDERS ARE SUCH SHOW-OFFS.
YEAH.
WISH I WAS ONE OF 'EM, THOUGH.
YEAH.
ENOUGH!
TIME TO DROP THE HAMMER!
HOG RIDERS!!
Ha ha! Are your eyeballs smacked, or what?!
MAKE 'EM SEE STARS, RIDERS!
POW POW POW
I'LL TREASURE THIS MOMENT FOREVERRR!
LET'S GO, PIM PIM!
PLEASE?!
MPH.
Wait. Why are you paying attention to that little guy on the hill?!

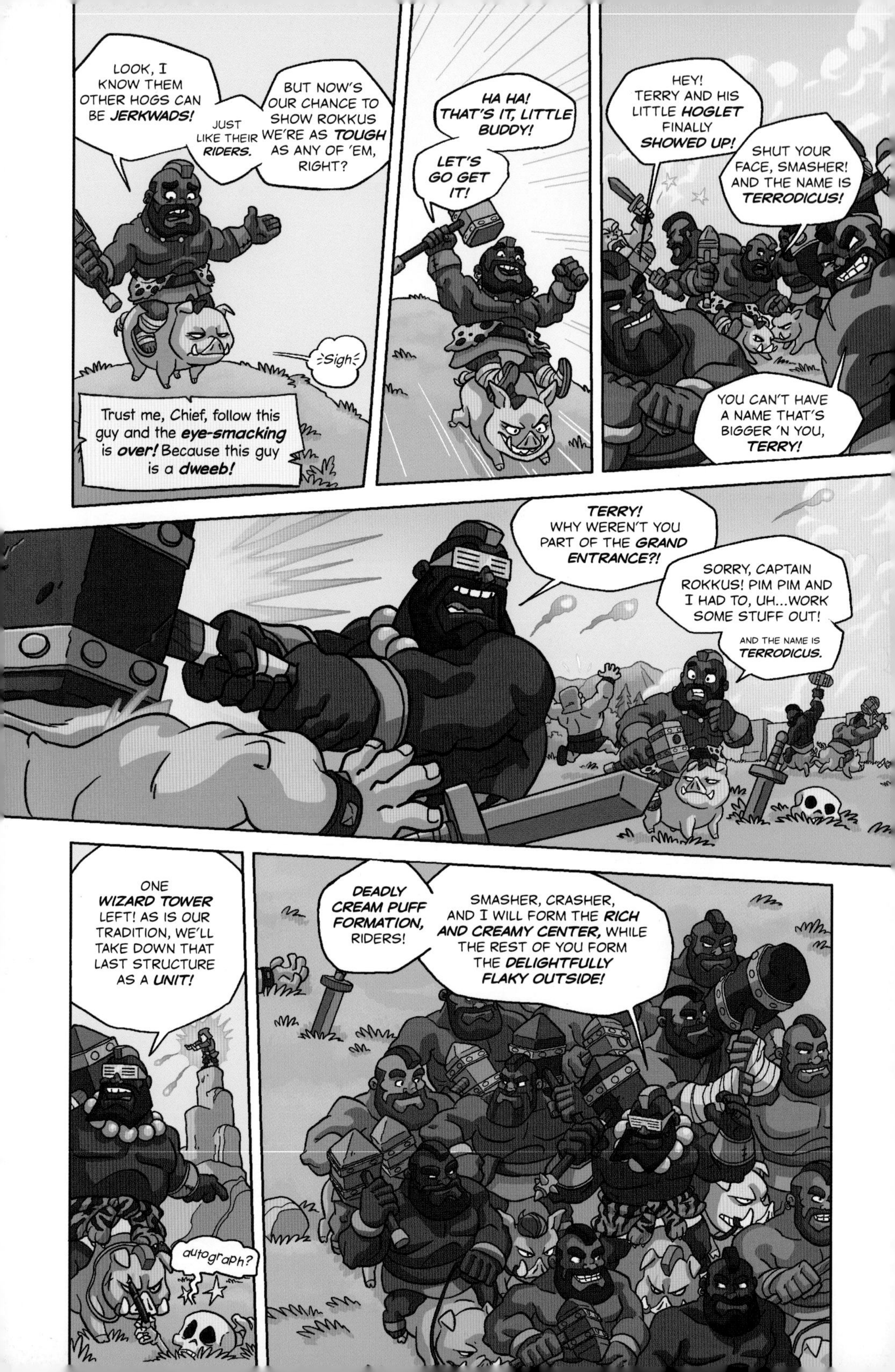
LOOK, I KNOW THEM OTHER HOGS CAN BE JERKWADS!
JUST LIKE THEIR RIDERS.
BUT NOW'S OUR CHANCE TO SHOW ROKKUS WE'RE AS TOUGH AS ANY OF 'EM, RIGHT?
Sigh
Trust me, Chief, follow this guy and the eye-smacking is over! Because this guy is a dweeb!
HA HA! THAT'S IT, LITTLE BUDDY!
LET'S GO GET IT!
HEY! TERRY AND HIS LITTLE HOGLET FINALLY SHOWED UP!
SHUT YOUR FACE, SMASHER! AND THE NAME IS TERRODICUS!
YOU CAN'T HAVE A NAME THAT'S BIGGER 'N YOU, TERRY!
TERRY! WHY WEREN'T YOU PART OF THE GRAND ENTRANCE?!
SORRY, CAPTAIN ROKKUS! PIM PIM AND I HAD TO, UH...WORK SOME STUFF OUT!
AND THE NAME IS TERRODICUS.
ONE WIZARD TOWER LEFT! AS IS OUR TRADITION, WE'LL TAKE DOWN THAT LAST STRUCTURE AS A UNIT!
autograph?
DEADLY CREAM PUFF FORMATION, RIDERS!
SMASHER, CRASHER, AND I WILL FORM THE RICH AND CREAMY CENTER, WHILE THE REST OF YOU FORM THE DELIGHTFULLY FLAKY OUTSIDE!

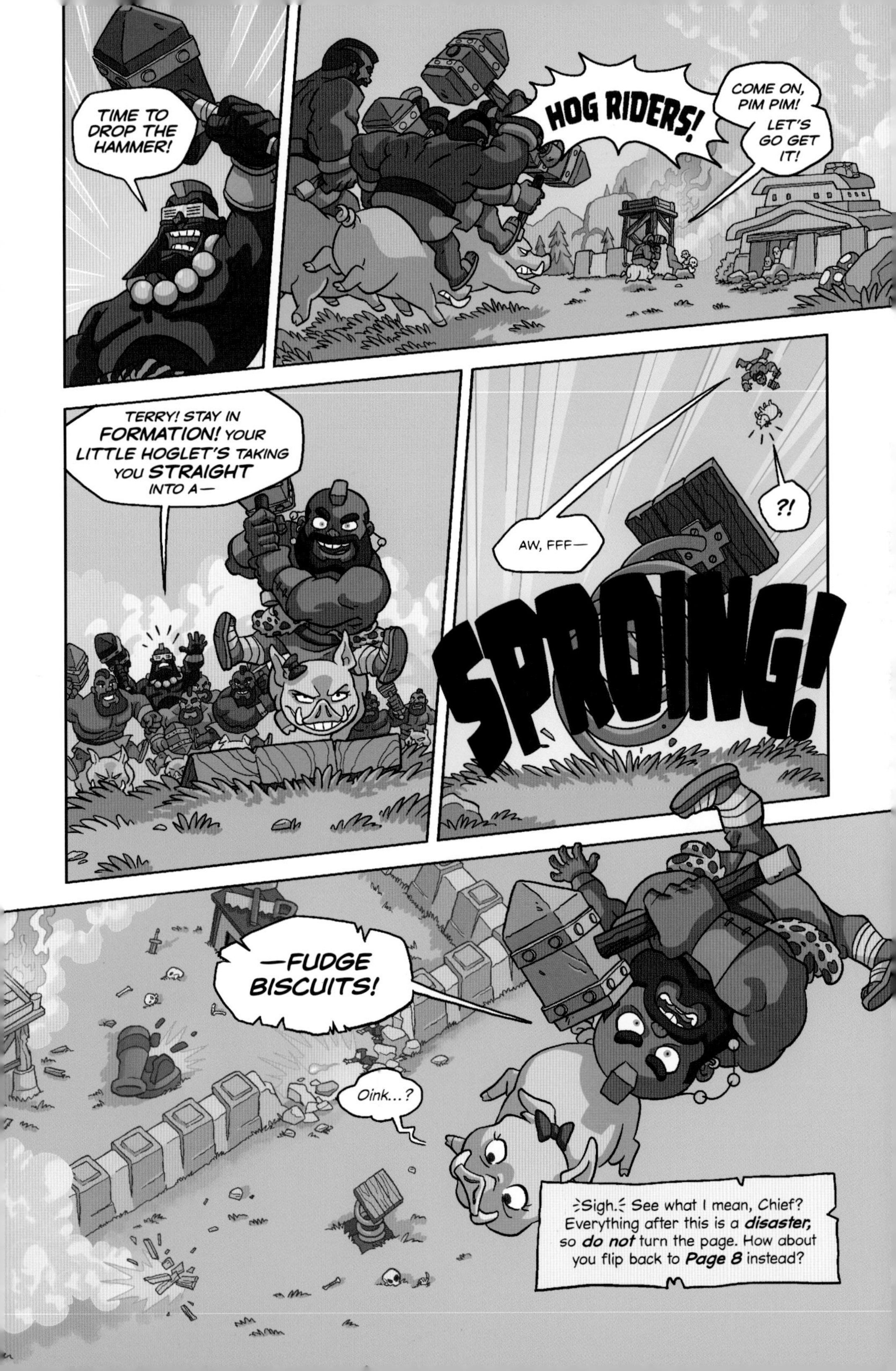

TIME TO DROP THE HAMMER!
HOG RIDERS!
COME ON, PIM PIM! LET'S GO GET IT!
TERRY! STAY IN FORMATION! YOUR LITTLE HOGLET'S TAKING YOU STRAIGHT INTO A—
AW, FFF—
?!
SPROING!
—FUDGE BISCUITS!
Oink...?
Sigh. See what I mean, Chief? Everything after this is a disaster, so do not turn the page. How about you flip back to Page 8 instead?

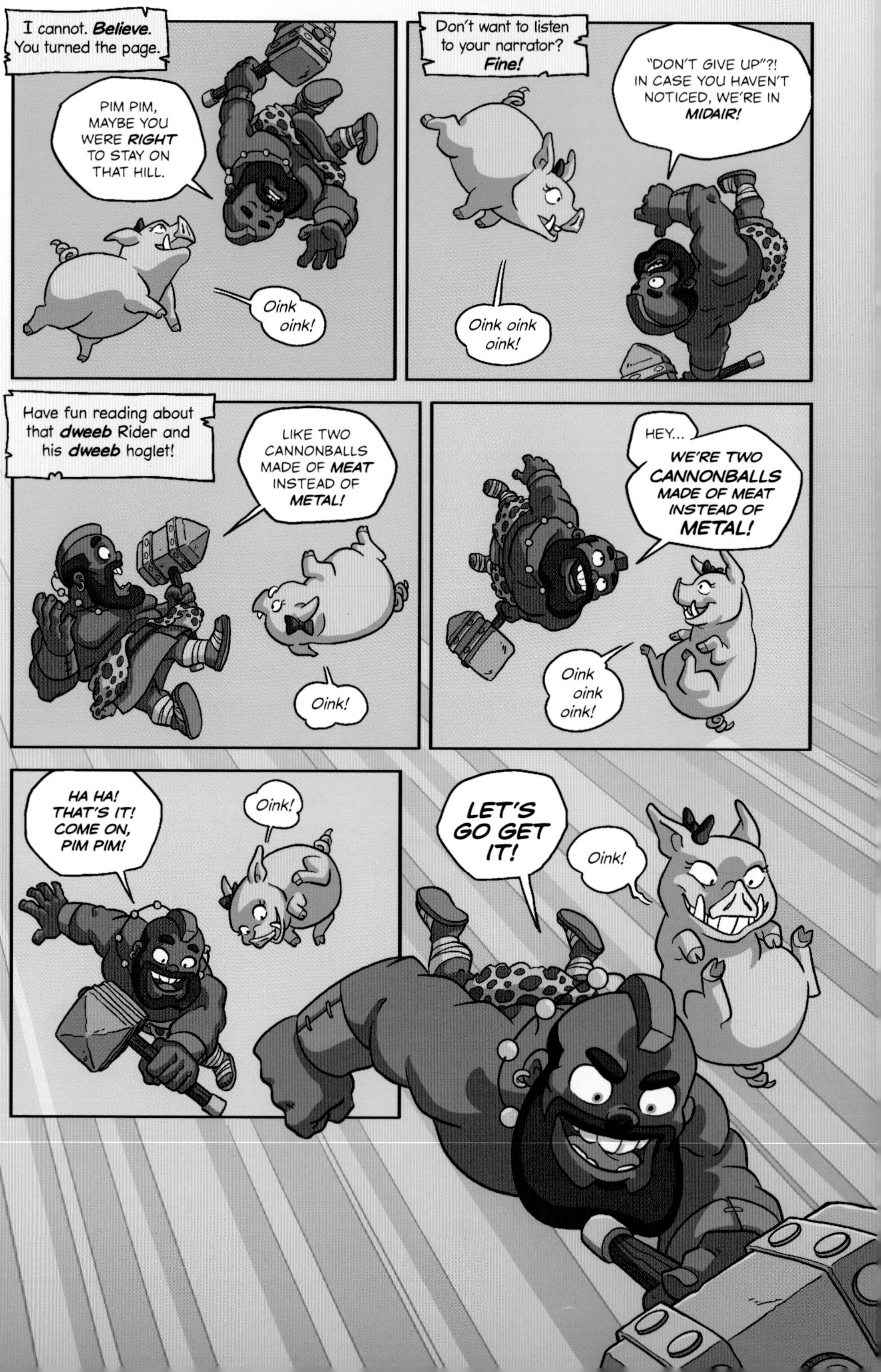
I cannot. Believe. You turned the page.
PIM PIM, MAYBE YOU WERE RIGHT TO STAY ON THAT HILL.
Oink oink!
Don't want to listen to your narrator? Fine!
"DON'T GIVE UP"?! IN CASE YOU HAVEN'T NOTICED, WE'RE IN MIDAIR!
Oink oink oink!
Have fun reading about that dweeb Rider and his dweeb hoglet!
LIKE TWO CANNONBALLS MADE OF MEAT INSTEAD OF METAL!
Oink!
HEY...
WE'RE TWO CANNONBALLS MADE OF MEAT INSTEAD OF METAL!
Oink oink oink!
HA HA! THAT'S IT! COME ON, PIM PIM!
Oink!
LET'S GO GET IT!
Oink!

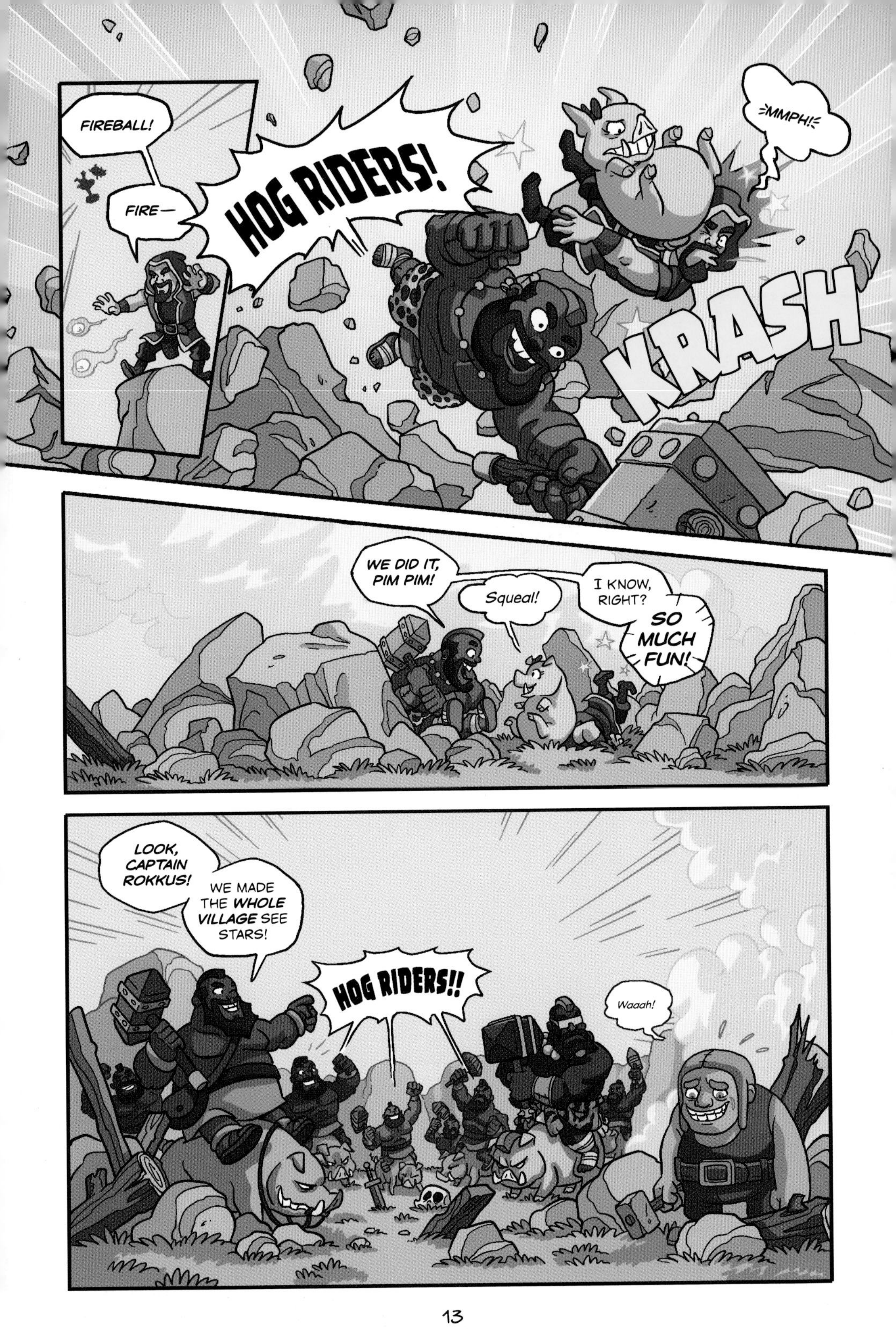
FIREBALL!
FIRE—
HOG RIDERS!
=MMPH!=
KRASH
WE DID IT, PIM PIM!
Squeal!
I KNOW, RIGHT?
SO MUCH FUN!
LOOK, CAPTAIN ROKKUS!
WE MADE THE WHOLE VILLAGE SEE STARS!
HOG RIDERS!!
Waaah!

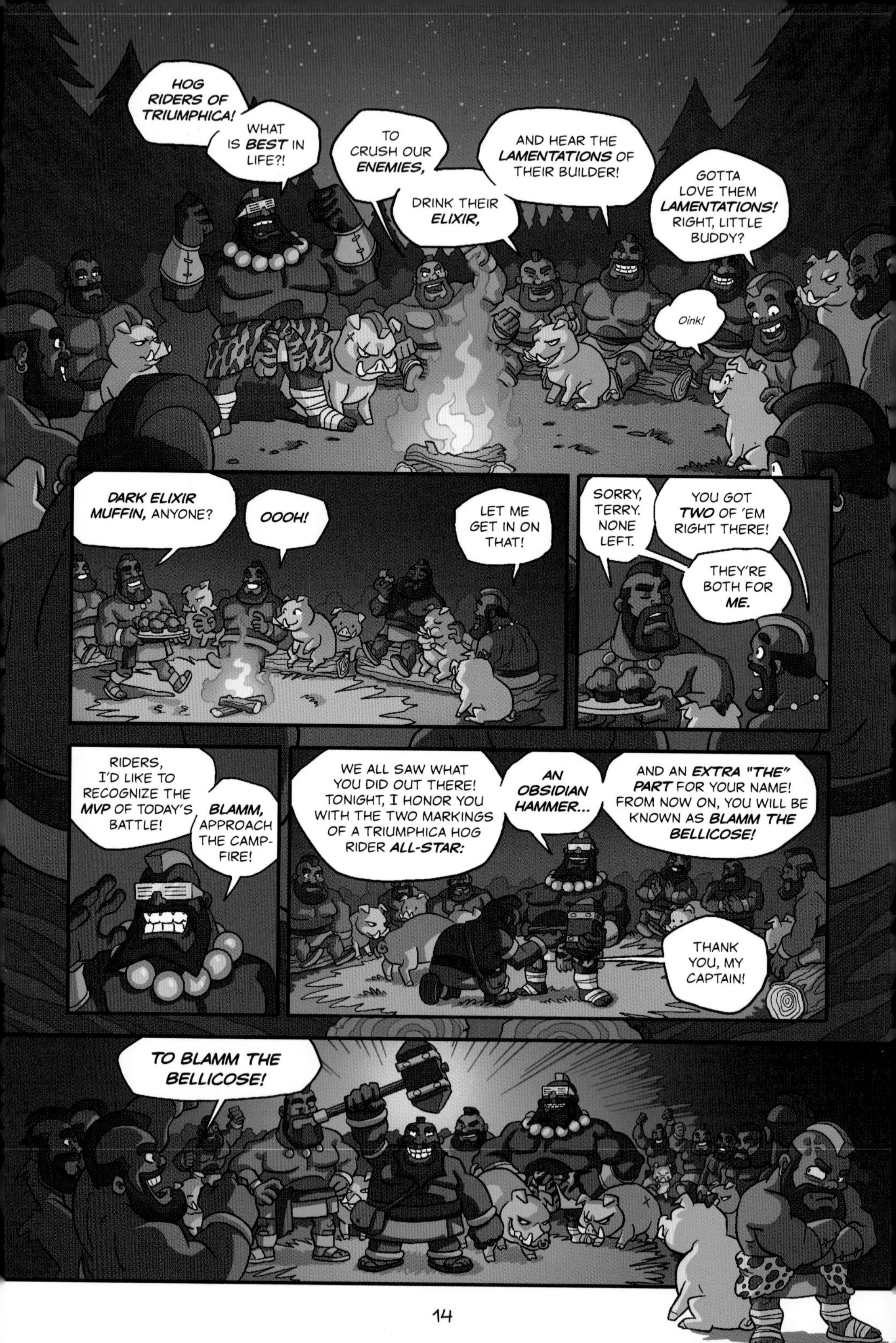
HOG RIDERS OF TRIUMPHICA!
WHAT IS BEST IN LIFE?!
TO CRUSH OUR ENEMIES,
DRINK THEIR ELIXIR,
AND HEAR THE LAMENTATIONS OF THEIR BUILDER!
GOTTA LOVE THEM LAMENTATIONS! RIGHT, LITTLE BUDDY?
Oink!
DARK ELIXIR MUFFIN, ANYONE?
OOOH!
LET ME GET IN ON THAT!
SORRY, TERRY. NONE LEFT.
YOU GOT TWO OF 'EM RIGHT THERE!
THEY'RE BOTH FOR ME.
RIDERS, I'D LIKE TO RECOGNIZE THE MVP OF TODAY'S BATTLE!
BLAMM, APPROACH THE CAMP-FIRE!
WE ALL SAW WHAT YOU DID OUT THERE! TONIGHT, I HONOR YOU WITH THE TWO MARKINGS OF A TRIUMPHICA HOG RIDER ALL-STAR:
AN OBSIDIAN HAMMER...
AND AN EXTRA "THE" PART FOR YOUR NAME! FROM NOW ON, YOU WILL BE KNOWN AS BLAMM THE BELLICOSE!
THANK YOU, MY CAPTAIN!
TO BLAMM THE BELLICOSE!

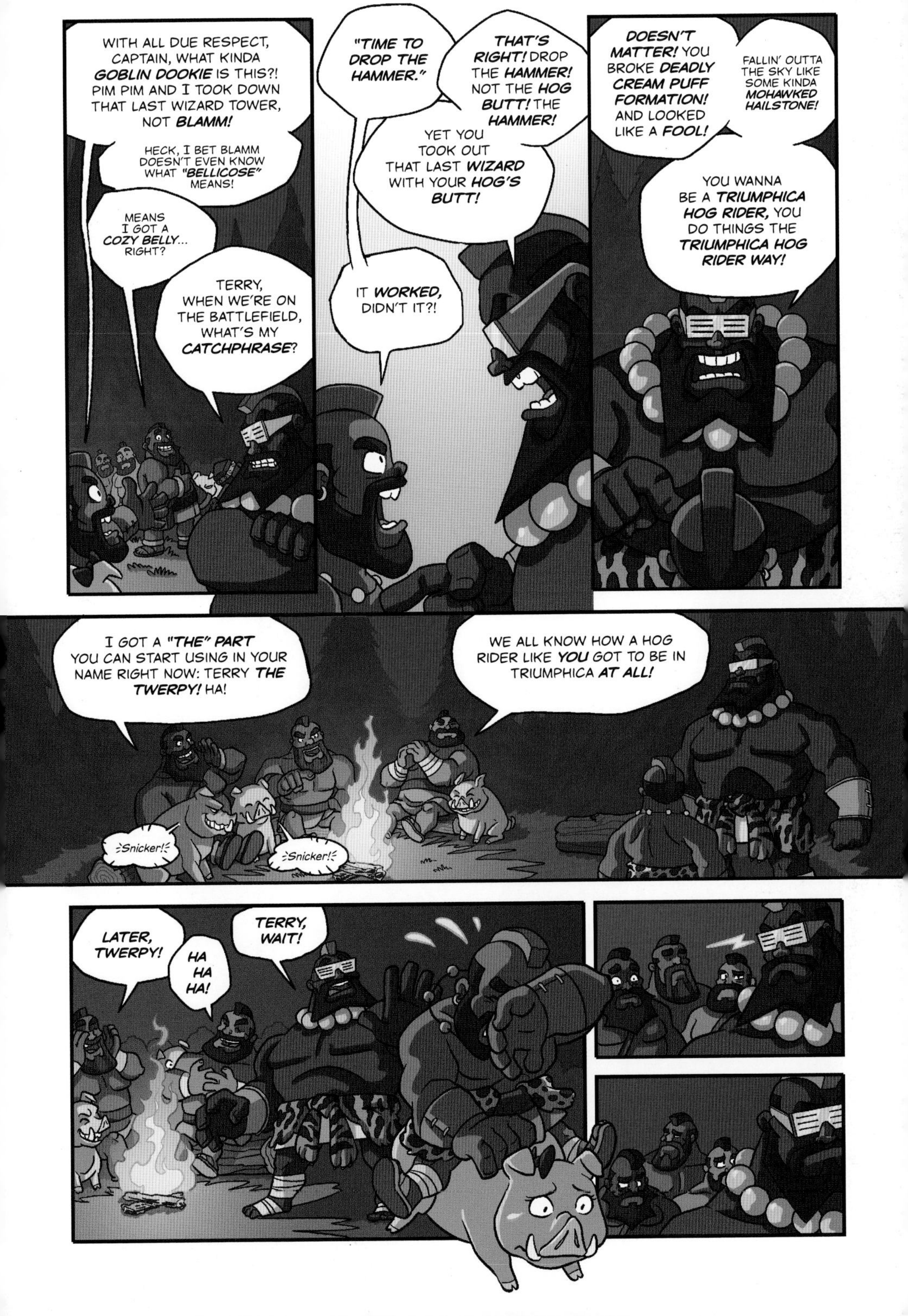
WITH ALL DUE RESPECT, CAPTAIN, WHAT KINDA GOBLIN DOOKIE IS THIS?! PIM PIM AND I TOOK DOWN THAT LAST WIZARD TOWER, NOT BLAMM!
HECK, I BET BLAMM DOESN'T EVEN KNOW WHAT "BELLICOSE" MEANS!
MEANS I GOT A COZY BELLY... RIGHT?
TERRY, WHEN WE'RE ON THE BATTLEFIELD, WHAT'S MY CATCHPHRASE?
"TIME TO DROP THE HAMMER."
THAT'S RIGHT! DROP THE HAMMER! NOT THE HOG BUTT! THE HAMMER!
YET YOU TOOK OUT THAT LAST WIZARD WITH YOUR HOG'S BUTT!
IT WORKED, DIDN'T IT?!
DOESN'T MATTER! YOU BROKE DEADLY CREAM PUFF FORMATION! AND LOOKED LIKE A FOOL!
FALLIN' OUTTA THE SKY LIKE SOME KINDA MOHAWKED HAILSTONE!
YOU WANNA BE A TRIUMPHICA HOG RIDER, YOU DO THINGS THE TRIUMPHICA HOG RIDER WAY!
I GOT A "THE" PART YOU CAN START USING IN YOUR NAME RIGHT NOW: TERRY THE TWERPY! HA!
Snicker!
Snicker!
WE ALL KNOW HOW A HOG RIDER LIKE YOU GOT TO BE IN TRIUMPHICA AT ALL!
LATER, TWERPY!
HA HA HA!
TERRY, WAIT!

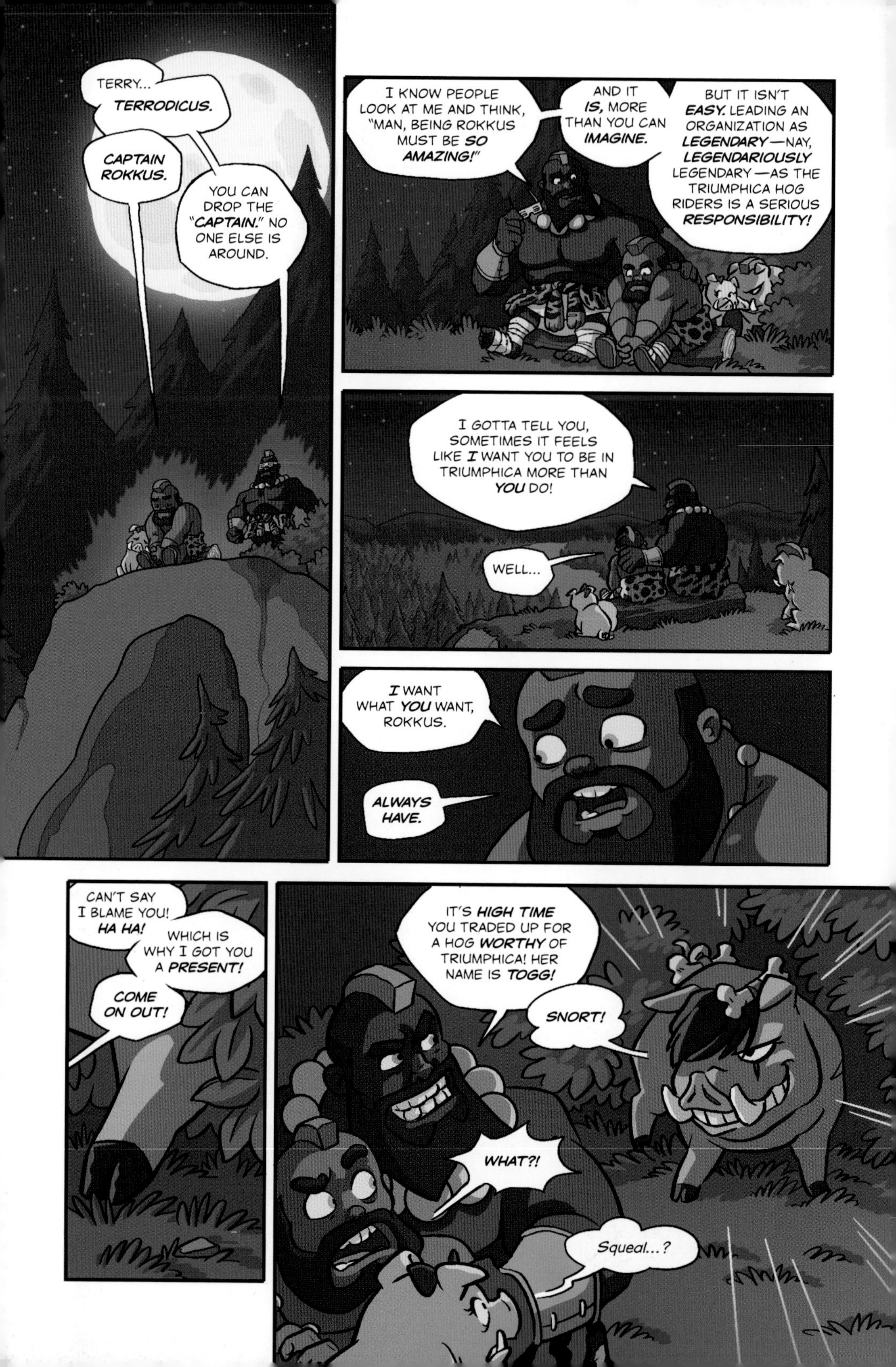
TERRY...
TERRODICUS.
CAPTAIN ROKKUS.
YOU CAN DROP THE "CAPTAIN." NO ONE ELSE IS AROUND.
I KNOW PEOPLE LOOK AT ME AND THINK, "MAN, BEING ROKKUS MUST BE SO AMAZING!"
AND IT IS, MORE THAN YOU CAN IMAGINE.
BUT IT ISN'T EASY. LEADING AN ORGANIZATION AS LEGENDARY—NAY, LEGENDARIOUSLY LEGENDARY—AS THE TRIUMPHICA HOG RIDERS IS A SERIOUS RESPONSIBILITY!
I GOTTA TELL YOU, SOMETIMES IT FEELS LIKE I WANT YOU TO BE IN TRIUMPHICA MORE THAN YOU DO!
WELL...
I WANT WHAT YOU WANT, ROKKUS.
ALWAYS HAVE.
CAN'T SAY I BLAME YOU! HA HA!
WHICH IS WHY I GOT YOU A PRESENT!
COME ON OUT!
IT'S HIGH TIME YOU TRADED UP FOR A HOG WORTHY OF TRIUMPHICA! HER NAME IS TOGG!
SNORT!
WHAT?!
Squeal...?

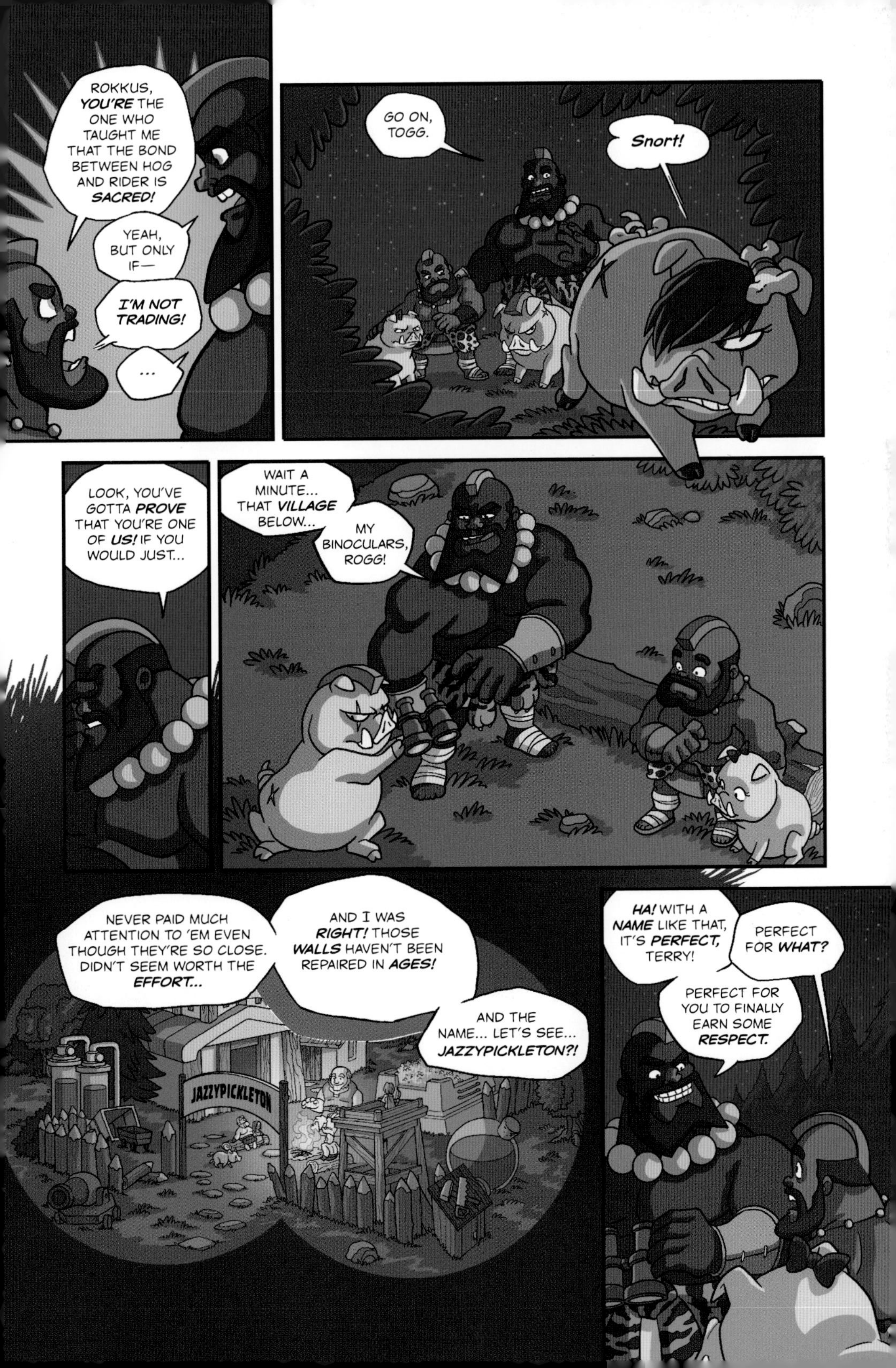
ROKKUS, ***YOU'RE*** THE ONE WHO TAUGHT ME THAT THE BOND BETWEEN HOG AND RIDER IS ***SACRED!***
YEAH, BUT ONLY IF—
I'M NOT TRADING!
...
GO ON, TOGG.
Snort!
LOOK, YOU'VE GOTTA ***PROVE*** THAT YOU'RE ONE OF ***US!*** IF YOU WOULD JUST...
WAIT A MINUTE... THAT ***VILLAGE*** BELOW...
MY BINOCULARS, ROGG!
NEVER PAID MUCH ATTENTION TO 'EM EVEN THOUGH THEY'RE SO CLOSE. DIDN'T SEEM WORTH THE ***EFFORT...***
AND I WAS ***RIGHT!*** THOSE ***WALLS*** HAVEN'T BEEN REPAIRED IN ***AGES!***
AND THE NAME... LET'S SEE... ***JAZZYPICKLETON?!***
JAZZYPICKLETON
HA! WITH A ***NAME*** LIKE THAT, IT'S ***PERFECT,*** TERRY!
PERFECT FOR ***WHAT?***
PERFECT FOR YOU TO FINALLY EARN SOME ***RESPECT.***

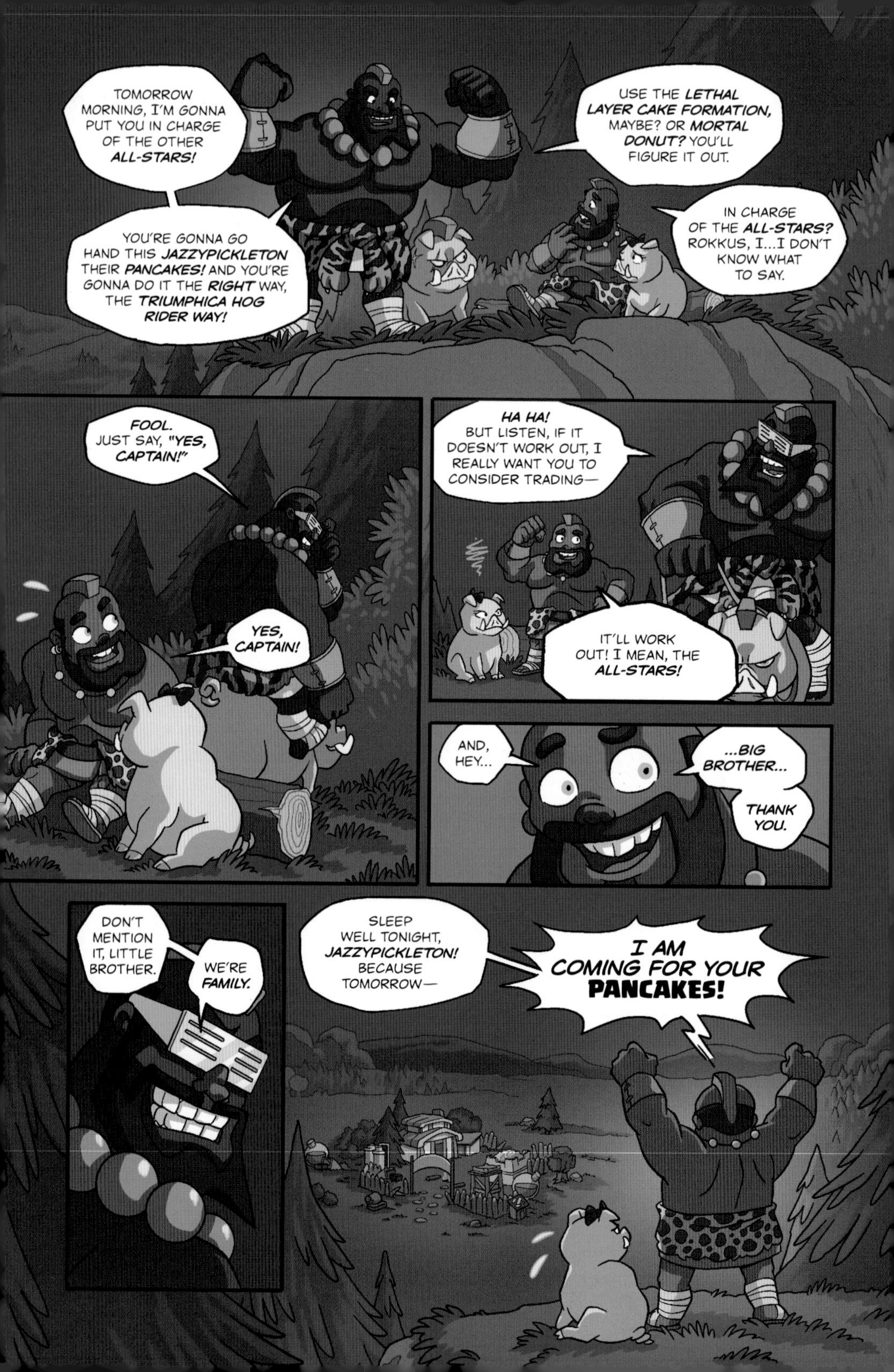
TOMORROW MORNING, I'M GONNA PUT YOU IN CHARGE OF THE OTHER ALL-STARS!
YOU'RE GONNA GO HAND THIS JAZZYPICKLETON THEIR PANCAKES! AND YOU'RE GONNA DO IT THE RIGHT WAY, THE TRIUMPHICA HOG RIDER WAY!
USE THE LETHAL LAYER CAKE FORMATION, MAYBE? OR MORTAL DONUT? YOU'LL FIGURE IT OUT.
IN CHARGE OF THE ALL-STARS? ROKKUS, I...I DON'T KNOW WHAT TO SAY.
FOOL. JUST SAY, "YES, CAPTAIN!"
YES, CAPTAIN!
HA HA! BUT LISTEN, IF IT DOESN'T WORK OUT, I REALLY WANT YOU TO CONSIDER TRADING—
IT'LL WORK OUT! I MEAN, THE ALL-STARS!
AND, HEY...
...BIG BROTHER...
THANK YOU.
DON'T MENTION IT, LITTLE BROTHER.
WE'RE FAMILY.
SLEEP WELL TONIGHT, JAZZYPICKLETON! BECAUSE TOMORROW—
I AM COMING FOR YOUR PANCAKES!

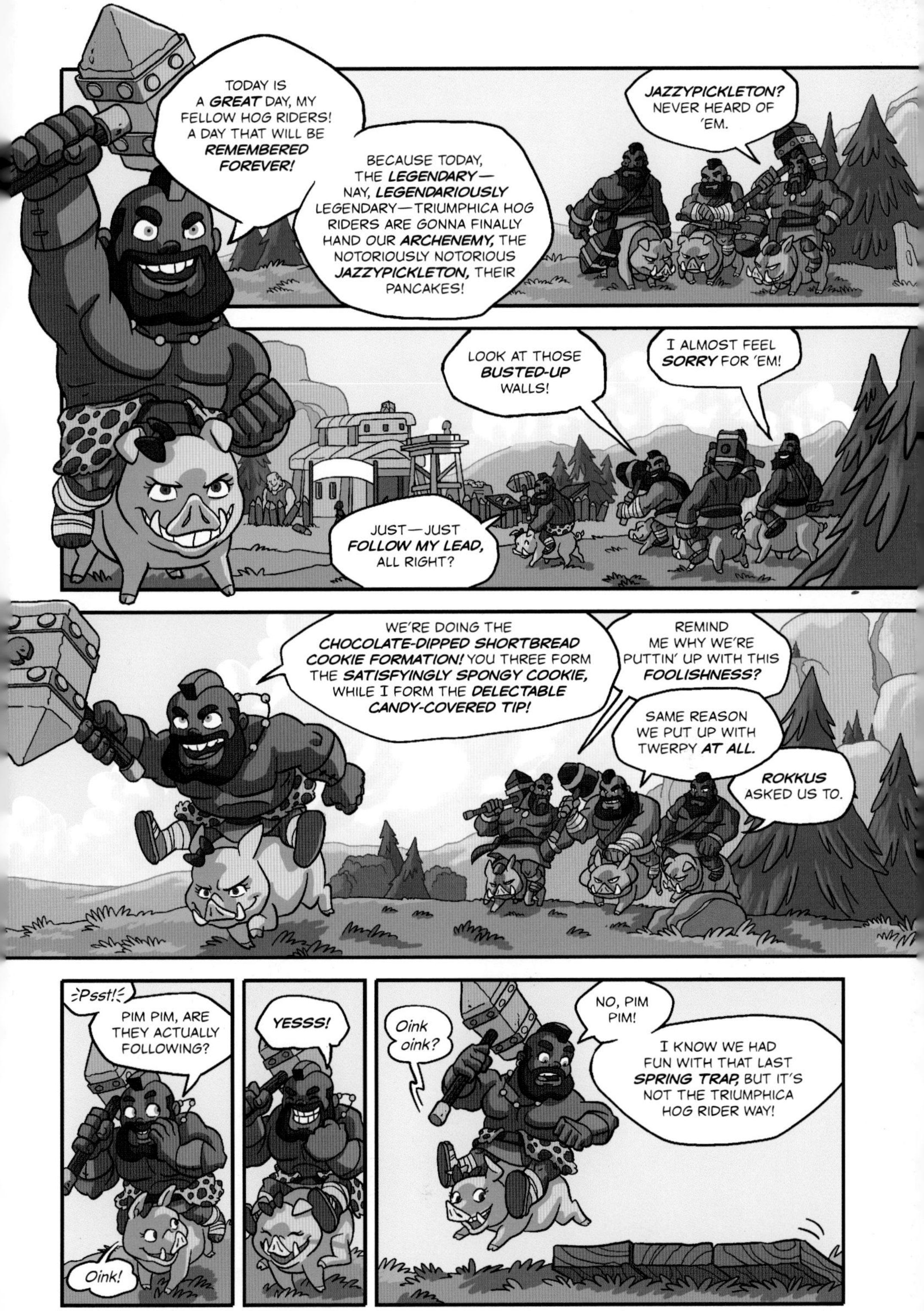
TODAY IS A GREAT DAY, MY FELLOW HOG RIDERS! A DAY THAT WILL BE REMEMBERED FOREVER!
BECAUSE TODAY, THE LEGENDARY—NAY, LEGENDARIOUSLY LEGENDARY—TRIUMPHICA HOG RIDERS ARE GONNA FINALLY HAND OUR ARCHENEMY, THE NOTORIOUSLY NOTORIOUS JAZZYPICKLETON, THEIR PANCAKES!
JAZZYPICKLETON? NEVER HEARD OF 'EM.
LOOK AT THOSE BUSTED-UP WALLS!
I ALMOST FEEL SORRY FOR 'EM!
JUST—JUST FOLLOW MY LEAD, ALL RIGHT?
WE'RE DOING THE CHOCOLATE-DIPPED SHORTBREAD COOKIE FORMATION! YOU THREE FORM THE SATISFYINGLY SPONGY COOKIE, WHILE I FORM THE DELECTABLE CANDY-COVERED TIP!
REMIND ME WHY WE'RE PUTTIN' UP WITH THIS FOOLISHNESS?
SAME REASON WE PUT UP WITH TWERPY AT ALL.
ROKKUS ASKED US TO.
Psst!
PIM PIM, ARE THEY ACTUALLY FOLLOWING?
Oink!
YESSS!
Oink oink?
NO, PIM PIM!
I KNOW WE HAD FUN WITH THAT LAST SPRING TRAP, BUT IT'S NOT THE TRIUMPHICA HOG RIDER WAY!

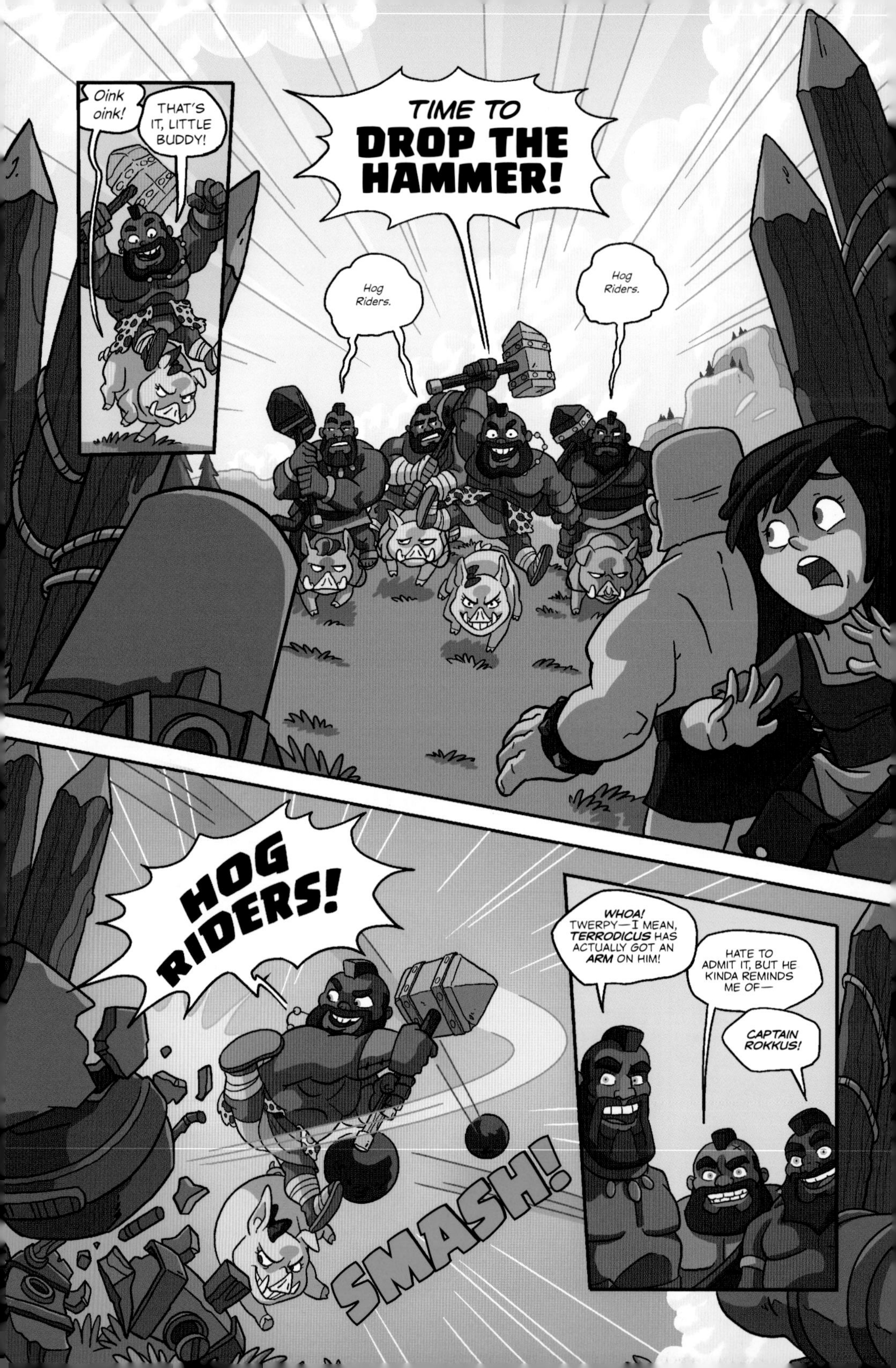

Oink oink!
THAT'S IT, LITTLE BUDDY!
TIME TO DROP THE HAMMER!
Hog Riders.
Hog Riders.
HOG RIDERS!
SMASH!
WHOA! TWERPY—I MEAN, TERRODICUS HAS ACTUALLY GOT AN ARM ON HIM!
HATE TO ADMIT IT, BUT HE KINDA REMINDS ME OF—
CAPTAIN ROKKUS!

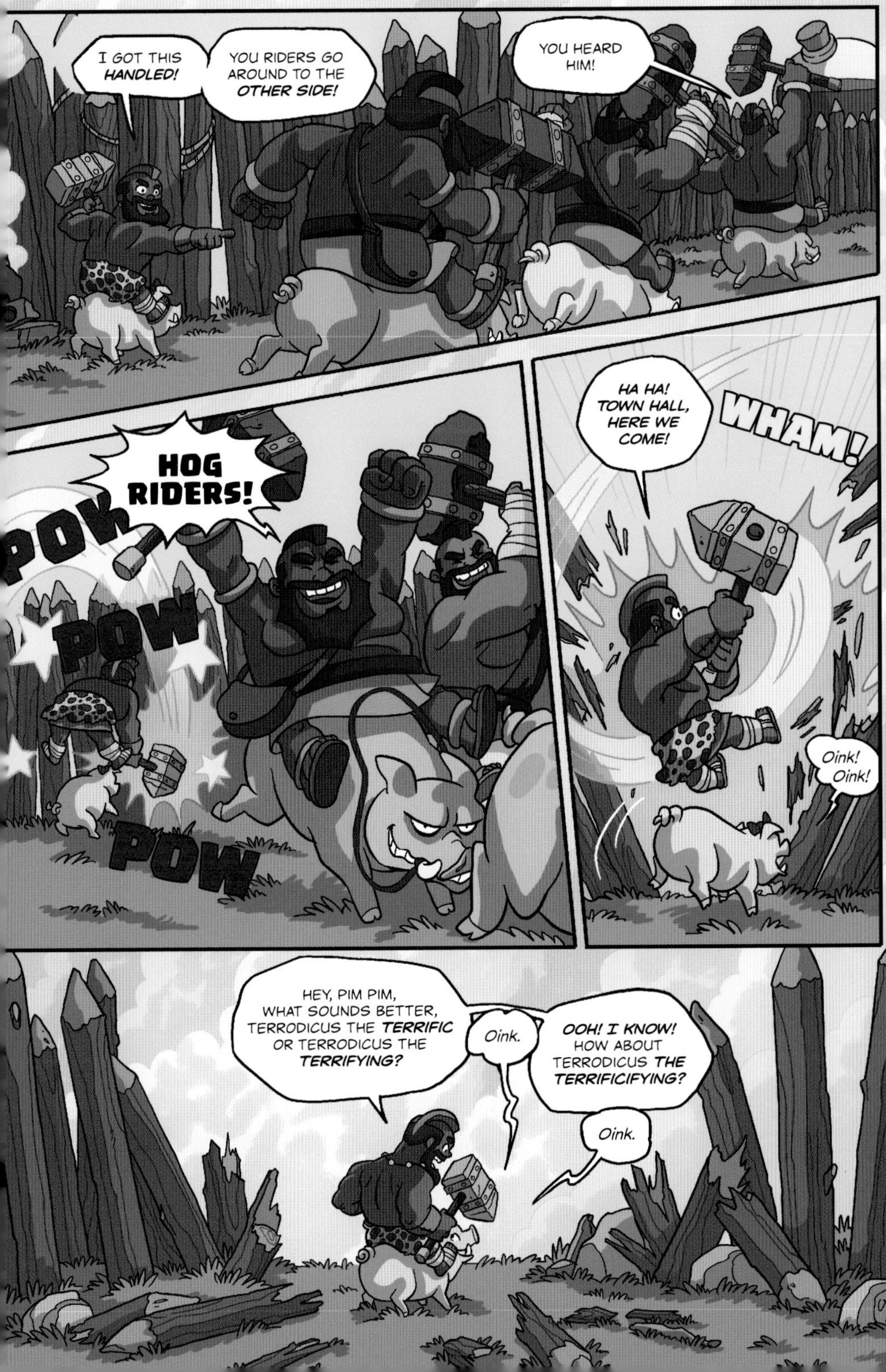
I GOT THIS HANDLED!
YOU RIDERS GO AROUND TO THE OTHER SIDE!
YOU HEARD HIM!
HOG RIDERS!
POK
POW
POW
HA HA! TOWN HALL, HERE WE COME!
WHAM!
Oink! Oink!
HEY, PIM PIM, WHAT SOUNDS BETTER, TERRODICUS THE TERRIFIC OR TERRODICUS THE TERRIFYING?
Oink.
OOH! I KNOW! HOW ABOUT TERRODICUS THE TERRIFICIFYING?
Oink.

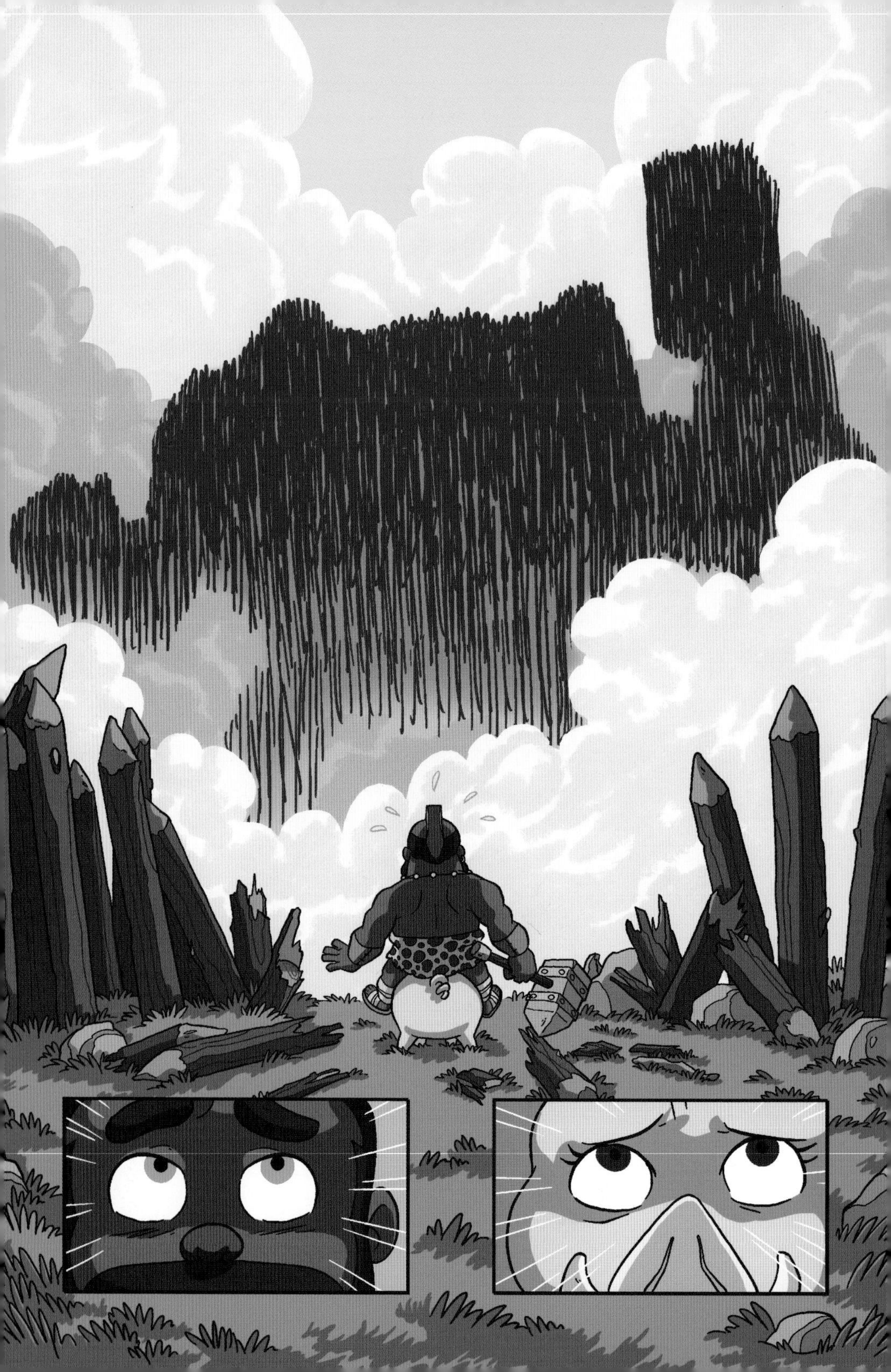

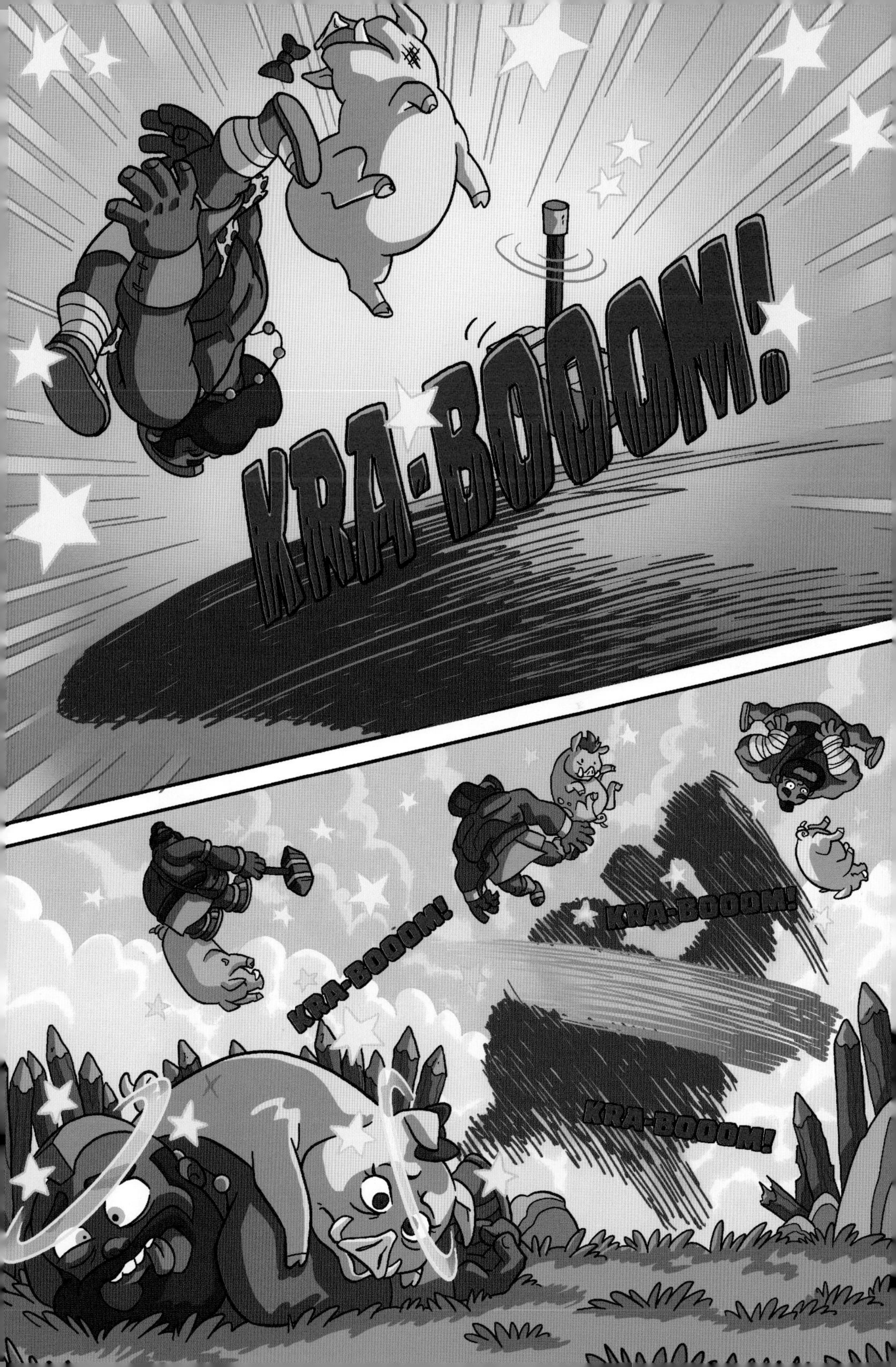
KRA-BOOOM!
KRA-BOOOM!
KRA-BOOOM!
KRA-BOOOM!

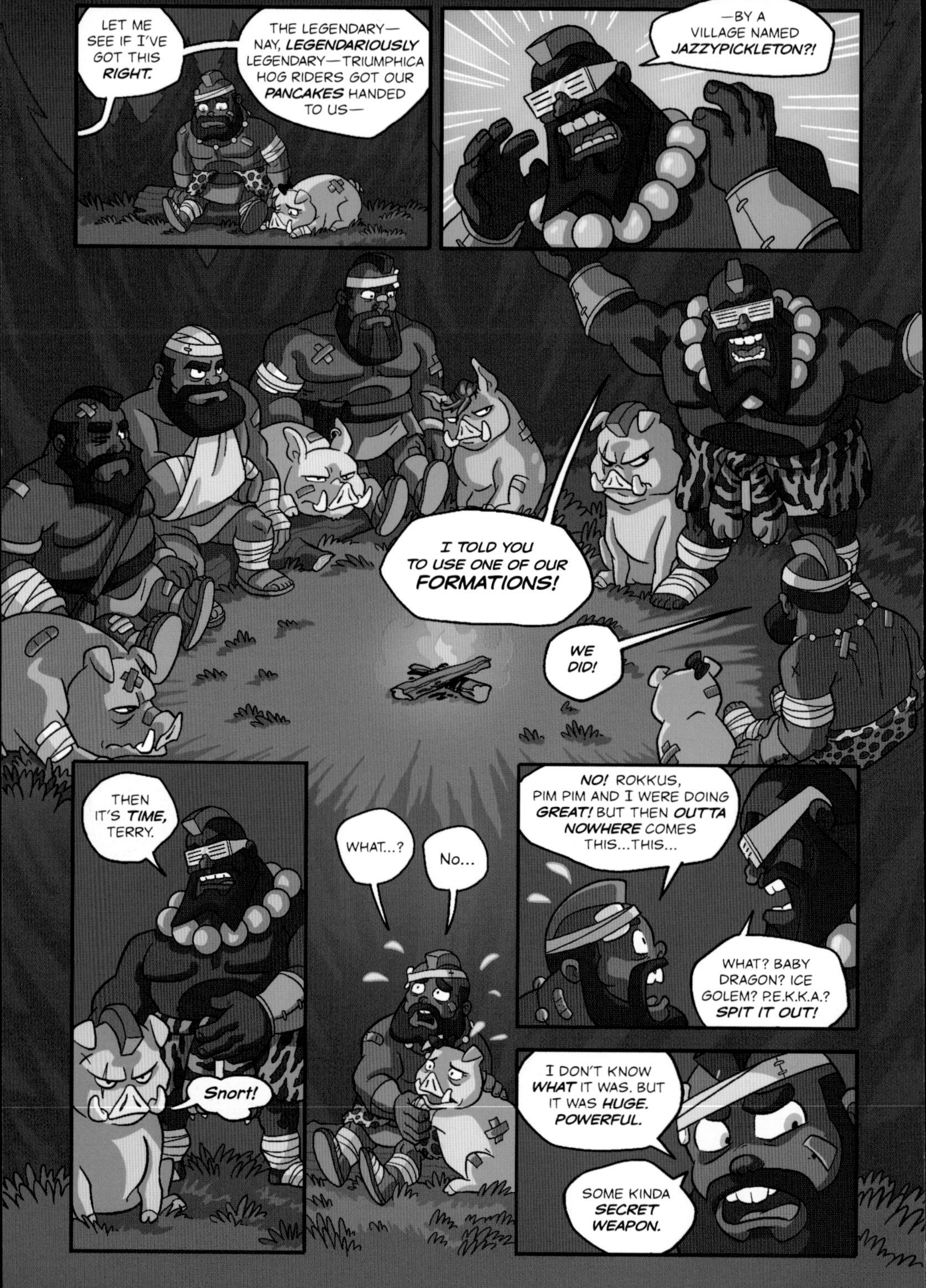

LET ME SEE IF I'VE GOT THIS **RIGHT.**
THE LEGENDARY—NAY, **LEGENDARIOUSLY** LEGENDARY—TRIUMPHICA HOG RIDERS GOT OUR **PANCAKES** HANDED TO US—
—BY A VILLAGE NAMED **JAZZYPICKLETON?!**
I TOLD YOU TO USE ONE OF OUR **FORMATIONS!**
WE DID!
THEN IT'S **TIME,** TERRY.
WHAT...?
No...
Snort!
NO! ROKKUS, PIM PIM AND I WERE DOING **GREAT!** BUT THEN **OUTTA NOWHERE** COMES THIS...THIS...
WHAT? BABY DRAGON? ICE GOLEM? P.E.K.K.A.? **SPIT IT OUT!**
I DON'T KNOW **WHAT** IT WAS. BUT IT WAS **HUGE. POWERFUL.**
SOME KINDA **SECRET WEAPON.**

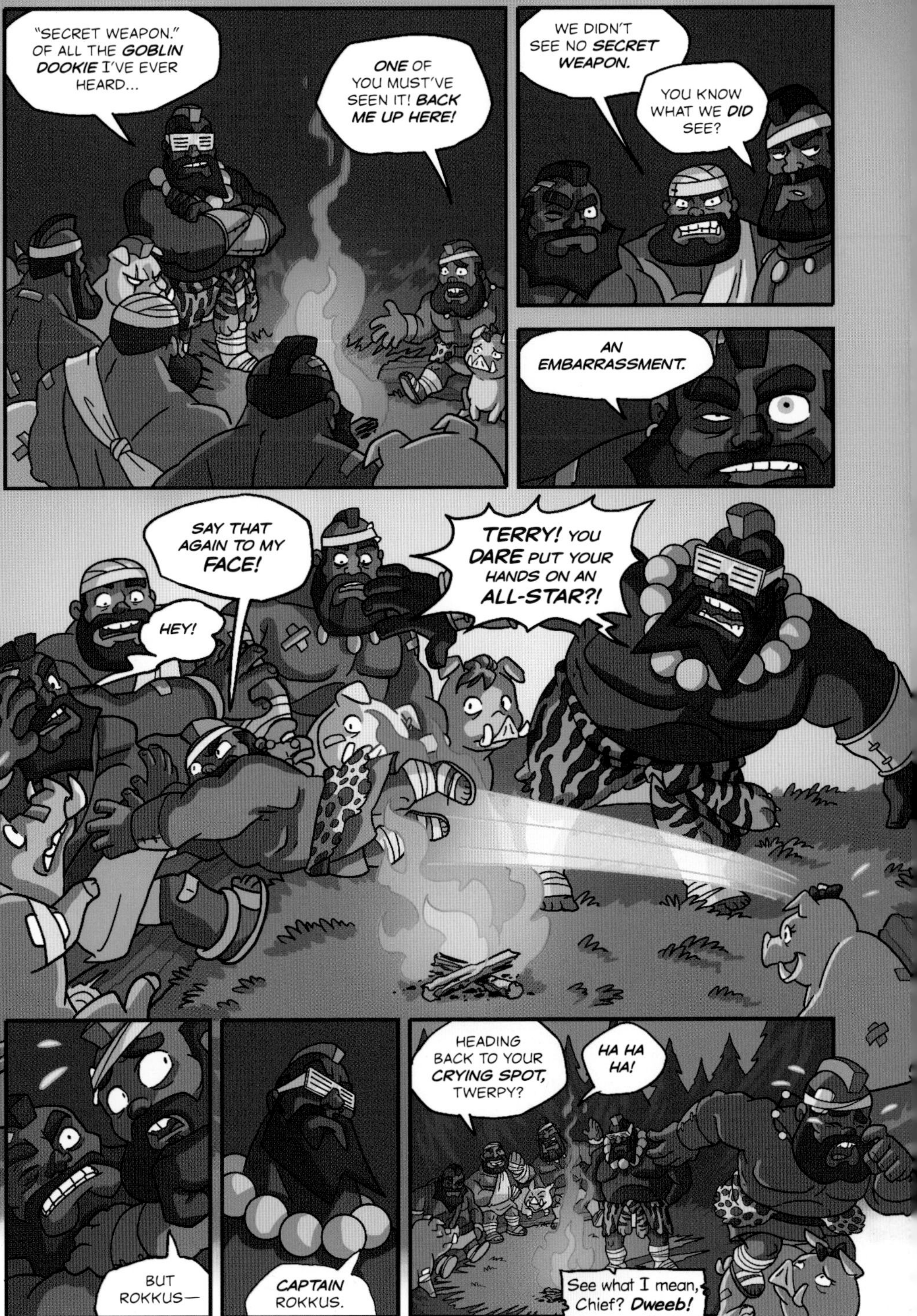
"SECRET WEAPON." OF ALL THE **GOBLIN DOOKIE** I'VE EVER HEARD...
ONE OF YOU MUST'VE SEEN IT! **BACK ME UP HERE!**
WE DIDN'T SEE NO **SECRET WEAPON.**
YOU KNOW WHAT WE **DID** SEE?
AN EMBARRASSMENT.
SAY THAT AGAIN TO MY **FACE!**
HEY!
TERRY! YOU **DARE** PUT YOUR HANDS ON AN **ALL-STAR?!**
BUT ROKKUS—
CAPTAIN ROKKUS.
HEADING BACK TO YOUR **CRYING SPOT,** TWERPY?
HA HA HA!
See what I mean, Chief? **Dweeb!**

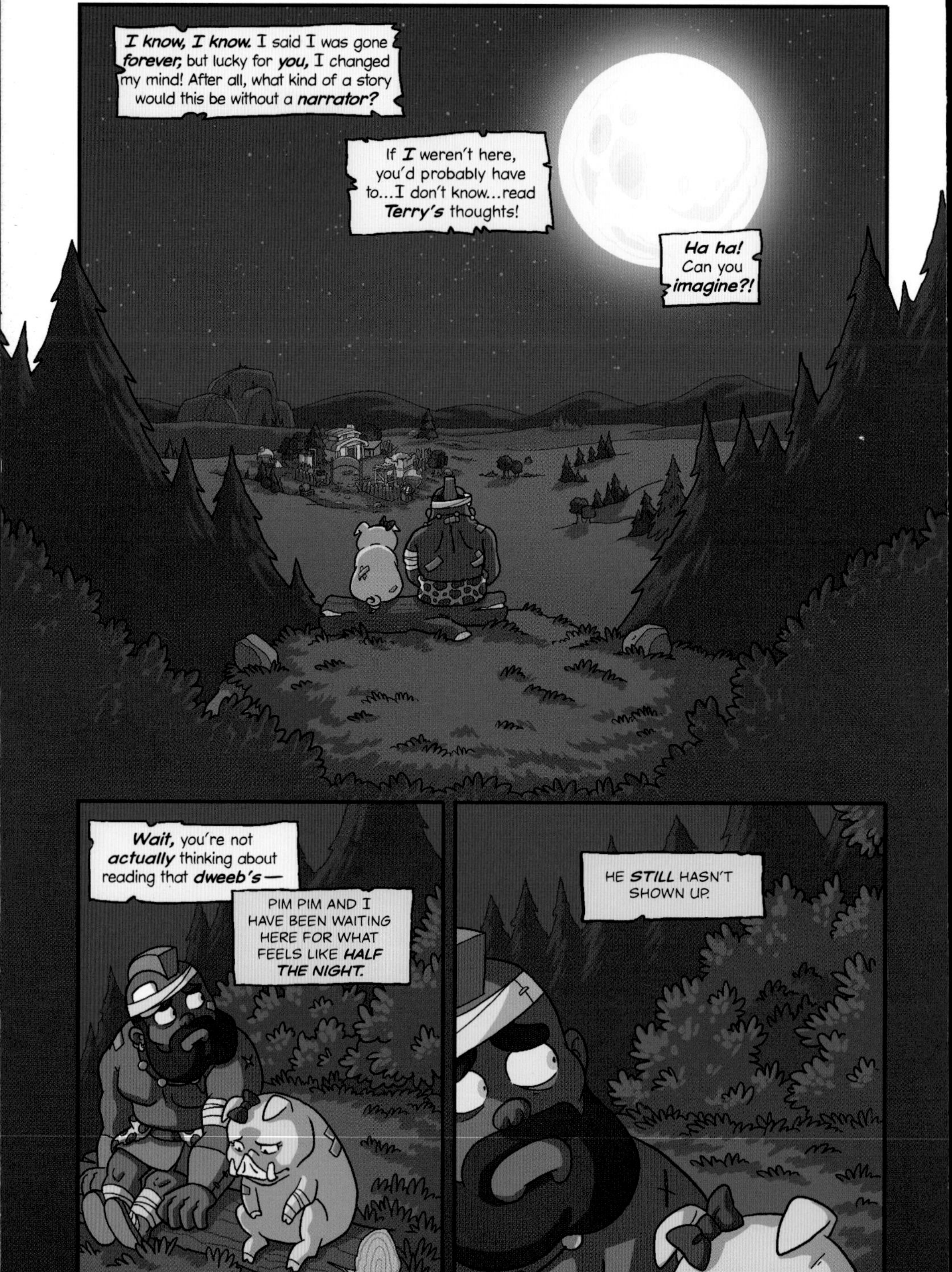

I know, I know. I said I was gone forever, but lucky for you, I changed my mind! After all, what kind of a story would this be without a narrator?
If I weren't here, you'd probably have to...I don't know...read Terry's thoughts!
Ha ha! Can you imagine?!
Wait, you're not actually thinking about reading that dweeb's—
PIM PIM AND I HAVE BEEN WAITING HERE FOR WHAT FEELS LIKE HALF THE NIGHT.
HE STILL HASN'T SHOWN UP.

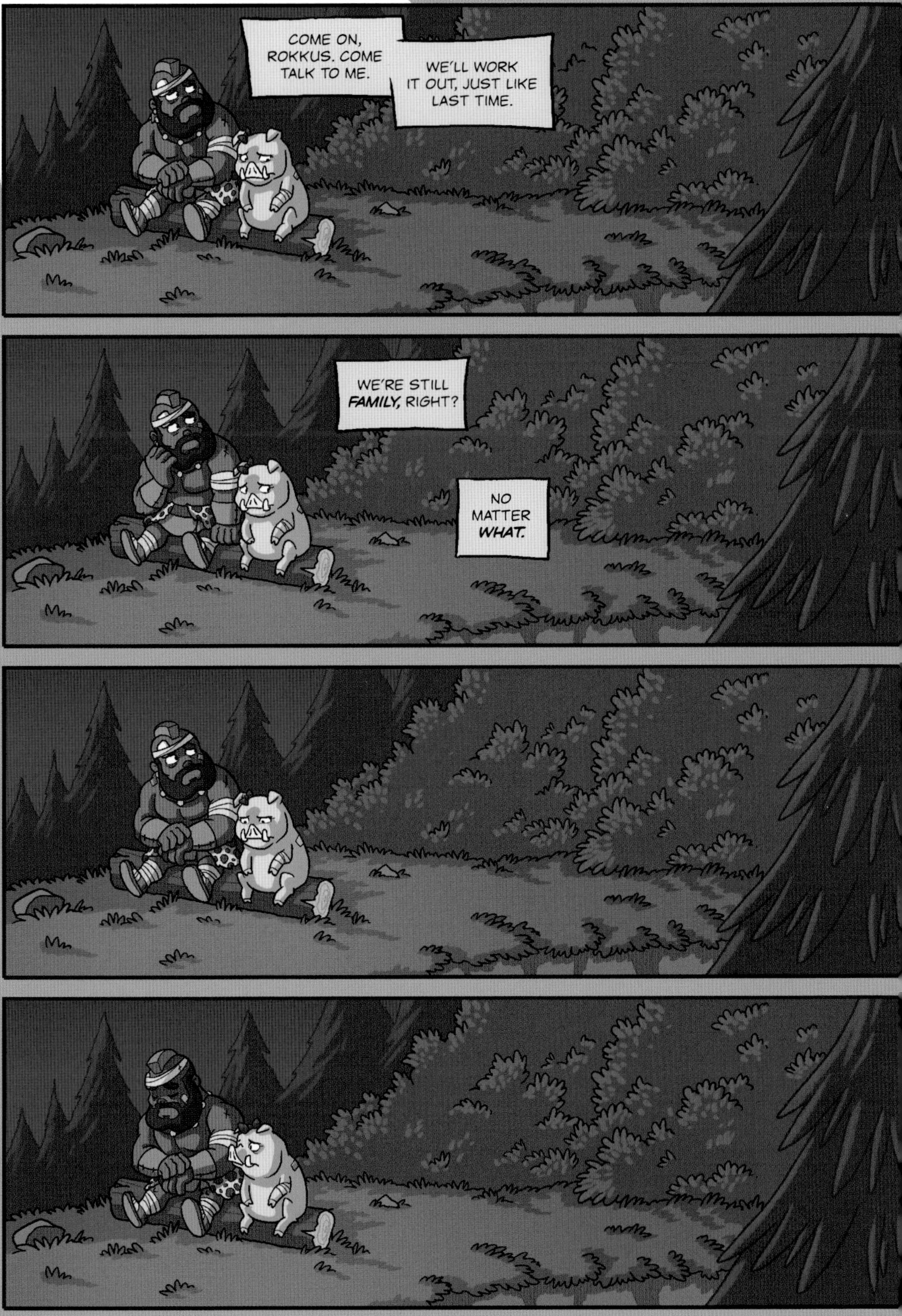
COME ON, ROKKUS. COME TALK TO ME.
WE'LL WORK IT OUT, JUST LIKE LAST TIME.
WE'RE STILL *FAMILY,* RIGHT?
NO MATTER *WHAT.*

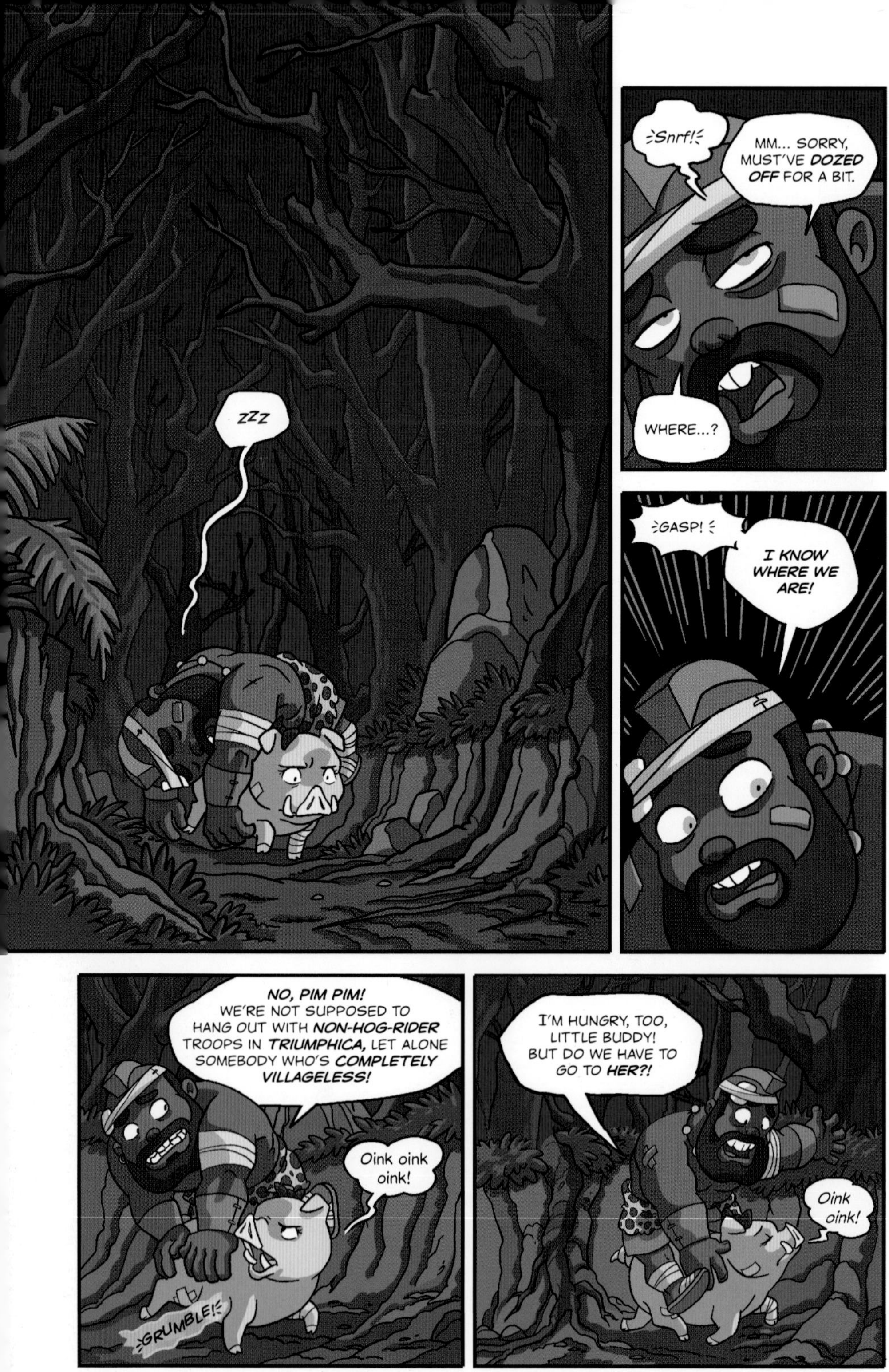
ZZZ
Snrf!
MM... SORRY, MUST'VE DOZED OFF FOR A BIT.
WHERE...?
GASP!
I KNOW WHERE WE ARE!
NO, PIM PIM! WE'RE NOT SUPPOSED TO HANG OUT WITH NON-HOG-RIDER TROOPS IN TRIUMPHICA, LET ALONE SOMEBODY WHO'S COMPLETELY VILLAGELESS!
Oink oink oink!
GRUMBLE!
I'M HUNGRY, TOO, LITTLE BUDDY! BUT DO WE HAVE TO GO TO HER?!
Oink oink!

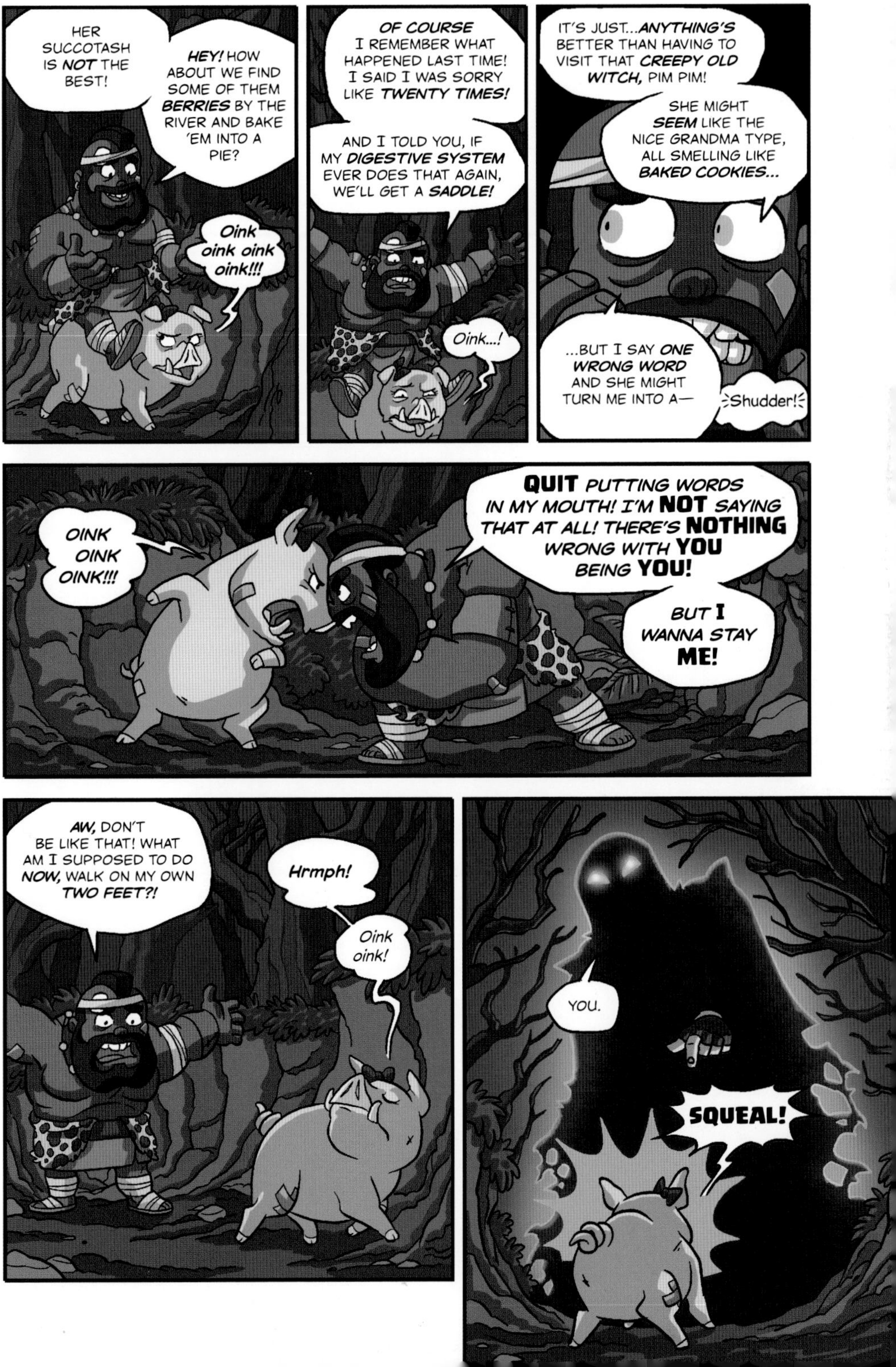
HER SUCCOTASH IS NOT THE BEST!
HEY! HOW ABOUT WE FIND SOME OF THEM BERRIES BY THE RIVER AND BAKE 'EM INTO A PIE?
Oink oink oink oink!!!
OF COURSE I REMEMBER WHAT HAPPENED LAST TIME! I SAID I WAS SORRY LIKE TWENTY TIMES!
AND I TOLD YOU, IF MY DIGESTIVE SYSTEM EVER DOES THAT AGAIN, WE'LL GET A SADDLE!
Oink...!
IT'S JUST...ANYTHING'S BETTER THAN HAVING TO VISIT THAT CREEPY OLD WITCH, PIM PIM!
SHE MIGHT SEEM LIKE THE NICE GRANDMA TYPE, ALL SMELLING LIKE BAKED COOKIES...
...BUT I SAY ONE WRONG WORD AND SHE MIGHT TURN ME INTO A—
Shudder!
OINK OINK OINK!!!
QUIT PUTTING WORDS IN MY MOUTH! I'M NOT SAYING THAT AT ALL! THERE'S NOTHING WRONG WITH YOU BEING YOU!
BUT I WANNA STAY ME!
AW, DON'T BE LIKE THAT! WHAT AM I SUPPOSED TO DO NOW, WALK ON MY OWN TWO FEET?!
Hrmph!
Oink oink!
YOU.
SQUEAL!

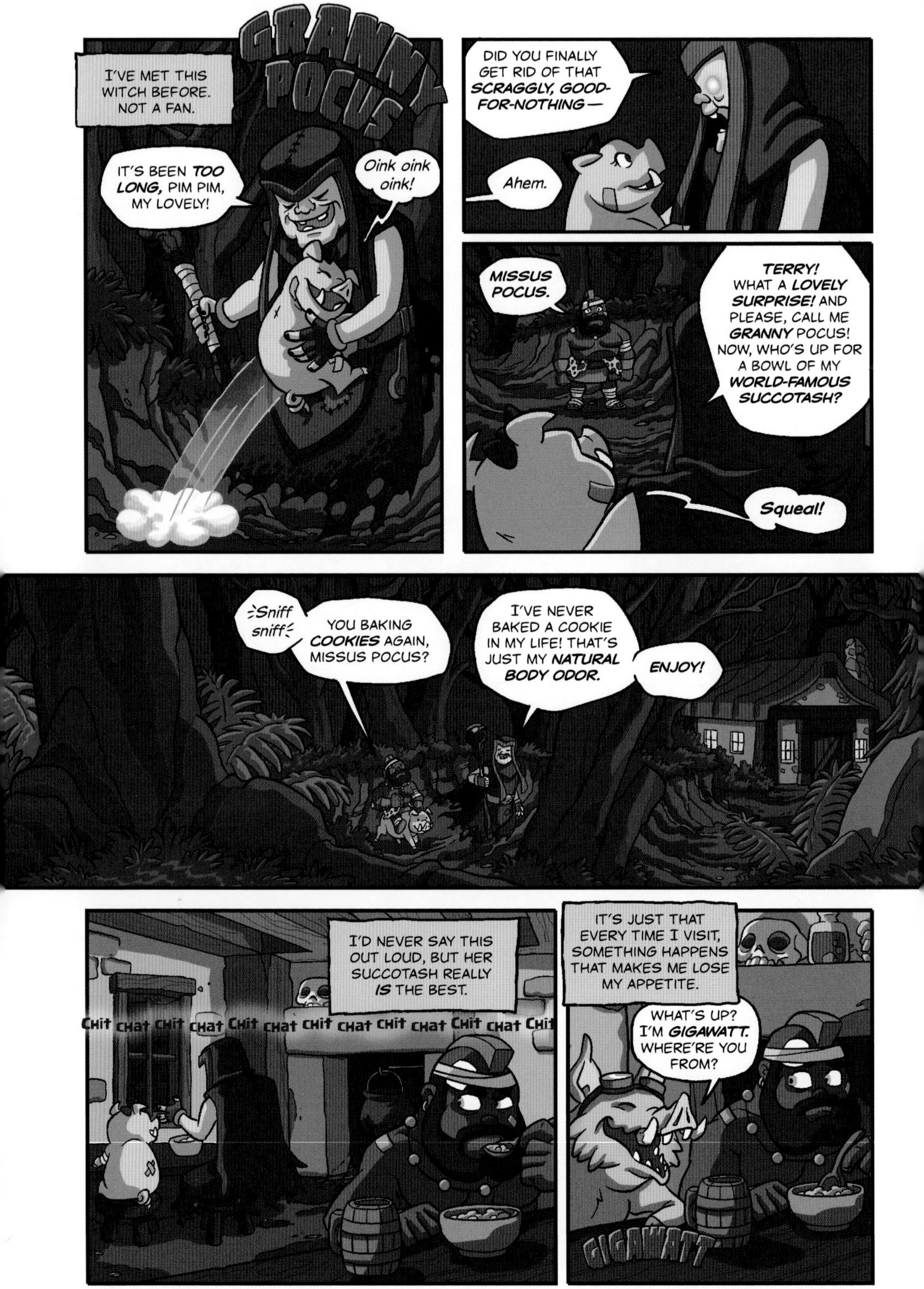
GRANNY POCUS
I'VE MET THIS WITCH BEFORE. NOT A FAN.
IT'S BEEN TOO LONG, PIM PIM, MY LOVELY!
Oink oink oink!
DID YOU FINALLY GET RID OF THAT SCRAGGLY, GOOD-FOR-NOTHING—
Ahem.
MISSUS POCUS.
TERRY! WHAT A LOVELY SURPRISE! AND PLEASE, CALL ME GRANNY POCUS! NOW, WHO'S UP FOR A BOWL OF MY WORLD-FAMOUS SUCCOTASH?
Squeal!
Sniff sniff
YOU BAKING COOKIES AGAIN, MISSUS POCUS?
I'VE NEVER BAKED A COOKIE IN MY LIFE! THAT'S JUST MY NATURAL BODY ODOR.
ENJOY!
I'D NEVER SAY THIS OUT LOUD, BUT HER SUCCOTASH REALLY IS THE BEST.
CHIT CHAT CHIT CHAT CHIT CHAT CHIT CHAT CHIT CHAT CHIT CHAT CHIT
IT'S JUST THAT EVERY TIME I VISIT, SOMETHING HAPPENS THAT MAKES ME LOSE MY APPETITE.
WHAT'S UP? I'M GIGAWATT. WHERE'RE YOU FROM?
GIGAWATT

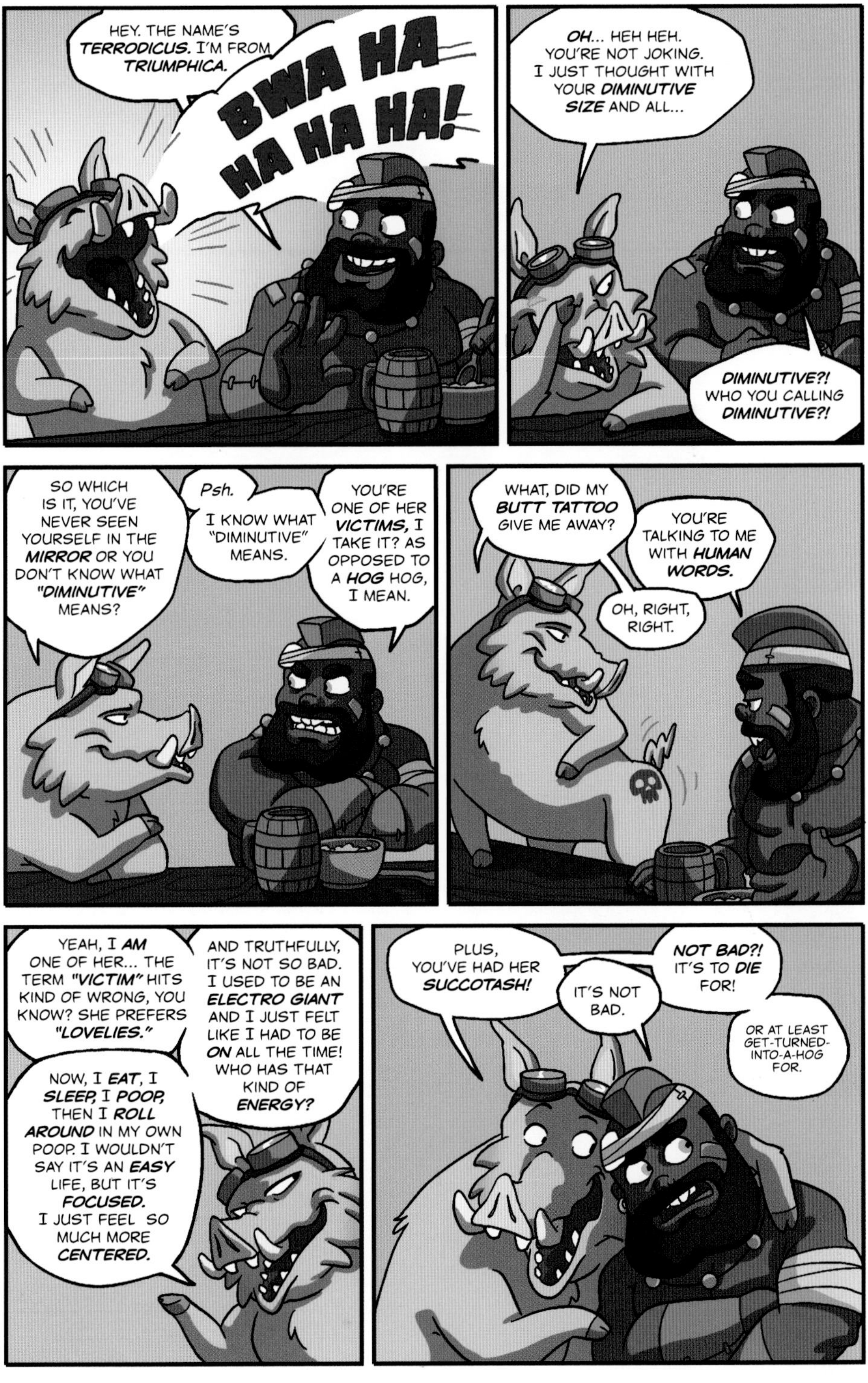
HEY. THE NAME'S TERRODICUS. I'M FROM TRIUMPHICA.
BWA HA HA HA HA!
OH... HEH HEH. YOU'RE NOT JOKING. I JUST THOUGHT WITH YOUR DIMINUTIVE SIZE AND ALL...
DIMINUTIVE?! WHO YOU CALLING DIMINUTIVE?!
SO WHICH IS IT, YOU'VE NEVER SEEN YOURSELF IN THE MIRROR OR YOU DON'T KNOW WHAT "DIMINUTIVE" MEANS?
Psh.
I KNOW WHAT "DIMINUTIVE" MEANS.
YOU'RE ONE OF HER VICTIMS, I TAKE IT? AS OPPOSED TO A HOG HOG, I MEAN.
WHAT, DID MY BUTT TATTOO GIVE ME AWAY?
YOU'RE TALKING TO ME WITH HUMAN WORDS.
OH, RIGHT, RIGHT.
YEAH, I AM ONE OF HER... THE TERM "VICTIM" HITS KIND OF WRONG, YOU KNOW? SHE PREFERS "LOVELIES."
AND TRUTHFULLY, IT'S NOT SO BAD. I USED TO BE AN ELECTRO GIANT AND I JUST FELT LIKE I HAD TO BE ON ALL THE TIME! WHO HAS THAT KIND OF ENERGY?
NOW, I EAT, I SLEEP, I POOP, THEN I ROLL AROUND IN MY OWN POOP. I WOULDN'T SAY IT'S AN EASY LIFE, BUT IT'S FOCUSED. I JUST FEEL SO MUCH MORE CENTERED.
PLUS, YOU'VE HAD HER SUCCOTASH!
IT'S NOT BAD.
NOT BAD?! IT'S TO DIE FOR!
OR AT LEAST GET-TURNED-INTO-A-HOG FOR.

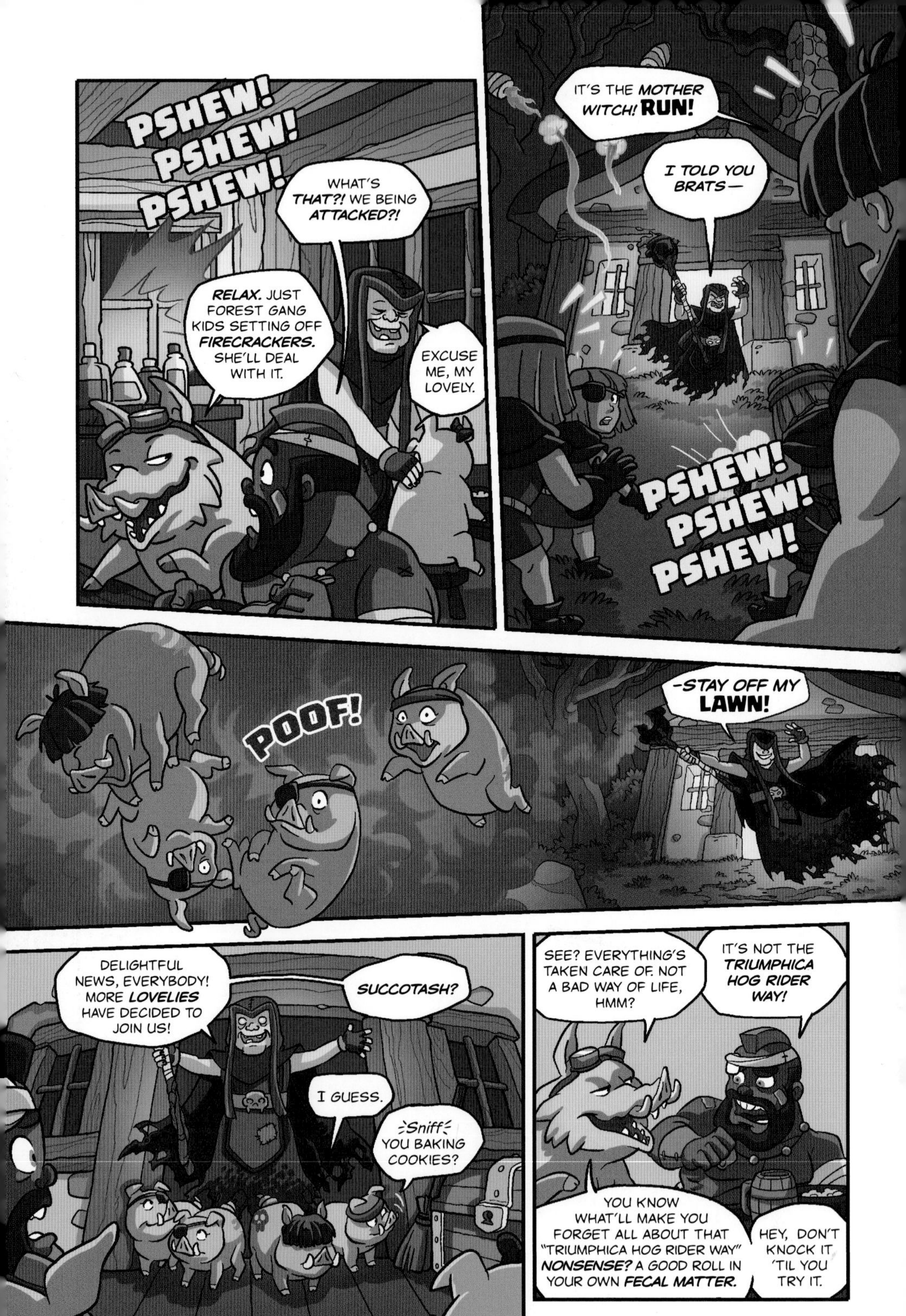
PSHEW! PSHEW! PSHEW!
WHAT'S THAT?! WE BEING ATTACKED?!
RELAX. JUST FOREST GANG KIDS SETTING OFF FIRECRACKERS. SHE'LL DEAL WITH IT.
EXCUSE ME, MY LOVELY.
IT'S THE MOTHER WITCH! RUN!
I TOLD YOU BRATS—
PSHEW! PSHEW! PSHEW!
POOF!
–STAY OFF MY LAWN!
DELIGHTFUL NEWS, EVERYBODY! MORE LOVELIES HAVE DECIDED TO JOIN US!
SUCCOTASH?
I GUESS.
Sniff YOU BAKING COOKIES?
SEE? EVERYTHING'S TAKEN CARE OF. NOT A BAD WAY OF LIFE, HMM?
IT'S NOT THE TRIUMPHICA HOG RIDER WAY!
YOU KNOW WHAT'LL MAKE YOU FORGET ALL ABOUT THAT "TRIUMPHICA HOG RIDER WAY" NONSENSE? A GOOD ROLL IN YOUR OWN FECAL MATTER.
HEY, DON'T KNOCK IT 'TIL YOU TRY IT.

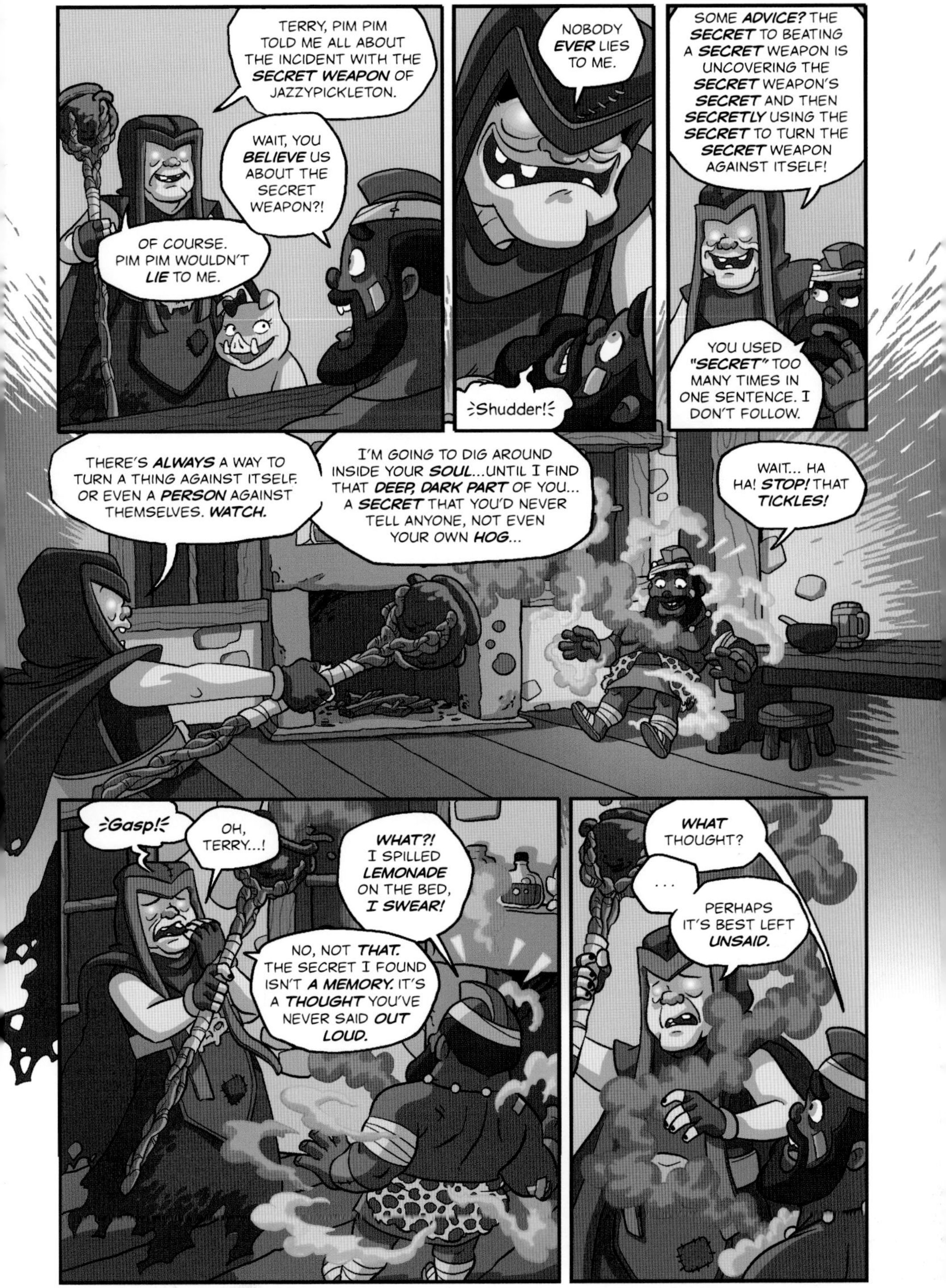
TERRY, PIM PIM TOLD ME ALL ABOUT THE INCIDENT WITH THE SECRET WEAPON OF JAZZYPICKLETON.
WAIT, YOU BELIEVE US ABOUT THE SECRET WEAPON?!
OF COURSE. PIM PIM WOULDN'T LIE TO ME.
NOBODY EVER LIES TO ME.
Shudder!
SOME ADVICE? THE SECRET TO BEATING A SECRET WEAPON IS UNCOVERING THE SECRET WEAPON'S SECRET AND THEN SECRETLY USING THE SECRET TO TURN THE SECRET WEAPON AGAINST ITSELF!
YOU USED "SECRET" TOO MANY TIMES IN ONE SENTENCE. I DON'T FOLLOW.
THERE'S ALWAYS A WAY TO TURN A THING AGAINST ITSELF. OR EVEN A PERSON AGAINST THEMSELVES. WATCH.
I'M GOING TO DIG AROUND INSIDE YOUR SOUL...UNTIL I FIND THAT DEEP, DARK PART OF YOU... A SECRET THAT YOU'D NEVER TELL ANYONE, NOT EVEN YOUR OWN HOG...
WAIT... HA HA! STOP! THAT TICKLES!
Gasp!
OH, TERRY...!
WHAT?! I SPILLED LEMONADE ON THE BED, I SWEAR!
NO, NOT THAT. THE SECRET I FOUND ISN'T A MEMORY. IT'S A THOUGHT YOU'VE NEVER SAID OUT LOUD.
WHAT THOUGHT?
...
PERHAPS IT'S BEST LEFT UNSAID.

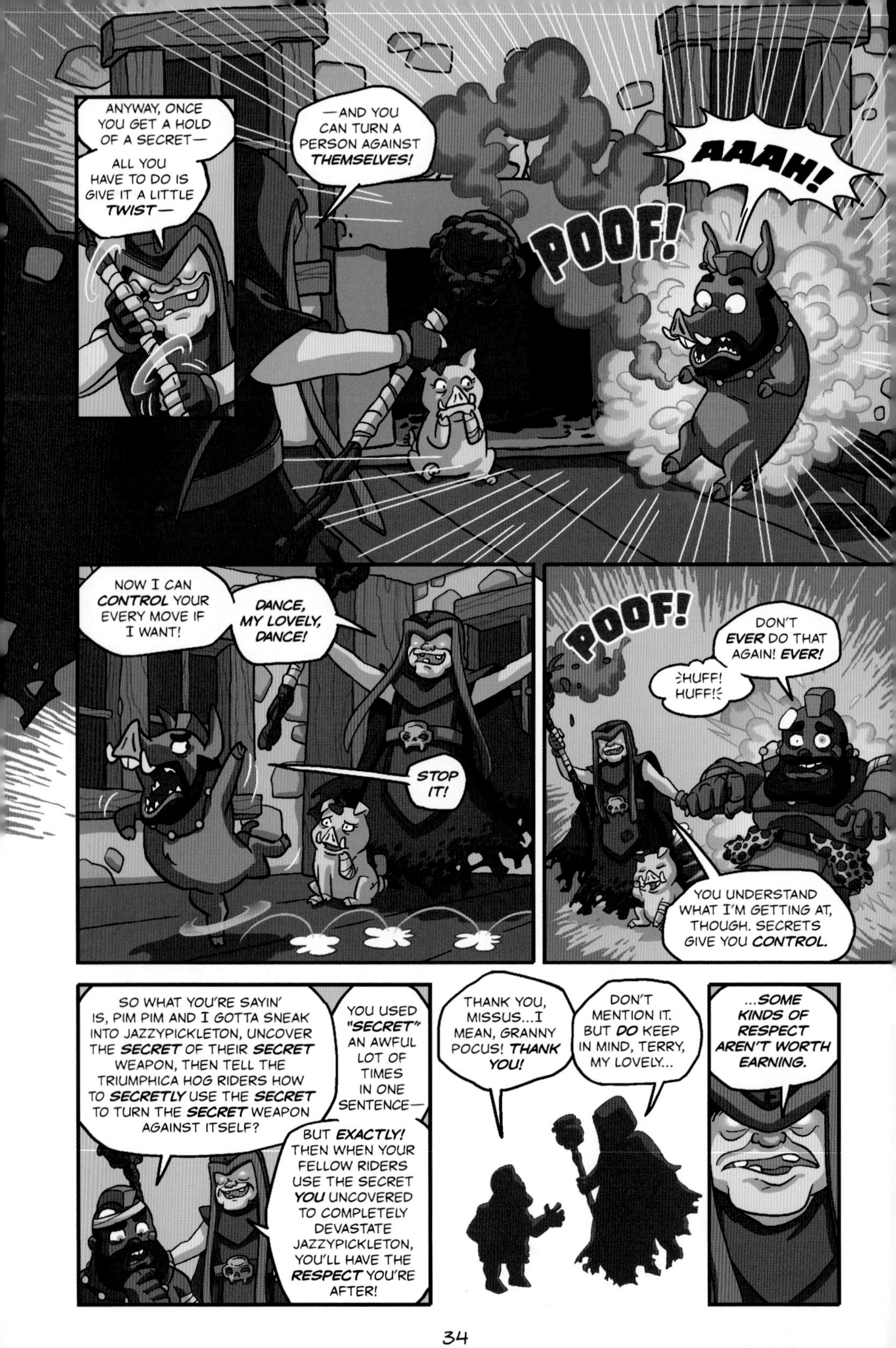

ANYWAY, ONCE YOU GET A HOLD OF A SECRET—
ALL YOU HAVE TO DO IS GIVE IT A LITTLE TWIST—
—AND YOU CAN TURN A PERSON AGAINST THEMSELVES!
AAAH!
POOF!
NOW I CAN CONTROL YOUR EVERY MOVE IF I WANT!
DANCE, MY LOVELY, DANCE!
STOP IT!
POOF!
DON'T EVER DO THAT AGAIN! EVER!
HUFF! HUFF!
YOU UNDERSTAND WHAT I'M GETTING AT, THOUGH. SECRETS GIVE YOU CONTROL.
SO WHAT YOU'RE SAYIN' IS, PIM PIM AND I GOTTA SNEAK INTO JAZZYPICKLETON, UNCOVER THE SECRET OF THEIR SECRET WEAPON, THEN TELL THE TRIUMPHICA HOG RIDERS HOW TO SECRETLY USE THE SECRET TO TURN THE SECRET WEAPON AGAINST ITSELF?
YOU USED "SECRET" AN AWFUL LOT OF TIMES IN ONE SENTENCE—
BUT EXACTLY! THEN WHEN YOUR FELLOW RIDERS USE THE SECRET YOU UNCOVERED TO COMPLETELY DEVASTATE JAZZYPICKLETON, YOU'LL HAVE THE RESPECT YOU'RE AFTER!
THANK YOU, MISSUS...I MEAN, GRANNY POCUS! THANK YOU!
DON'T MENTION IT. BUT DO KEEP IN MIND, TERRY, MY LOVELY...
...SOME KINDS OF RESPECT AREN'T WORTH EARNING.

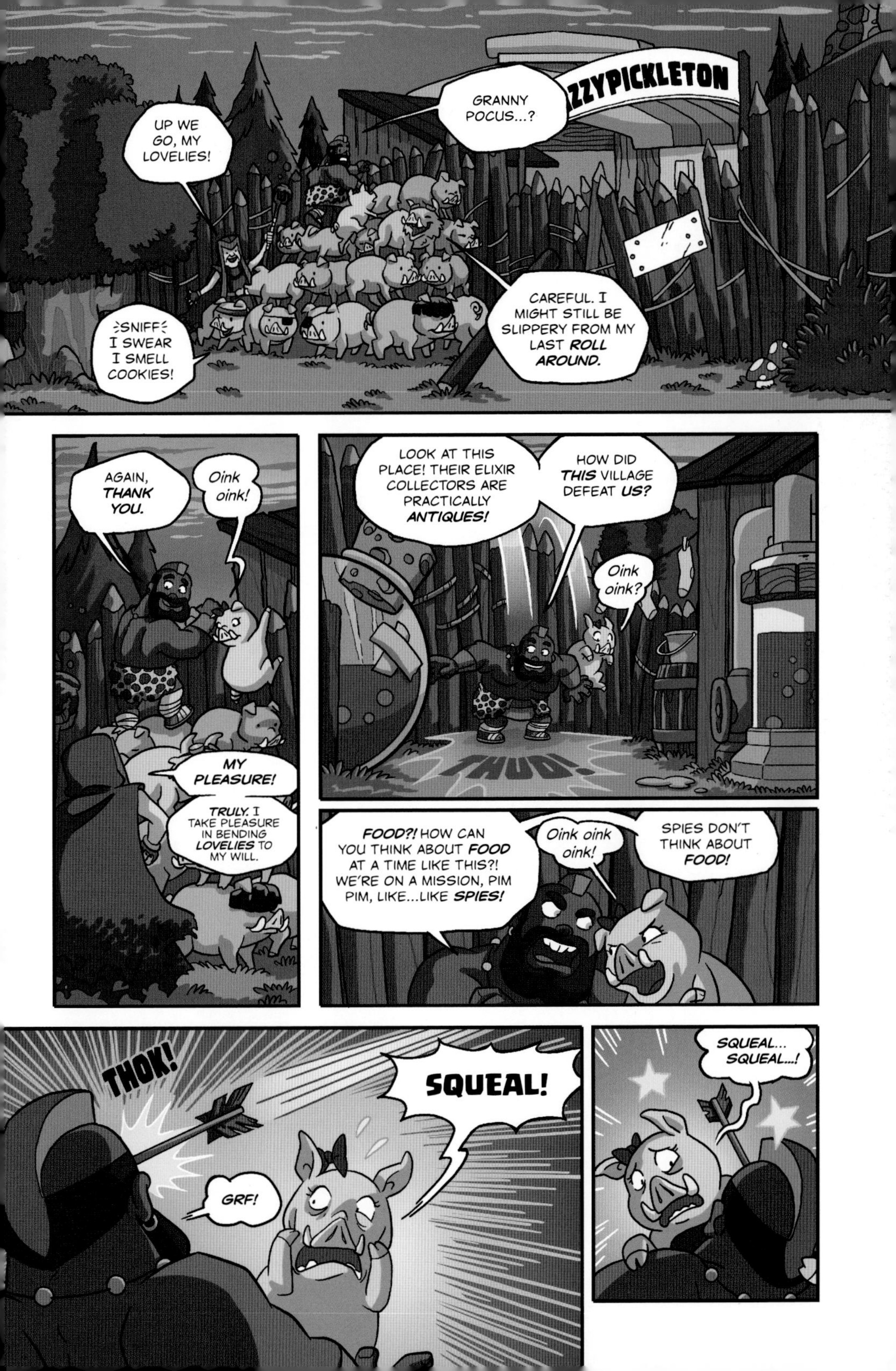
ZZYPICKLETON
UP WE GO, MY LOVELIES!
GRANNY POCUS...?
SNIFF I SWEAR I SMELL COOKIES!
CAREFUL. I MIGHT STILL BE SLIPPERY FROM MY LAST ROLL AROUND.
AGAIN, THANK YOU.
Oink oink!
MY PLEASURE!
TRULY. I TAKE PLEASURE IN BENDING LOVELIES TO MY WILL.
LOOK AT THIS PLACE! THEIR ELIXIR COLLECTORS ARE PRACTICALLY ANTIQUES!
HOW DID THIS VILLAGE DEFEAT US?
Oink oink?
THUD!
FOOD?! HOW CAN YOU THINK ABOUT FOOD AT A TIME LIKE THIS?! WE'RE ON A MISSION, PIM PIM, LIKE...LIKE SPIES!
Oink oink oink!
SPIES DON'T THINK ABOUT FOOD!
THOK!
SQUEAL!
GRF!
SQUEAL... SQUEAL...!

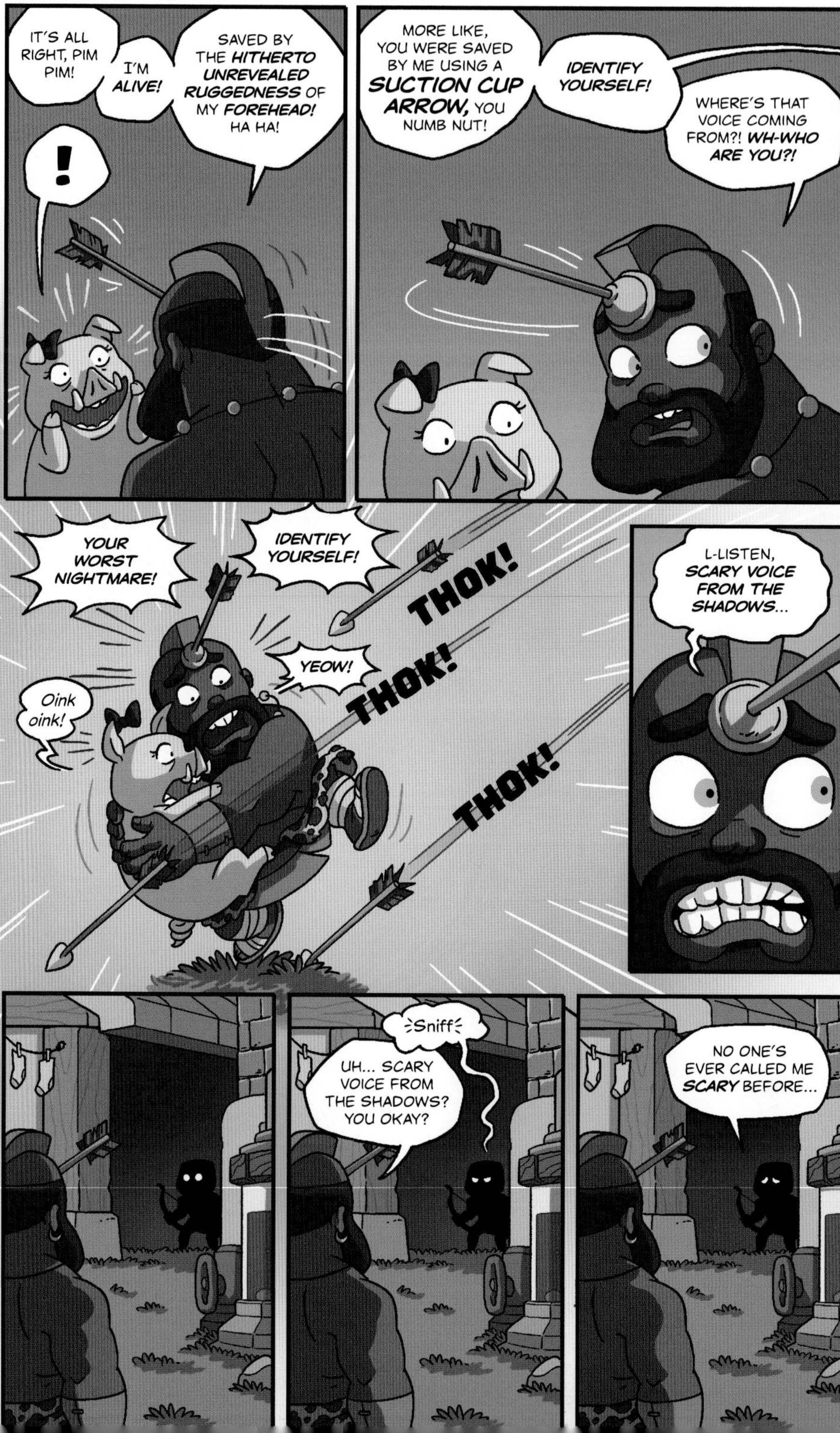
IT'S ALL RIGHT, PIM PIM!
I'M ALIVE!
SAVED BY THE HITHERTO UNREVEALED RUGGEDNESS OF MY FOREHEAD! HA HA!
!
MORE LIKE, YOU WERE SAVED BY ME USING A SUCTION CUP ARROW, YOU NUMB NUT!
IDENTIFY YOURSELF!
WHERE'S THAT VOICE COMING FROM?! WH-WHO ARE YOU?!
YOUR WORST NIGHTMARE!
IDENTIFY YOURSELF!
YEOW!
Oink oink!
THOK!
THOK!
THOK!
L-LISTEN, SCARY VOICE FROM THE SHADOWS...
Sniff
UH... SCARY VOICE FROM THE SHADOWS? YOU OKAY?
NO ONE'S EVER CALLED ME SCARY BEFORE...

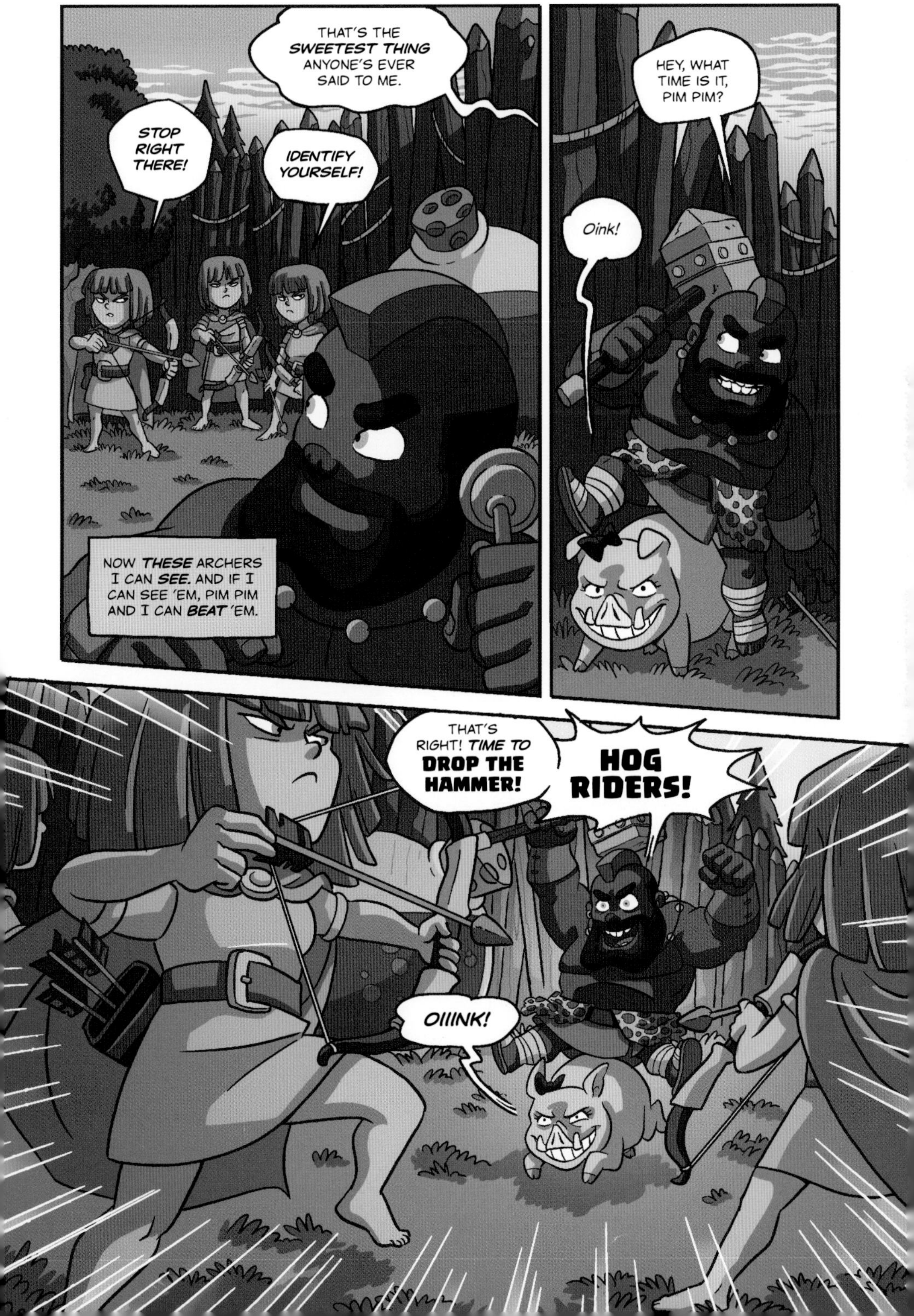
THAT'S THE **SWEETEST THING** ANYONE'S EVER SAID TO ME.
STOP RIGHT THERE!
IDENTIFY YOURSELF!
NOW **THESE** ARCHERS I CAN **SEE.** AND IF I CAN SEE 'EM, PIM PIM AND I CAN **BEAT** 'EM.
HEY, WHAT TIME IS IT, PIM PIM?
Oink!
THAT'S RIGHT! **TIME TO DROP THE HAMMER!**
HOG RIDERS!
OIIINK!

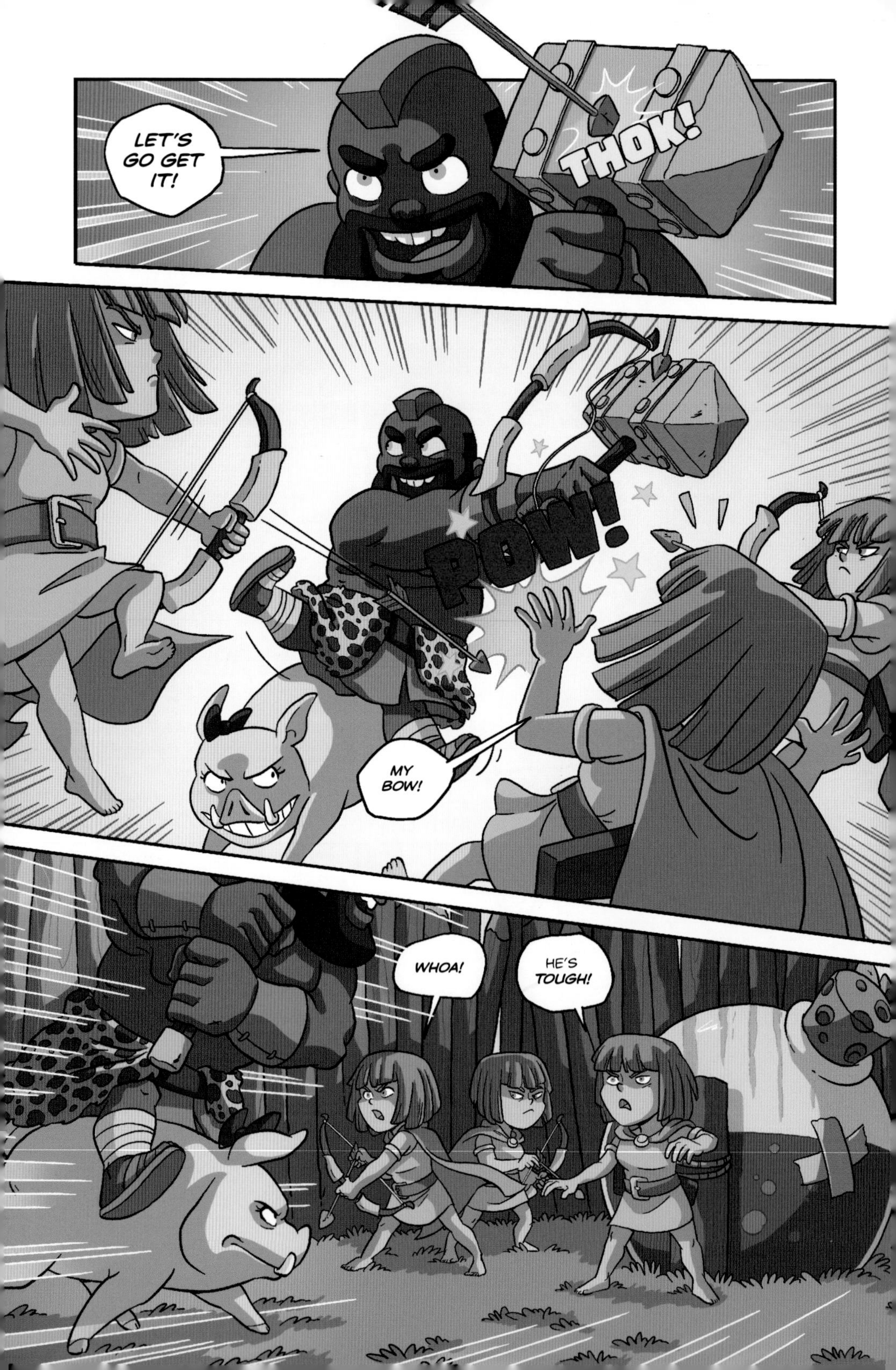
LET'S GO GET IT!
THOK!
POW!
MY BOW!
WHOA!
HE'S TOUGH!

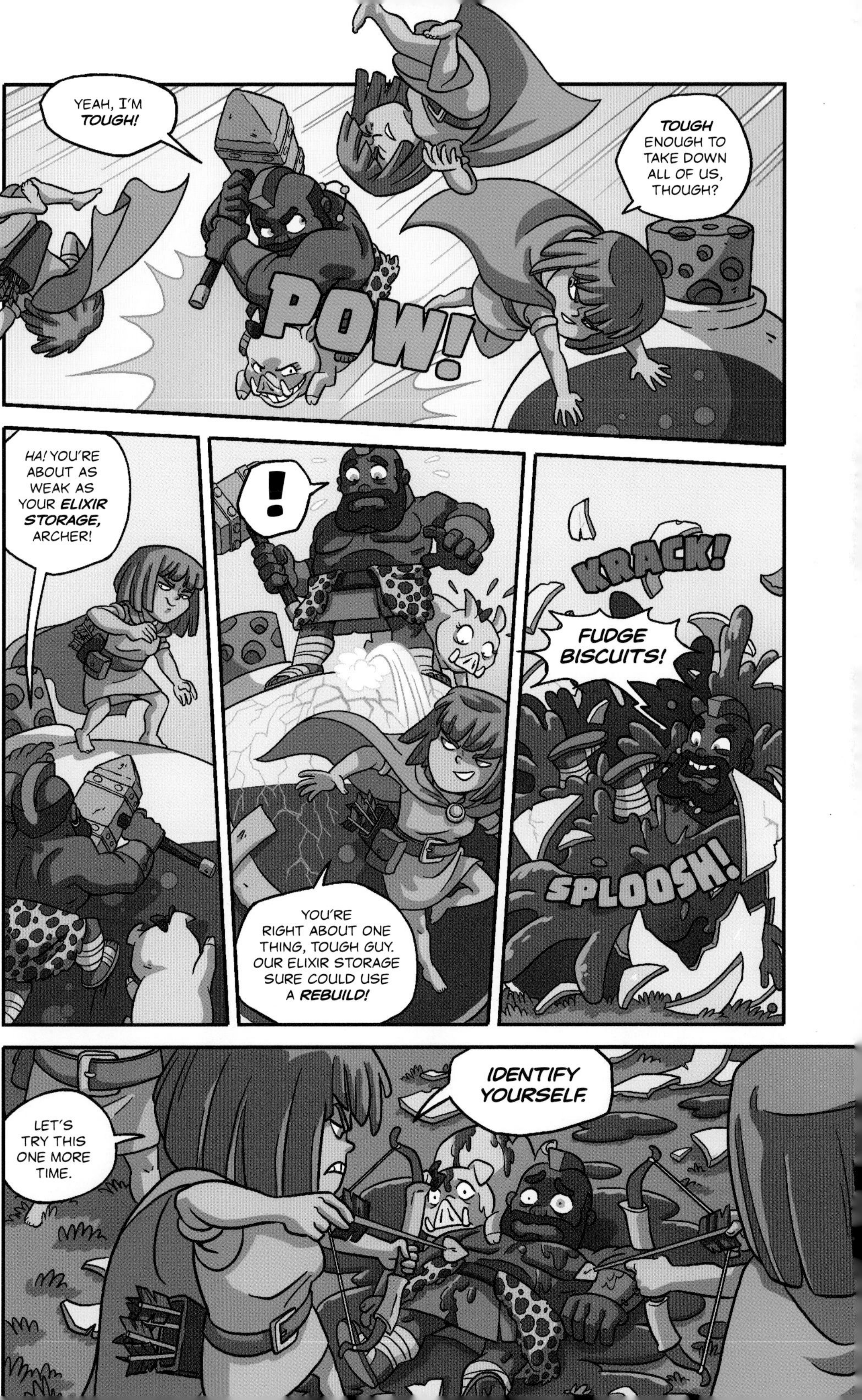
YEAH, I'M *TOUGH!*
TOUGH ENOUGH TO TAKE DOWN ALL OF US, THOUGH?
POW!
HA! YOU'RE ABOUT AS WEAK AS YOUR *ELIXIR STORAGE,* ARCHER!
!
YOU'RE RIGHT ABOUT ONE THING, TOUGH GUY. OUR ELIXIR STORAGE SURE COULD USE A *REBUILD!*
KRACK!
FUDGE BISCUITS!
SPLOOSH!
LET'S TRY THIS ONE MORE TIME.
IDENTIFY YOURSELF.

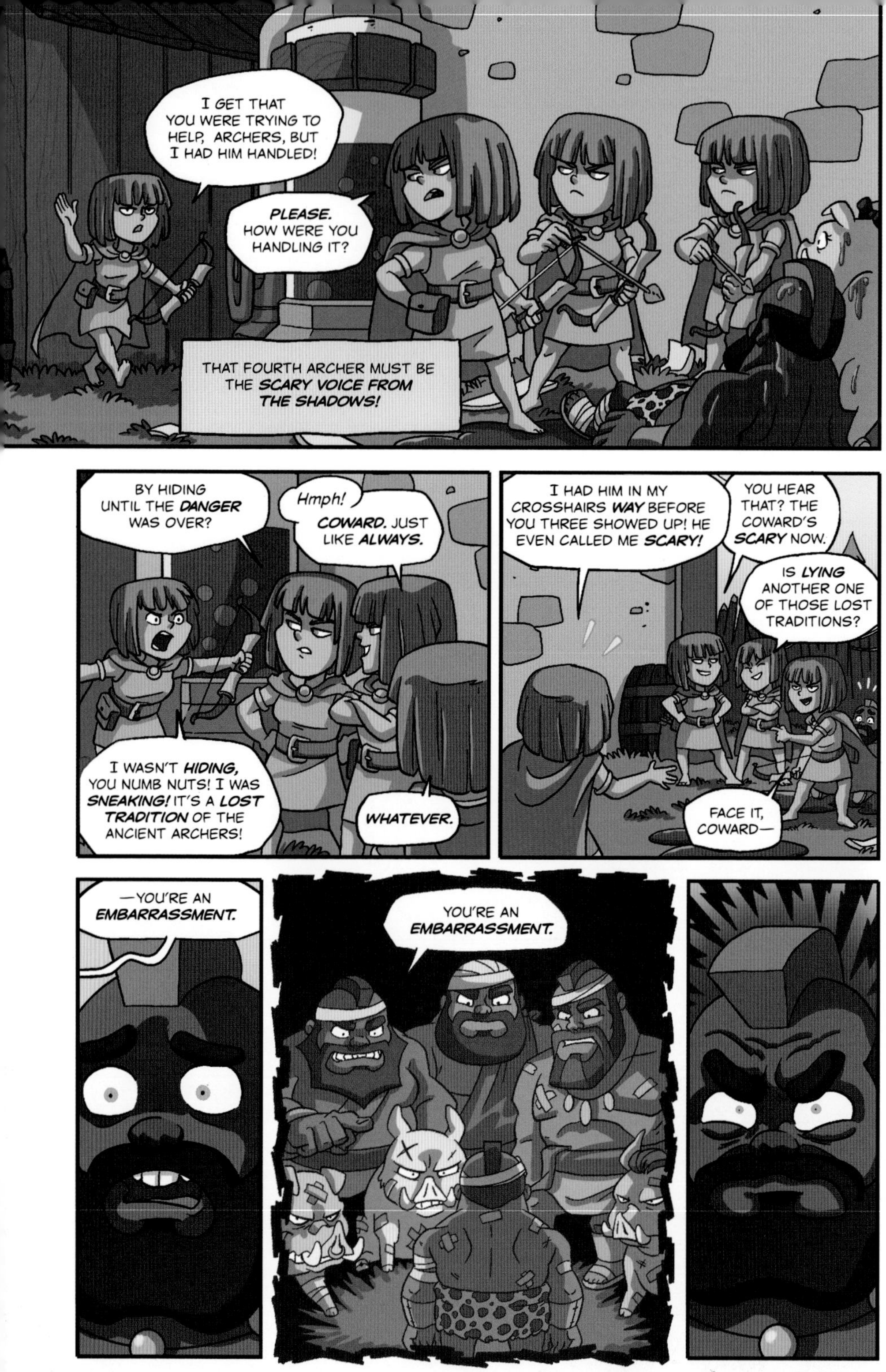

I GET THAT YOU WERE TRYING TO HELP, ARCHERS, BUT I HAD HIM HANDLED!
PLEASE. HOW WERE YOU HANDLING IT?
THAT FOURTH ARCHER MUST BE THE SCARY VOICE FROM THE SHADOWS!
BY HIDING UNTIL THE DANGER WAS OVER?
Hmph!
COWARD. JUST LIKE ALWAYS.
I WASN'T HIDING, YOU NUMB NUTS! I WAS SNEAKING! IT'S A LOST TRADITION OF THE ANCIENT ARCHERS!
WHATEVER.
I HAD HIM IN MY CROSSHAIRS WAY BEFORE YOU THREE SHOWED UP! HE EVEN CALLED ME SCARY!
YOU HEAR THAT? THE COWARD'S SCARY NOW.
IS LYING ANOTHER ONE OF THOSE LOST TRADITIONS?
FACE IT, COWARD—
—YOU'RE AN EMBARRASSMENT.
YOU'RE AN EMBARRASSMENT.

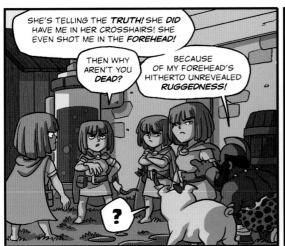

SHE'S TELLING THE **TRUTH!** SHE **DID** HAVE ME IN HER CROSSHAIRS! SHE EVEN SHOT ME IN THE **FOREHEAD!**

THEN WHY AREN'T YOU **DEAD?**

BECAUSE OF MY FOREHEAD'S HITHERTO UNREVEALED **RUGGEDNESS!**

?

YOU MEAN BECAUSE OF MY **SUCTION CUP ARROW,** BUT HOLD ON—

YOU'RE BACKING ME UP?

YOU'RE BACKING HER UP?

YEAH. I'M BACKING HER UP.

ARCHERS, ARE WE GONNA BELIEVE THIS...THIS **SPY?!**

SPY?! PSH. **ME?!**

NAW!

YOU'D THINK A SPY WOULD **TALK** WAY LESS.

AND **SWEAT** WAY LESS.

WHY ARE YOU HERE, THEN?

I'M...I'M...A **NEW RECRUIT!**

YEAH, **THAT'S RIGHT!** I'M ONE OF JAZZYPICKLETON'S NEW RECRUITS!

THEN SHOULDN'T YOU BE COMING FROM THE **BARRACKS?**

MAYBE HE GOT TURNED AROUND!

I TOLD YOU ALL, I'VE GOT HIM **HANDLED!**

Hmph.

WHATEVER.

END OF OUR SHIFT, ANYWAY.

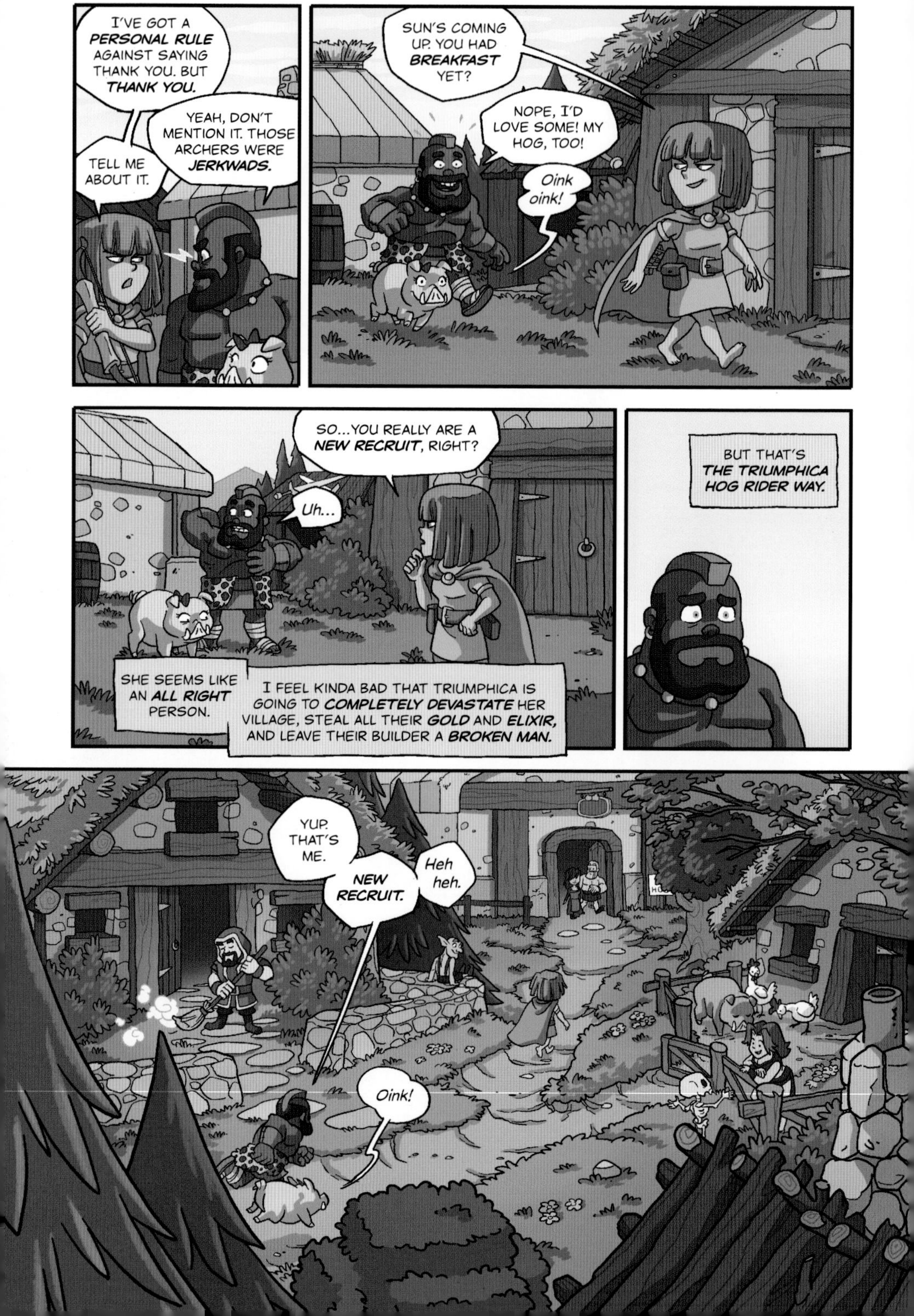

I'VE GOT A PERSONAL RULE AGAINST SAYING THANK YOU. BUT THANK YOU.
YEAH, DON'T MENTION IT. THOSE ARCHERS WERE JERKWADS.
TELL ME ABOUT IT.
SUN'S COMING UP. YOU HAD BREAKFAST YET?
NOPE, I'D LOVE SOME! MY HOG, TOO!
Oink oink!
SO...YOU REALLY ARE A NEW RECRUIT, RIGHT?
Uh...
SHE SEEMS LIKE AN ALL RIGHT PERSON.
I FEEL KINDA BAD THAT TRIUMPHICA IS GOING TO COMPLETELY DEVASTATE HER VILLAGE, STEAL ALL THEIR GOLD AND ELIXIR, AND LEAVE THEIR BUILDER A BROKEN MAN.
BUT THAT'S THE TRIUMPHICA HOG RIDER WAY.
YUP. THAT'S ME.
NEW RECRUIT.
Heh heh.
Oink!

Chapter 2

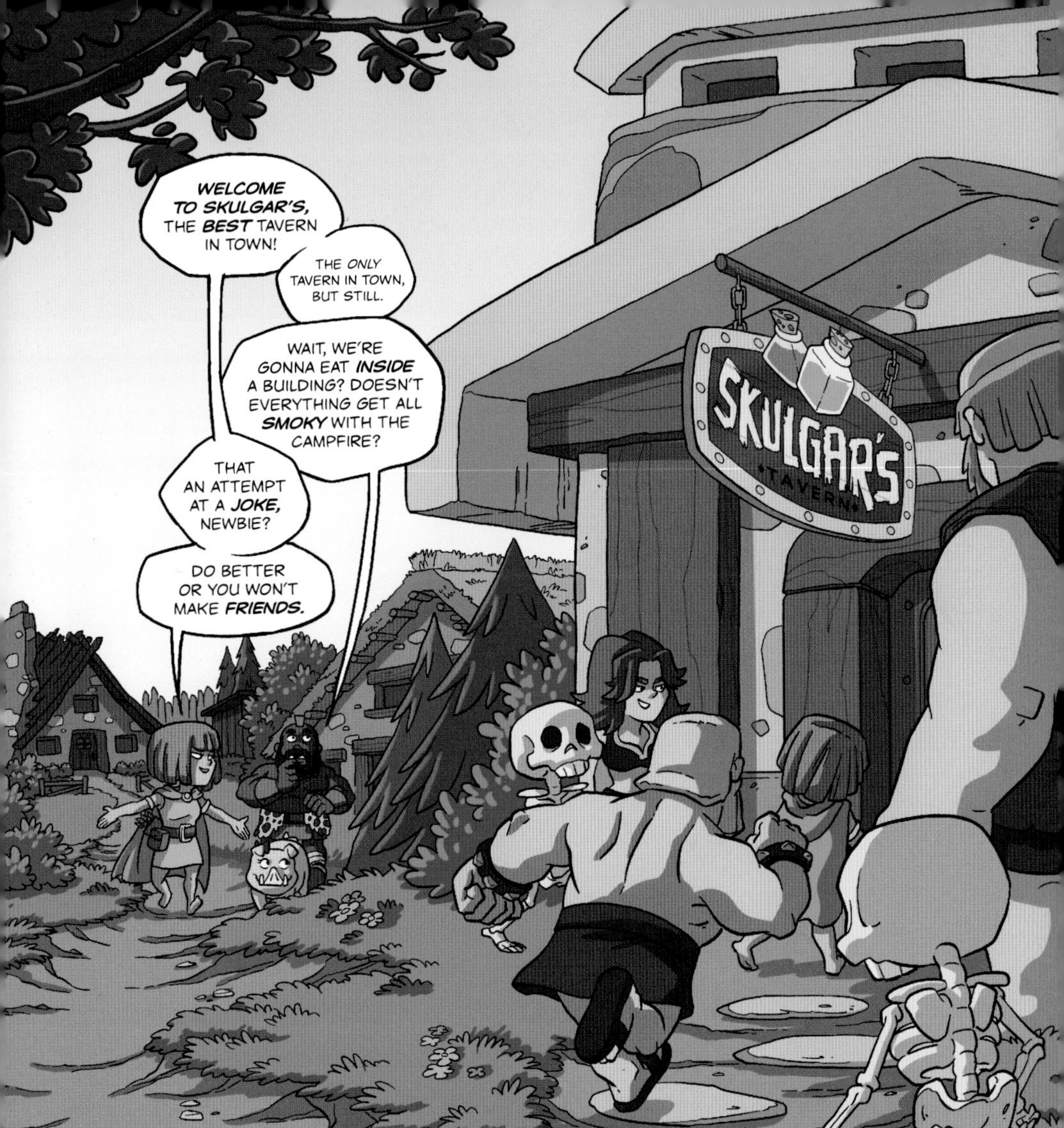
WELCOME TO SKULGAR'S, THE BEST TAVERN IN TOWN!
THE ONLY TAVERN IN TOWN, BUT STILL.
WAIT, WE'RE GONNA EAT INSIDE A BUILDING? DOESN'T EVERYTHING GET ALL SMOKY WITH THE CAMPFIRE?
THAT AN ATTEMPT AT A JOKE, NEWBIE?
DO BETTER OR YOU WON'T MAKE FRIENDS.
SKULGAR'S
TAVERN

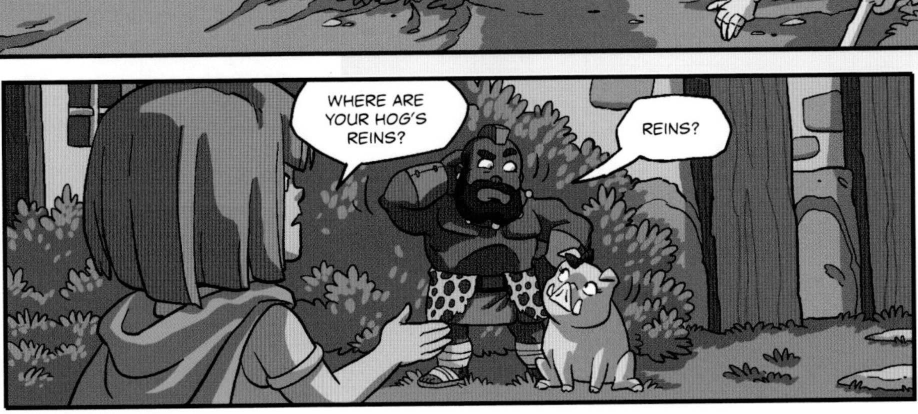
WHERE ARE YOUR HOG'S REINS?
REINS?

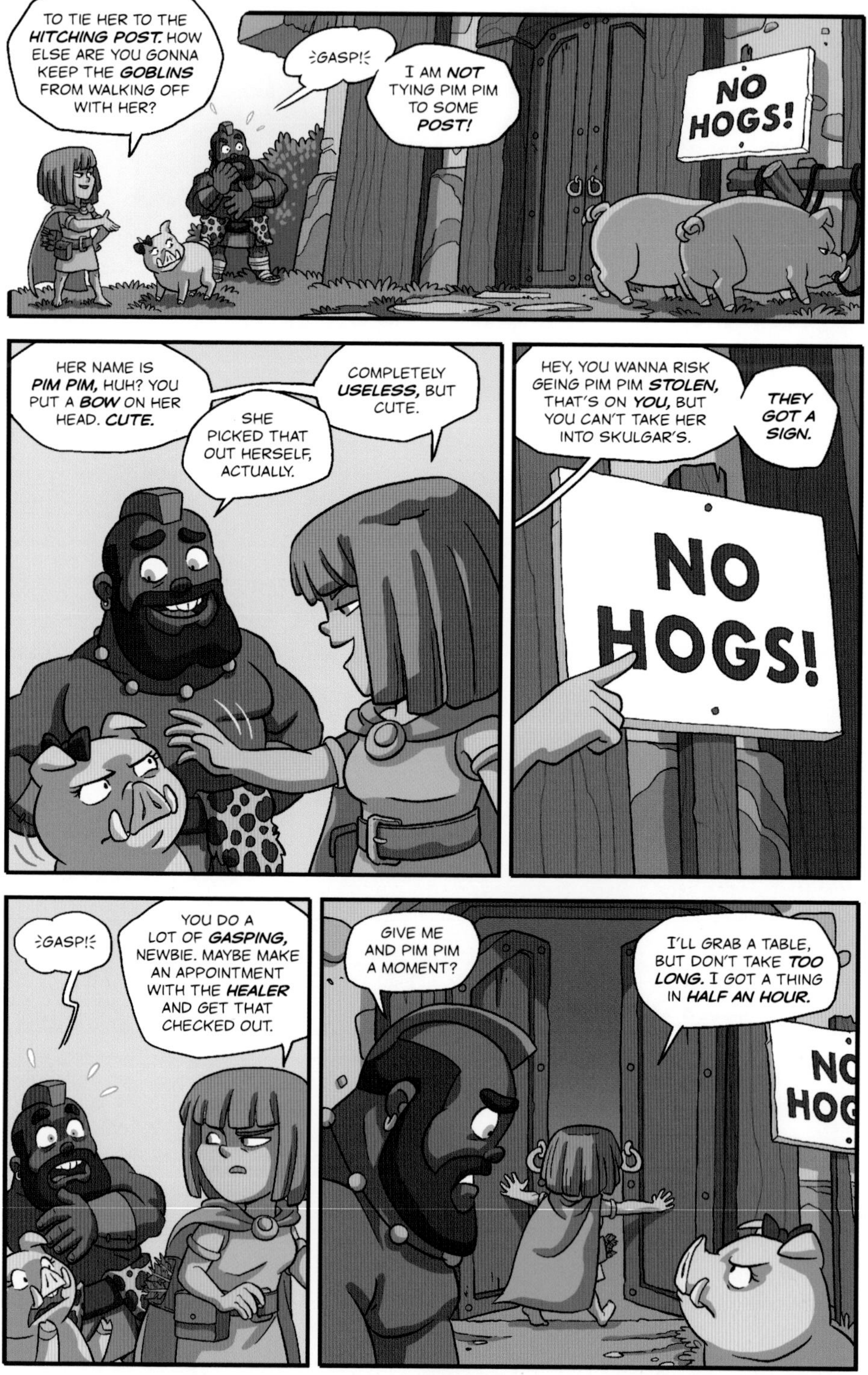
TO TIE HER TO THE HITCHING POST. HOW ELSE ARE YOU GONNA KEEP THE GOBLINS FROM WALKING OFF WITH HER?
GASP!
I AM NOT TYING PIM PIM TO SOME POST!
NO HOGS!
HER NAME IS PIM PIM, HUH? YOU PUT A BOW ON HER HEAD. CUTE.
SHE PICKED THAT OUT HERSELF, ACTUALLY.
COMPLETELY USELESS, BUT CUTE.
HEY, YOU WANNA RISK GEING PIM PIM STOLEN, THAT'S ON YOU, BUT YOU CAN'T TAKE HER INTO SKULGAR'S.
THEY GOT A SIGN.
NO HOGS!
GASP!
YOU DO A LOT OF GASPING, NEWBIE. MAYBE MAKE AN APPOINTMENT WITH THE HEALER AND GET THAT CHECKED OUT.
GIVE ME AND PIM PIM A MOMENT?
I'LL GRAB A TABLE, BUT DON'T TAKE TOO LONG. I GOT A THING IN HALF AN HOUR.

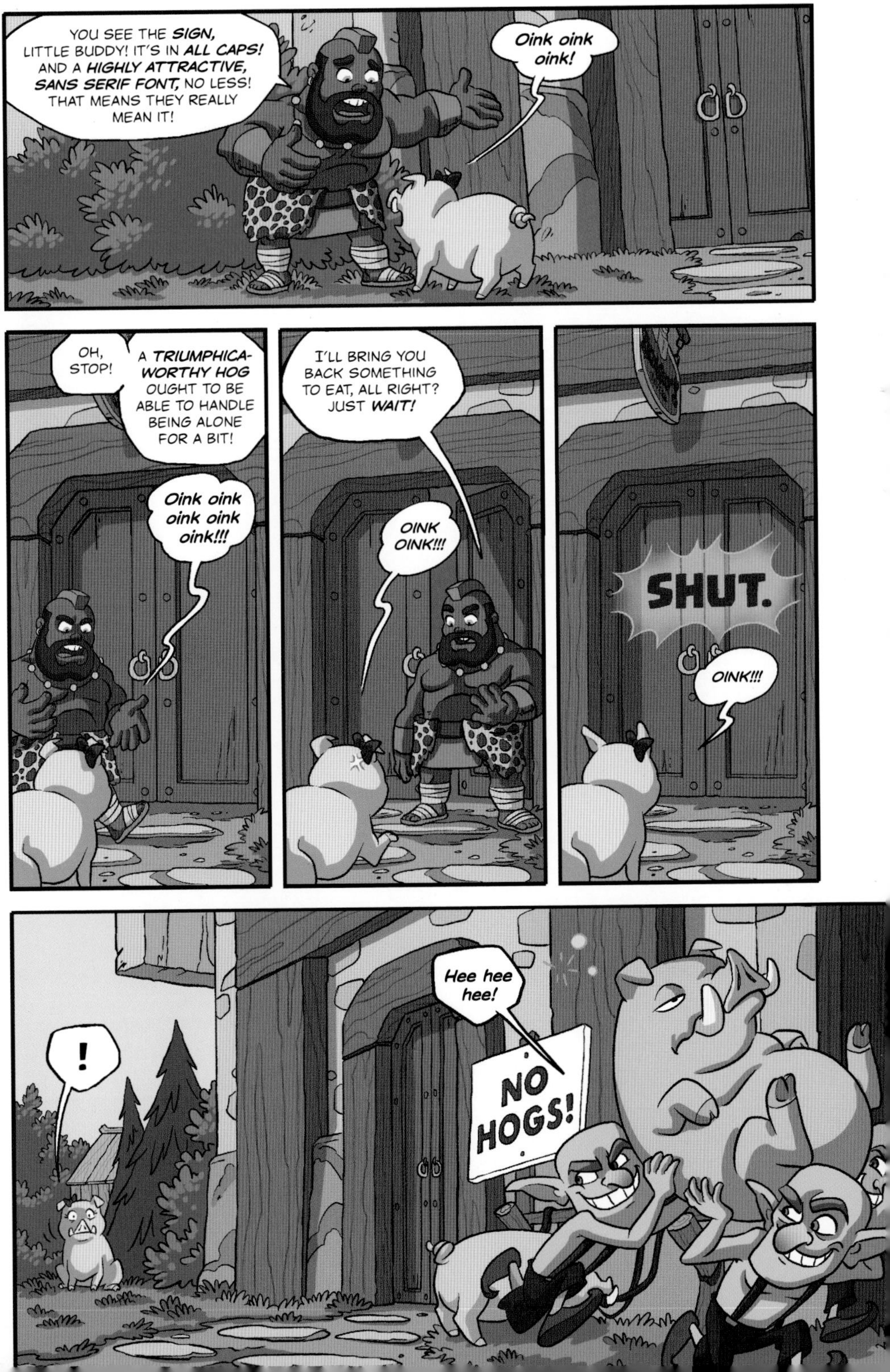
YOU SEE THE SIGN, LITTLE BUDDY! IT'S IN ALL CAPS! AND A HIGHLY ATTRACTIVE, SANS SERIF FONT, NO LESS! THAT MEANS THEY REALLY MEAN IT!
Oink oink oink!
OH, STOP!
A TRIUMPHICA-WORTHY HOG OUGHT TO BE ABLE TO HANDLE BEING ALONE FOR A BIT!
Oink oink oink oink oink!!!
I'LL BRING YOU BACK SOMETHING TO EAT, ALL RIGHT? JUST WAIT!
OINK OINK!!!
SHUT.
OINK!!!
!
Hee hee hee!
NO HOGS!

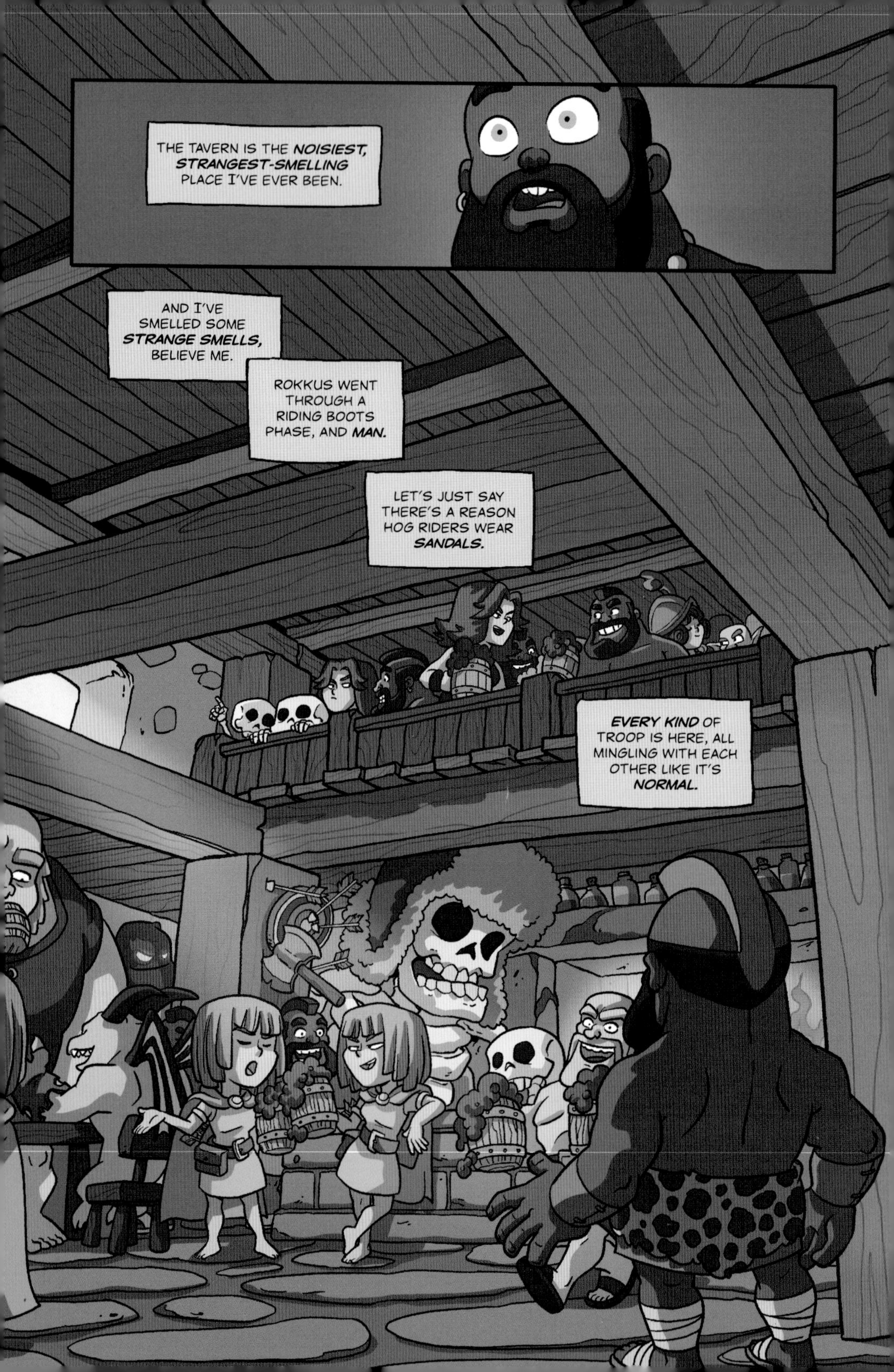
THE TAVERN IS THE **NOISIEST, STRANGEST-SMELLING** PLACE I'VE EVER BEEN.
AND I'VE SMELLED SOME ***STRANGE SMELLS,*** BELIEVE ME.
ROKKUS WENT THROUGH A RIDING BOOTS PHASE, AND ***MAN.***
LET'S JUST SAY THERE'S A REASON HOG RIDERS WEAR ***SANDALS.***
EVERY KIND OF TROOP IS HERE, ALL MINGLING WITH EACH OTHER LIKE IT'S ***NORMAL.***

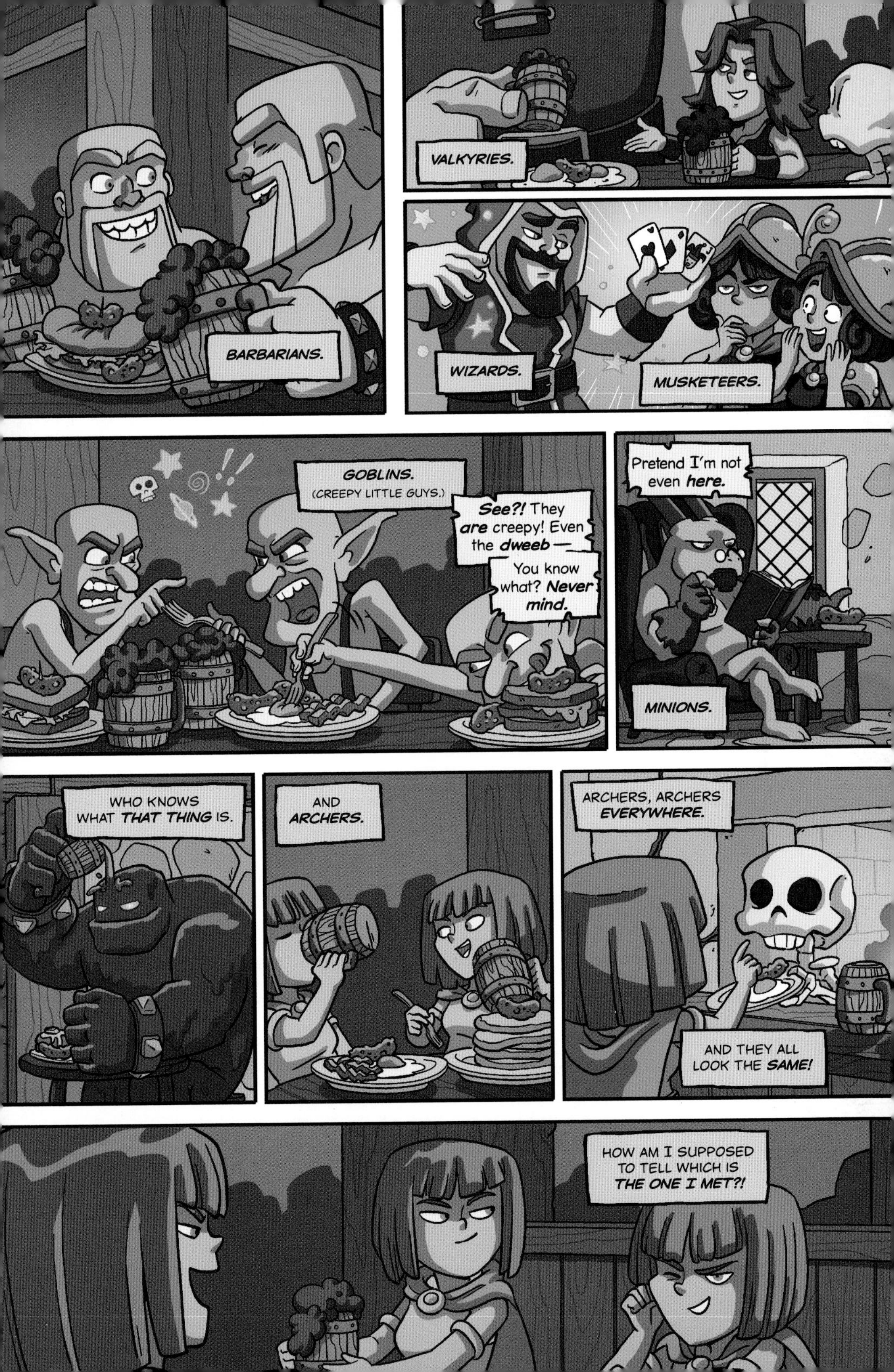
BARBARIANS.
VALKYRIES.
WIZARDS.
MUSKETEERS.
GOBLINS.
(CREEPY LITTLE GUYS.)
See?! They are creepy! Even the dweeb—
You know what? Never mind.
Pretend I'm not even here.
MINIONS.
WHO KNOWS WHAT THAT THING IS.
AND ARCHERS.
ARCHERS, ARCHERS EVERYWHERE.
AND THEY ALL LOOK THE SAME!
HOW AM I SUPPOSED TO TELL WHICH IS THE ONE I MET?!

I NEVER CAUGHT HER *NAME.*

HI, THERE!

ARE YOU... THE *SCARY VOICE FROM THE SHADOWS?*

HA HA. MY NAME'S *STACY!*

AFTER STACY INTRODUCES HERSELF, I START TO NOTICE THINGS ABOUT HER. LIKE, HER HAIR IS SHORTER THAN THE OTHER ARCHERS'.

...AND NOBODY'S EVER ... MY VOICE SCARY BEFOR... SUPPOSE IT CAN BE WHE... ...OODY LIKE THE OTHER DAY I ...AS ...NE OF THE SKELETONS ... ...E A BOWL OF OATMEA... ...E SLICES ON TOP WHE... ...Y ORDERED A BOWL... ...H PICKLE SLICES O... ...WAS I STEAMED! W... ...ELETON CAME BACK TO ... ...UAL, "HOW ARE THINGS... ...RE GAVE M... ...AR...

LISTEN, I'M—

AND SHE WEARS A *HAIR CLIP.*

WHICH IS IMPR... ...WHEN YOU THIN... BECAUSE SKELE... EVEN HAVE EARS! ...ONDER, THOUGH, D... ...O THEY HEAR... ...D THEY HAVE LITT... ... THE SIDES OF THEIR ... ...WHERE THE SOUND CAN... ...D GUESS THAT THEY D... ...M NOT SURE BECAUSE ... ...E NEVER GOTTEN AN... ...P-CLO...E LOOK...

TRUE, TRUE, BUT I'M LOOKING FOR—

AND SHE'S GOT THAT *MOLE* ON HER CHEEK.

...M CURIOUS, OF COU... ...ND IF OFFERED THE... SUPPOSE I'D TAKE I... NOT JUST GOING TO ... ...HAT'D BE AWFULLY RUDE... ...THINK? I MEAN, THEY MIGHT... ...AVE INTERNAL ORGANS ... ...EY PROBABLY STILL HAVE... ...WHICH BRINGS ME BA... ...T INCIDENT I TOLD YO... ...EARLIER, THE ONE I RE... ...S THE CASE OF THE MISTA... ...ATMEAL ORDER WHEN I'M... ...CUSSING IT WITH TH... ...HER ARCHERS...

NOT TO BE RUDE, BUT I GOTTA—

I CAN *DEFINITELY* PICK STACY OUT OF A CROWD NOW.

YOU KNOW WHAT I MEAN?

AND I CAN *DEFINITELY* SAY THAT SHE'S *NOT* THE ARCHER I MET EARLIER.

...S FUNNY, THOUGH. THE OTHER ARCHE... ...NER SEEM TO KNOW WHAT I'M TALKING AB... ...OUGH I'VE BROUGHT IT UP OVER A... ...D OVER AGAIN. YOU'D THINK THE... ...AY ATTENTION TO A THING I SA... ...BE IRONIC BECAUSE UNLIKE SKEL... ...RS DO HAVE EARS! ONES THAT WO... ...AD...MADE OF FLESH AND BONE! Y'K... ...I THINK ABOUT IT, MAYBE THAT'S ... ...EARS AREN'T MADE OF FLESH AND BO... ...HEY? FLESH AND CARTILAGE, MAY...

⸘SIGH⸘

PLEASE, SOMEBODY DROP SOMETHING HEAVY ON ME.

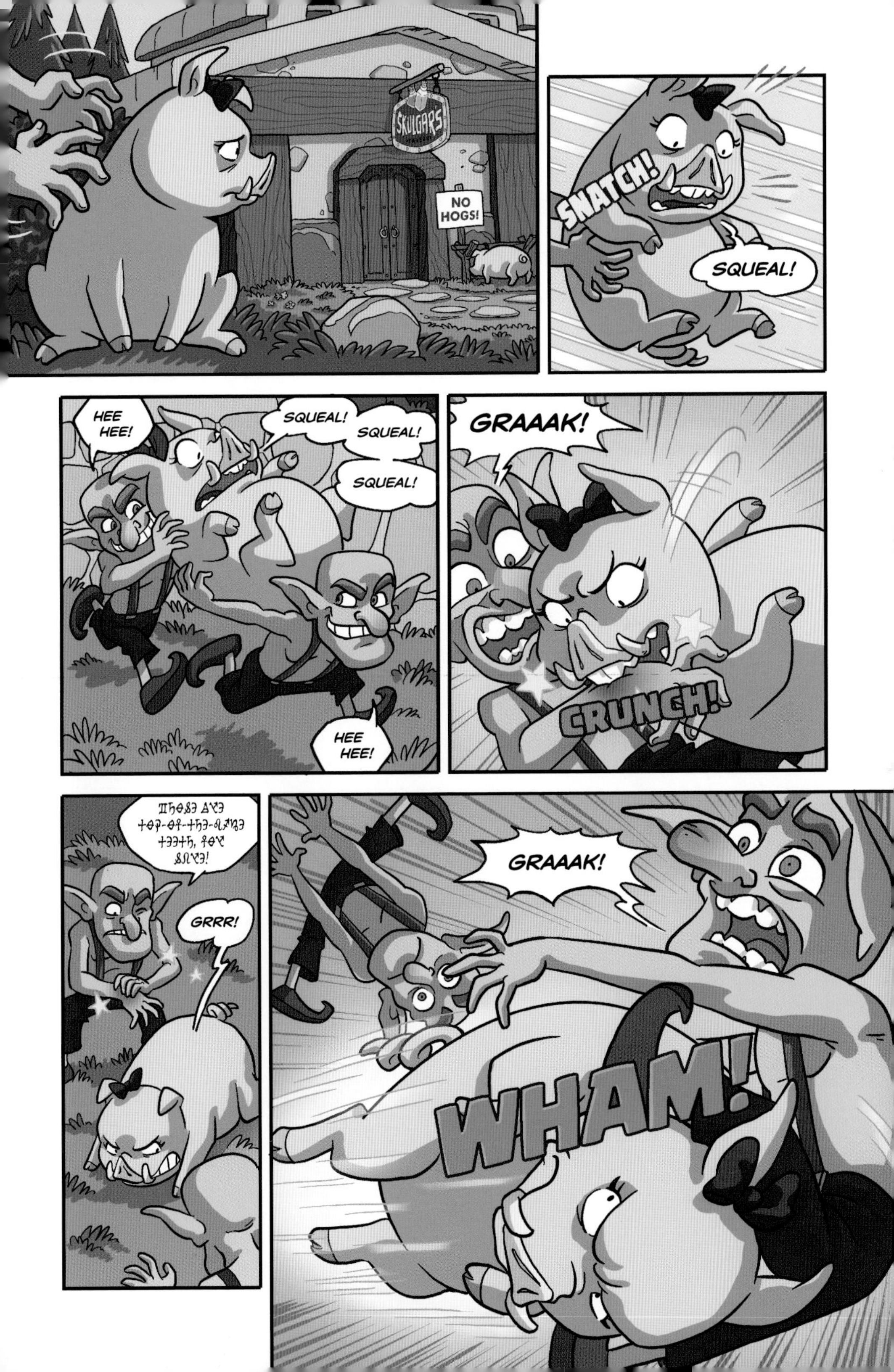
SKULGARS
NO HOGS!
SNATCH!
SQUEAL!
HEE HEE!
SQUEAL!
SQUEAL!
SQUEAL!
HEE HEE!
GRAAAK!
CRUNCH!
GRRR!
GRAAAK!
WHAM!

DOESN'T MATTER! A COMPLETE WORM LIKE THAT ISN'T WORTH THE TROUBLE!

MAYBE!

!

SNIFF SNIFF¿

WELCOME, ONE AND ALL, TO THE ROYAL ARENA!

HAVE YOUR TICKETS READY, FOLKS! THE MATCH IS ABOUT TO START!

I GOTTA FIND A WAY OUT OF THIS. A DISTRACTION, MAYBE.

WHAT IS THE DIVIDING LINE BETWEEN CARTILAGE AND BONE, ANYWA... ALWAYS WONDERED. LIKE... HARD DOES CART... GET BEFORE... NG TO IT AS B... THAT'S TH... N ALTOGE... TEGORICALLY... OR ARE THEY... ALE OF SOME... SORT?

MINION ATTACK!

WHERE?!

?

ZHIIIIIIIIP!

SIR!

WHY, PRAY TELL, DID YOU CHOOSE **MINIONS** AS YOUR IMAGINARY ASSAILANTS? DO YOU FIND SOME SORT OF **PERVERSE PLEASURE** IN PERPETUATING **TIRED OLD STEREOTYPES** ABOUT MY KIND?

OH! UH... I DIDN'T MEAN ANY **OFFENSE!**

BUT OFFENSE WAS **TAKEN,** GOOD SIR! OFFENSE WAS SURELY TAKEN!

HOG RIDERS!

FINALLY, SOME FRIENDLY FACES!

YOU A **NEW RECRUIT?**

YEP! THAT'S **ME!**

NEW RECRUIT!

PULL UP A CHAIR.

WAIT, WAIT—

53

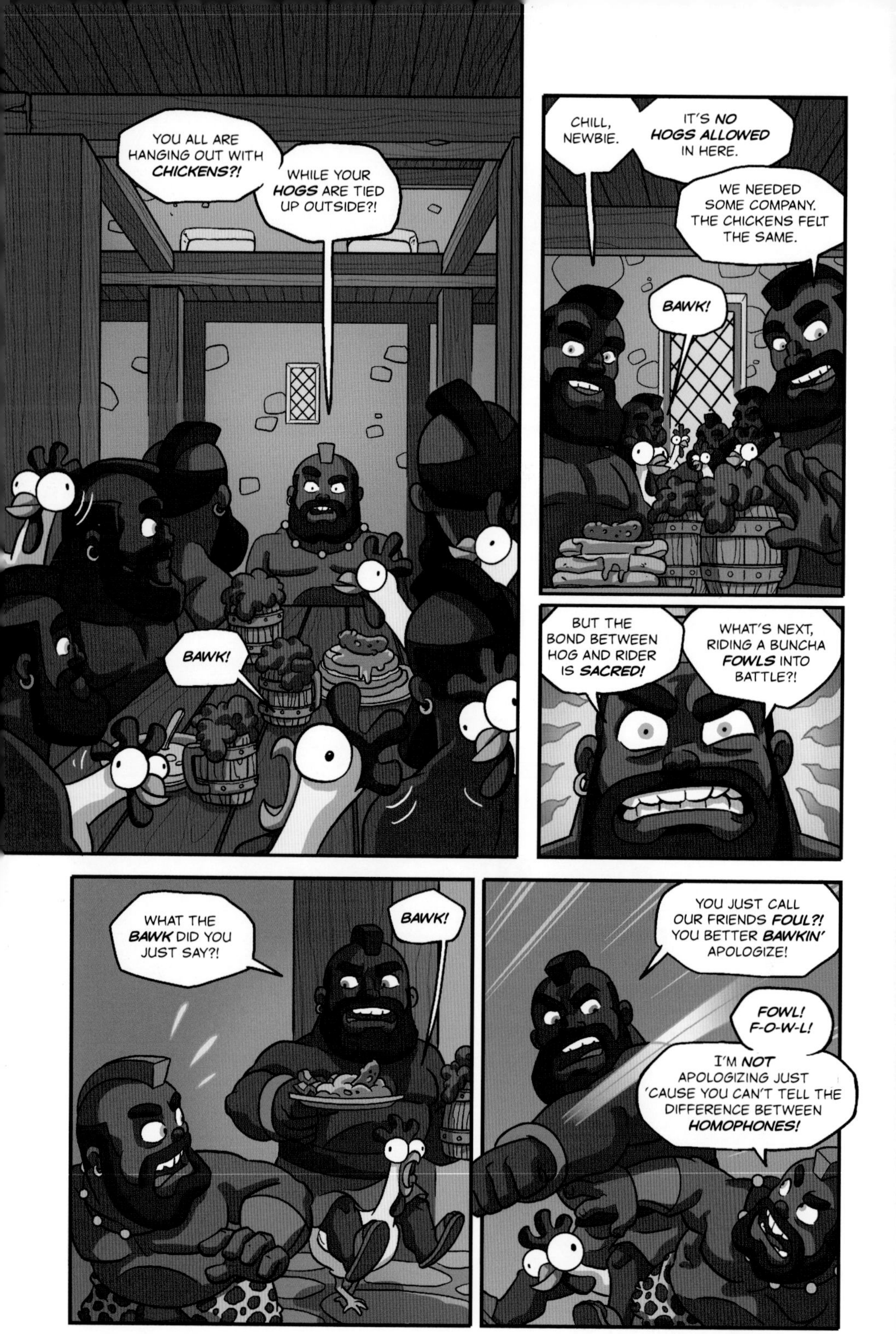
YOU ALL ARE HANGING OUT WITH **CHICKENS?!**
WHILE YOUR **HOGS** ARE TIED UP OUTSIDE?!
BAWK!
CHILL, NEWBIE.
IT'S **NO HOGS ALLOWED** IN HERE.
WE NEEDED SOME COMPANY. THE CHICKENS FELT THE SAME.
BAWK!
BUT THE BOND BETWEEN HOG AND RIDER IS **SACRED!**
WHAT'S NEXT, RIDING A BUNCHA **FOWLS** INTO BATTLE?!
WHAT THE **BAWK** DID YOU JUST SAY?!
BAWK!
YOU JUST CALL OUR FRIENDS **FOUL?!** YOU BETTER **BAWKIN'** APOLOGIZE!
FOWL! F-O-W-L!
I'M **NOT** APOLOGIZING JUST 'CAUSE YOU CAN'T TELL THE DIFFERENCE BETWEEN **HOMOPHONES!**

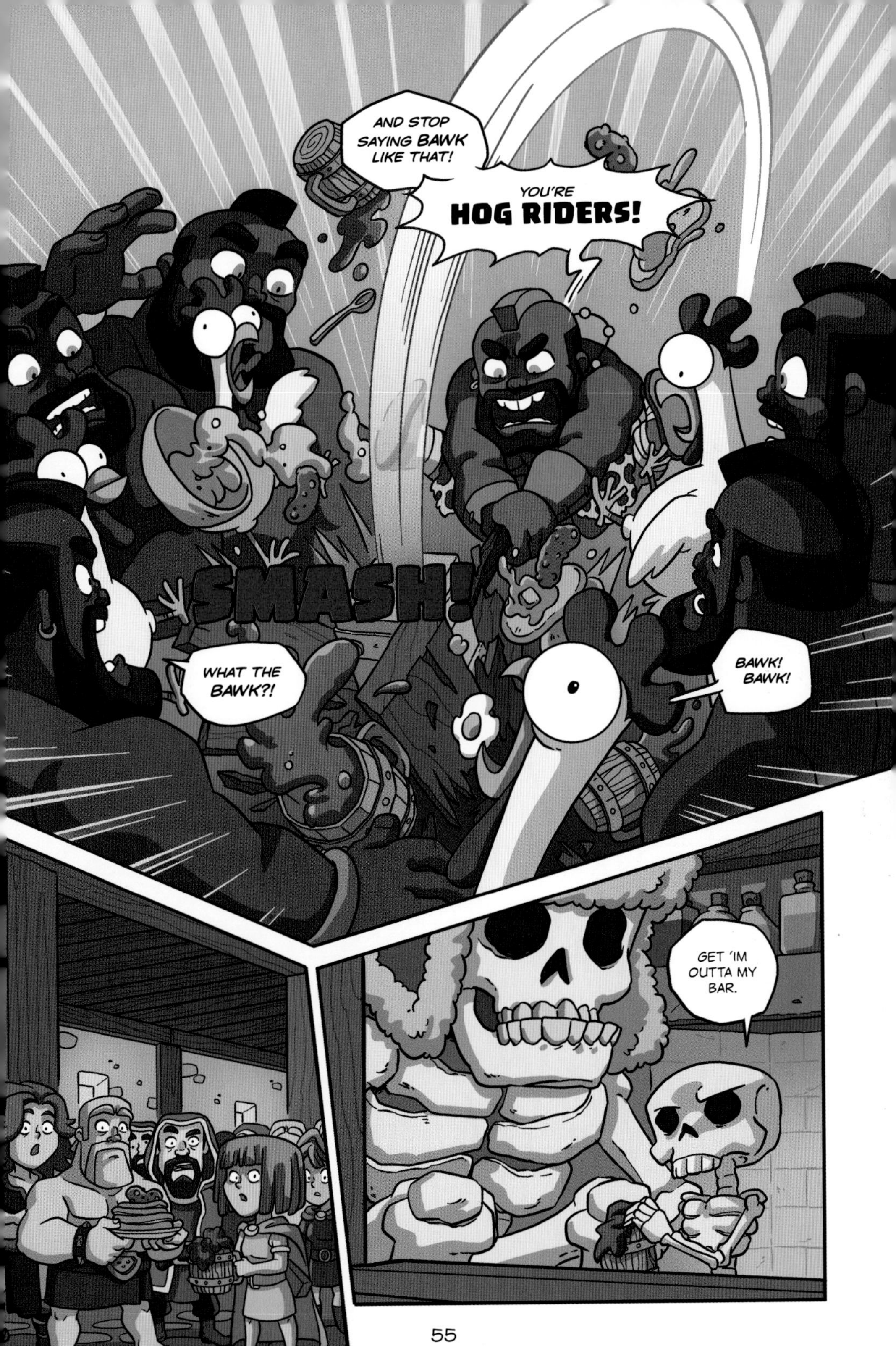

AND STOP SAYING BAWK LIKE THAT!
YOU'RE HOG RIDERS!
SMASH!
WHAT THE BAWK?!
BAWK! BAWK!
GET 'IM OUTTA MY BAR.

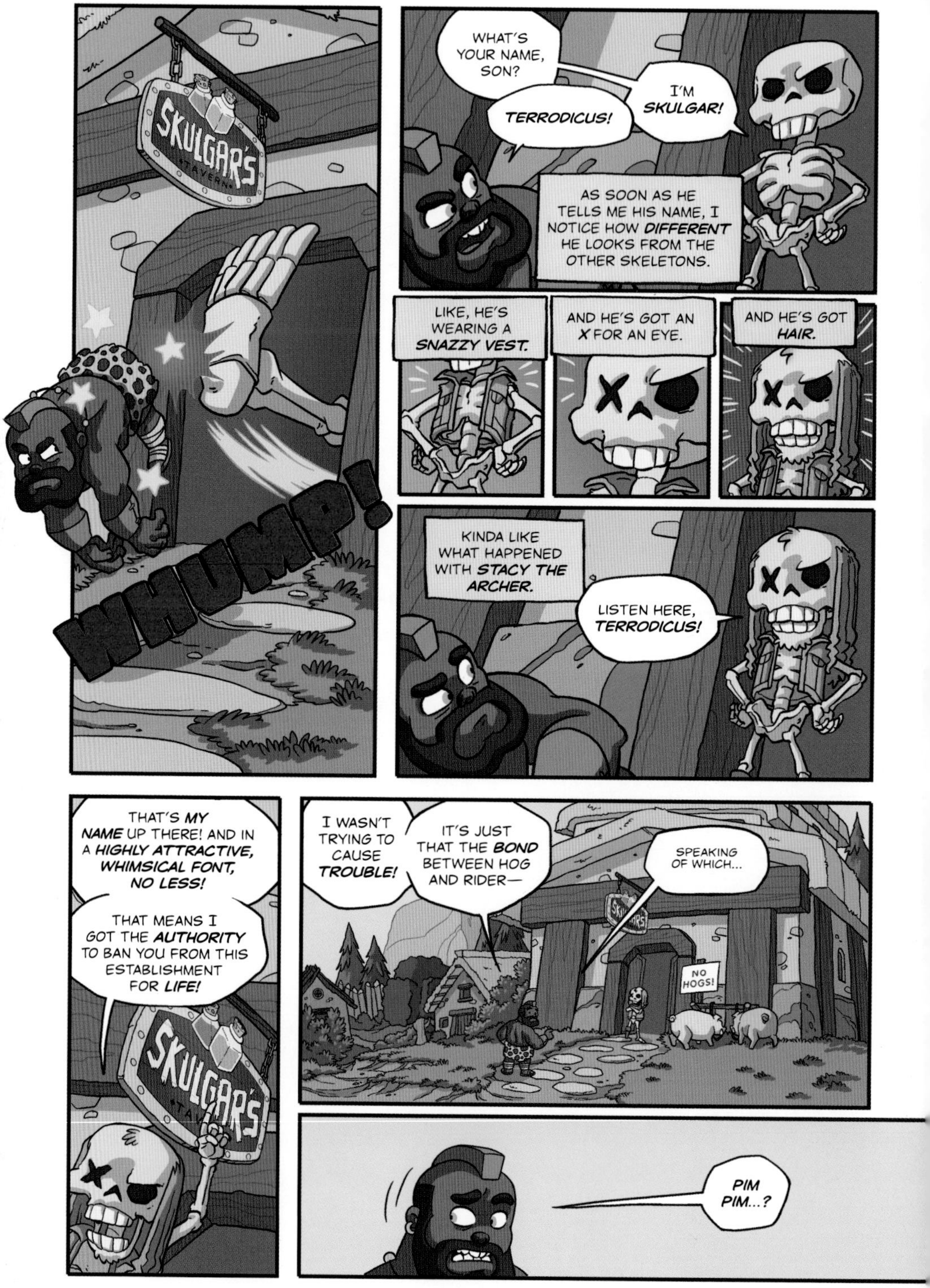
SKULGAR'S TAVERN
WHUMP!
WHAT'S YOUR NAME, SON?
TERRODICUS!
I'M SKULGAR!
AS SOON AS HE TELLS ME HIS NAME, I NOTICE HOW DIFFERENT HE LOOKS FROM THE OTHER SKELETONS.
LIKE, HE'S WEARING A SNAZZY VEST.
AND HE'S GOT AN X FOR AN EYE.
AND HE'S GOT HAIR.
KINDA LIKE WHAT HAPPENED WITH STACY THE ARCHER.
LISTEN HERE, TERRODICUS!
THAT'S MY NAME UP THERE! AND IN A HIGHLY ATTRACTIVE, WHIMSICAL FONT, NO LESS!
THAT MEANS I GOT THE AUTHORITY TO BAN YOU FROM THIS ESTABLISHMENT FOR LIFE!
SKULGAR'S
I WASN'T TRYING TO CAUSE TROUBLE!
IT'S JUST THAT THE BOND BETWEEN HOG AND RIDER—
SPEAKING OF WHICH...
NO HOGS!
PIM PIM...?

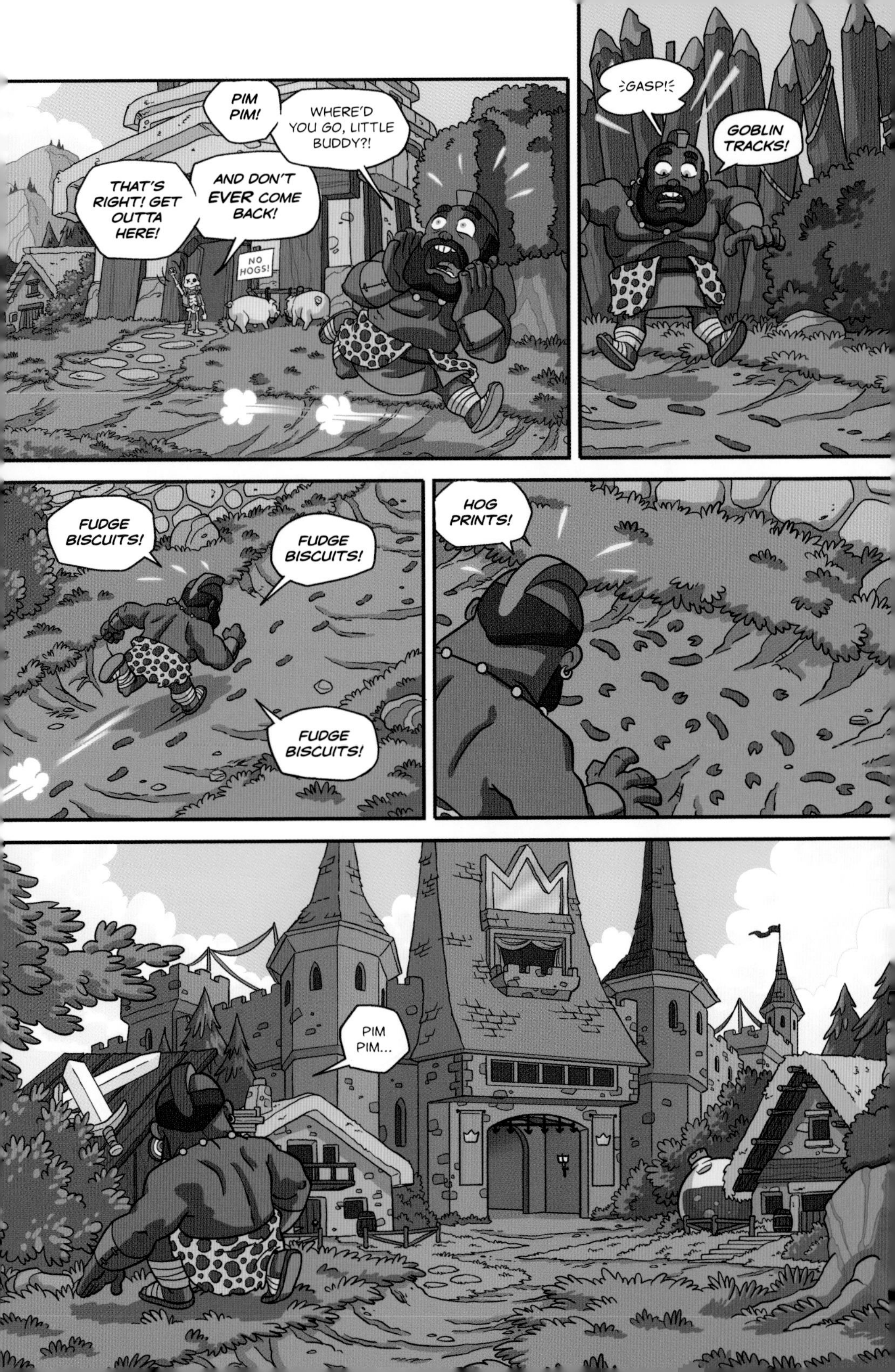
PIM PIM!
WHERE'D YOU GO, LITTLE BUDDY?!
THAT'S RIGHT! GET OUTTA HERE!
AND DON'T EVER COME BACK!
NO HOGS!
GASP!
GOBLIN TRACKS!
FUDGE BISCUITS!
FUDGE BISCUITS!
FUDGE BISCUITS!
HOG PRINTS!
PIM PIM...

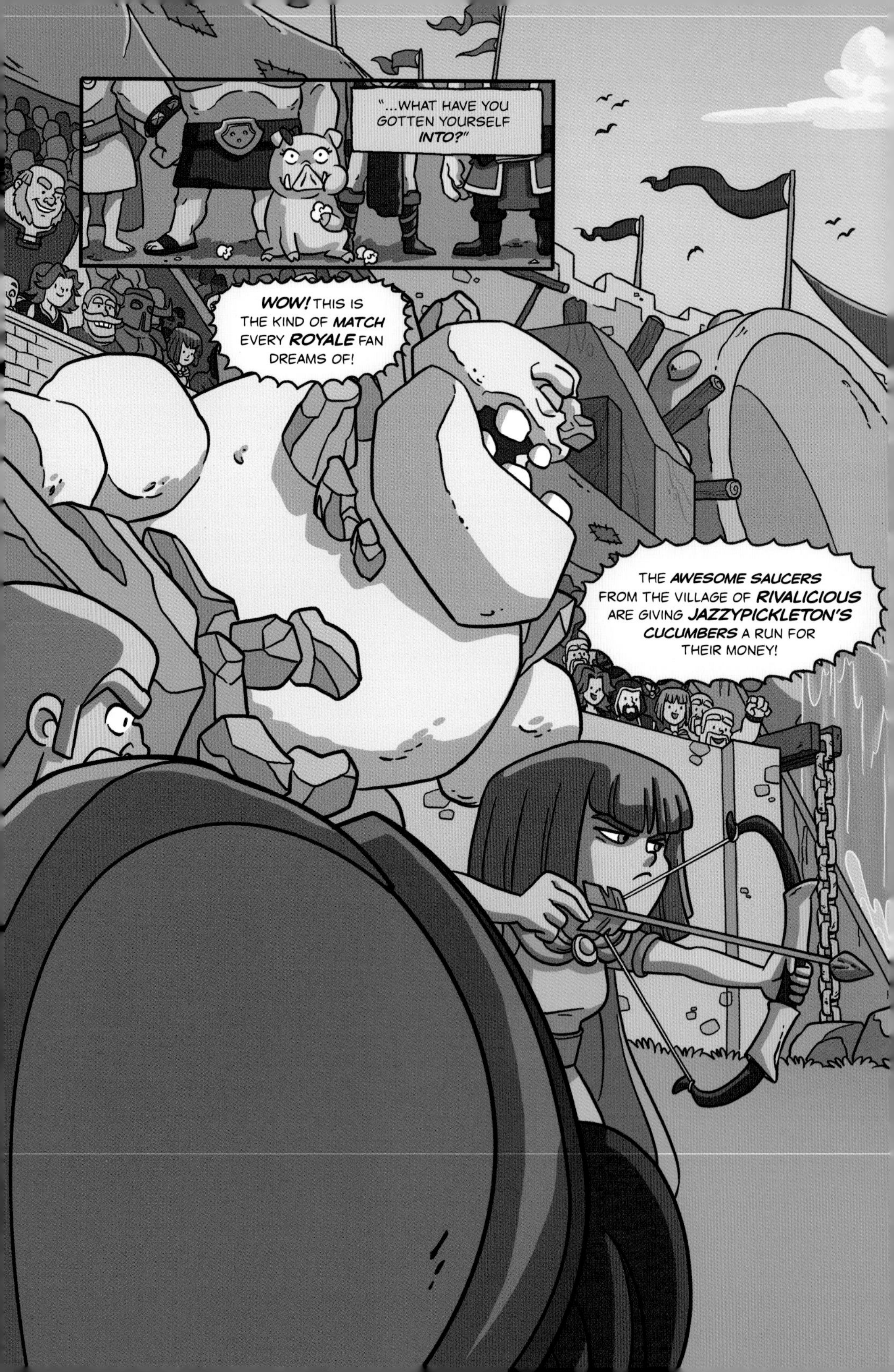
"...WHAT HAVE YOU GOTTEN YOURSELF INTO?"
WOW! THIS IS THE KIND OF MATCH EVERY ROYALE FAN DREAMS OF!
THE AWESOME SAUCERS FROM THE VILLAGE OF RIVALICIOUS ARE GIVING JAZZYPICKLETON'S CUCUMBERS A RUN FOR THEIR MONEY!

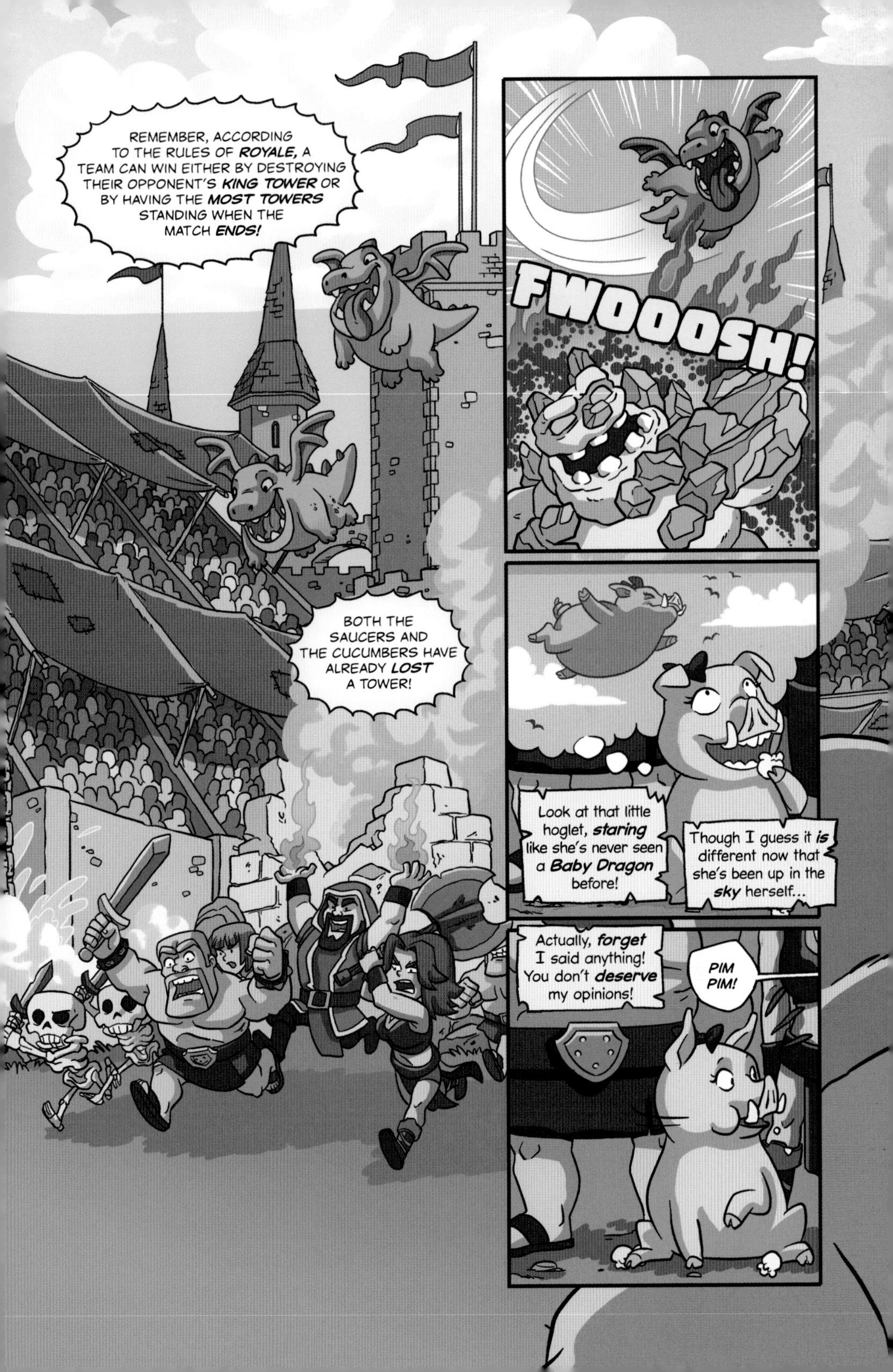

REMEMBER, ACCORDING TO THE RULES OF ROYALE, A TEAM CAN WIN EITHER BY DESTROYING THEIR OPPONENT'S KING TOWER OR BY HAVING THE MOST TOWERS STANDING WHEN THE MATCH ENDS!
BOTH THE SAUCERS AND THE CUCUMBERS HAVE ALREADY LOST A TOWER!
FWOOOSH!
Look at that little hoglet, staring like she's never seen a Baby Dragon before!
Though I guess it is different now that she's been up in the sky herself...
Actually, forget I said anything! You don't deserve my opinions!
PIM PIM!

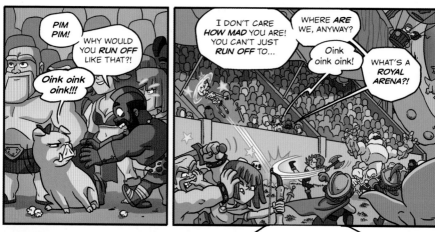

PIM PIM!

WHY WOULD YOU **RUN OFF** LIKE THAT?!

Oink oink oink!!!

I DON'T CARE **HOW MAD** YOU ARE! YOU CAN'T JUST **RUN OFF** TO...

WHERE **ARE** WE, ANYWAY?

Oink oink oink!

WHAT'S A **ROYAL ARENA?!**

Oink oink oink oink!

YEAH, I CAN SEE THEY'RE **BATTLING**, BUT OVER **WHAT?** A COUPLE OF **TOWERS** INSTEAD OF A WHOLE **VILLAGE?**

THERE'S NO **ELIXIR STORAGE!** WHAT'RE THEY GONNA **DRINK** WHEN THEY WIN?!

NO **BUILDER**, EITHER! WHO'S GONNA DO THE **LAMENTING?!**

PIM PIM, NONE OF THIS IS THE **TRIUMPHICA HOG RIDER WAY!**

LET'S GO!

Oink oink oink!

OVER THERE!

HALT WHERE YOU ARE!

Oink?!

DOOR, I MEAN. NOT TICKET.

THEY WOULDN'T LET ME THROUGH THE **DOOR** BECAUSE I DIDN'T HAVE A **TICKET**, SO I KINDA SORTA MADE **MY OWN.**

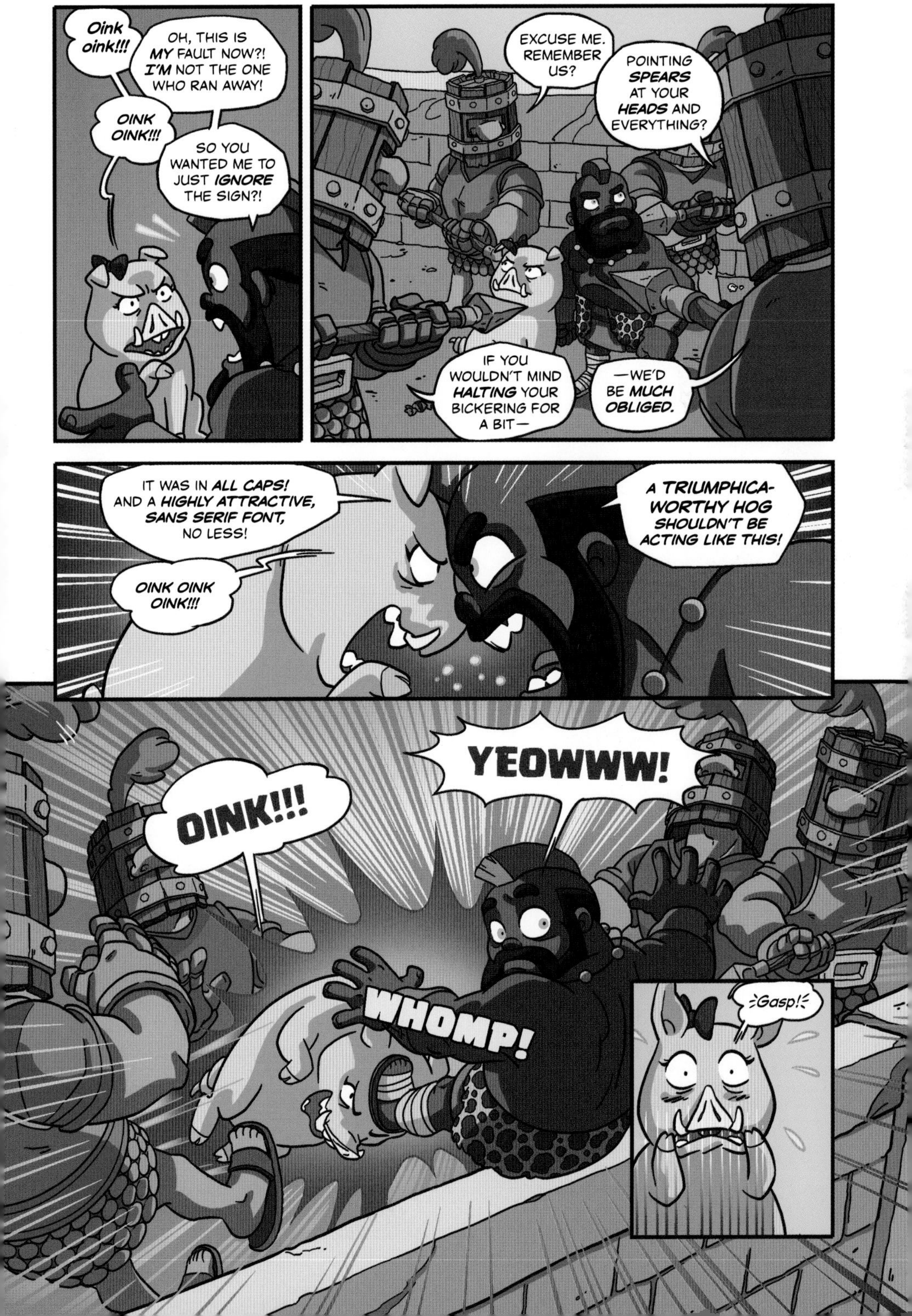
Oink oink!!!
OH, THIS IS MY FAULT NOW?! I'M NOT THE ONE WHO RAN AWAY!
OINK OINK!!!
SO YOU WANTED ME TO JUST IGNORE THE SIGN?!
EXCUSE ME. REMEMBER US?
POINTING SPEARS AT YOUR HEADS AND EVERYTHING?
IF YOU WOULDN'T MIND HALTING YOUR BICKERING FOR A BIT—
—WE'D BE MUCH OBLIGED.
IT WAS IN ALL CAPS! AND A HIGHLY ATTRACTIVE, SANS SERIF FONT, NO LESS!
OINK OINK OINK!!!
A TRIUMPHICA-WORTHY HOG SHOULDN'T BE ACTING LIKE THIS!
YEOWWW!
OINK!!!
WHOMP!
Gasp!

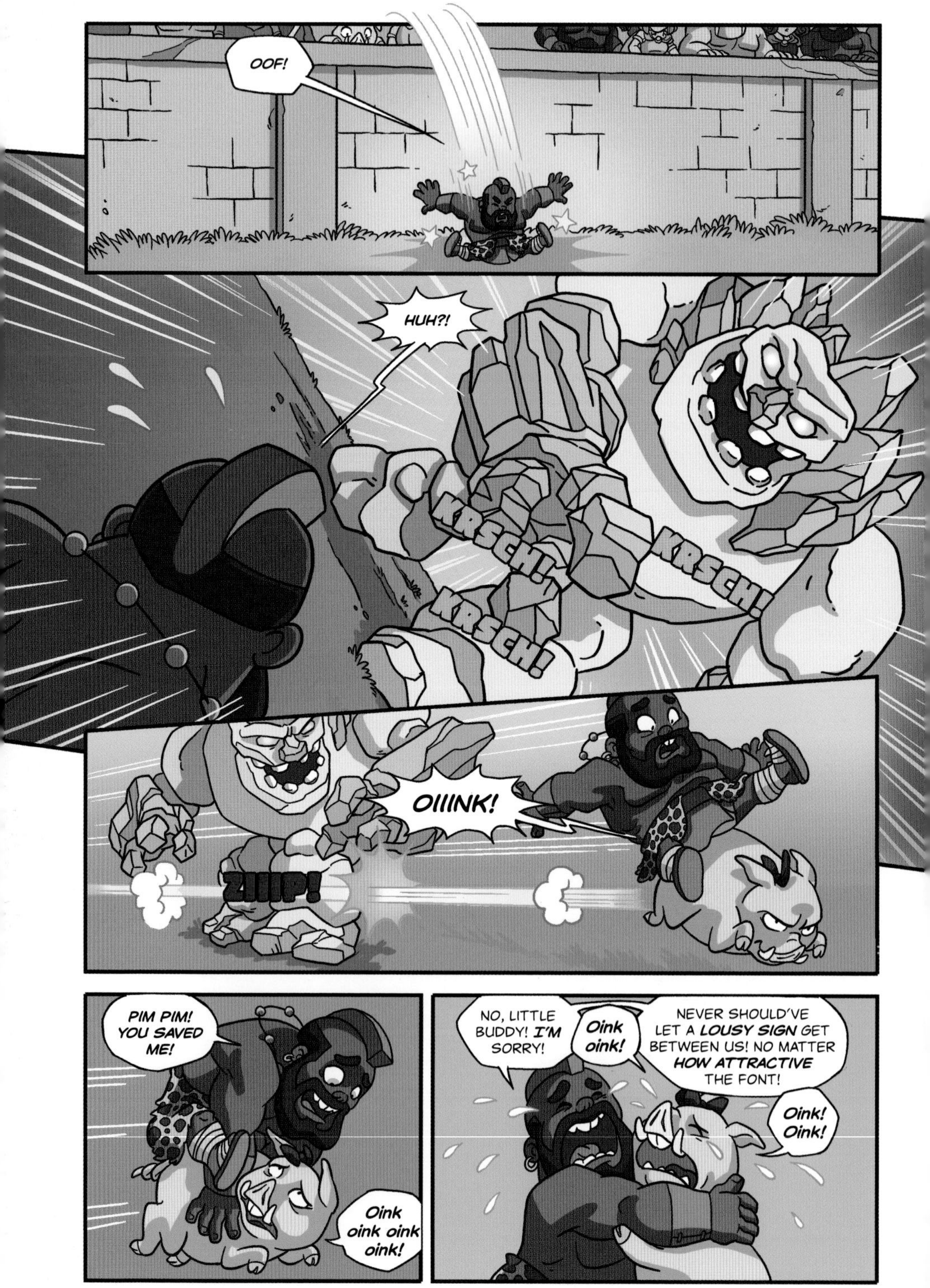
OOF!
HUH?!
KRSCH!
KRSCH!
KRSCH!
OIIINK!
ZIIIP!
PIM PIM! YOU SAVED ME!
Oink oink oink oink!
NO, LITTLE BUDDY! I'M SORRY!
Oink oink!
NEVER SHOULD'VE LET A LOUSY SIGN GET BETWEEN US! NO MATTER HOW ATTRACTIVE THE FONT!
Oink! Oink!

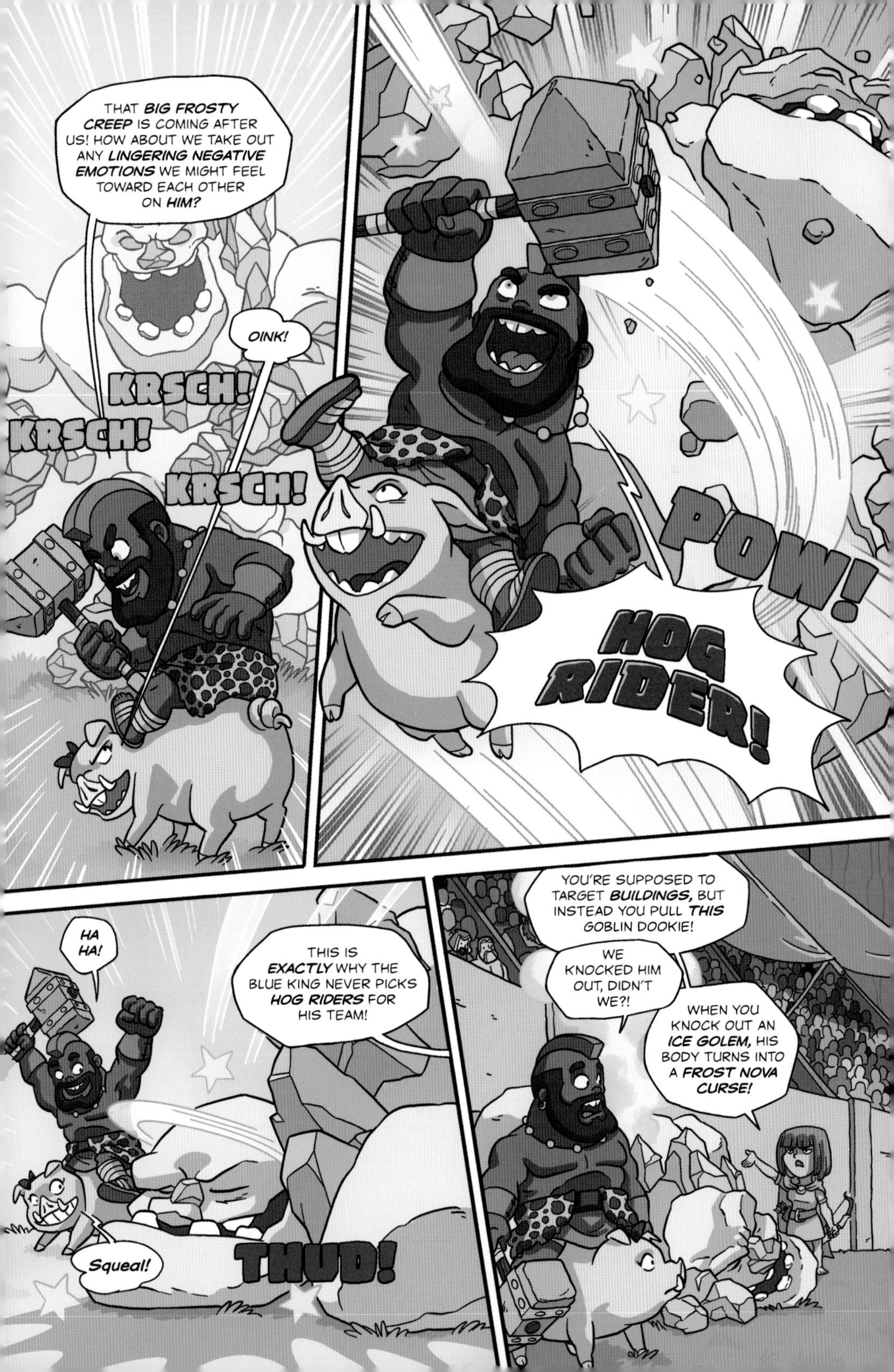

THAT BIG FROSTY CREEP IS COMING AFTER US! HOW ABOUT WE TAKE OUT ANY LINGERING NEGATIVE EMOTIONS WE MIGHT FEEL TOWARD EACH OTHER ON HIM?
OINK!
KRSCH!
KRSCH!
KRSCH!
POW!
HOG RIDER!
HA HA!
THIS IS EXACTLY WHY THE BLUE KING NEVER PICKS HOG RIDERS FOR HIS TEAM!
Squeal!
THUD!
YOU'RE SUPPOSED TO TARGET BUILDINGS, BUT INSTEAD YOU PULL THIS GOBLIN DOOKIE!
WE KNOCKED HIM OUT, DIDN'T WE?!
WHEN YOU KNOCK OUT AN ICE GOLEM, HIS BODY TURNS INTO A FROST NOVA CURSE!

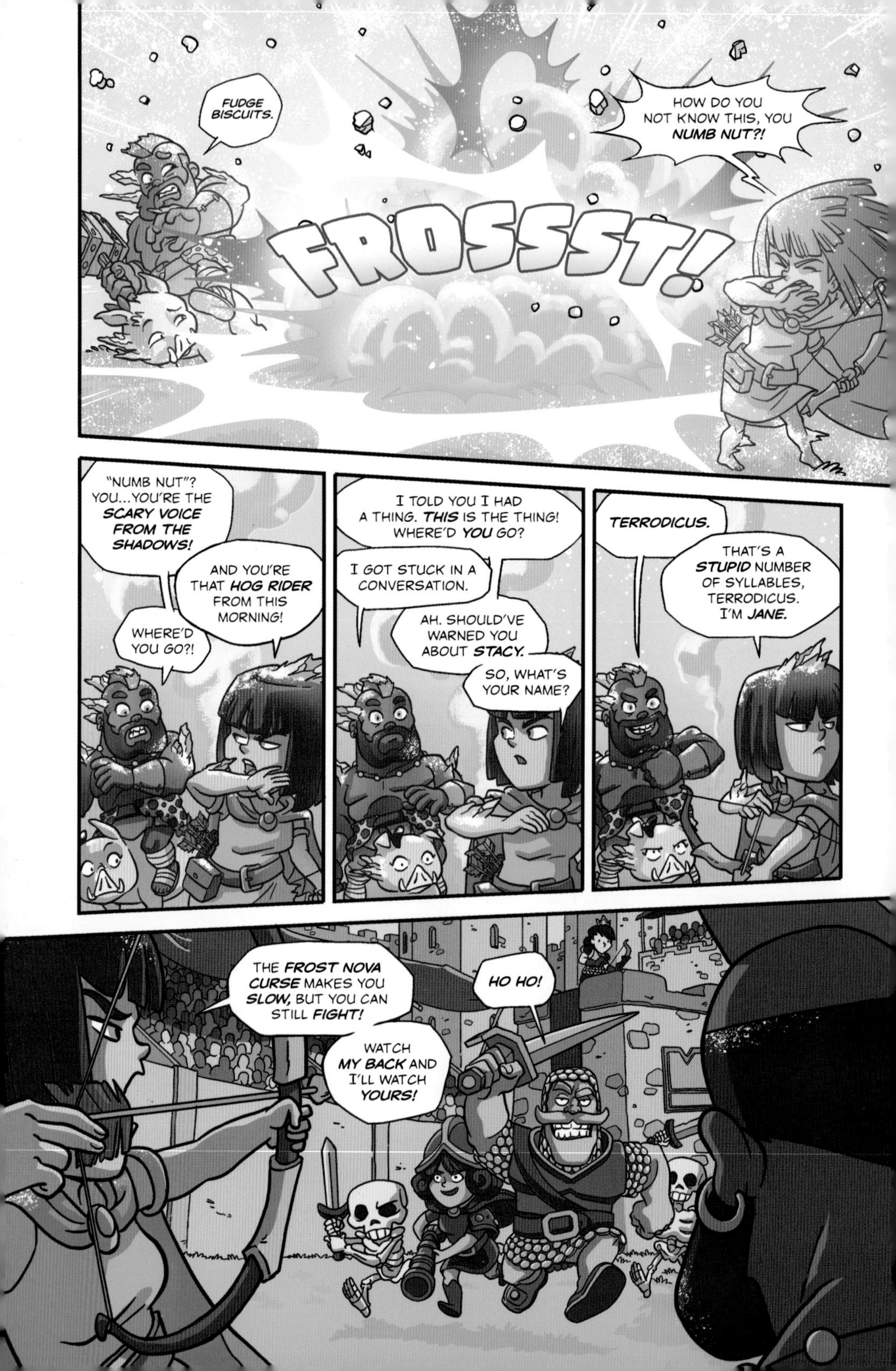
FUDGE BISCUITS.
HOW DO YOU NOT KNOW THIS, YOU NUMB NUT?!
FROSSST!
"NUMB NUT"? YOU...YOU'RE THE SCARY VOICE FROM THE SHADOWS!
AND YOU'RE THAT HOG RIDER FROM THIS MORNING!
WHERE'D YOU GO?!
I TOLD YOU I HAD A THING. THIS IS THE THING! WHERE'D YOU GO?
I GOT STUCK IN A CONVERSATION.
AH. SHOULD'VE WARNED YOU ABOUT STACY.
SO, WHAT'S YOUR NAME?
TERRODICUS.
THAT'S A STUPID NUMBER OF SYLLABLES, TERRODICUS. I'M JANE.
THE FROST NOVA CURSE MAKES YOU SLOW, BUT YOU CAN STILL FIGHT!
HO HO!
WATCH MY BACK AND I'LL WATCH YOURS!

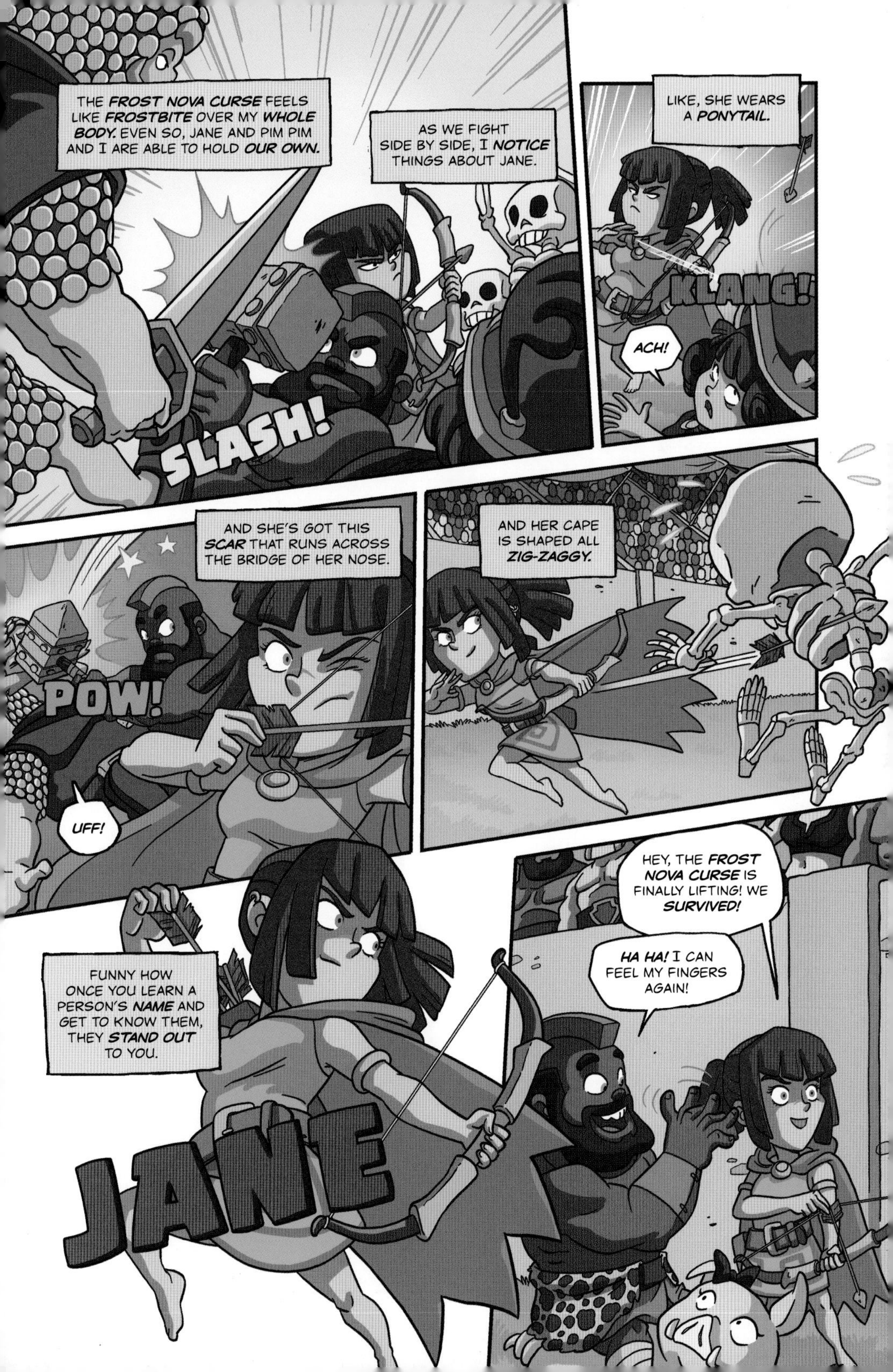

THE FROST NOVA CURSE FEELS LIKE FROSTBITE OVER MY WHOLE BODY. EVEN SO, JANE AND PIM PIM AND I ARE ABLE TO HOLD OUR OWN.
AS WE FIGHT SIDE BY SIDE, I NOTICE THINGS ABOUT JANE.
SLASH!
LIKE, SHE WEARS A PONYTAIL.
KLANG!
ACH!
AND SHE'S GOT THIS SCAR THAT RUNS ACROSS THE BRIDGE OF HER NOSE.
POW!
UFF!
AND HER CAPE IS SHAPED ALL ZIG-ZAGGY.
FUNNY HOW ONCE YOU LEARN A PERSON'S NAME AND GET TO KNOW THEM, THEY STAND OUT TO YOU.
JANE
HEY, THE FROST NOVA CURSE IS FINALLY LIFTING! WE SURVIVED!
HA HA! I CAN FEEL MY FINGERS AGAIN!

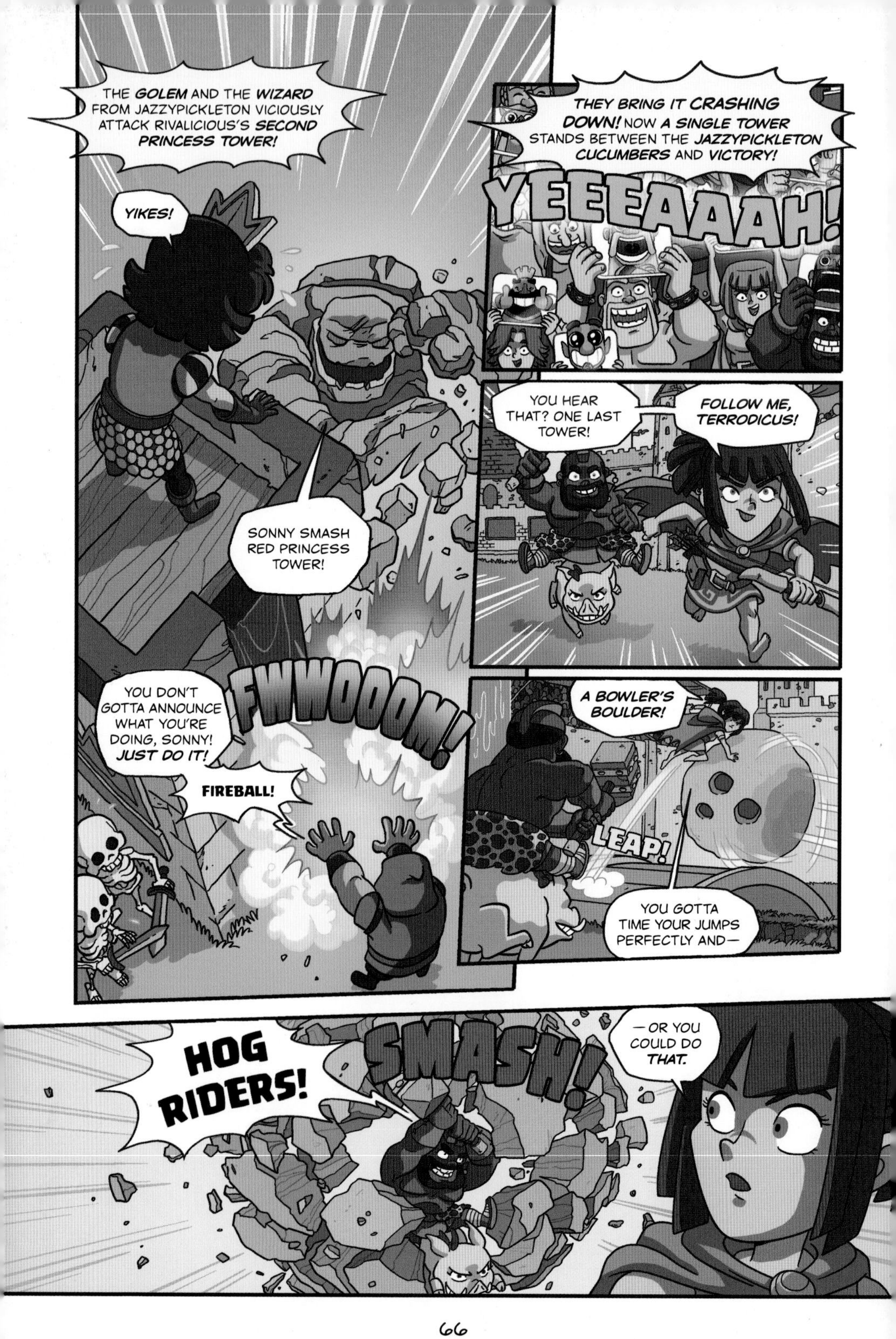
THE GOLEM AND THE WIZARD FROM JAZZYPICKLETON VICIOUSLY ATTACK RIVALICIOUS'S SECOND PRINCESS TOWER!
YIKES!
SONNY SMASH RED PRINCESS TOWER!
THEY BRING IT CRASHING DOWN! NOW A SINGLE TOWER STANDS BETWEEN THE JAZZYPICKLETON CUCUMBERS AND VICTORY!
YEEEAAAH!
YOU HEAR THAT? ONE LAST TOWER!
FOLLOW ME, TERRODICUS!
FWWOOOM!
YOU DON'T GOTTA ANNOUNCE WHAT YOU'RE DOING, SONNY! JUST DO IT!
FIREBALL!
A BOWLER'S BOULDER!
LEAP!
YOU GOTTA TIME YOUR JUMPS PERFECTLY AND—
HOG RIDERS!
SMASH!
—OR YOU COULD DO THAT.

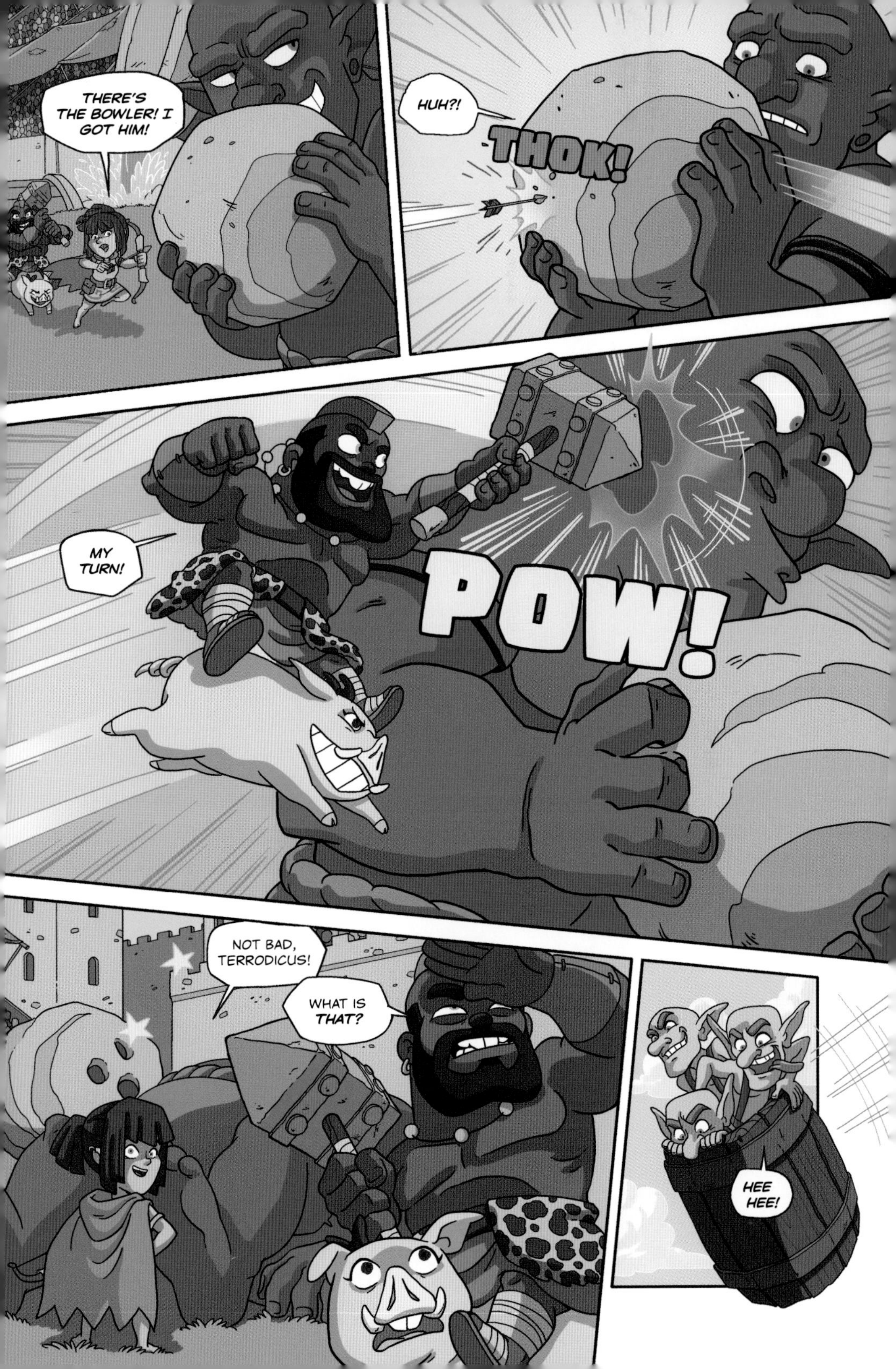
THERE'S THE BOWLER! I GOT HIM!
HUH?!
THOK!
MY TURN!
POW!
NOT BAD, TERRODICUS!
WHAT IS THAT?
HEE HEE!

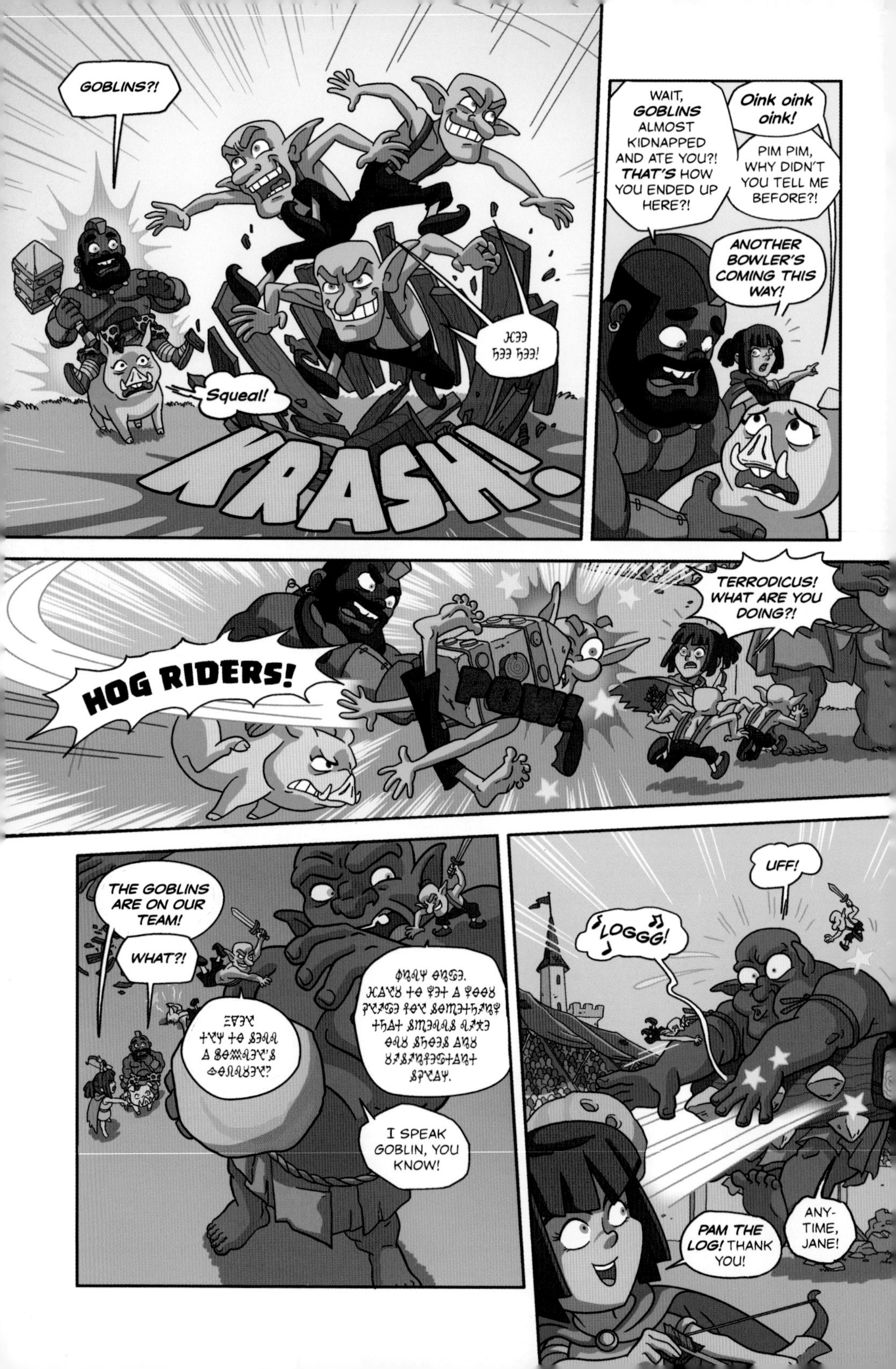
GOBLINS?!
Squeal!
KRASH!
WAIT, GOBLINS ALMOST KIDNAPPED AND ATE YOU?! THAT'S HOW YOU ENDED UP HERE?!
Oink oink oink!
PIM PIM, WHY DIDN'T YOU TELL ME BEFORE?!
ANOTHER BOWLER'S COMING THIS WAY!
HOG RIDERS!
POW!
TERRODICUS! WHAT ARE YOU DOING?!
THE GOBLINS ARE ON OUR TEAM!
WHAT?!
I SPEAK GOBLIN, YOU KNOW!
UFF!
LOGGG!
PAM THE LOG! THANK YOU!
ANY-TIME, JANE!

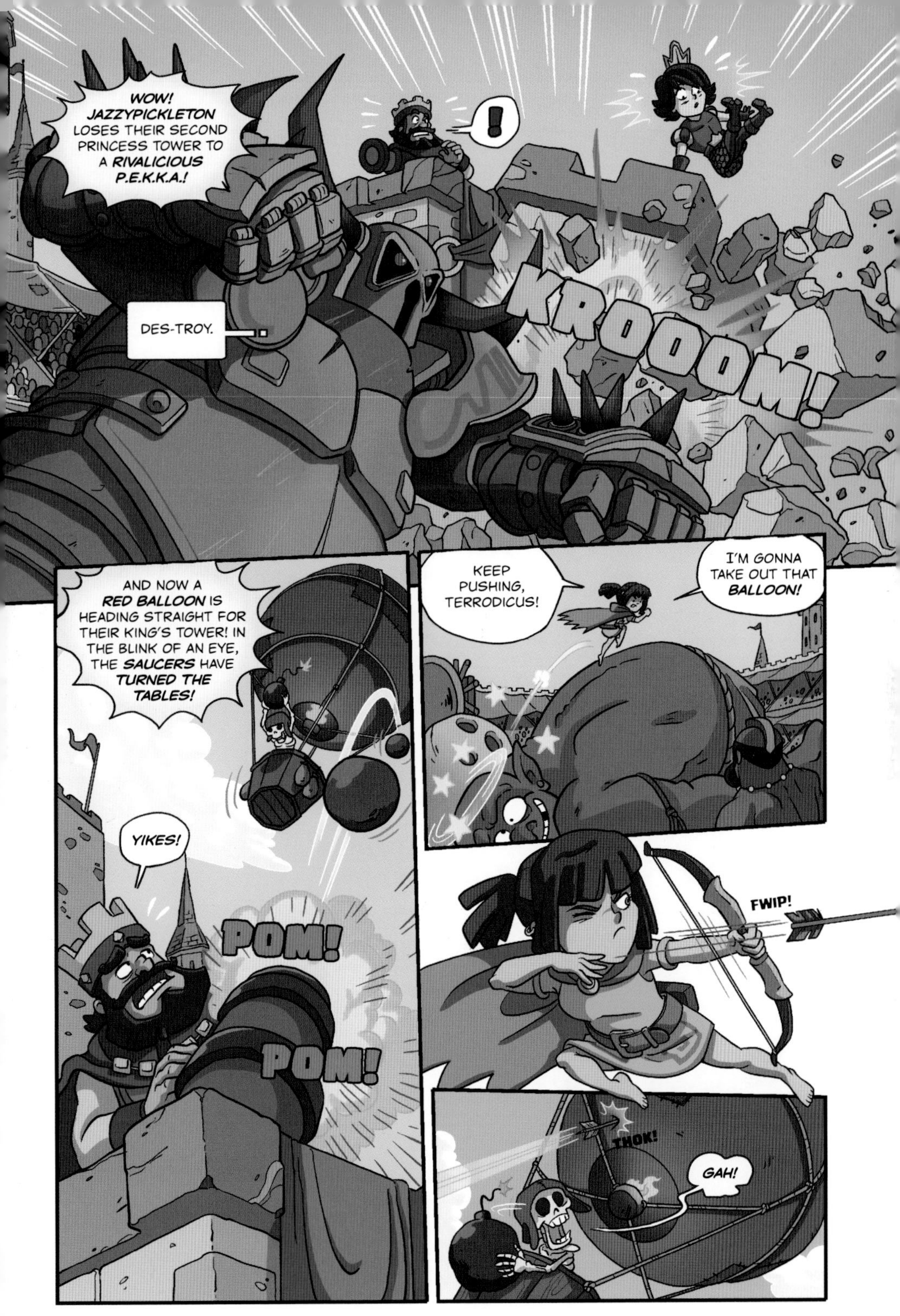
WOW! JAZZYPICKLETON LOSES THEIR SECOND PRINCESS TOWER TO A RIVALICIOUS P.E.K.K.A.!
!
DES-TROY.
KROOOOM!
AND NOW A RED BALLOON IS HEADING STRAIGHT FOR THEIR KING'S TOWER! IN THE BLINK OF AN EYE, THE SAUCERS HAVE TURNED THE TABLES!
YIKES!
POM!
POM!
KEEP PUSHING, TERRODICUS!
I'M GONNA TAKE OUT THAT BALLOON!
FWIP!
THOK!
GAH!

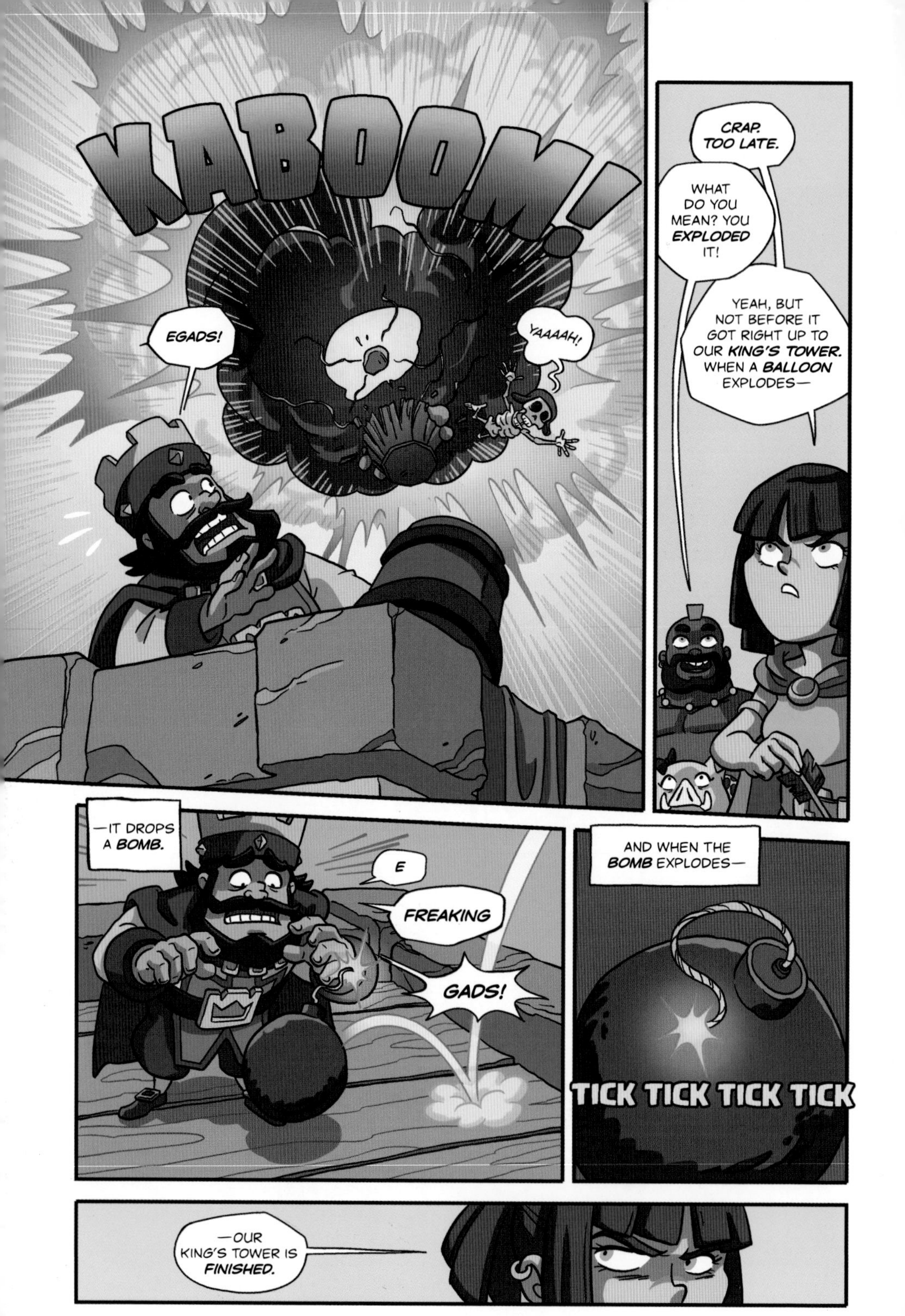
KABOOM!
EGADS!
YAAAAH!
CRAP. TOO LATE.
WHAT DO YOU MEAN? YOU EXPLODED IT!
YEAH, BUT NOT BEFORE IT GOT RIGHT UP TO OUR KING'S TOWER. WHEN A BALLOON EXPLODES—
—IT DROPS A BOMB.
E
FREAKING
GADS!
AND WHEN THE BOMB EXPLODES—
TICK TICK TICK TICK
—OUR KING'S TOWER IS FINISHED.

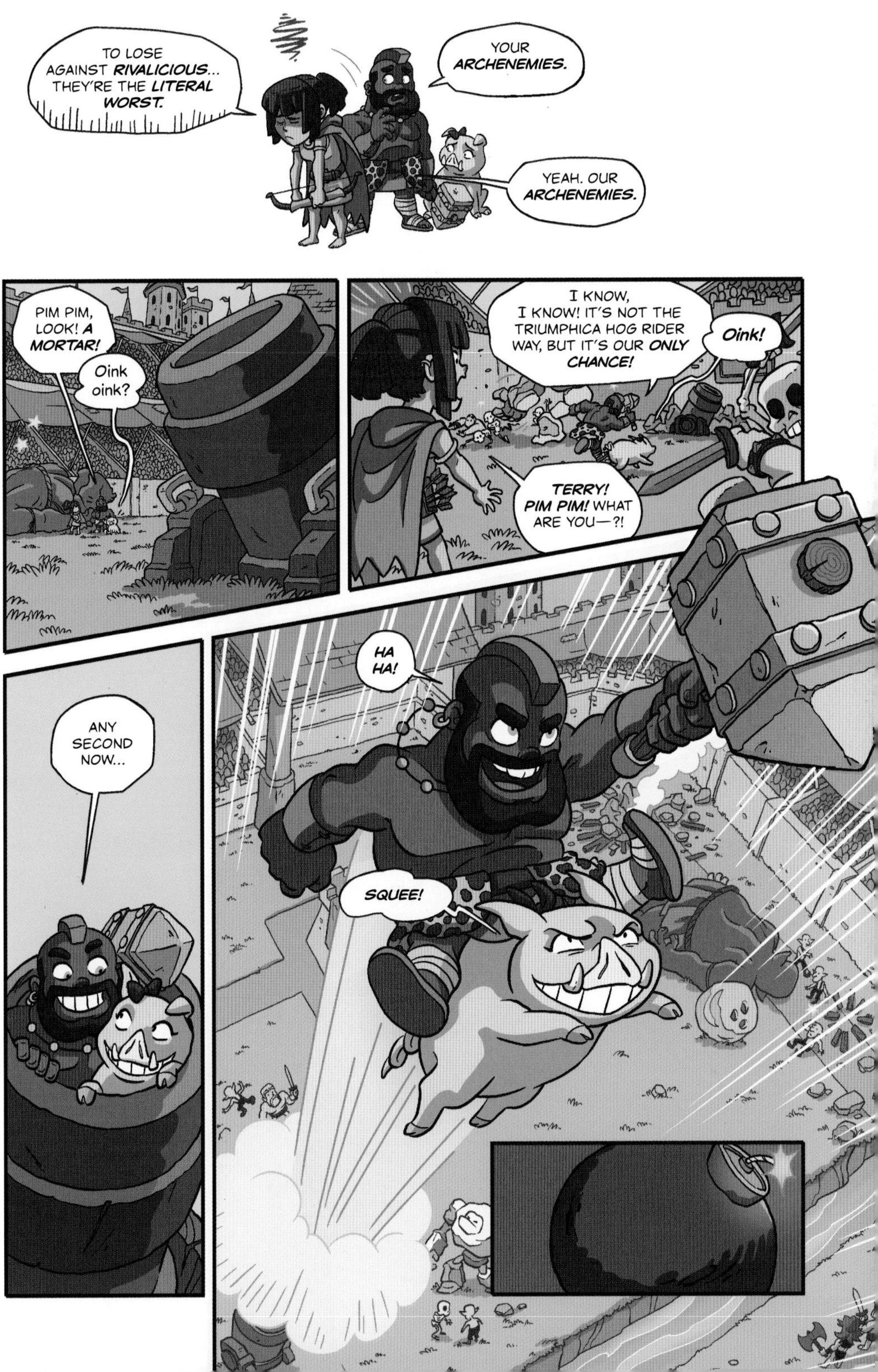
TO LOSE AGAINST RIVALICIOUS... THEY'RE THE LITERAL WORST.
YOUR ARCHENEMIES.
YEAH. OUR ARCHENEMIES.
PIM PIM, LOOK! A MORTAR!
Oink oink?
I KNOW, I KNOW! IT'S NOT THE TRIUMPHICA HOG RIDER WAY, BUT IT'S OUR ONLY CHANCE!
Oink!
TERRY! PIM PIM! WHAT ARE YOU—?!
ANY SECOND NOW...
HA HA!
SQUEE!

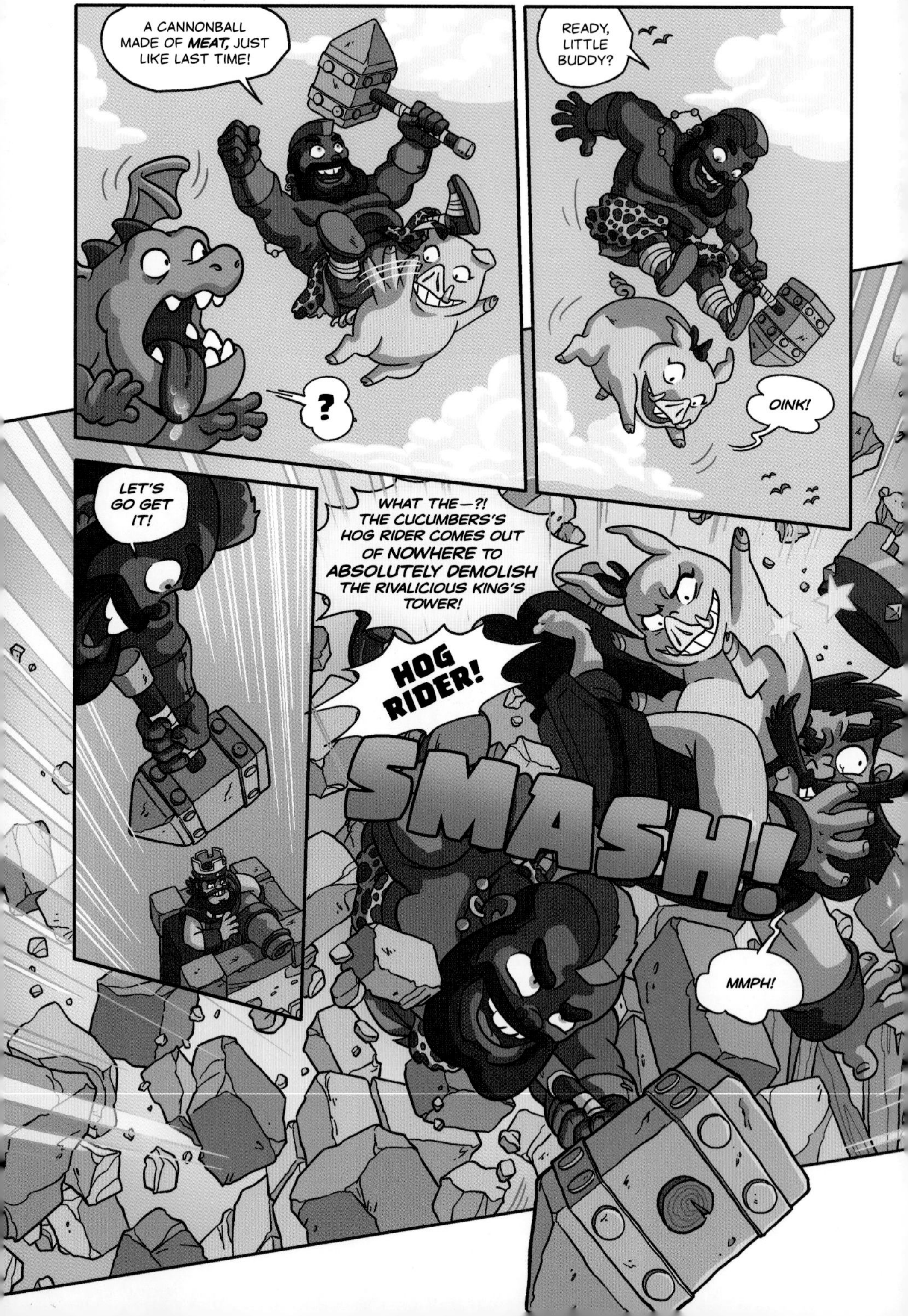
A CANNONBALL MADE OF MEAT, JUST LIKE LAST TIME!
?
READY, LITTLE BUDDY?
OINK!
LET'S GO GET IT!
WHAT THE—?! THE CUCUMBERS'S HOG RIDER COMES OUT OF NOWHERE TO ABSOLUTELY DEMOLISH THE RIVALICIOUS KING'S TOWER!
HOG RIDER!
SMASH!
MMPH!

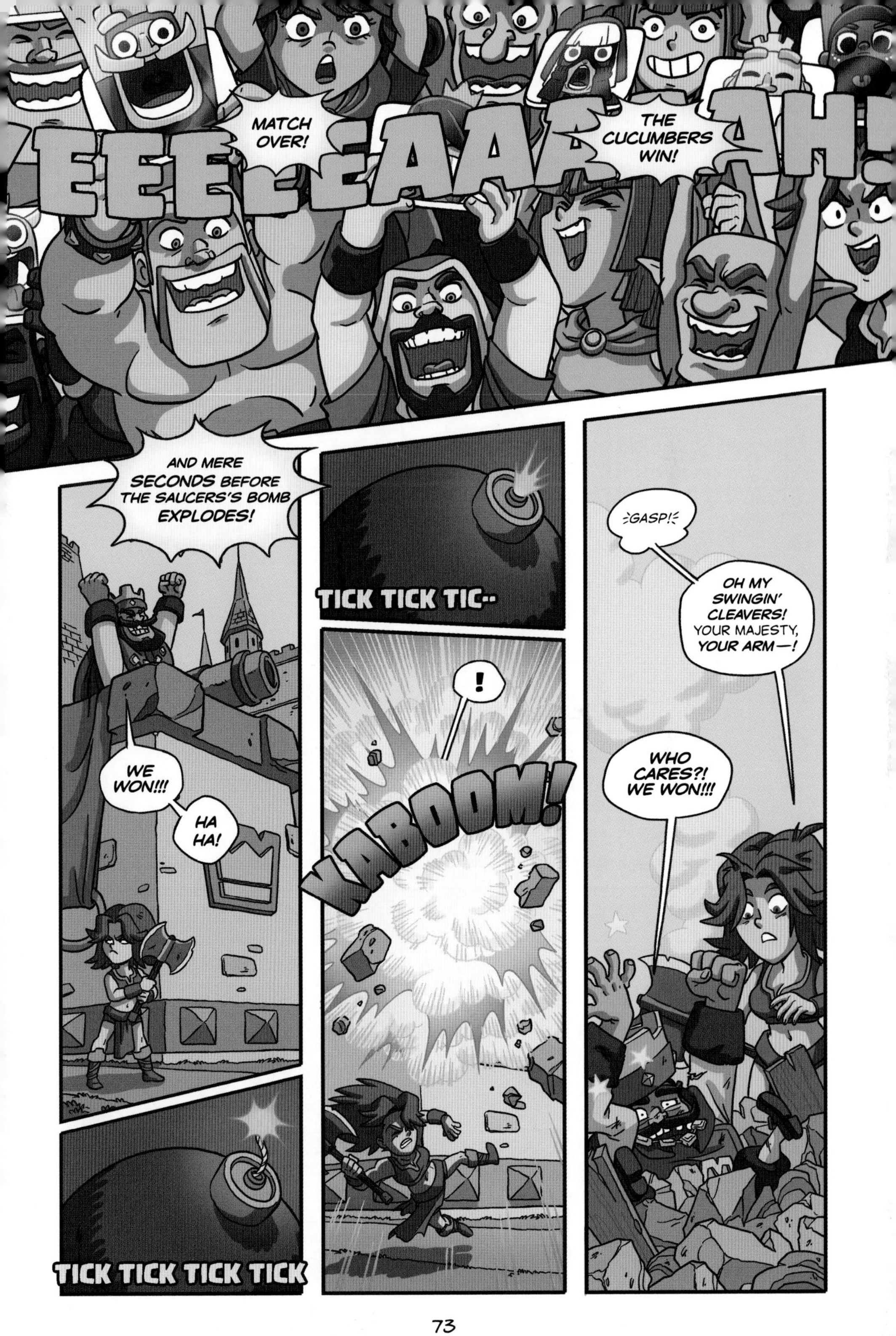
EEEEAAAAAH!
MATCH OVER!
THE CUCUMBERS WIN!
AND MERE SECONDS BEFORE THE SAUCERS'S BOMB EXPLODES!
WE WON!!!
HA HA!
TICK TICK TICK TICK
TICK TICK TIC--
!
KABOOM!
GASP!
OH MY SWINGIN' CLEAVERS! YOUR MAJESTY, YOUR ARM—!
WHO CARES?! WE WON!!!

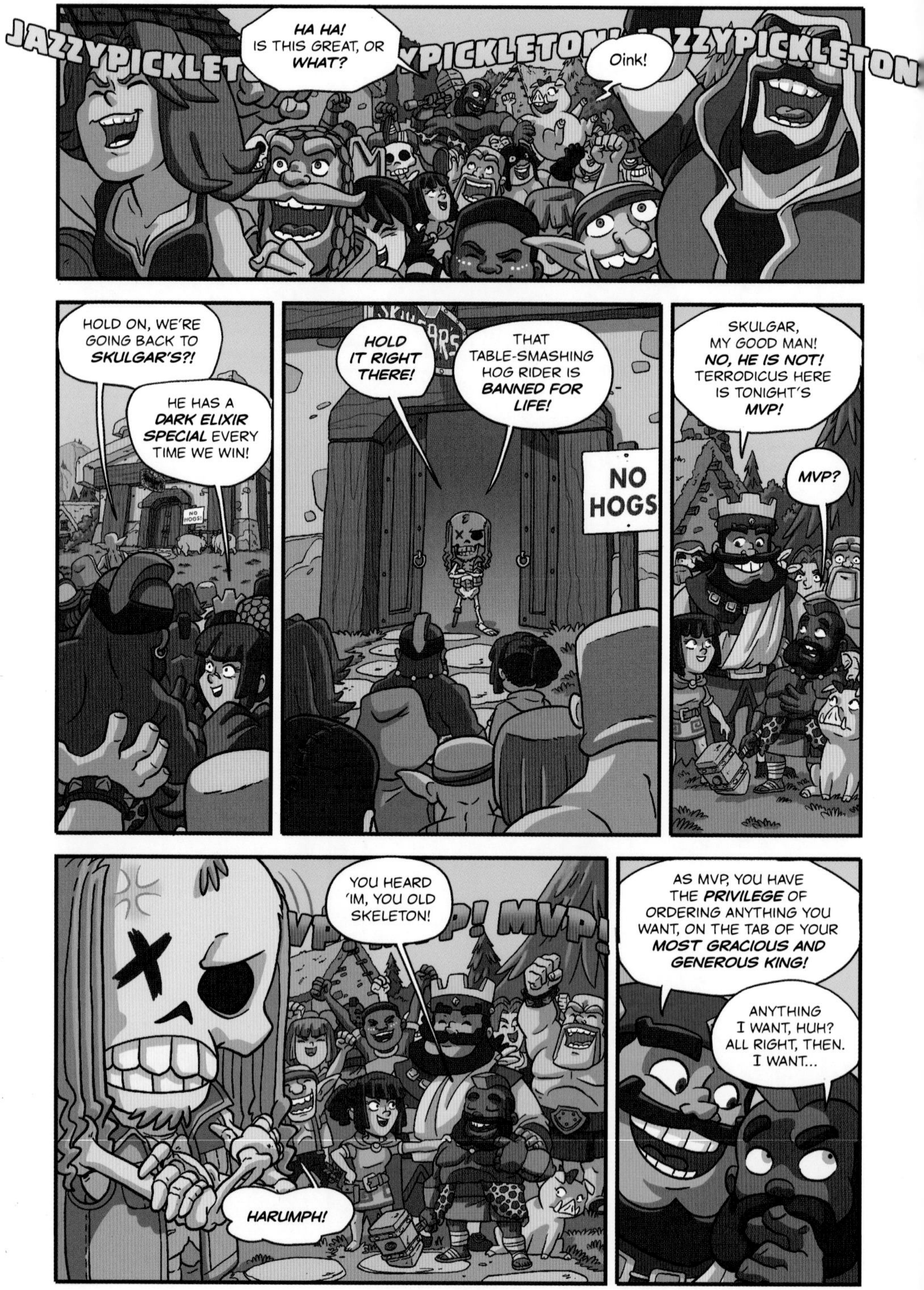
JAZZYPICKLETON! JAZZYPICKLETON! JAZZYPICKLETON!
HA HA! IS THIS GREAT, OR WHAT?
Oink!
HOLD ON, WE'RE GOING BACK TO SKULGAR'S?!
HE HAS A DARK ELIXIR SPECIAL EVERY TIME WE WIN!
NO HOGS!
HOLD IT RIGHT THERE!
THAT TABLE-SMASHING HOG RIDER IS BANNED FOR LIFE!
NO HOGS
SKULGAR, MY GOOD MAN! NO, HE IS NOT! TERRODICUS HERE IS TONIGHT'S MVP!
MVP?
MVP! MVP! MVP!
YOU HEARD 'IM, YOU OLD SKELETON!
HARUMPH!
AS MVP, YOU HAVE THE PRIVILEGE OF ORDERING ANYTHING YOU WANT, ON THE TAB OF YOUR MOST GRACIOUS AND GENEROUS KING!
ANYTHING I WANT, HUH? ALL RIGHT, THEN. I WANT...

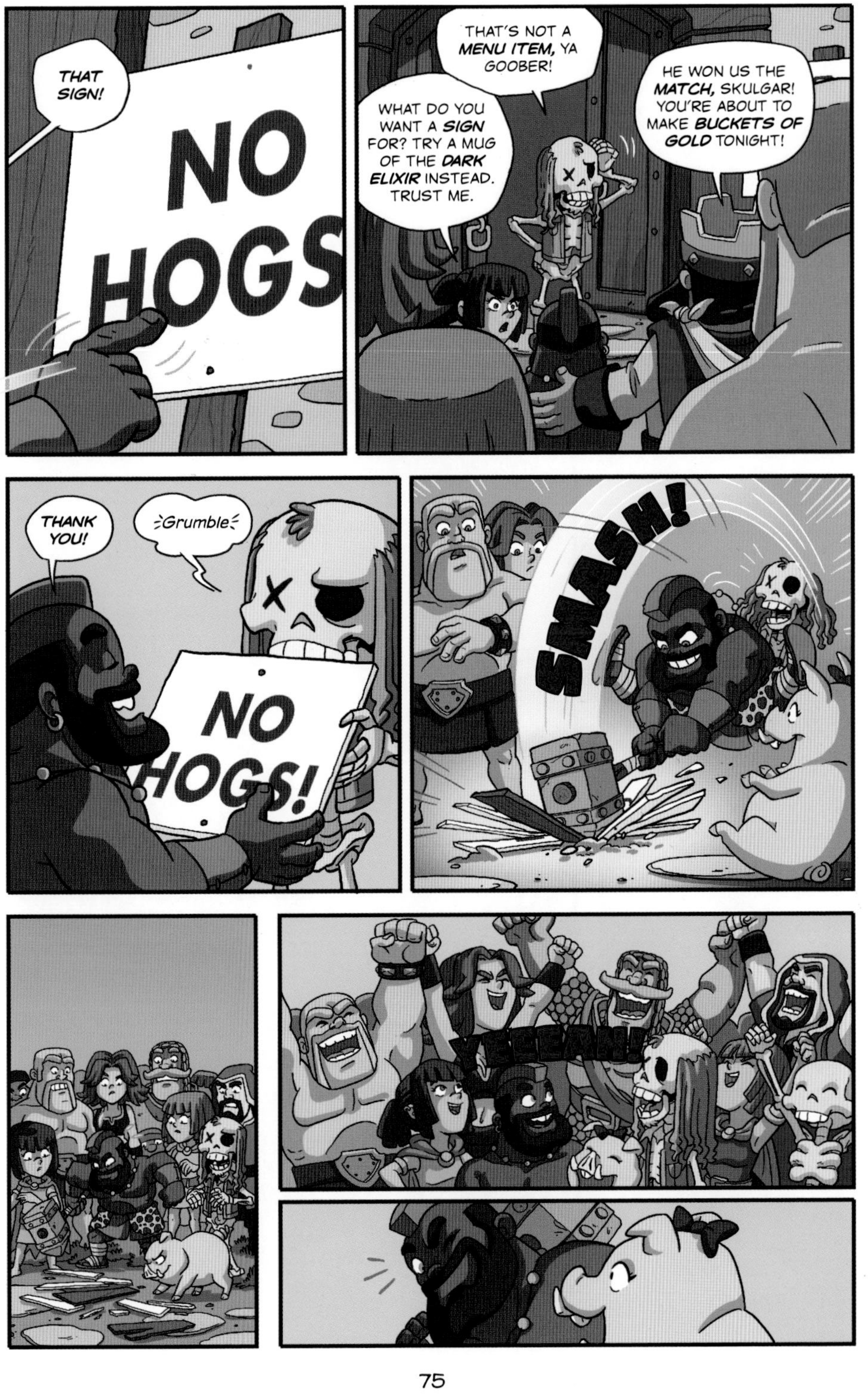
THAT SIGN!
NO HOGS
WHAT DO YOU WANT A **SIGN** FOR? TRY A MUG OF THE **DARK ELIXIR** INSTEAD. TRUST ME.
THAT'S NOT A **MENU ITEM,** YA GOOBER!
HE WON US THE **MATCH,** SKULGAR! YOU'RE ABOUT TO MAKE **BUCKETS OF GOLD** TONIGHT!
THANK YOU!
Grumble
NO HOGS!
SMASH!
YEEEAH!

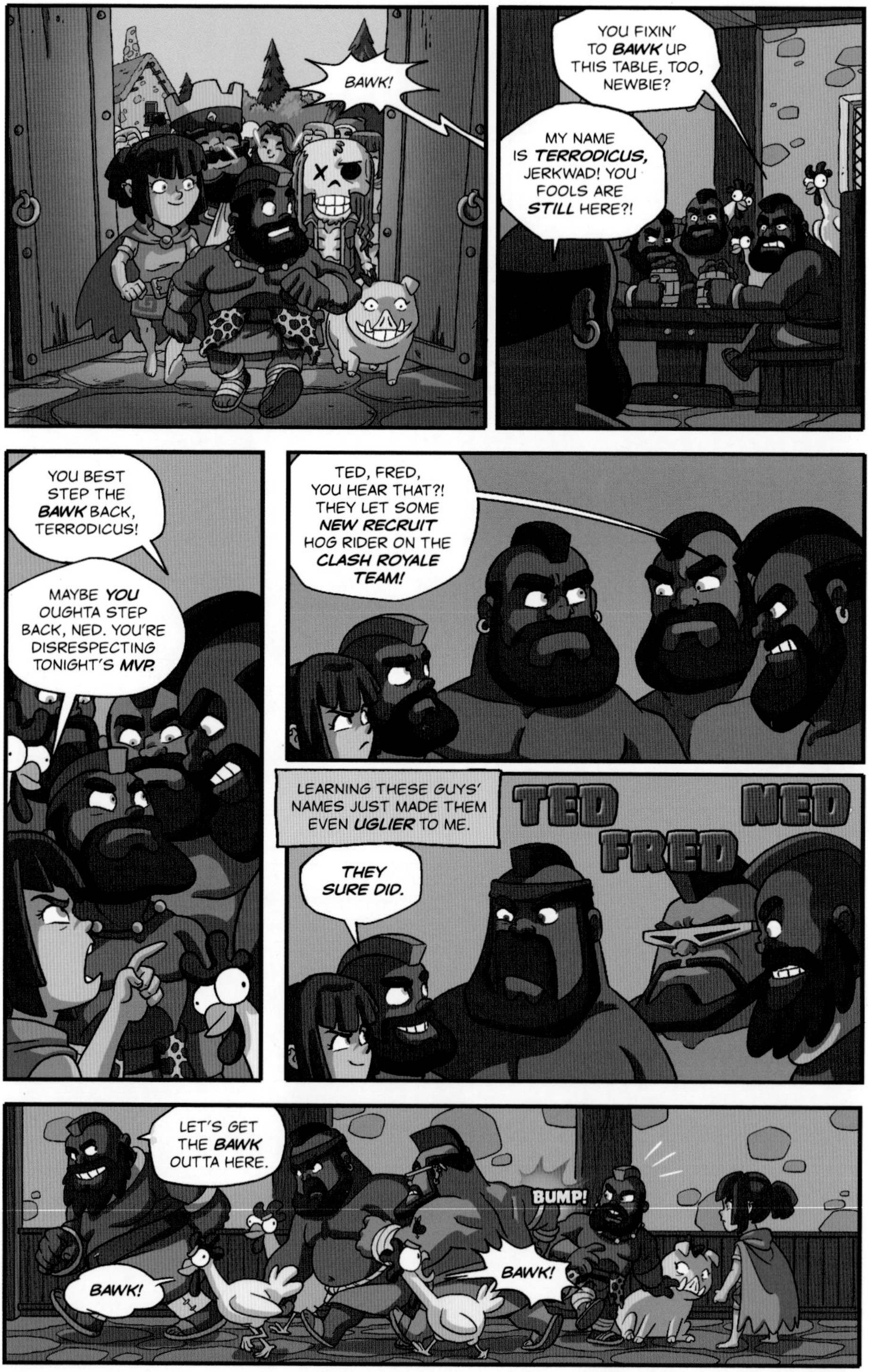

BAWK!
YOU FIXIN' TO BAWK UP THIS TABLE, TOO, NEWBIE?
MY NAME IS TERRODICUS, JERKWAD! YOU FOOLS ARE STILL HERE?!
YOU BEST STEP THE BAWK BACK, TERRODICUS!
MAYBE YOU OUGHTA STEP BACK, NED. YOU'RE DISRESPECTING TONIGHT'S MVP.
TED, FRED, YOU HEAR THAT?! THEY LET SOME NEW RECRUIT HOG RIDER ON THE CLASH ROYALE TEAM!
LEARNING THESE GUYS' NAMES JUST MADE THEM EVEN UGLIER TO ME.
TED
NED
FRED
THEY SURE DID.
LET'S GET THE BAWK OUTTA HERE.
BUMP!
BAWK!
BAWK!

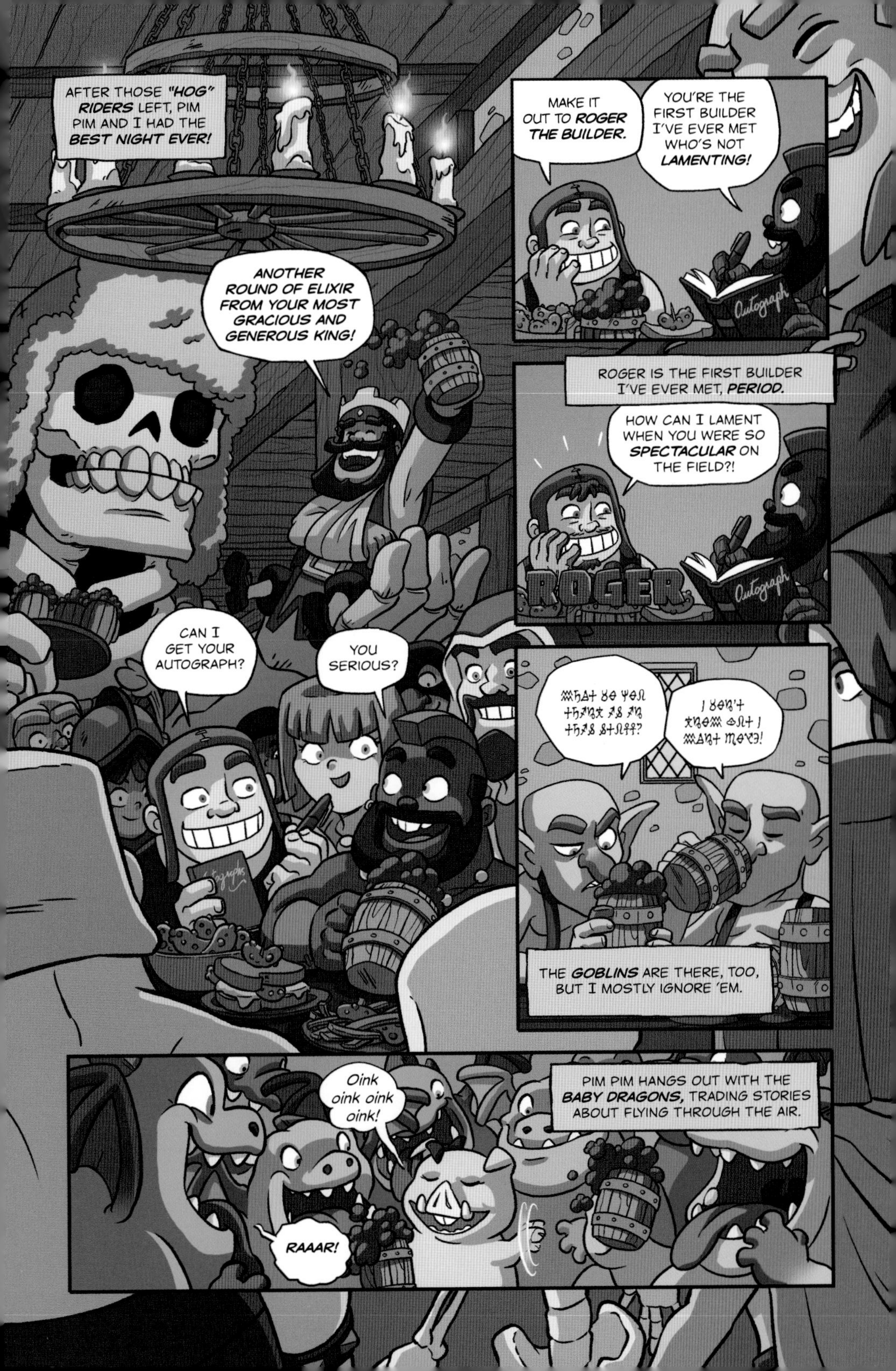
AFTER THOSE "HOG" RIDERS LEFT, PIM PIM AND I HAD THE BEST NIGHT EVER!
ANOTHER ROUND OF ELIXIR FROM YOUR MOST GRACIOUS AND GENEROUS KING!
CAN I GET YOUR AUTOGRAPH?
YOU SERIOUS?
MAKE IT OUT TO ROGER THE BUILDER.
YOU'RE THE FIRST BUILDER I'VE EVER MET WHO'S NOT LAMENTING!
Autograph
ROGER IS THE FIRST BUILDER I'VE EVER MET, PERIOD.
HOW CAN I LAMENT WHEN YOU WERE SO SPECTACULAR ON THE FIELD?!
ROGER
Autograph
THE GOBLINS ARE THERE, TOO, BUT I MOSTLY IGNORE 'EM.
Oink oink oink oink!
PIM PIM HANGS OUT WITH THE BABY DRAGONS, TRADING STORIES ABOUT FLYING THROUGH THE AIR.
RAAAR!

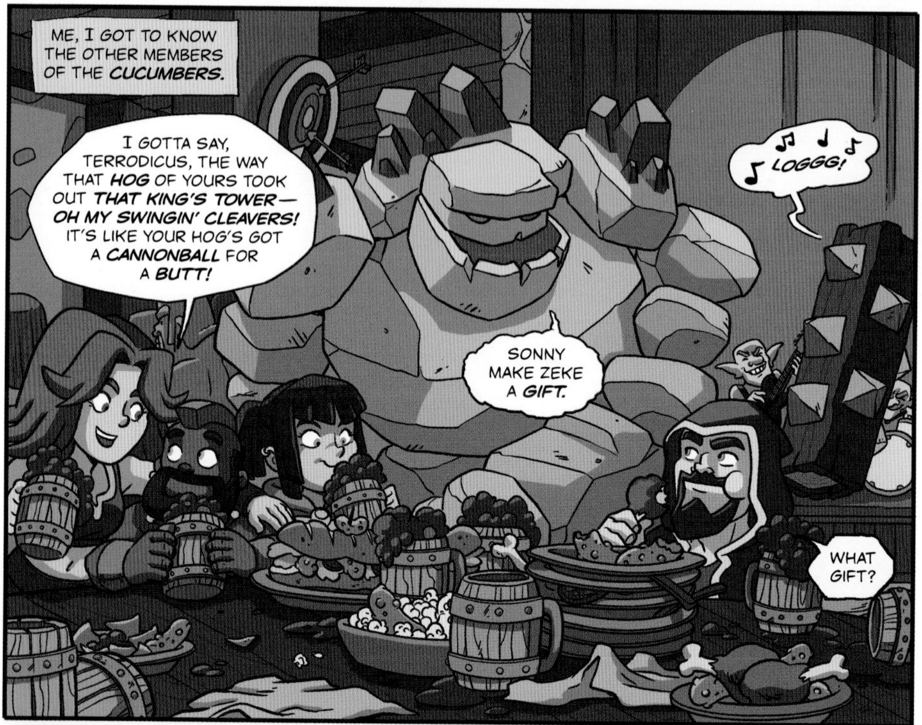

ME, I GOT TO KNOW THE OTHER MEMBERS OF THE CUCUMBERS.
I GOTTA SAY, TERRODICUS, THE WAY THAT HOG OF YOURS TOOK OUT THAT KING'S TOWER— OH MY SWINGIN' CLEAVERS! IT'S LIKE YOUR HOG'S GOT A CANNONBALL FOR A BUTT!
LOGGG!
SONNY MAKE ZEKE A GIFT.
WHAT GIFT?

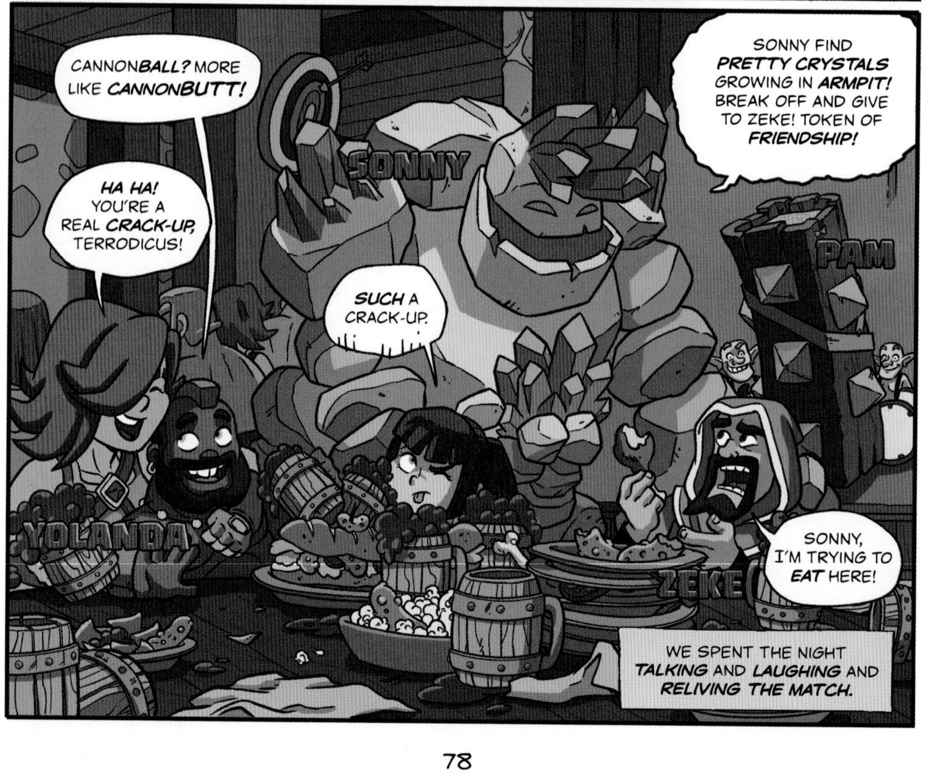

CANNONBALL? MORE LIKE CANNONBUTT!
SONNY FIND PRETTY CRYSTALS GROWING IN ARMPIT! BREAK OFF AND GIVE TO ZEKE! TOKEN OF FRIENDSHIP!
SONNY
HA HA! YOU'RE A REAL CRACK-UP, TERRODICUS!
PAM
SUCH A CRACK-UP.
YOLANDA
ZEKE
SONNY, I'M TRYING TO EAT HERE!
WE SPENT THE NIGHT TALKING AND LAUGHING AND RELIVING THE MATCH.

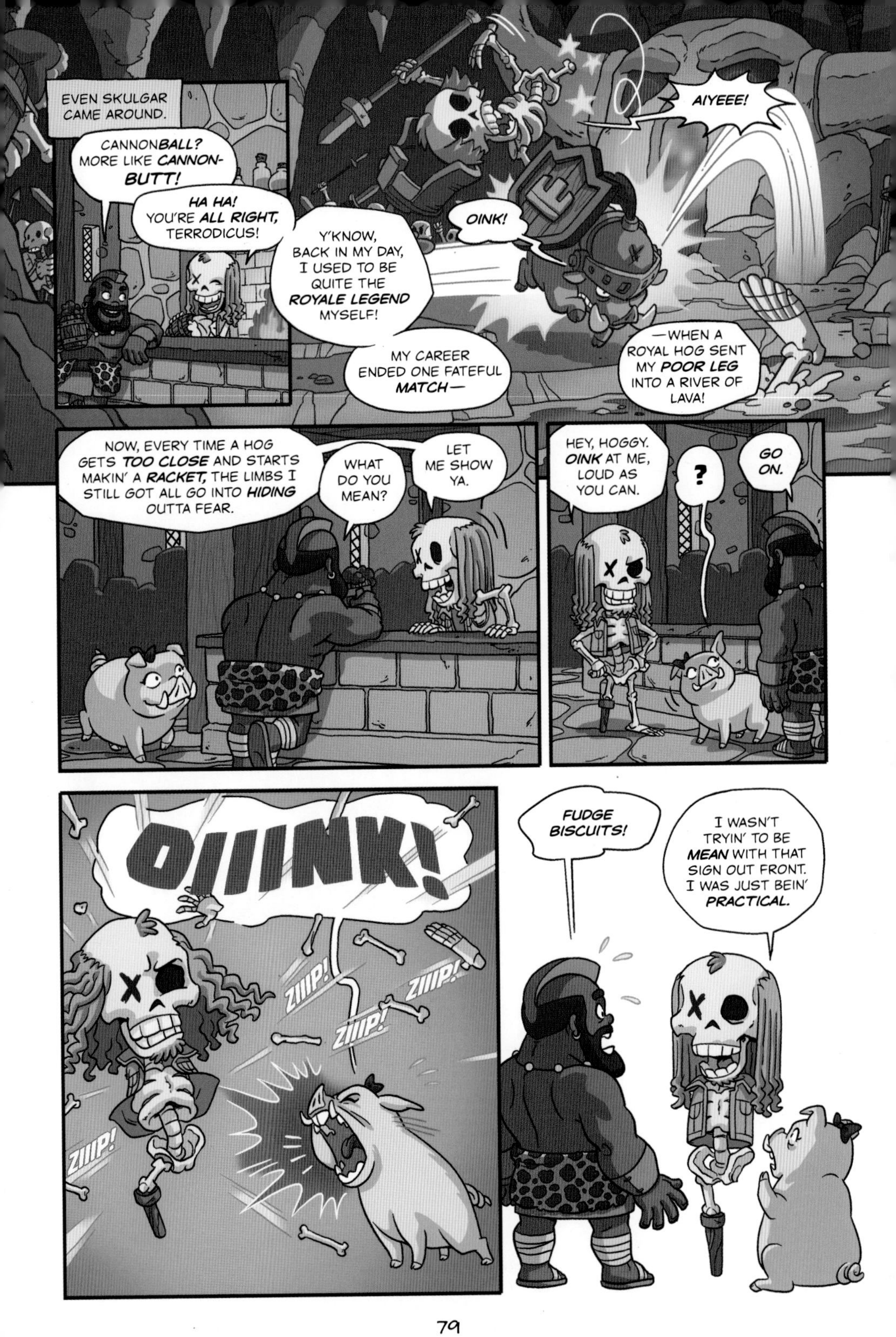
EVEN SKULGAR CAME AROUND.
CANNONBALL? MORE LIKE CANNON-BUTT!
HA HA! YOU'RE ALL RIGHT, TERRODICUS!
Y'KNOW, BACK IN MY DAY, I USED TO BE QUITE THE ROYALE LEGEND MYSELF!
OINK!
AIYEEE!
MY CAREER ENDED ONE FATEFUL MATCH—
—WHEN A ROYAL HOG SENT MY POOR LEG INTO A RIVER OF LAVA!
NOW, EVERY TIME A HOG GETS TOO CLOSE AND STARTS MAKIN' A RACKET, THE LIMBS I STILL GOT ALL GO INTO HIDING OUTTA FEAR.
WHAT DO YOU MEAN?
LET ME SHOW YA.
HEY, HOGGY. OINK AT ME, LOUD AS YOU CAN.
?
GO ON.
OIIINK!
ZIIIP!
ZIIIP!
ZIIIP!
ZIIIP!
FUDGE BISCUITS!
I WASN'T TRYIN' TO BE MEAN WITH THAT SIGN OUT FRONT. I WAS JUST BEIN' PRACTICAL.

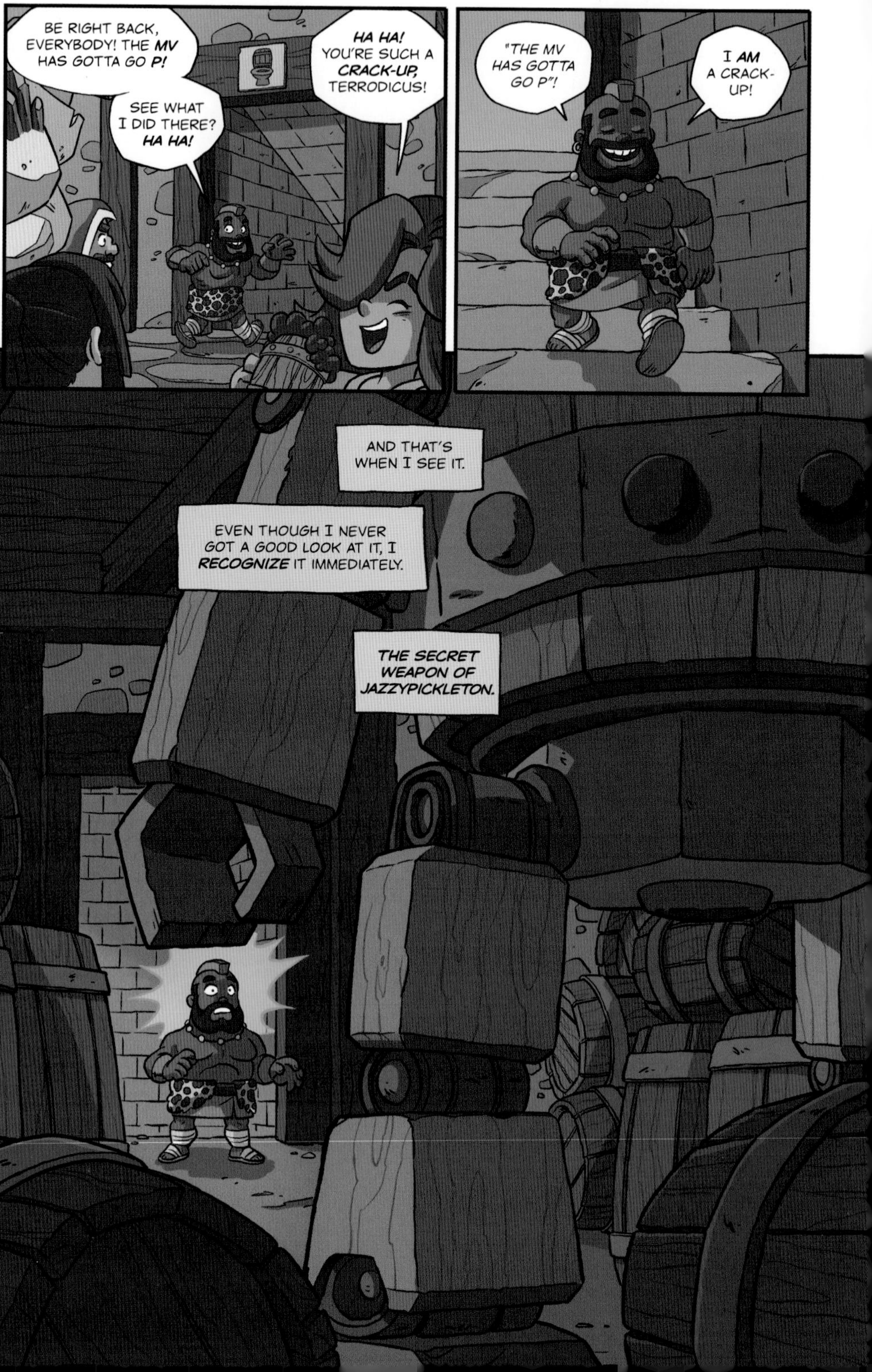
BE RIGHT BACK, EVERYBODY! THE **MV** HAS GOTTA GO **P!**
SEE WHAT I DID THERE? **HA HA!**
HA HA! YOU'RE SUCH A **CRACK-UP,** TERRODICUS!
"THE MV HAS GOTTA GO P"!
I **AM** A CRACK-UP!
AND THAT'S WHEN I SEE IT.
EVEN THOUGH I NEVER GOT A *GOOD* LOOK AT IT, I ***RECOGNIZE*** IT IMMEDIATELY.
THE SECRET WEAPON OF JAZZYPICKLETON.

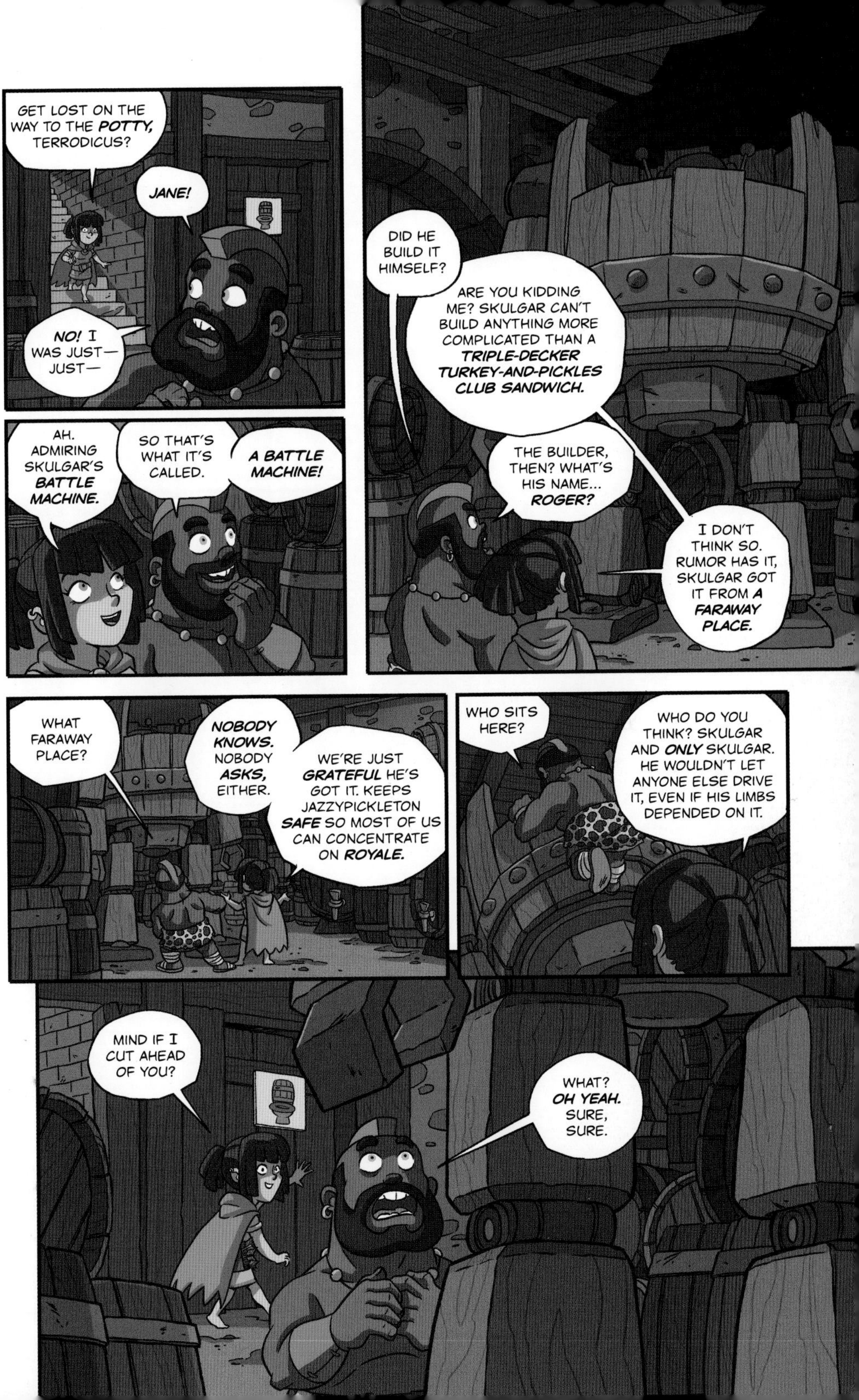
GET LOST ON THE WAY TO THE POTTY, TERRODICUS?
JANE!
NO! I WAS JUST— JUST—
AH. ADMIRING SKULGAR'S BATTLE MACHINE.
SO THAT'S WHAT IT'S CALLED.
A BATTLE MACHINE!
DID HE BUILD IT HIMSELF?
ARE YOU KIDDING ME? SKULGAR CAN'T BUILD ANYTHING MORE COMPLICATED THAN A TRIPLE-DECKER TURKEY-AND-PICKLES CLUB SANDWICH.
THE BUILDER, THEN? WHAT'S HIS NAME... ROGER?
I DON'T THINK SO. RUMOR HAS IT, SKULGAR GOT IT FROM A FARAWAY PLACE.
WHAT FARAWAY PLACE?
NOBODY KNOWS. NOBODY ASKS, EITHER.
WE'RE JUST GRATEFUL HE'S GOT IT. KEEPS JAZZYPICKLETON SAFE SO MOST OF US CAN CONCENTRATE ON ROYALE.
WHO SITS HERE?
WHO DO YOU THINK? SKULGAR AND ONLY SKULGAR. HE WOULDN'T LET ANYONE ELSE DRIVE IT, EVEN IF HIS LIMBS DEPENDED ON IT.
MIND IF I CUT AHEAD OF YOU?
WHAT? OH YEAH. SURE, SURE.

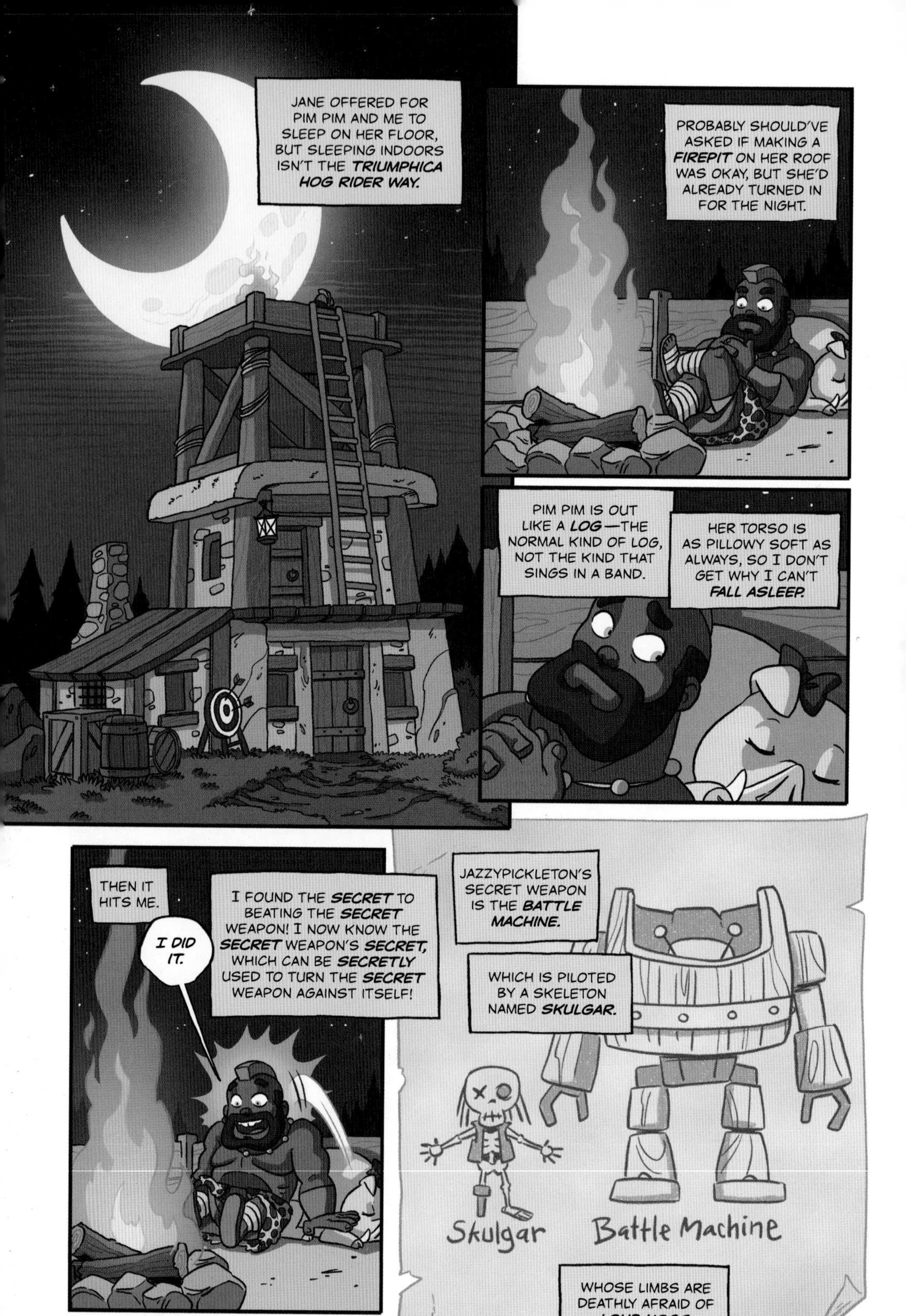

JANE OFFERED FOR PIM PIM AND ME TO SLEEP ON HER FLOOR, BUT SLEEPING INDOORS ISN'T THE TRIUMPHICA HOG RIDER WAY.
PROBABLY SHOULD'VE ASKED IF MAKING A FIREPIT ON HER ROOF WAS OKAY, BUT SHE'D ALREADY TURNED IN FOR THE NIGHT.
PIM PIM IS OUT LIKE A LOG—THE NORMAL KIND OF LOG, NOT THE KIND THAT SINGS IN A BAND.
HER TORSO IS AS PILLOWY SOFT AS ALWAYS, SO I DON'T GET WHY I CAN'T FALL ASLEEP.
THEN IT HITS ME.
I FOUND THE SECRET TO BEATING THE SECRET WEAPON! I NOW KNOW THE SECRET WEAPON'S SECRET, WHICH CAN BE SECRETLY USED TO TURN THE SECRET WEAPON AGAINST ITSELF!
I DID IT.
JAZZYPICKLETON'S SECRET WEAPON IS THE BATTLE MACHINE.
WHICH IS PILOTED BY A SKELETON NAMED SKULGAR.
Skulgar
Battle Machine
WHOSE LIMBS ARE DEATHLY AFRAID OF LOUD HOGS.

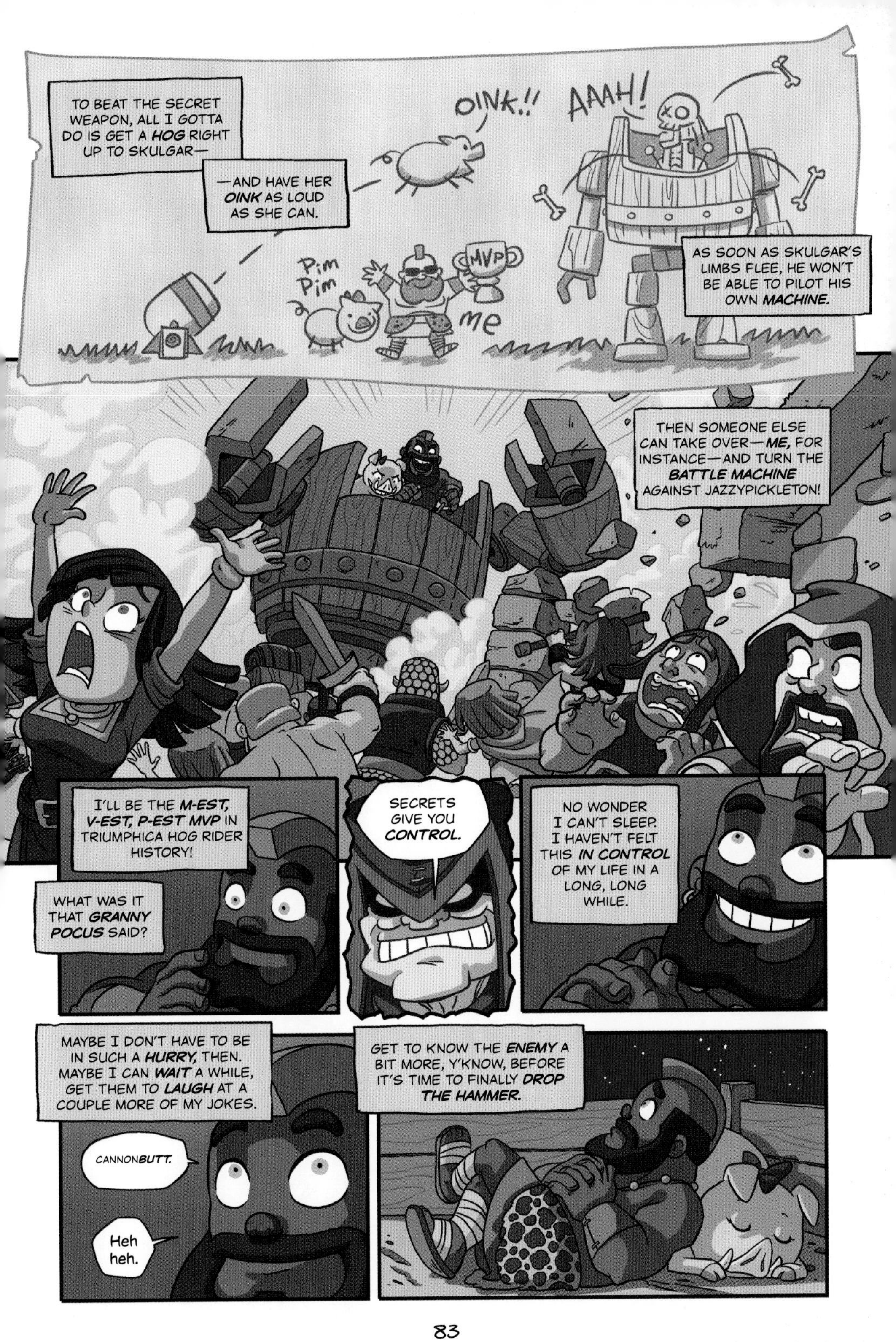
TO BEAT THE SECRET WEAPON, ALL I GOTTA DO IS GET A HOG RIGHT UP TO SKULGAR—
—AND HAVE HER OINK AS LOUD AS SHE CAN.
OINK!!
AAAH!
Pim Pim
MVP
me
AS SOON AS SKULGAR'S LIMBS FLEE, HE WON'T BE ABLE TO PILOT HIS OWN MACHINE.
THEN SOMEONE ELSE CAN TAKE OVER—ME, FOR INSTANCE—AND TURN THE BATTLE MACHINE AGAINST JAZZYPICKLETON!
I'LL BE THE M-EST, V-EST, P-EST MVP IN TRIUMPHICA HOG RIDER HISTORY!
WHAT WAS IT THAT GRANNY POCUS SAID?
SECRETS GIVE YOU CONTROL.
NO WONDER I CAN'T SLEEP. I HAVEN'T FELT THIS IN CONTROL OF MY LIFE IN A LONG, LONG WHILE.
MAYBE I DON'T HAVE TO BE IN SUCH A HURRY, THEN. MAYBE I CAN WAIT A WHILE, GET THEM TO LAUGH AT A COUPLE MORE OF MY JOKES.
CANNONBUTT.
Heh heh.
GET TO KNOW THE ENEMY A BIT MORE, Y'KNOW, BEFORE IT'S TIME TO FINALLY DROP THE HAMMER.

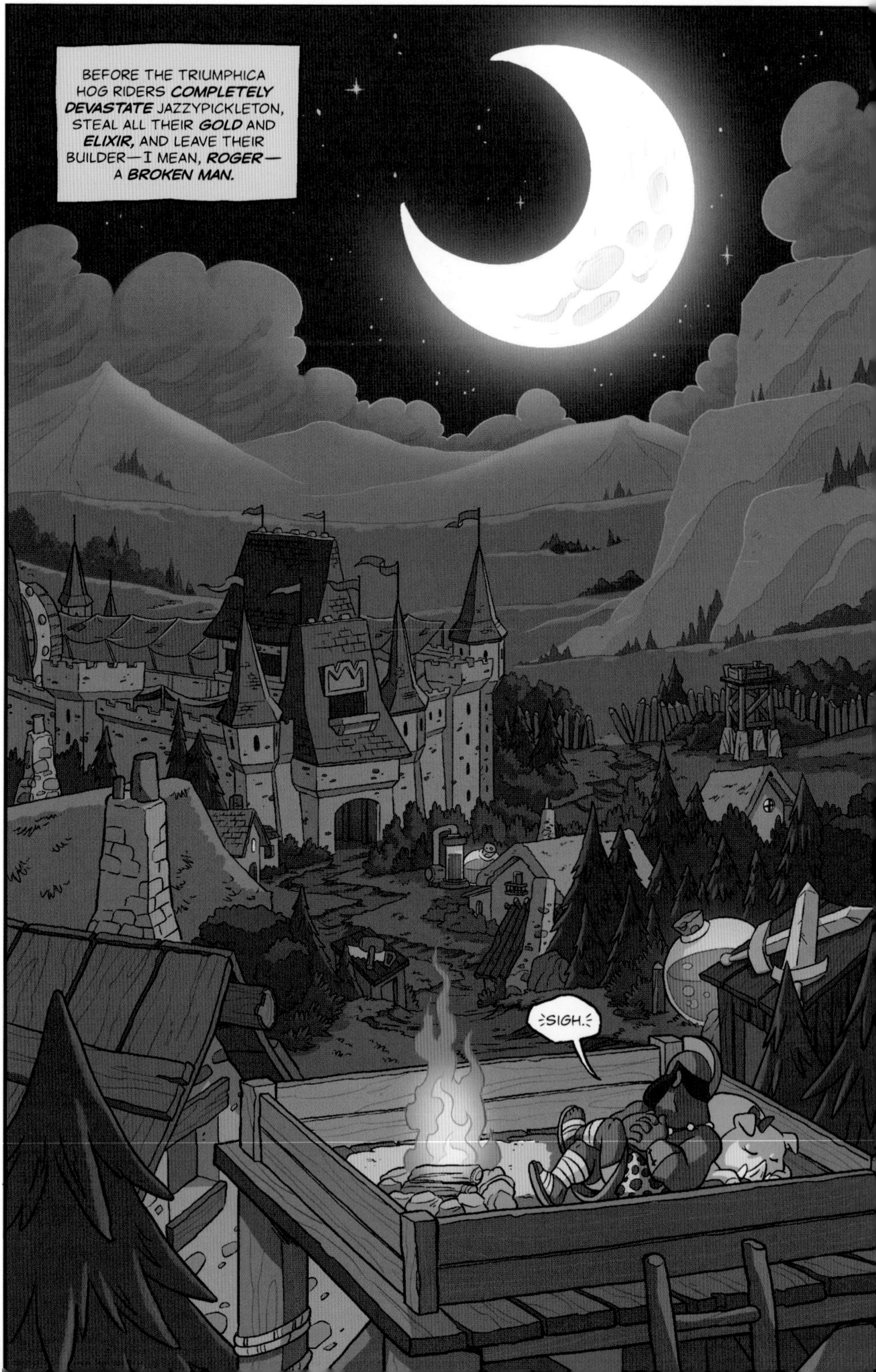
BEFORE THE TRIUMPHICA HOG RIDERS **COMPLETELY DEVASTATE** JAZZYPICKLETON, STEAL ALL THEIR **GOLD** AND **ELIXIR,** AND LEAVE THEIR BUILDER—I MEAN, **ROGER**—A **BROKEN MAN.**
SIGH.

Chapter 3

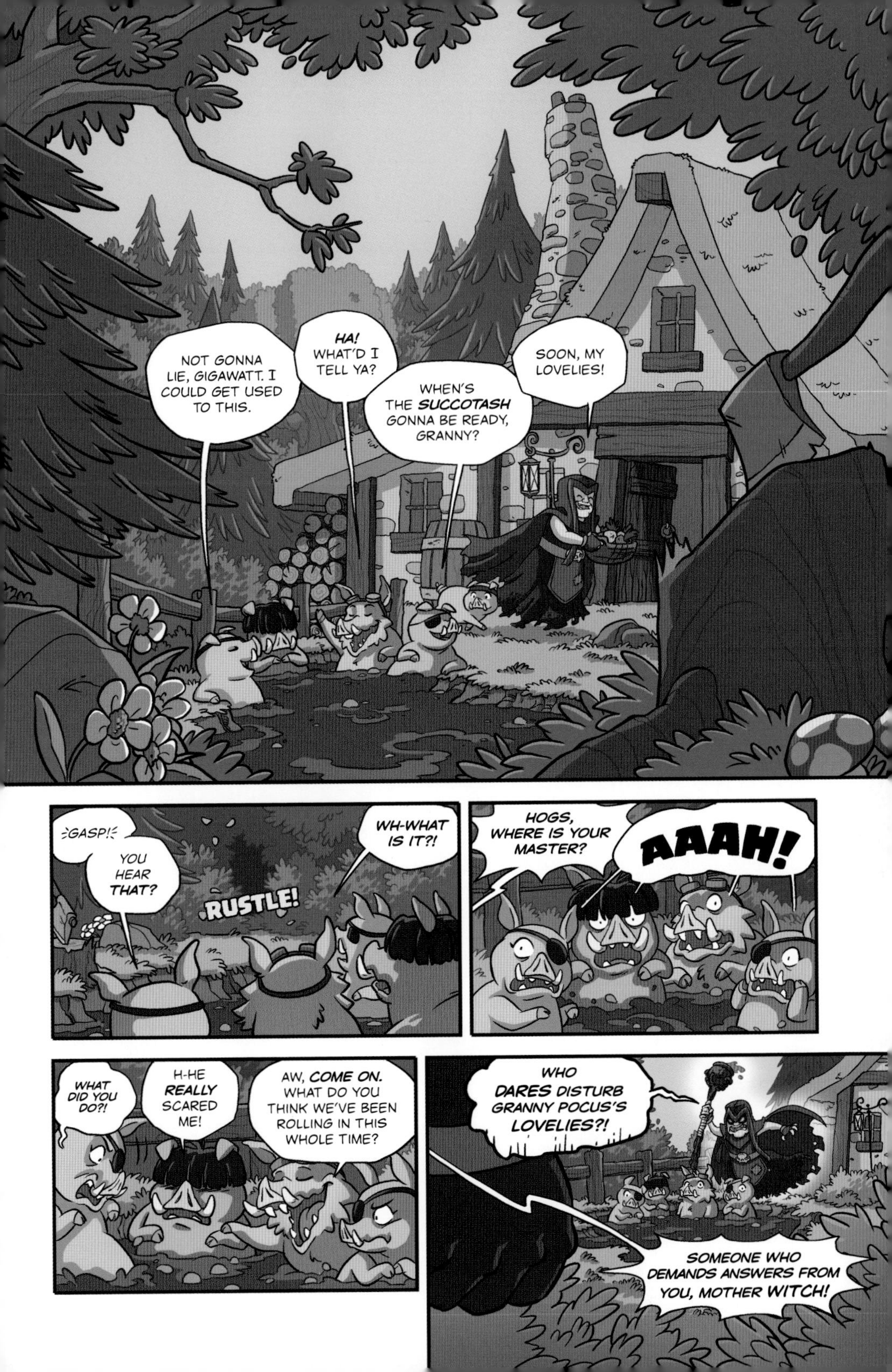
NOT GONNA LIE, GIGAWATT. I COULD GET USED TO THIS.
HA! WHAT'D I TELL YA?
WHEN'S THE SUCCOTASH GONNA BE READY, GRANNY?
SOON, MY LOVELIES!
GASP!
YOU HEAR THAT?
RUSTLE!
WH-WHAT IS IT?!
HOGS, WHERE IS YOUR MASTER?
AAAH!
WHAT DID YOU DO?!
H-HE REALLY SCARED ME!
AW, COME ON. WHAT DO YOU THINK WE'VE BEEN ROLLING IN THIS WHOLE TIME?
WHO DARES DISTURB GRANNY POCUS'S LOVELIES?!
SOMEONE WHO DEMANDS ANSWERS FROM YOU, MOTHER WITCH!

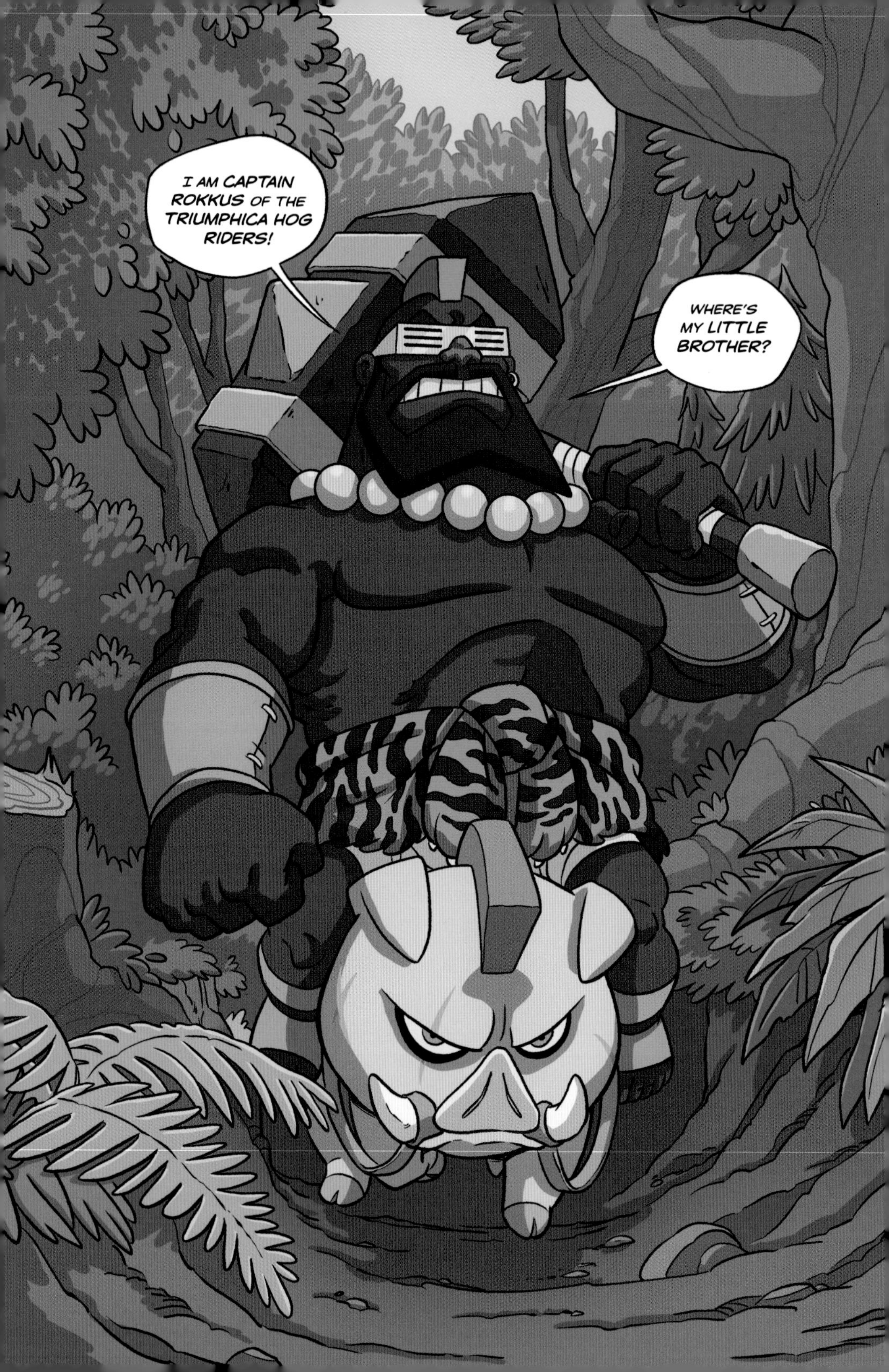
I AM CAPTAIN ROKKUS OF THE TRIUMPHICA HOG RIDERS!
WHERE'S MY LITTLE BROTHER?

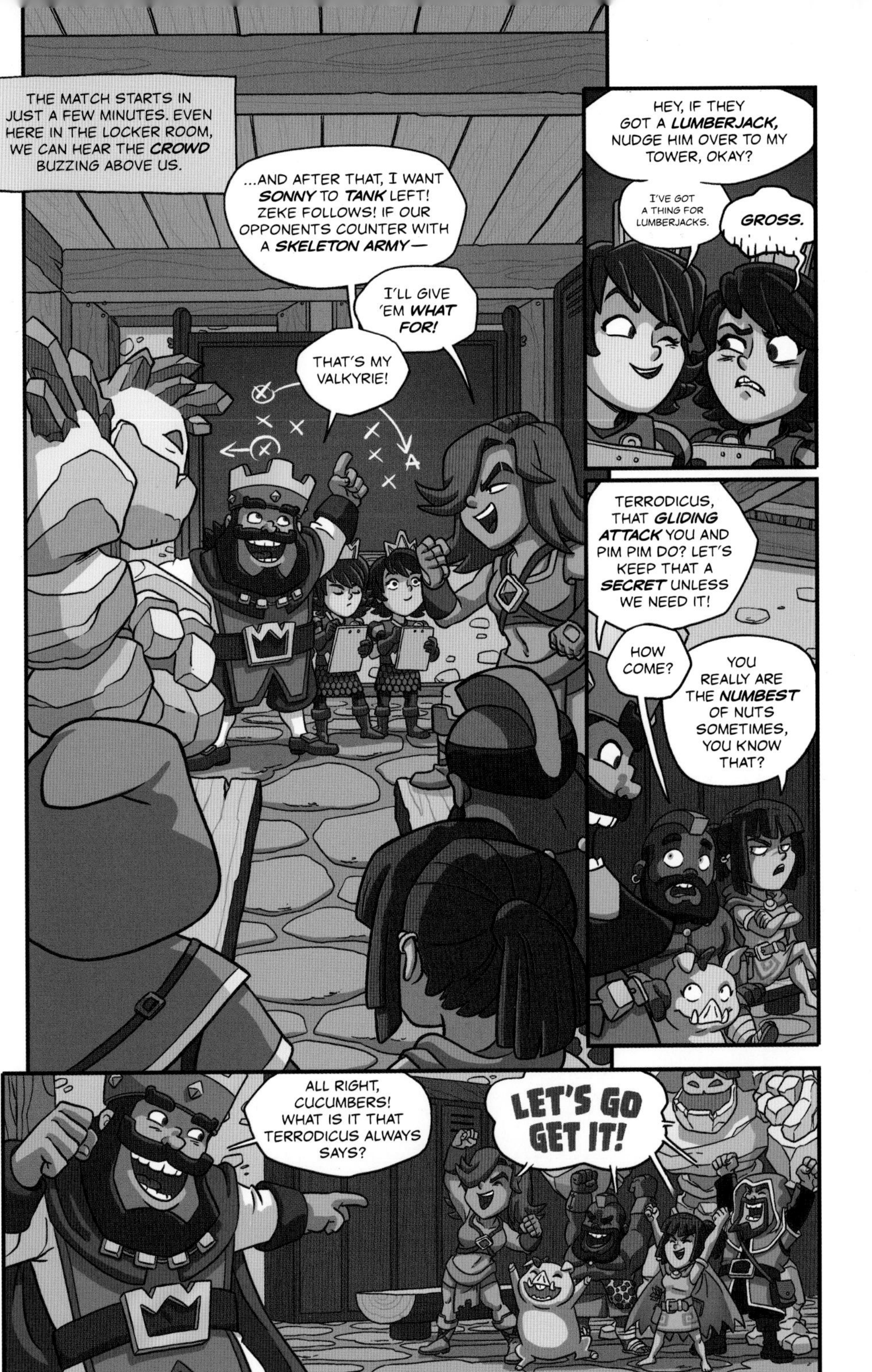
THE MATCH STARTS IN JUST A FEW MINUTES. EVEN HERE IN THE LOCKER ROOM, WE CAN HEAR THE CROWD BUZZING ABOVE US.
...AND AFTER THAT, I WANT SONNY TO TANK LEFT! ZEKE FOLLOWS! IF OUR OPPONENTS COUNTER WITH A SKELETON ARMY—
I'LL GIVE 'EM WHAT FOR!
THAT'S MY VALKYRIE!
HEY, IF THEY GOT A LUMBERJACK, NUDGE HIM OVER TO MY TOWER, OKAY?
I'VE GOT A THING FOR LUMBERJACKS.
GROSS.
TERRODICUS, THAT GLIDING ATTACK YOU AND PIM PIM DO? LET'S KEEP THAT A SECRET UNLESS WE NEED IT!
HOW COME?
YOU REALLY ARE THE NUMBEST OF NUTS SOMETIMES, YOU KNOW THAT?
ALL RIGHT, CUCUMBERS! WHAT IS IT THAT TERRODICUS ALWAYS SAYS?
LET'S GO GET IT!

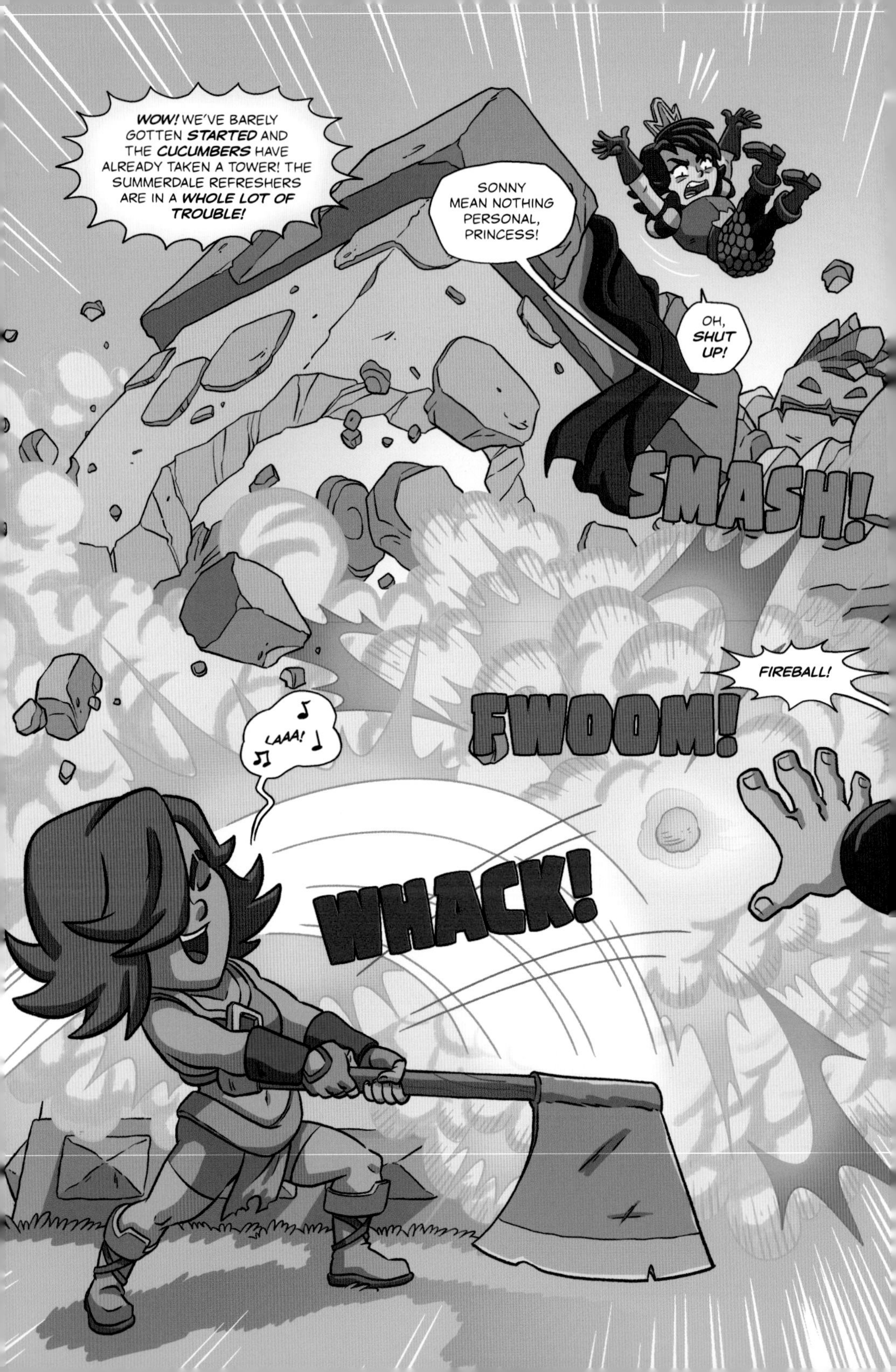
WOW! WE'VE BARELY GOTTEN STARTED AND THE CUCUMBERS HAVE ALREADY TAKEN A TOWER! THE SUMMERDALE REFRESHERS ARE IN A WHOLE LOT OF TROUBLE!
SONNY MEAN NOTHING PERSONAL, PRINCESS!
OH, SHUT UP!
SMASH!
FIREBALL!
FWOOM!
LAAA!
WHACK!

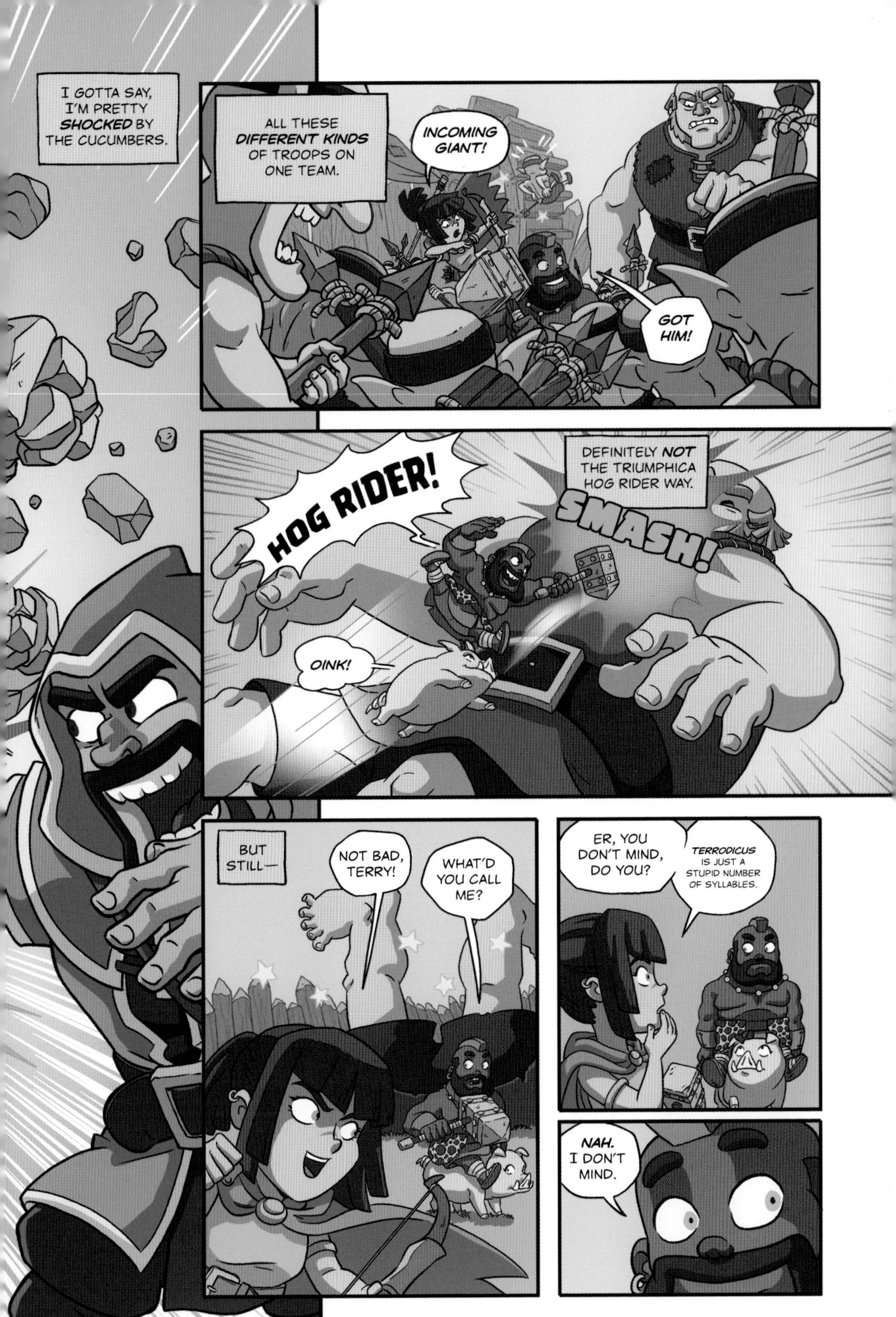
I GOTTA SAY, I'M PRETTY SHOCKED BY THE CUCUMBERS.
ALL THESE DIFFERENT KINDS OF TROOPS ON ONE TEAM.
INCOMING GIANT!
GOT HIM!
HOG RIDER!
DEFINITELY NOT THE TRIUMPHICA HOG RIDER WAY.
SMASH!
OINK!
BUT STILL—
NOT BAD, TERRY!
WHAT'D YOU CALL ME?
ER, YOU DON'T MIND, DO YOU?
TERRODICUS IS JUST A STUPID NUMBER OF SYLLABLES.
NAH. I DON'T MIND.

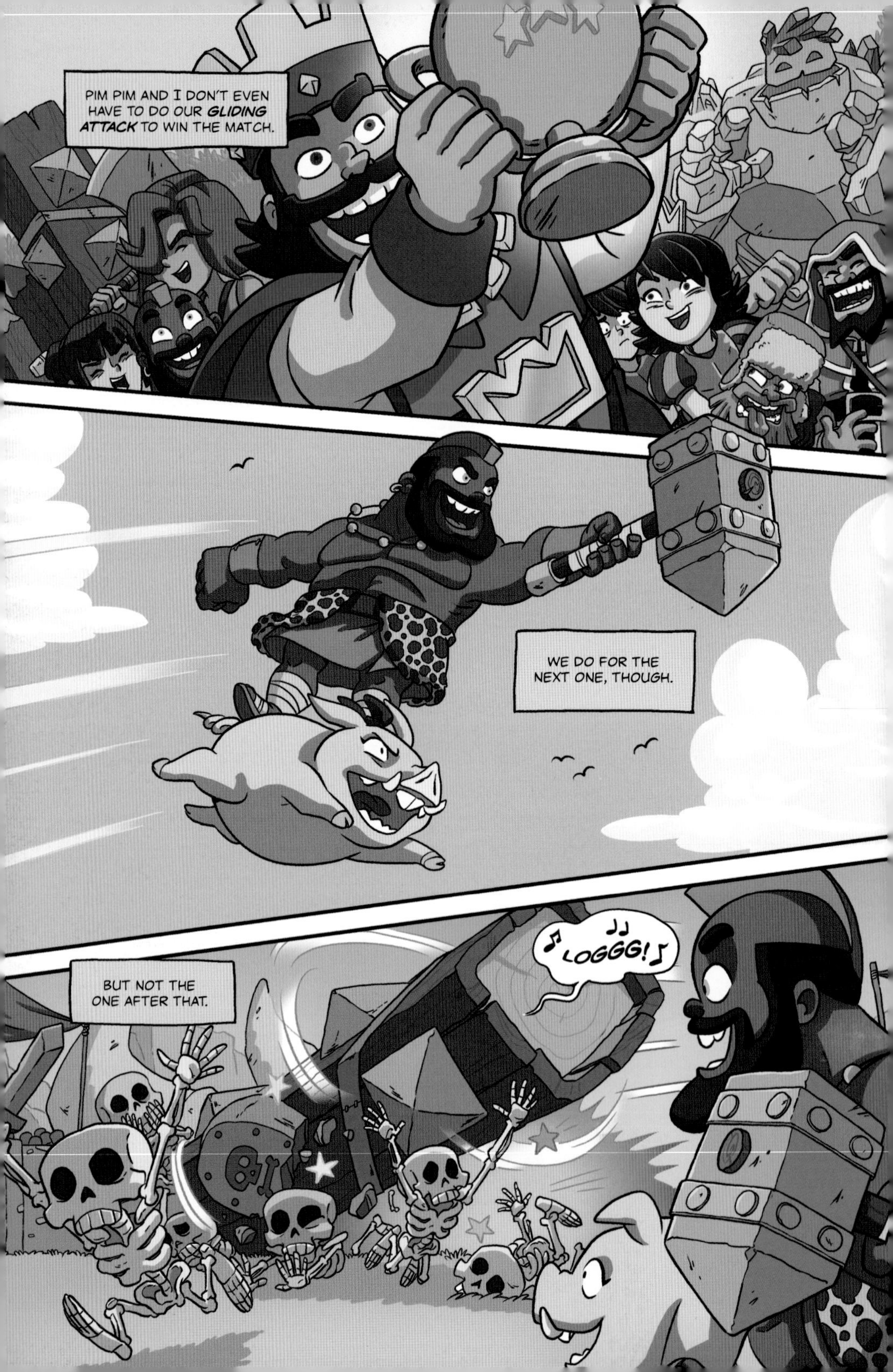
PIM PIM AND I DON'T EVEN HAVE TO DO OUR **GLIDING ATTACK** TO WIN THE MATCH.
WE DO FOR THE NEXT ONE, THOUGH.
BUT NOT THE ONE AFTER THAT.
LOGGG!

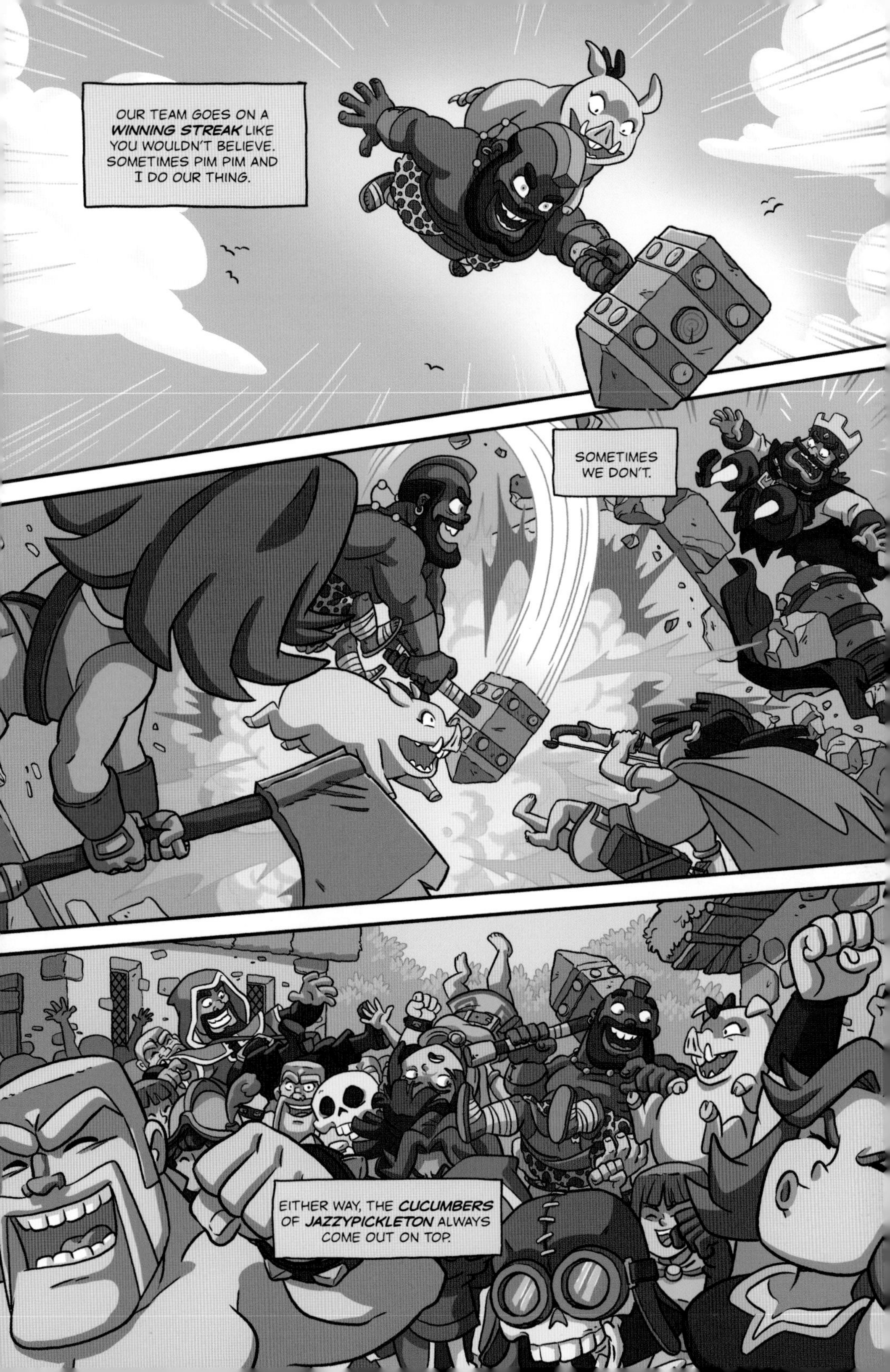
OUR TEAM GOES ON A *WINNING STREAK* LIKE YOU WOULDN'T BELIEVE. SOMETIMES PIM PIM AND I DO OUR THING.
SOMETIMES WE DON'T.
EITHER WAY, THE *CUCUMBERS* OF *JAZZYPICKLETON* ALWAYS COME OUT ON TOP.

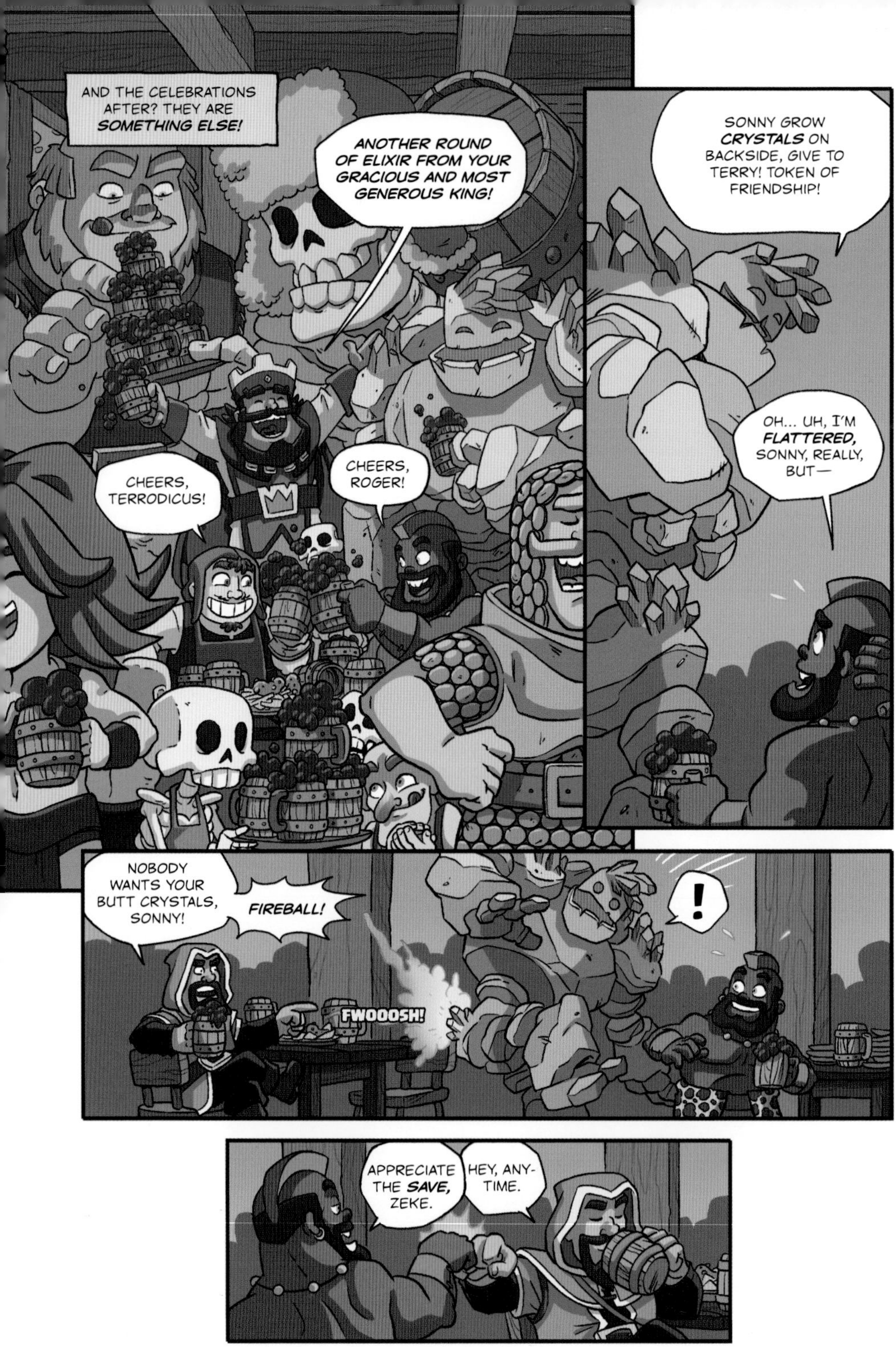

AND THE CELEBRATIONS AFTER? THEY ARE *SOMETHING ELSE!*
ANOTHER ROUND OF ELIXIR FROM YOUR GRACIOUS AND MOST GENEROUS KING!
CHEERS, TERRODICUS!
CHEERS, ROGER!
SONNY GROW **CRYSTALS** ON BACKSIDE, GIVE TO TERRY! TOKEN OF FRIENDSHIP!
OH... UH, I'M ***FLATTERED,*** SONNY, REALLY, BUT—
NOBODY WANTS YOUR BUTT CRYSTALS, SONNY!
FIREBALL!
FWOOOSH!
!
APPRECIATE THE ***SAVE,*** ZEKE.
HEY, ANY-TIME.

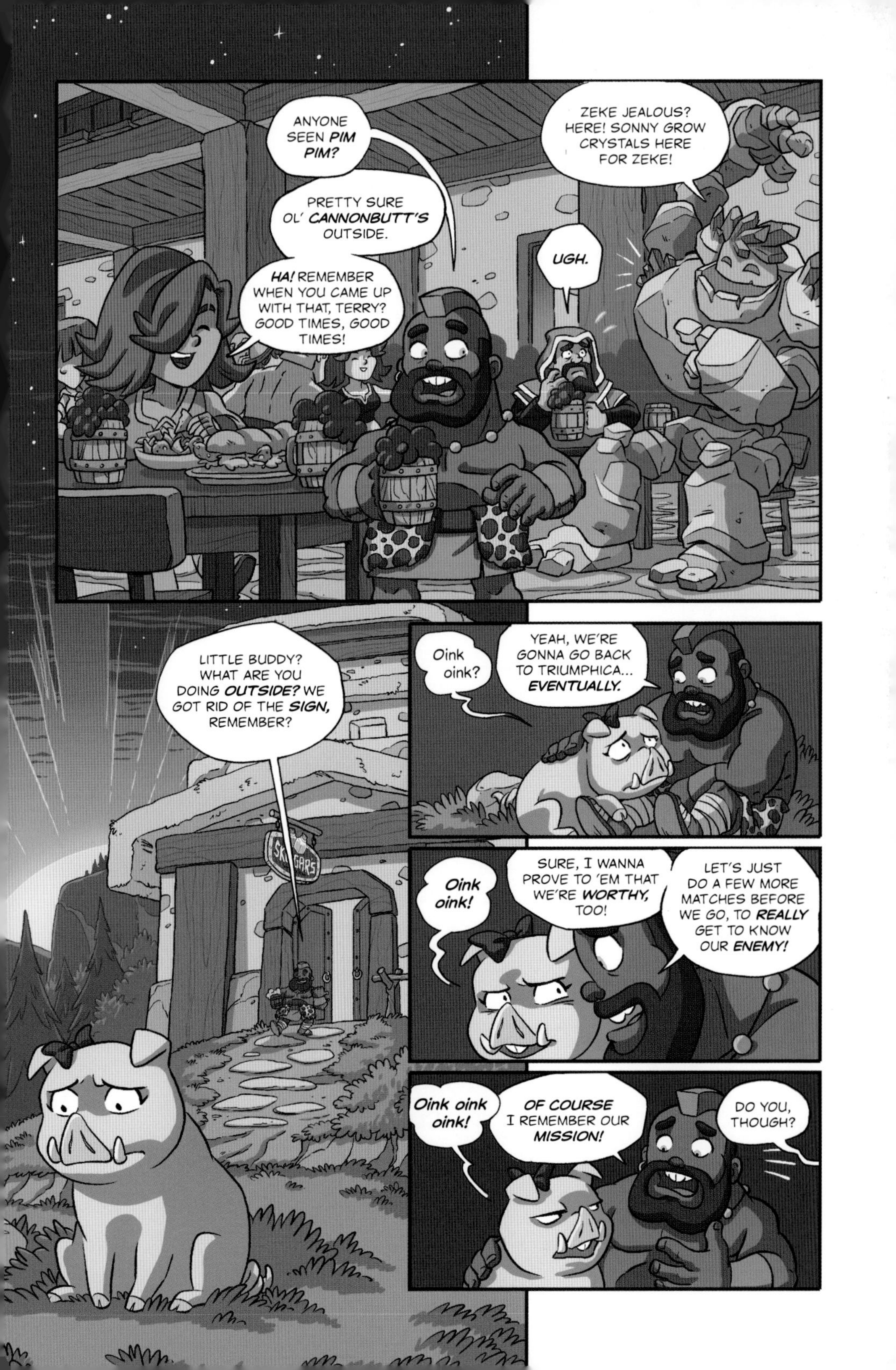
ANYONE SEEN PIM PIM?
PRETTY SURE OL' CANNONBUTT'S OUTSIDE.
HA! REMEMBER WHEN YOU CAME UP WITH THAT, TERRY? GOOD TIMES, GOOD TIMES!
UGH.
ZEKE JEALOUS? HERE! SONNY GROW CRYSTALS HERE FOR ZEKE!
LITTLE BUDDY? WHAT ARE YOU DOING OUTSIDE? WE GOT RID OF THE SIGN, REMEMBER?
Oink oink?
YEAH, WE'RE GONNA GO BACK TO TRIUMPHICA... EVENTUALLY.
Oink oink!
SURE, I WANNA PROVE TO 'EM THAT WE'RE WORTHY, TOO!
LET'S JUST DO A FEW MORE MATCHES BEFORE WE GO, TO REALLY GET TO KNOW OUR ENEMY!
Oink oink oink!
OF COURSE I REMEMBER OUR MISSION!
DO YOU, THOUGH?

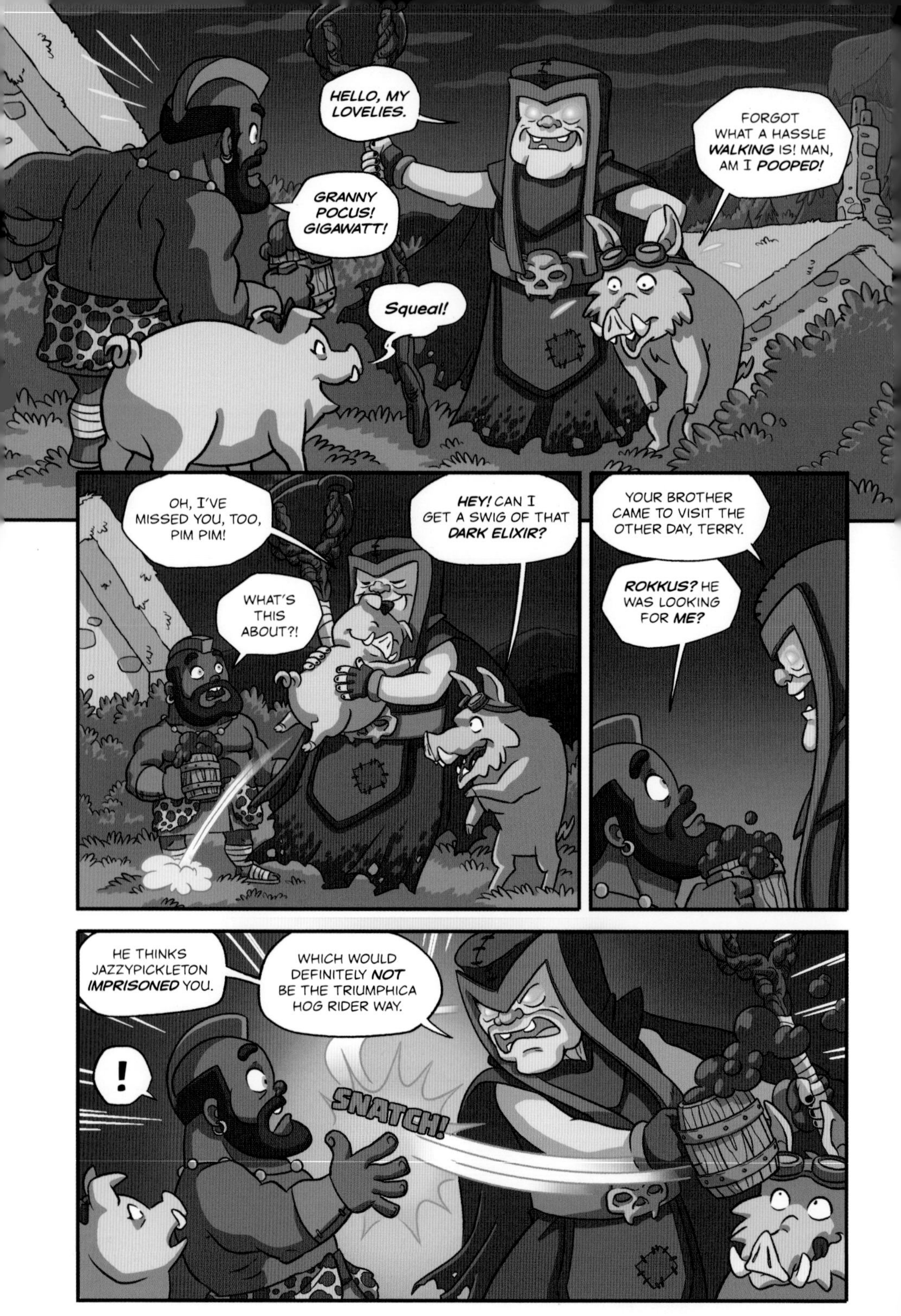
HELLO, MY LOVELIES.
GRANNY POCUS! GIGAWATT!
FORGOT WHAT A HASSLE WALKING IS! MAN, AM I POOPED!
Squeal!
OH, I'VE MISSED YOU, TOO, PIM PIM!
WHAT'S THIS ABOUT?!
HEY! CAN I GET A SWIG OF THAT DARK ELIXIR?
YOUR BROTHER CAME TO VISIT THE OTHER DAY, TERRY.
ROKKUS? HE WAS LOOKING FOR ME?
HE THINKS JAZZYPICKLETON IMPRISONED YOU.
WHICH WOULD DEFINITELY NOT BE THE TRIUMPHICA HOG RIDER WAY.
!
SNATCH!

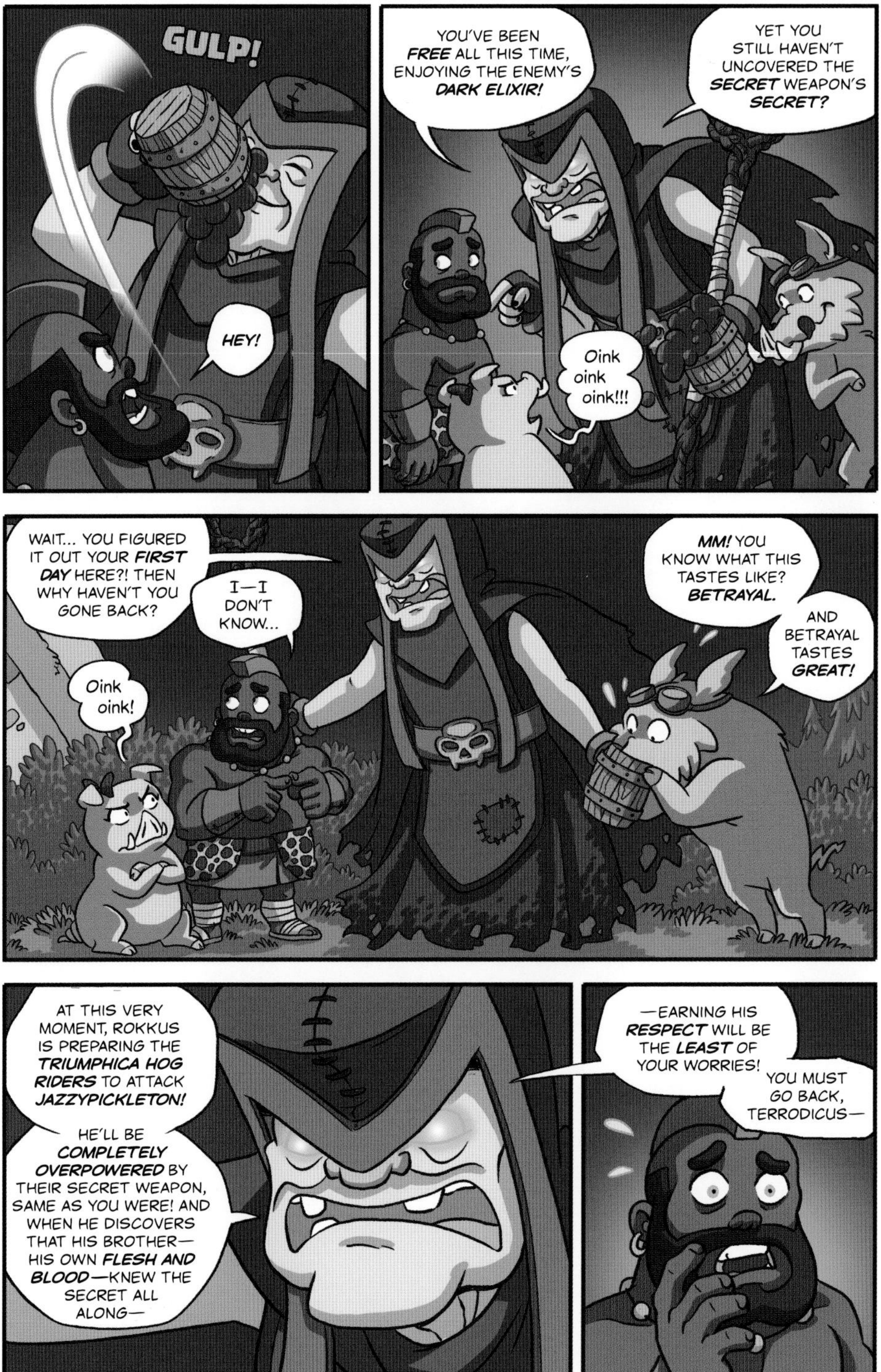
GULP!
HEY!
YOU'VE BEEN FREE ALL THIS TIME, ENJOYING THE ENEMY'S DARK ELIXIR!
YET YOU STILL HAVEN'T UNCOVERED THE SECRET WEAPON'S SECRET?
Oink oink oink!!!
WAIT... YOU FIGURED IT OUT YOUR FIRST DAY HERE?! THEN WHY HAVEN'T YOU GONE BACK?
I—I DON'T KNOW...
Oink oink!
MM! YOU KNOW WHAT THIS TASTES LIKE? BETRAYAL.
AND BETRAYAL TASTES GREAT!
AT THIS VERY MOMENT, ROKKUS IS PREPARING THE TRIUMPHICA HOG RIDERS TO ATTACK JAZZYPICKLETON!
HE'LL BE COMPLETELY OVERPOWERED BY THEIR SECRET WEAPON, SAME AS YOU WERE! AND WHEN HE DISCOVERS THAT HIS BROTHER—HIS OWN FLESH AND BLOOD—KNEW THE SECRET ALL ALONG—
—EARNING HIS RESPECT WILL BE THE LEAST OF YOUR WORRIES!
YOU MUST GO BACK, TERRODICUS—

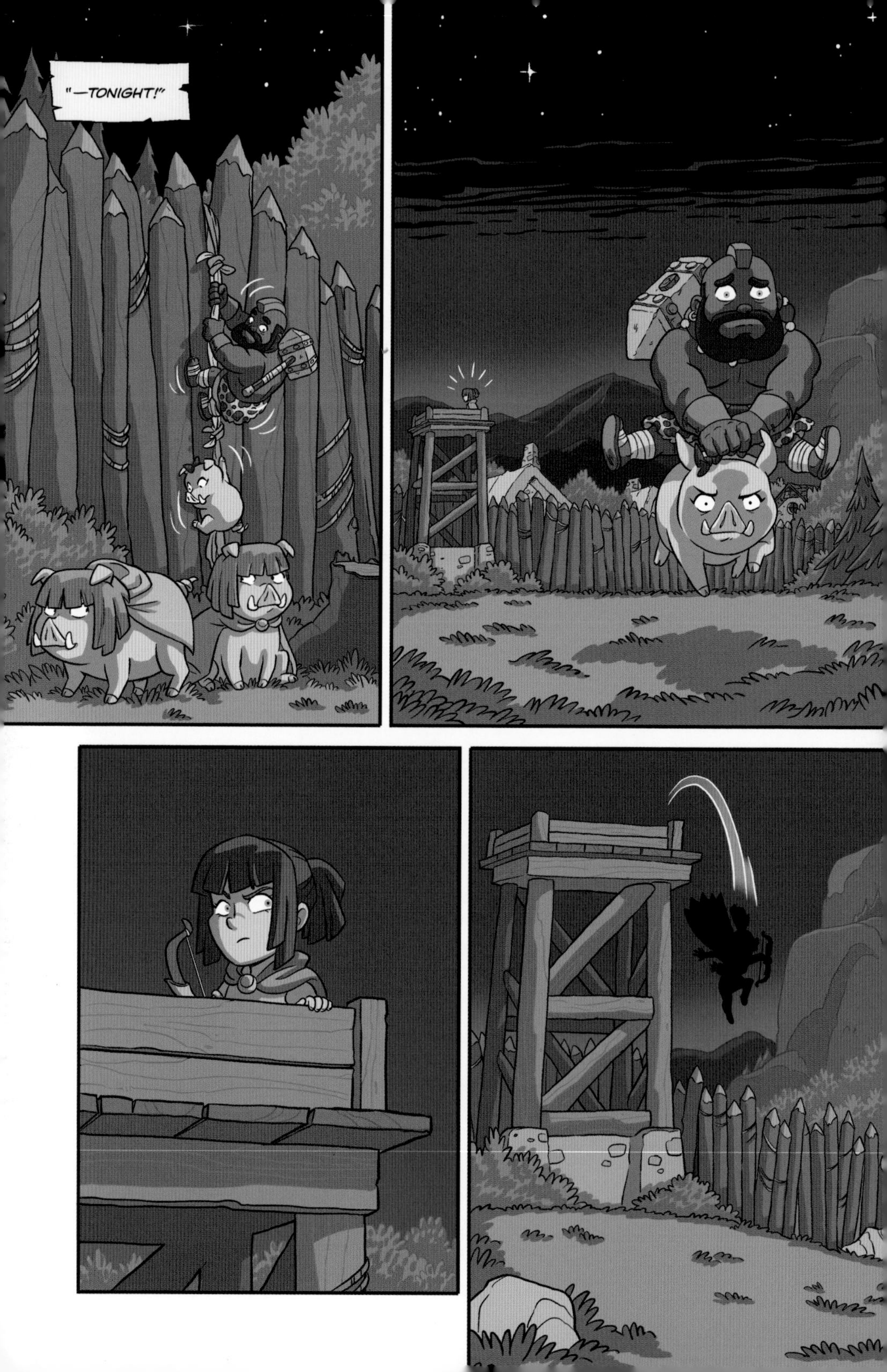
"—TONIGHT!"

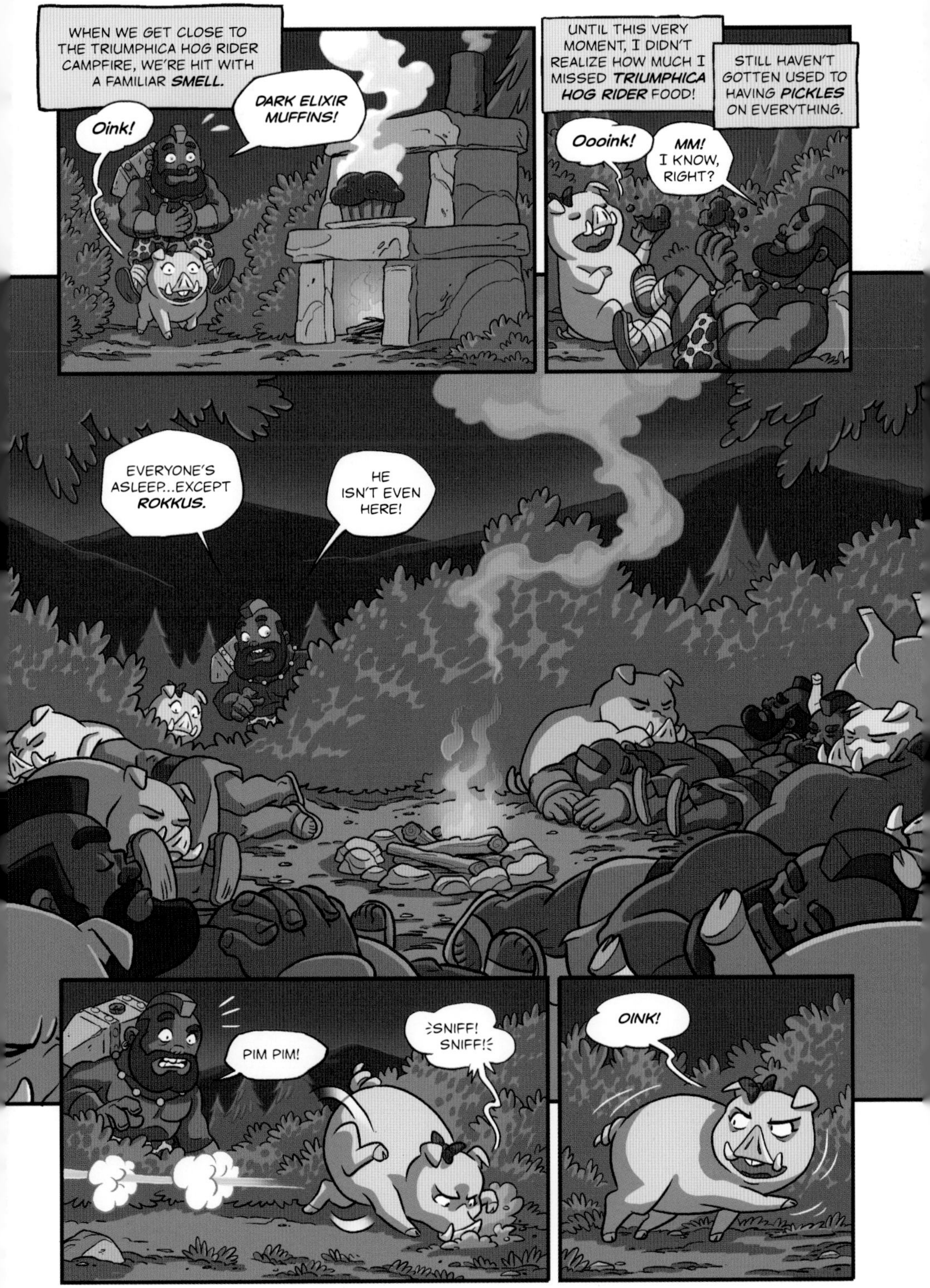
WHEN WE GET CLOSE TO THE TRIUMPHICA HOG RIDER CAMPFIRE, WE'RE HIT WITH A FAMILIAR SMELL.
Oink!
DARK ELIXIR MUFFINS!
UNTIL THIS VERY MOMENT, I DIDN'T REALIZE HOW MUCH I MISSED TRIUMPHICA HOG RIDER FOOD!
STILL HAVEN'T GOTTEN USED TO HAVING PICKLES ON EVERYTHING.
Oooink!
MM! I KNOW, RIGHT?
EVERYONE'S ASLEEP...EXCEPT ROKKUS.
HE ISN'T EVEN HERE!
PIM PIM!
SNIFF! SNIFF!
OINK!

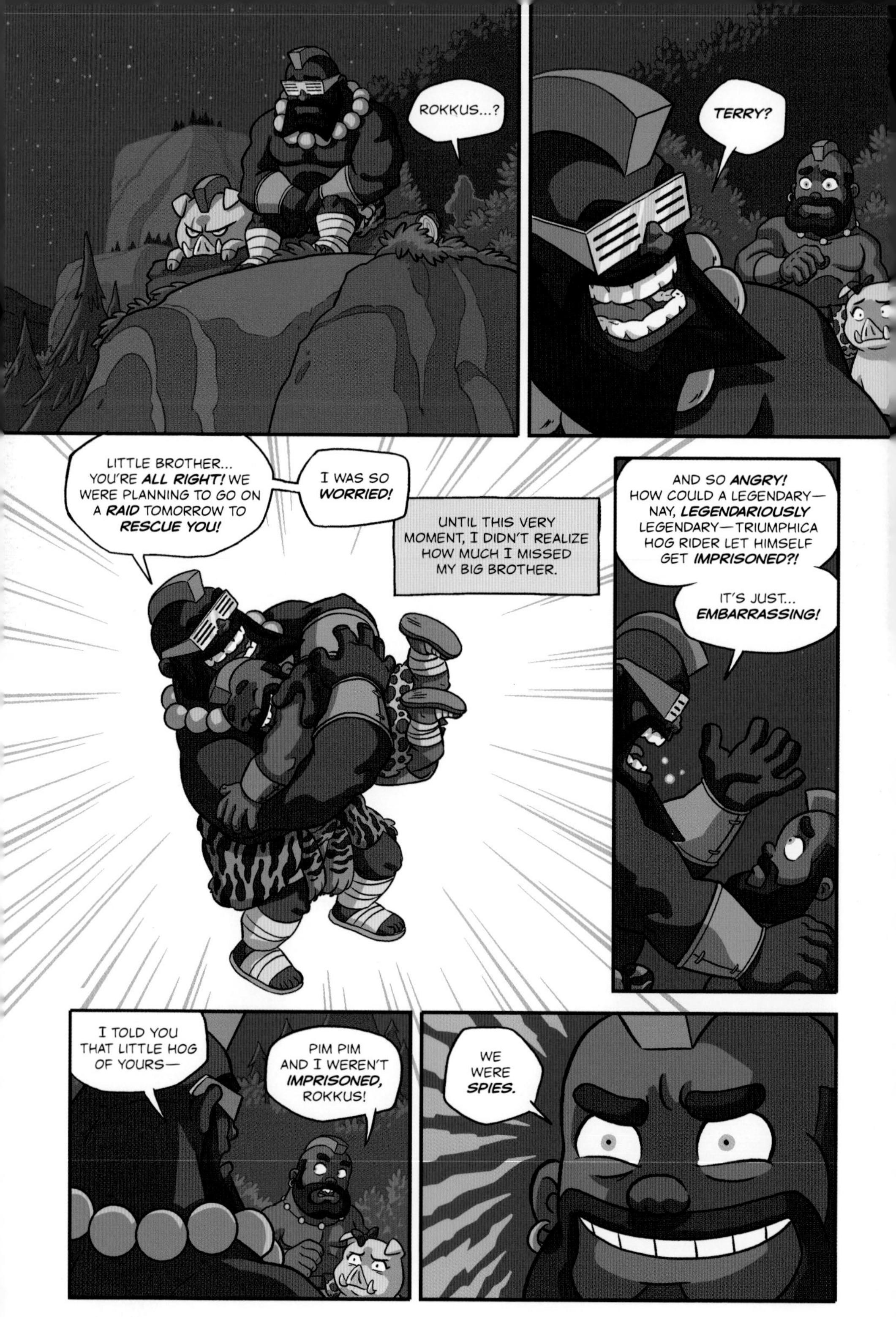
ROKKUS...?
TERRY?
LITTLE BROTHER... YOU'RE ALL RIGHT! WE WERE PLANNING TO GO ON A RAID TOMORROW TO RESCUE YOU!
I WAS SO WORRIED!
UNTIL THIS VERY MOMENT, I DIDN'T REALIZE HOW MUCH I MISSED MY BIG BROTHER.
AND SO ANGRY! HOW COULD A LEGENDARY— NAY, LEGENDARIOUSLY LEGENDARY—TRIUMPHICA HOG RIDER LET HIMSELF GET IMPRISONED?!
IT'S JUST... EMBARRASSING!
I TOLD YOU THAT LITTLE HOG OF YOURS—
PIM PIM AND I WEREN'T IMPRISONED, ROKKUS!
WE WERE SPIES.

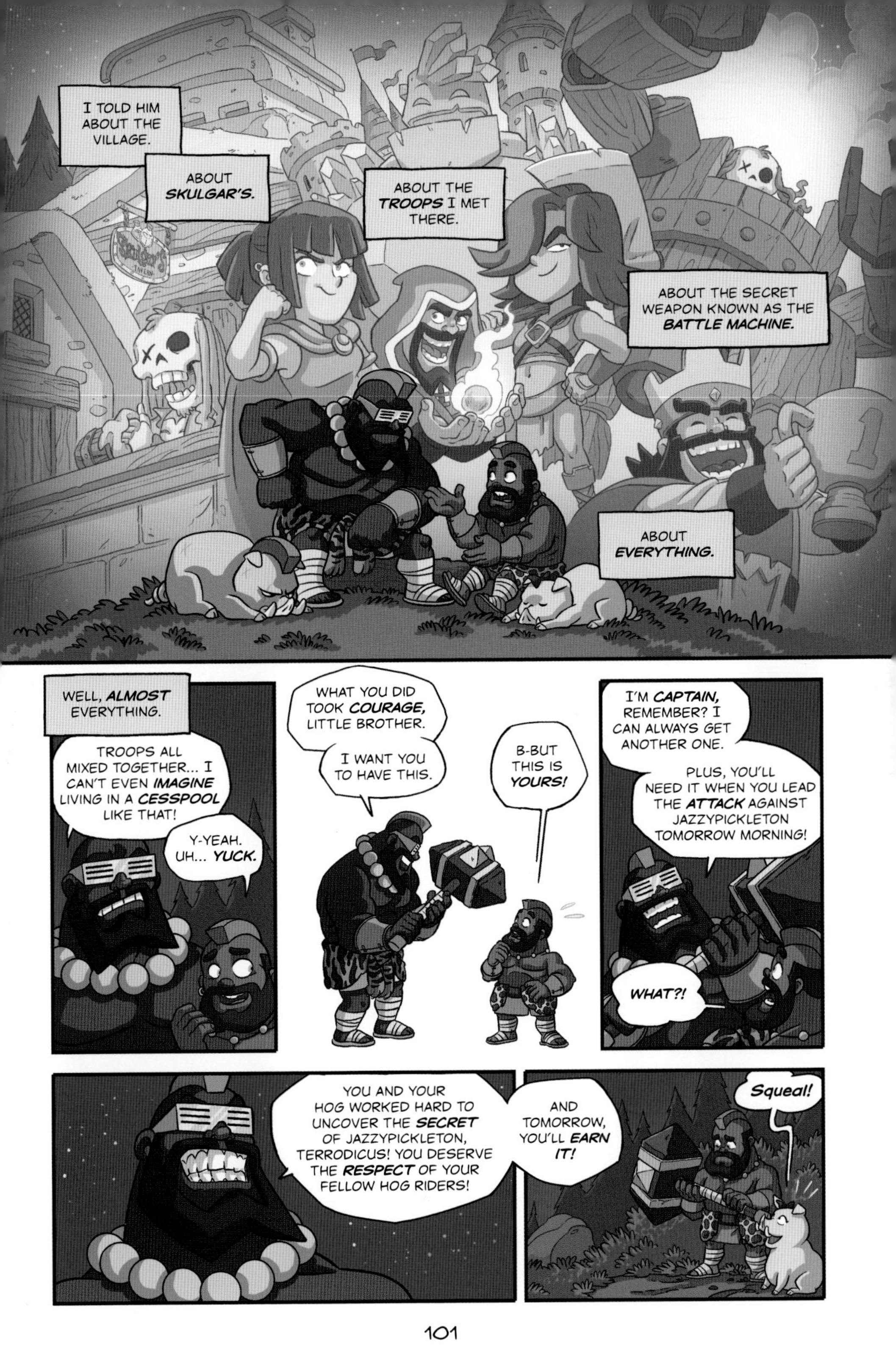
I TOLD HIM ABOUT THE VILLAGE.
ABOUT SKULGAR'S.
Skulgar's
ABOUT THE TROOPS I MET THERE.
ABOUT THE SECRET WEAPON KNOWN AS THE BATTLE MACHINE.
ABOUT EVERYTHING.
WELL, ALMOST EVERYTHING.
TROOPS ALL MIXED TOGETHER... I CAN'T EVEN IMAGINE LIVING IN A CESSPOOL LIKE THAT!
Y-YEAH. UH... YUCK.
WHAT YOU DID TOOK COURAGE, LITTLE BROTHER.
I WANT YOU TO HAVE THIS.
B-BUT THIS IS YOURS!
I'M CAPTAIN, REMEMBER? I CAN ALWAYS GET ANOTHER ONE.
PLUS, YOU'LL NEED IT WHEN YOU LEAD THE ATTACK AGAINST JAZZYPICKLETON TOMORROW MORNING!
WHAT?!
YOU AND YOUR HOG WORKED HARD TO UNCOVER THE SECRET OF JAZZYPICKLETON, TERRODICUS! YOU DESERVE THE RESPECT OF YOUR FELLOW HOG RIDERS!
AND TOMORROW, YOU'LL EARN IT!
Squeal!

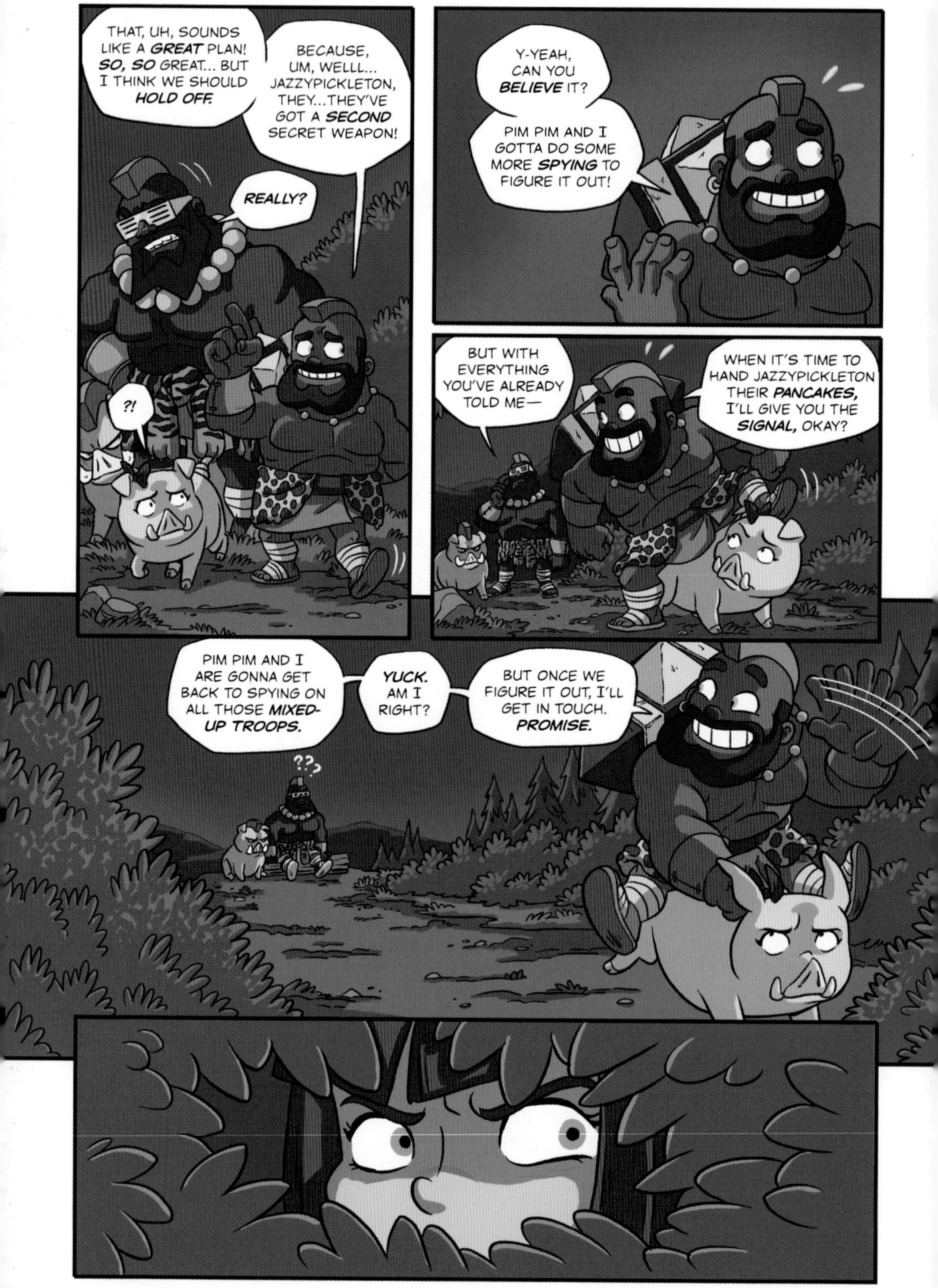

THAT, UH, SOUNDS LIKE A **GREAT** PLAN! **SO, SO** GREAT... BUT I THINK WE SHOULD **HOLD OFF.**
BECAUSE, UM, WELLL... JAZZYPICKLETON, THEY...THEY'VE GOT A **SECOND** SECRET WEAPON!
REALLY?
?!
Y-YEAH, CAN YOU **BELIEVE** IT?
PIM PIM AND I GOTTA DO SOME MORE **SPYING** TO FIGURE IT OUT!
BUT WITH EVERYTHING YOU'VE ALREADY TOLD ME—
WHEN IT'S TIME TO HAND JAZZYPICKLETON THEIR **PANCAKES,** I'LL GIVE YOU THE **SIGNAL,** OKAY?
PIM PIM AND I ARE GONNA GET BACK TO SPYING ON ALL THOSE **MIXED-UP TROOPS.**
YUCK. AM I RIGHT?
BUT ONCE WE FIGURE IT OUT, I'LL GET IN TOUCH. **PROMISE.**
???

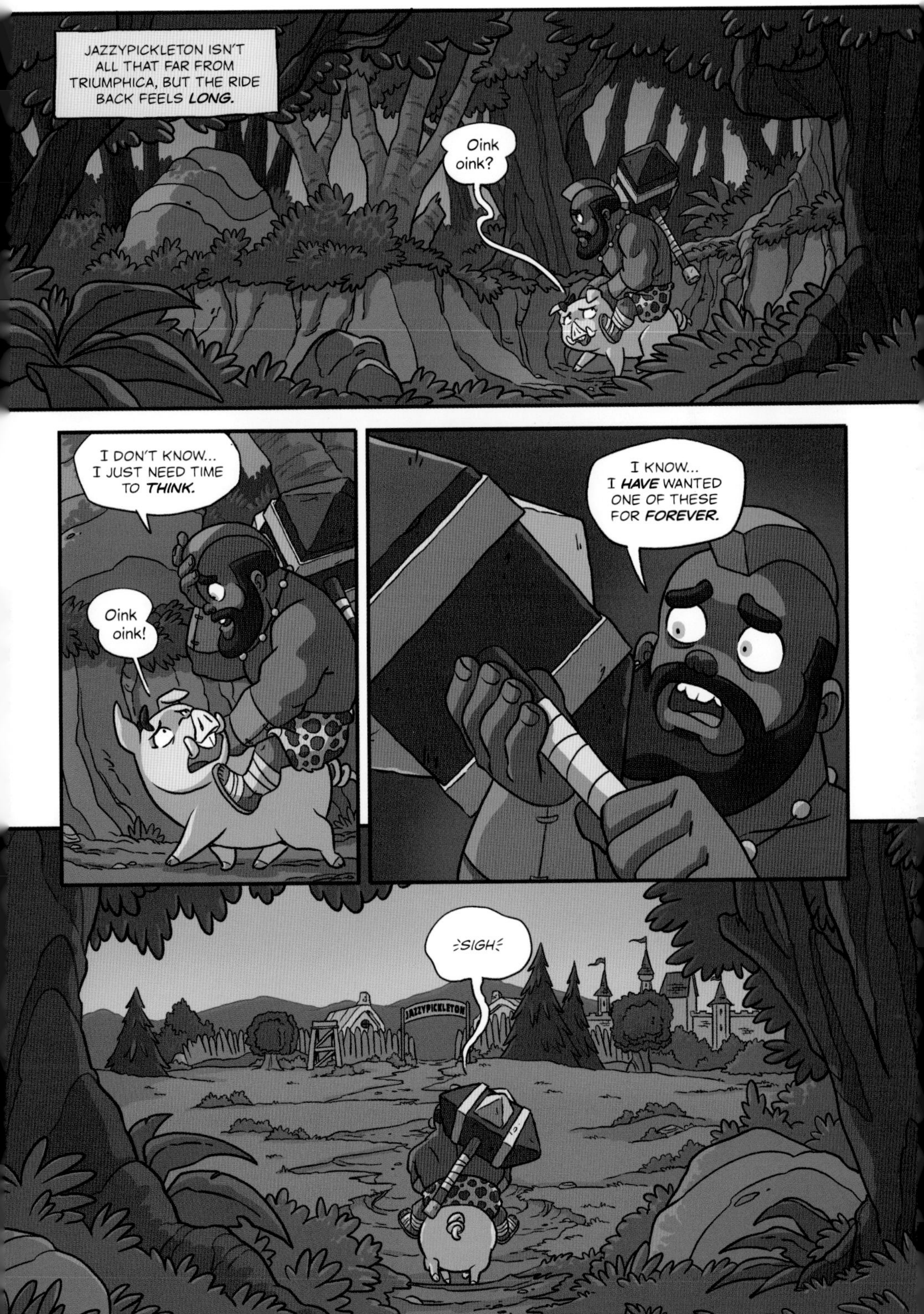
JAZZYPICKLETON ISN'T ALL THAT FAR FROM TRIUMPHICA, BUT THE RIDE BACK FEELS **LONG.**
Oink oink?
I DON'T KNOW... I JUST NEED TIME TO **THINK.**
Oink oink!
I KNOW... I **HAVE** WANTED ONE OF THESE FOR **FOREVER.**
JAZZYPICKLETON
SIGH

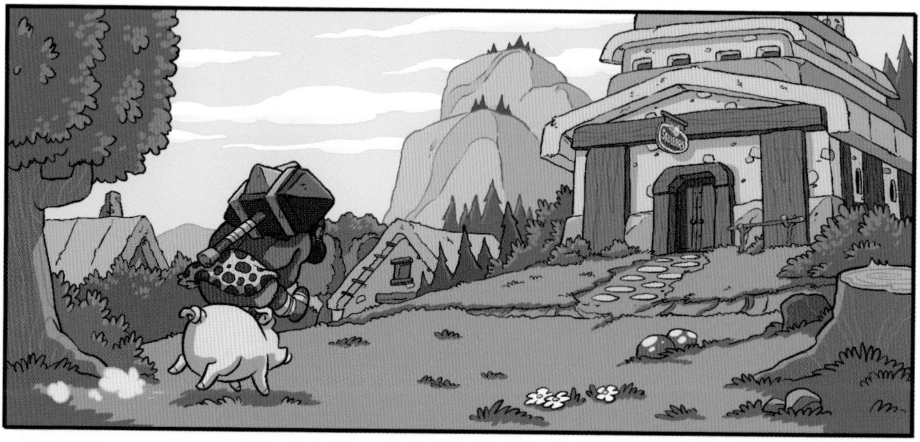
SKULGAR'S

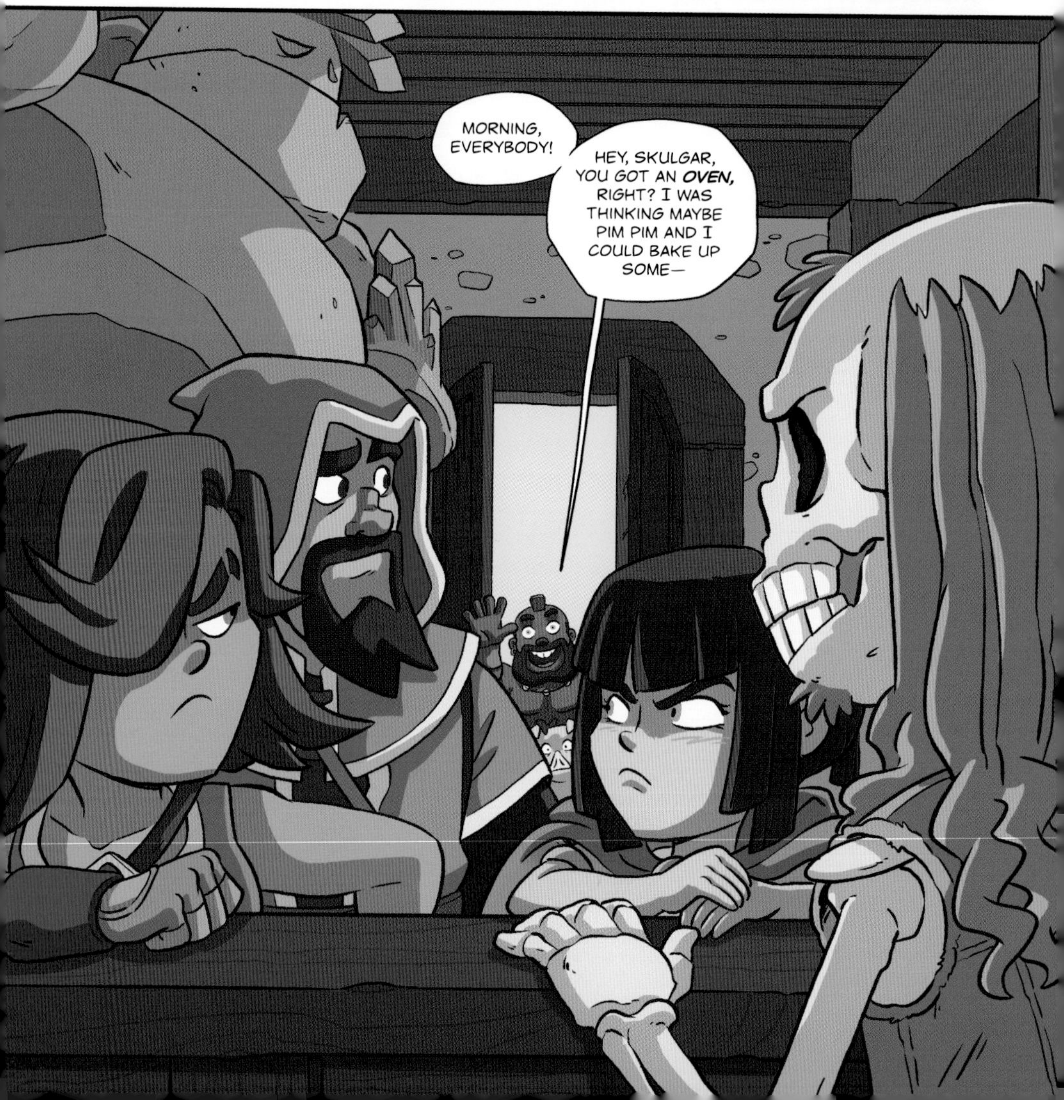
MORNING, EVERYBODY!
HEY, SKULGAR, YOU GOT AN **OVEN,** RIGHT? I WAS THINKING MAYBE PIM PIM AND I COULD BAKE UP SOME—

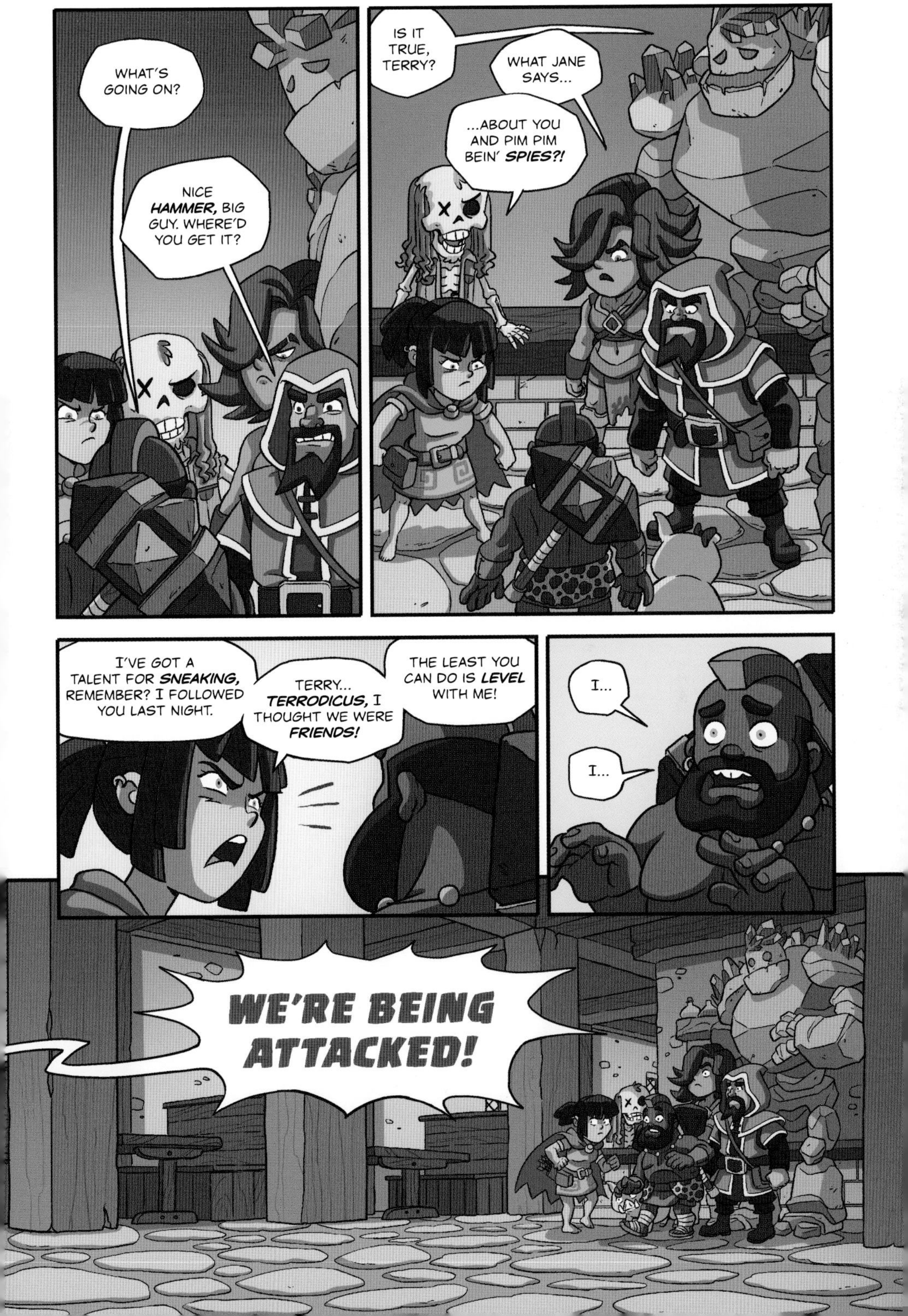
WHAT'S GOING ON?
NICE **HAMMER,** BIG GUY. WHERE'D YOU GET IT?
IS IT TRUE, TERRY?
WHAT JANE SAYS...
...ABOUT YOU AND PIM PIM BEIN' **SPIES?!**
I'VE GOT A TALENT FOR **SNEAKING,** REMEMBER? I FOLLOWED YOU LAST NIGHT.
TERRY... **TERRODICUS,** I THOUGHT WE WERE **FRIENDS!**
THE LEAST YOU CAN DO IS **LEVEL** WITH ME!
I...
I...
WE'RE BEING ATTACKED!

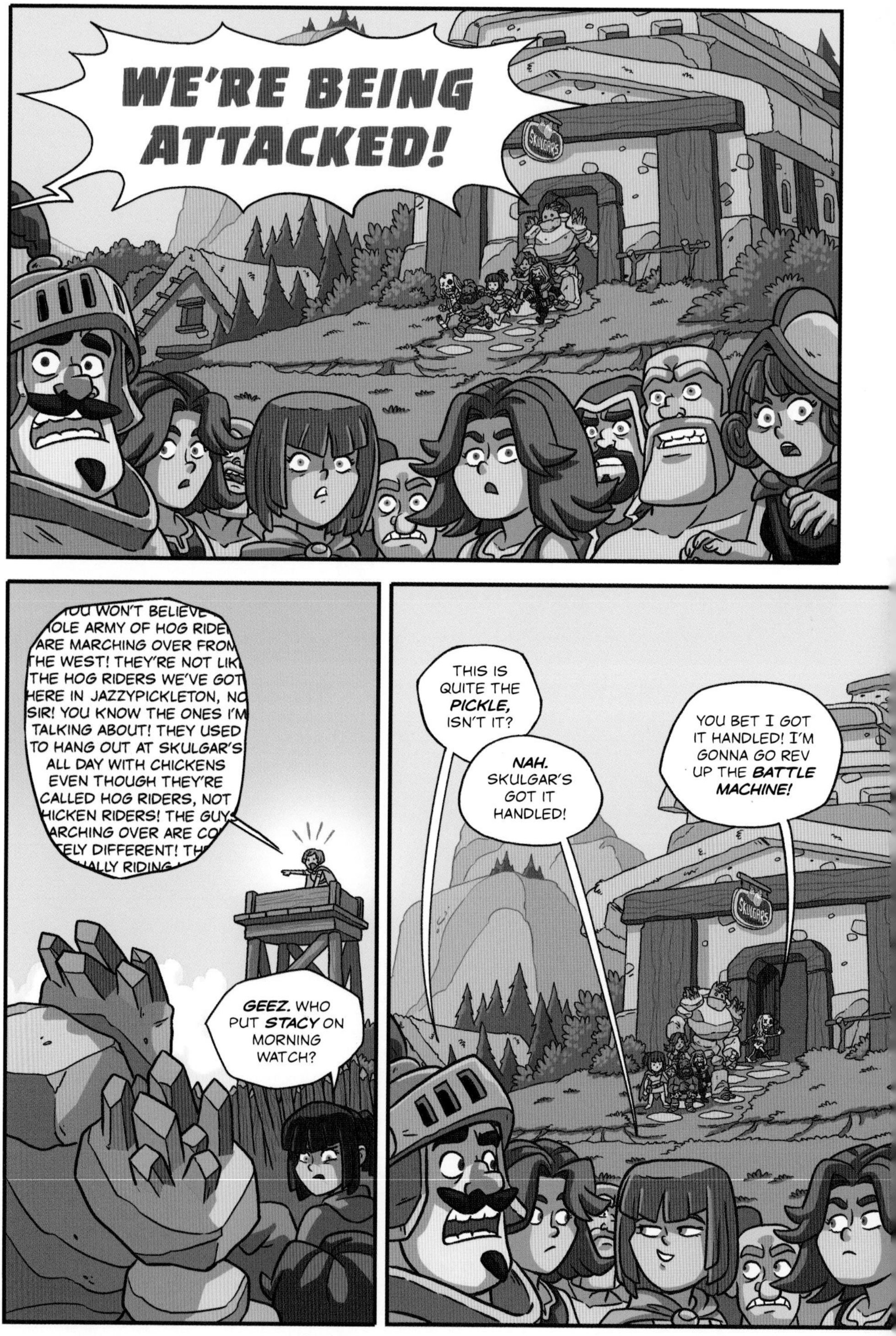
WE'RE BEING ATTACKED!
SKULGAR'S
YOU WON'T BELIEVE HOLE ARMY OF HOG RIDER ARE MARCHING OVER FROM THE WEST! THEY'RE NOT LIK THE HOG RIDERS WE'VE GOT HERE IN JAZZYPICKLETON, NO SIR! YOU KNOW THE ONES I'M TALKING ABOUT! THEY USED TO HANG OUT AT SKULGAR'S ALL DAY WITH CHICKENS EVEN THOUGH THEY'RE CALLED HOG RIDERS, NOT HICKEN RIDERS! THE GUYS ARCHING OVER ARE CO TELY DIFFERENT! TH ALLY RIDING
GEEZ. WHO PUT STACY ON MORNING WATCH?
THIS IS QUITE THE PICKLE, ISN'T IT?
NAH. SKULGAR'S GOT IT HANDLED!
YOU BET I GOT IT HANDLED! I'M GONNA GO REV UP THE BATTLE MACHINE!
SKULGAR'S

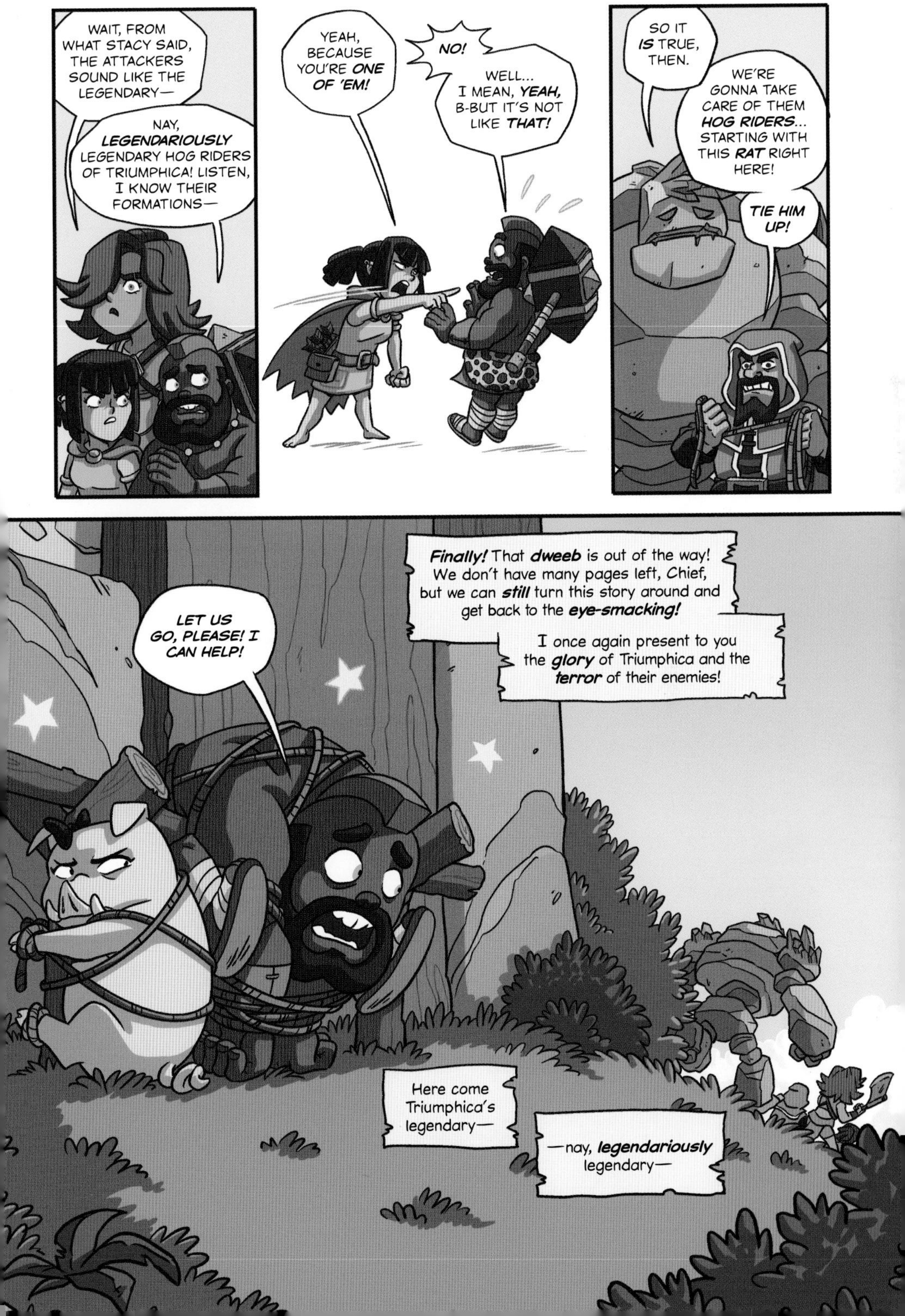

WAIT, FROM WHAT STACY SAID, THE ATTACKERS SOUND LIKE THE LEGENDARY—
NAY, LEGENDARIOUSLY LEGENDARY HOG RIDERS OF TRIUMPHICA! LISTEN, I KNOW THEIR FORMATIONS—
YEAH, BECAUSE YOU'RE ONE OF 'EM!
NO!
WELL... I MEAN, YEAH, B-BUT IT'S NOT LIKE THAT!
SO IT IS TRUE, THEN.
WE'RE GONNA TAKE CARE OF THEM HOG RIDERS... STARTING WITH THIS RAT RIGHT HERE!
TIE HIM UP!
Finally! That dweeb is out of the way! We don't have many pages left, Chief, but we can still turn this story around and get back to the eye-smacking!
I once again present to you the glory of Triumphica and the terror of their enemies!
LET US GO, PLEASE! I CAN HELP!
Here come Triumphica's legendary—
—nay, legendariously legendary—

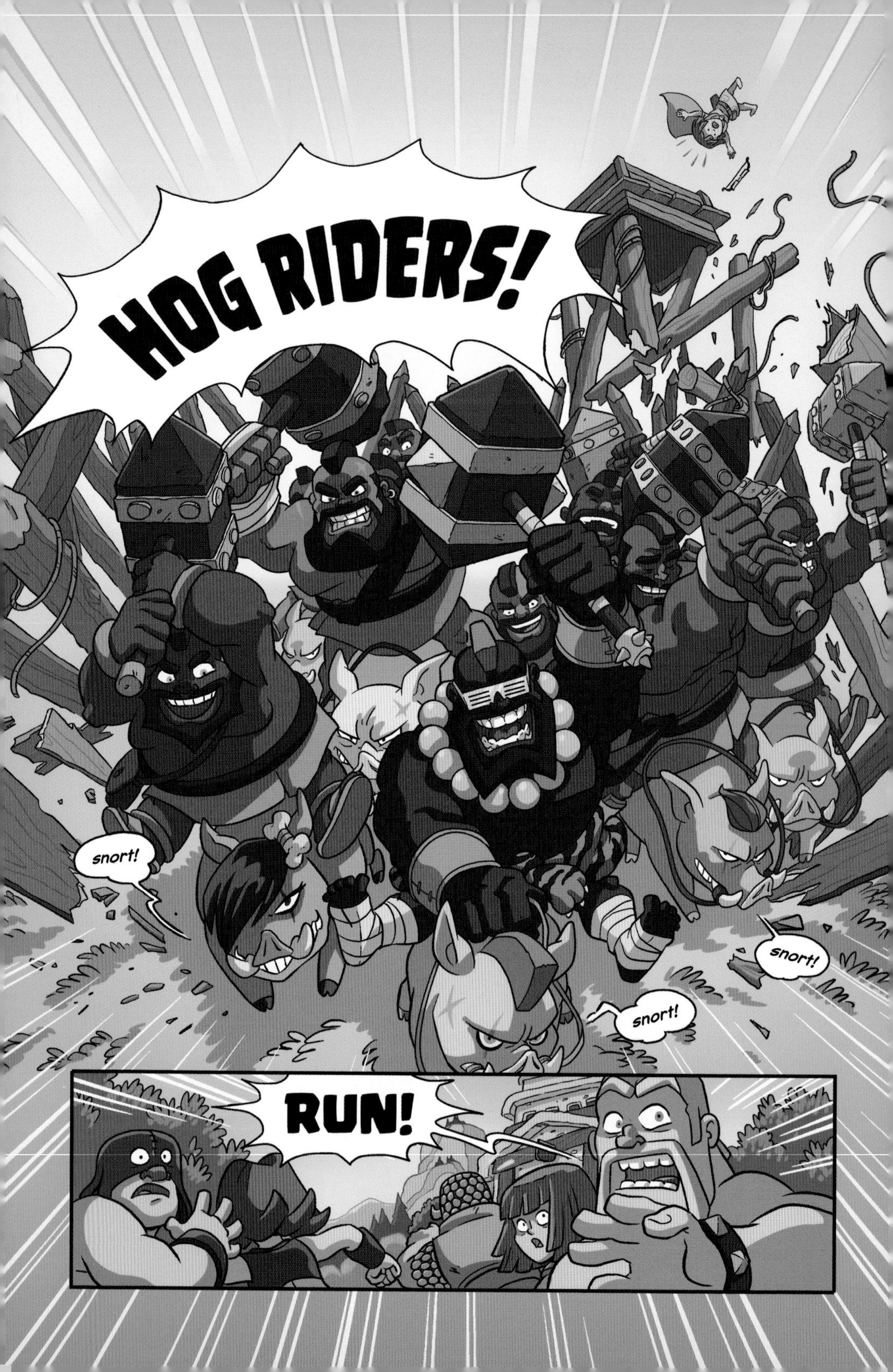
HOG RIDERS!
snort!
snort!
snort!
RUN!

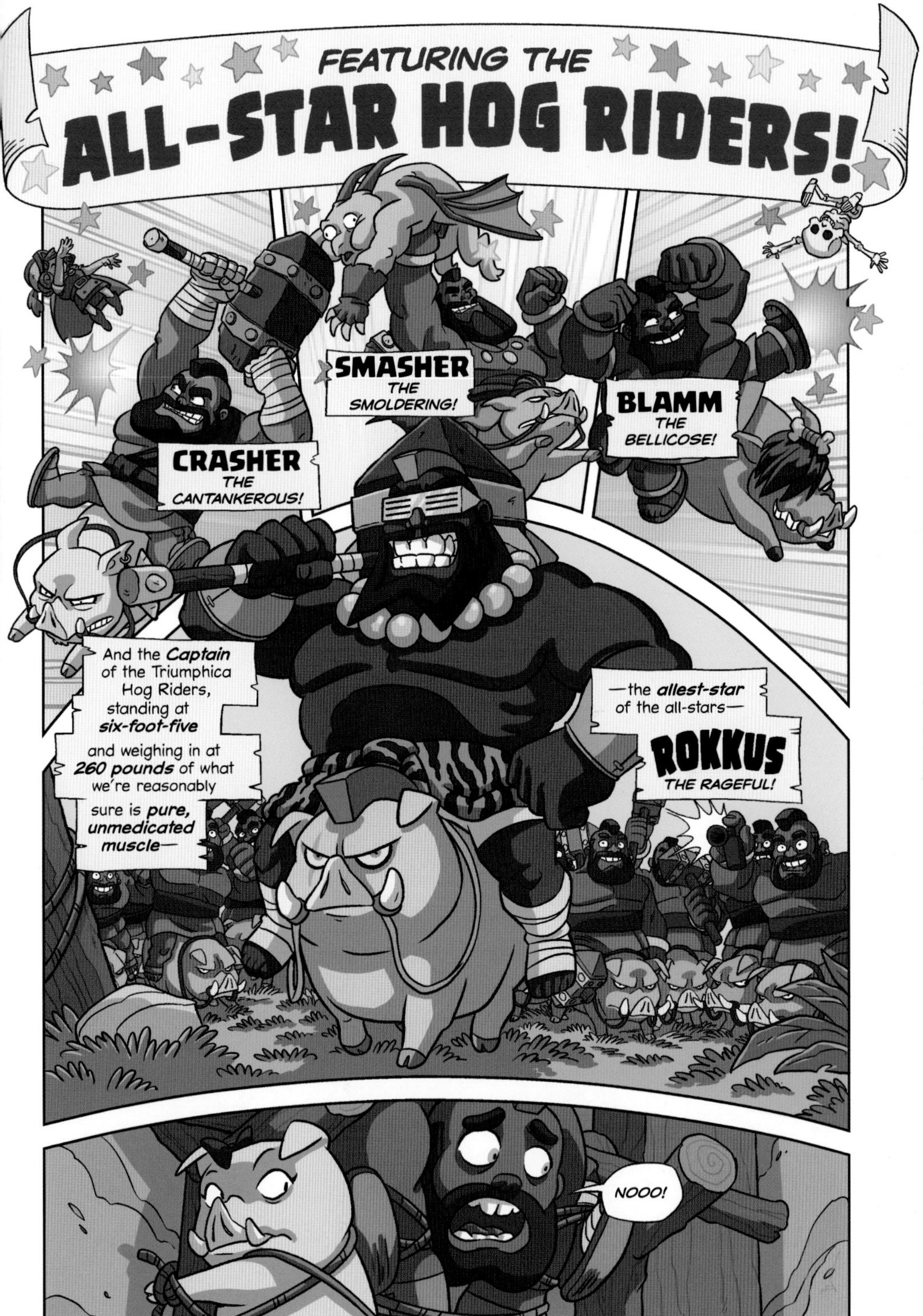
FEATURING THE
ALL-STAR HOG RIDERS!
SMASHER THE SMOLDERING!
BLAMM THE BELLICOSE!
CRASHER THE CANTANKEROUS!
And the Captain of the Triumphica Hog Riders, standing at six-foot-five
and weighing in at 260 pounds of what we're reasonably
sure is pure, unmedicated muscle—
—the allest-star of the all-stars—
ROKKUS THE RAGEFUL!
NOOO!

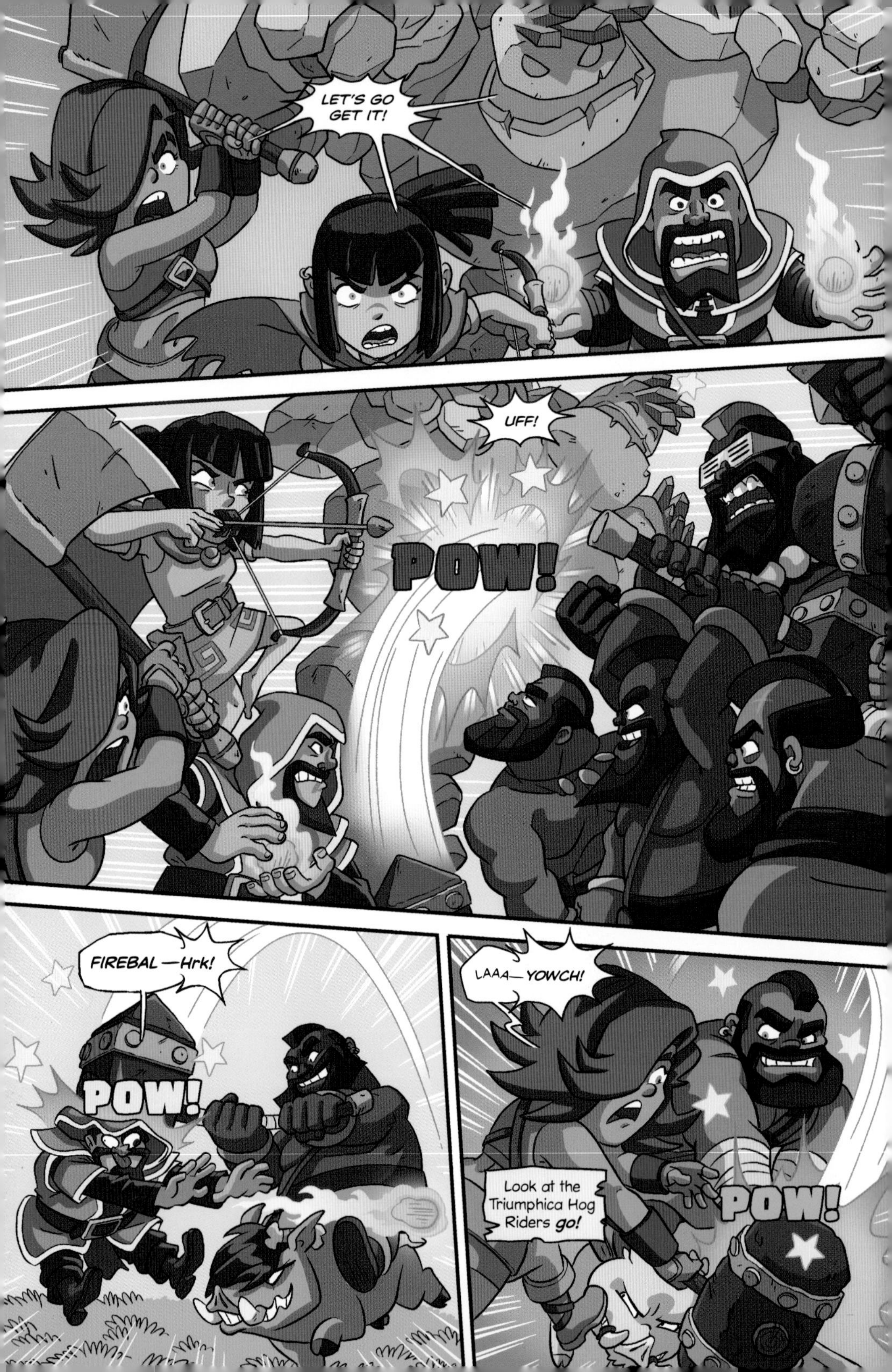
LET'S GO GET IT!
UFF!
POW!
FIREBAL—Hrk!
POW!
LAAA—YOWCH!
Look at the Triumphica Hog Riders go!
POW!

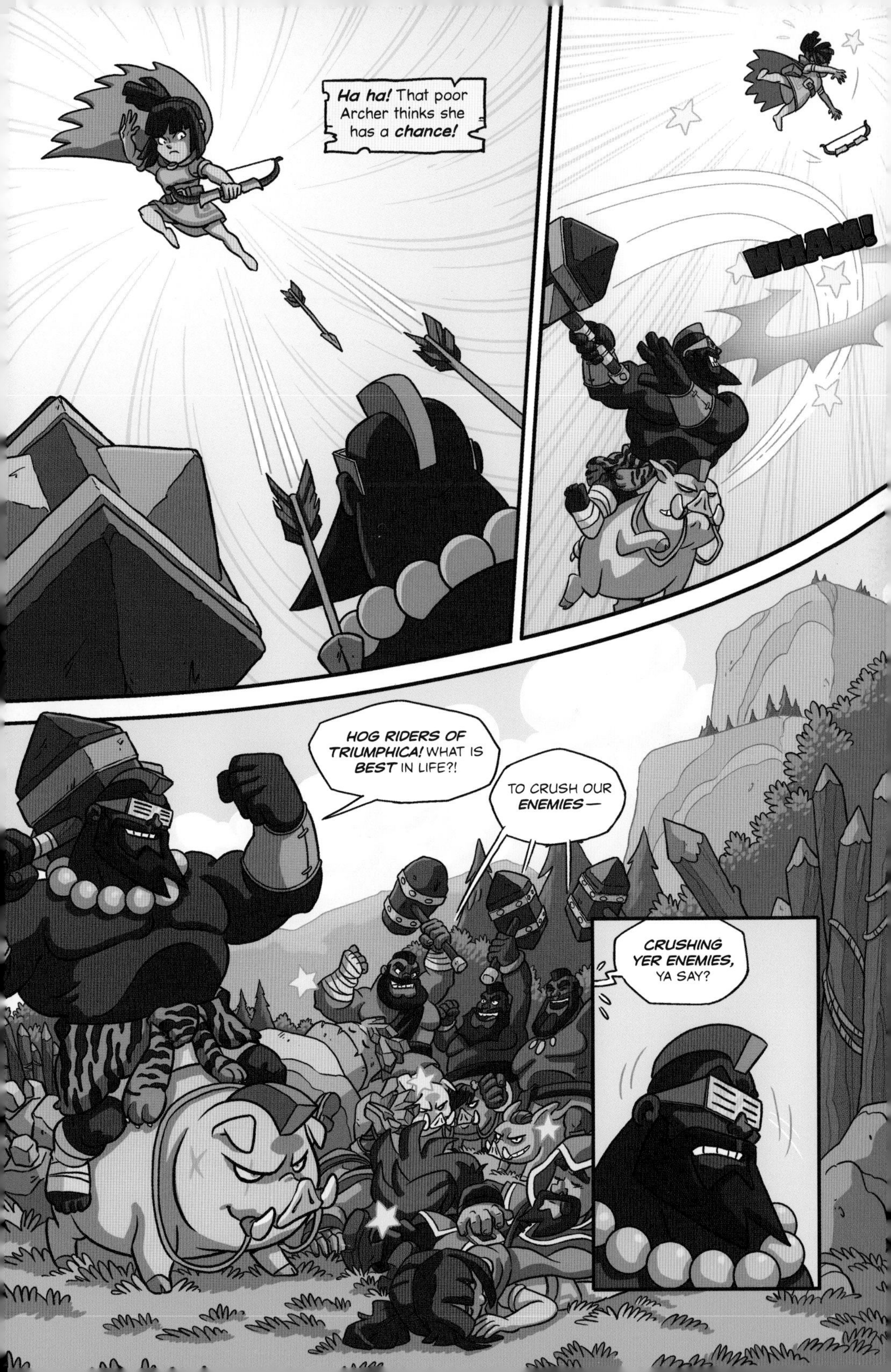

Ha ha! That poor Archer thinks she has a chance!
WHAM!
HOG RIDERS OF TRIUMPHICA! WHAT IS BEST IN LIFE?!
TO CRUSH OUR ENEMIES—
CRUSHING YER ENEMIES, YA SAY?

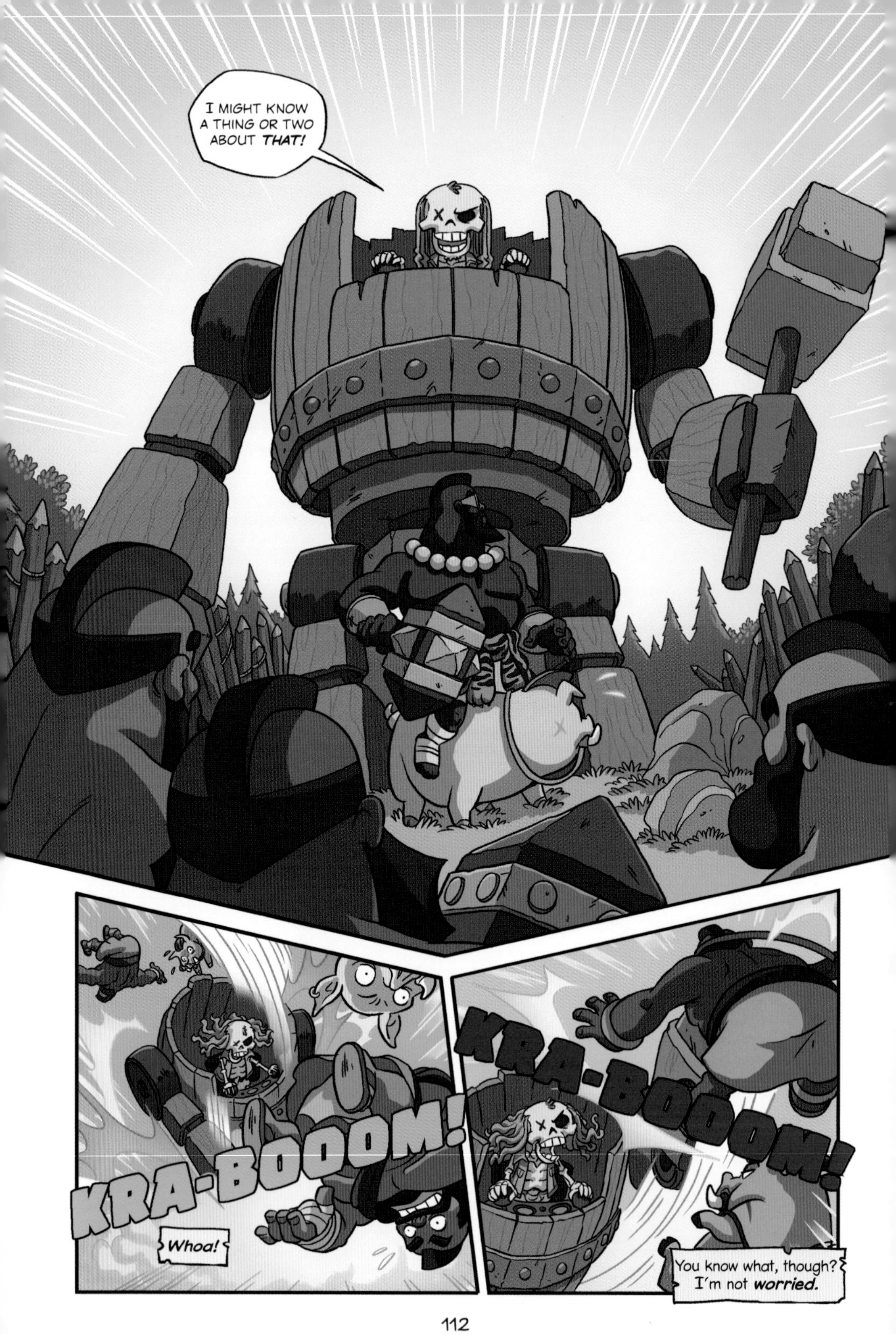
I MIGHT KNOW A THING OR TWO ABOUT *THAT!*
KRA-BOOOM!
Whoa!
KRA-BOOOM!
You know what, though? I'm not *worried.*

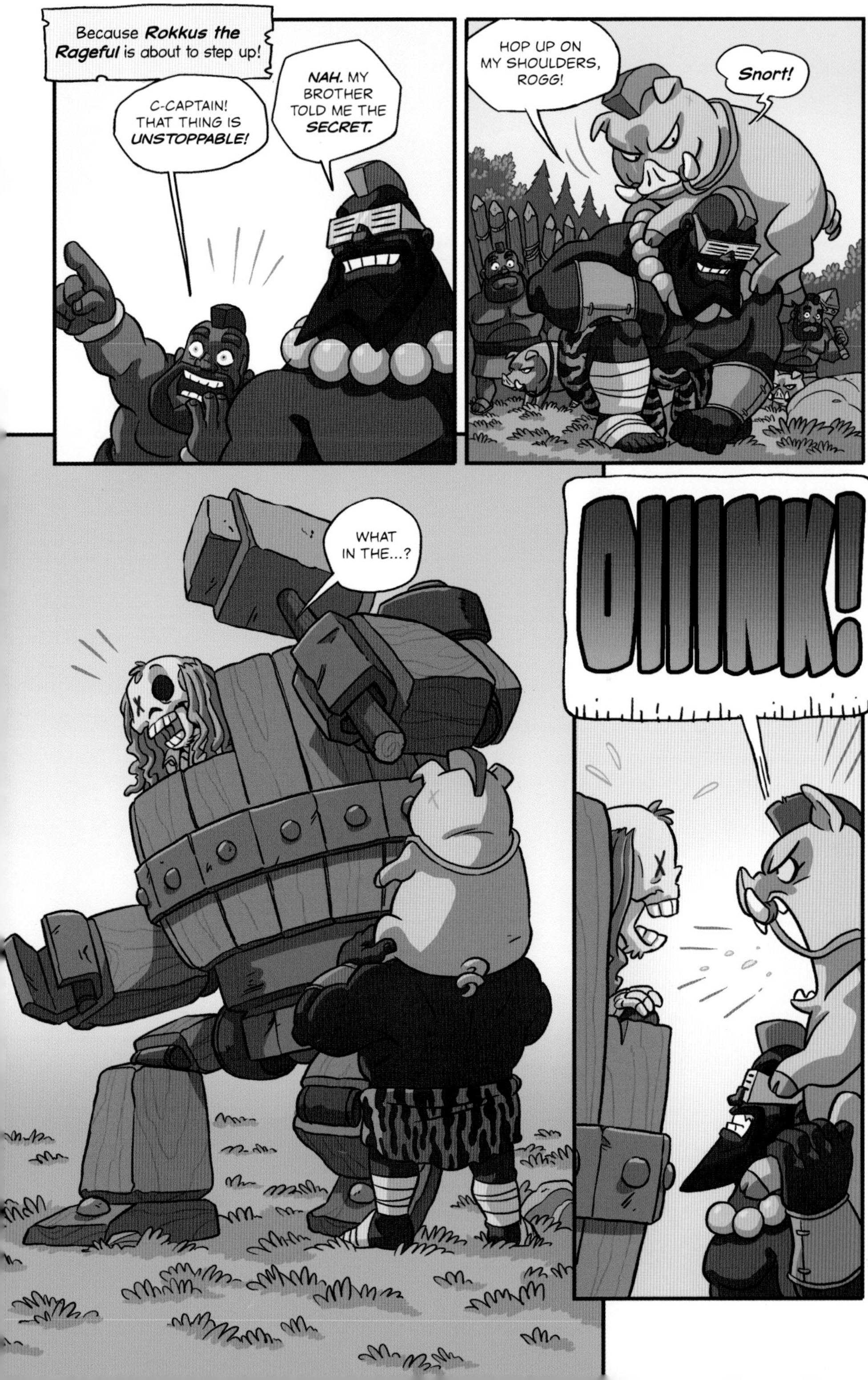
Because Rokkus the Rageful is about to step up!
C-CAPTAIN! THAT THING IS UNSTOPPABLE!
NAH. MY BROTHER TOLD ME THE SECRET.
HOP UP ON MY SHOULDERS, ROGG!
Snort!
WHAT IN THE...?
OIIINK!

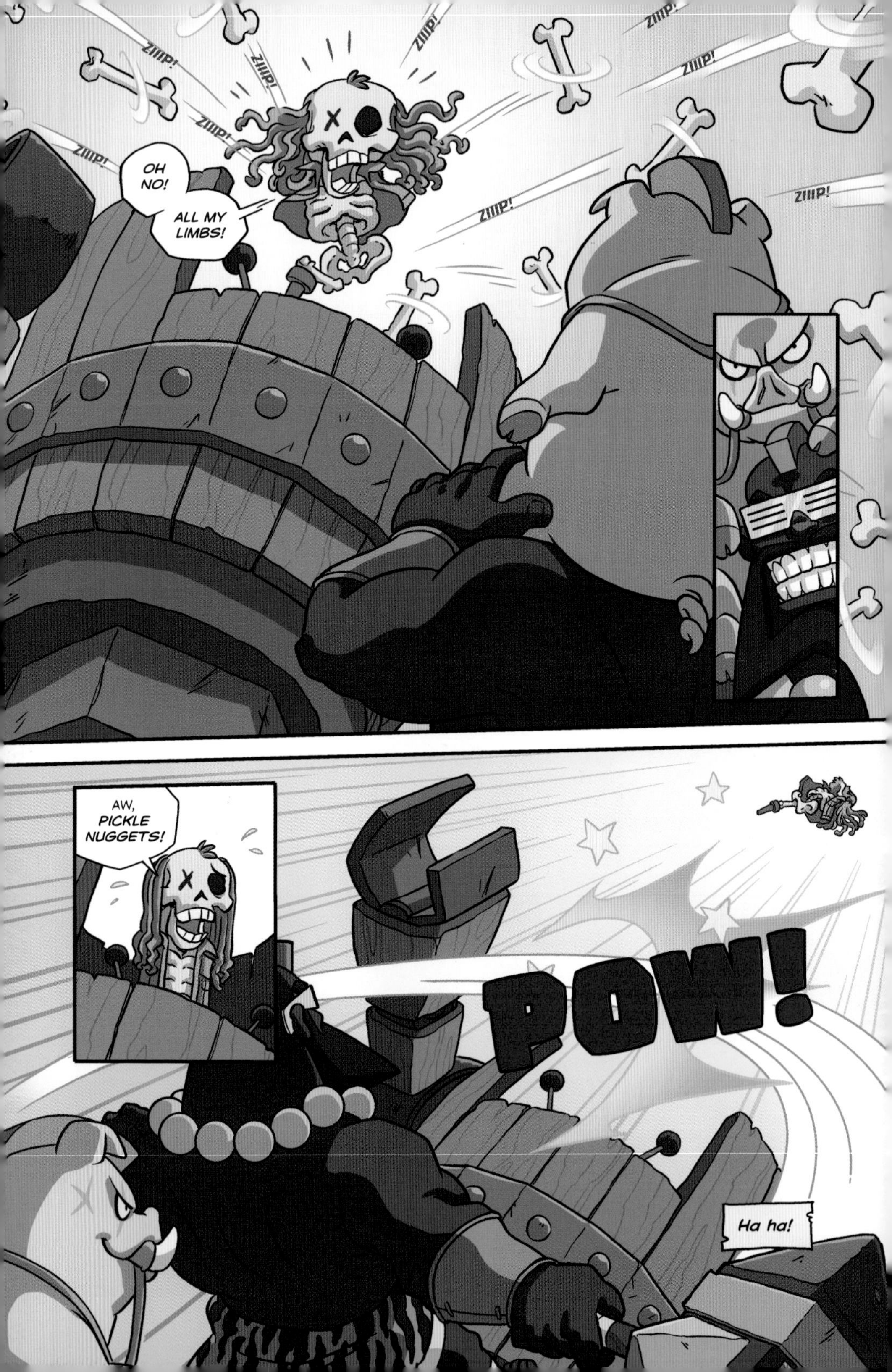

ZIIIP!
ZIIIP!
ZIIIP!
ZIIIP!
ZIIIP!
ZIIIP!
ZIIIP!
ZIIIP!
OH NO!
ALL MY LIMBS!
AW, PICKLE NUGGETS!
POW!
Ha ha!

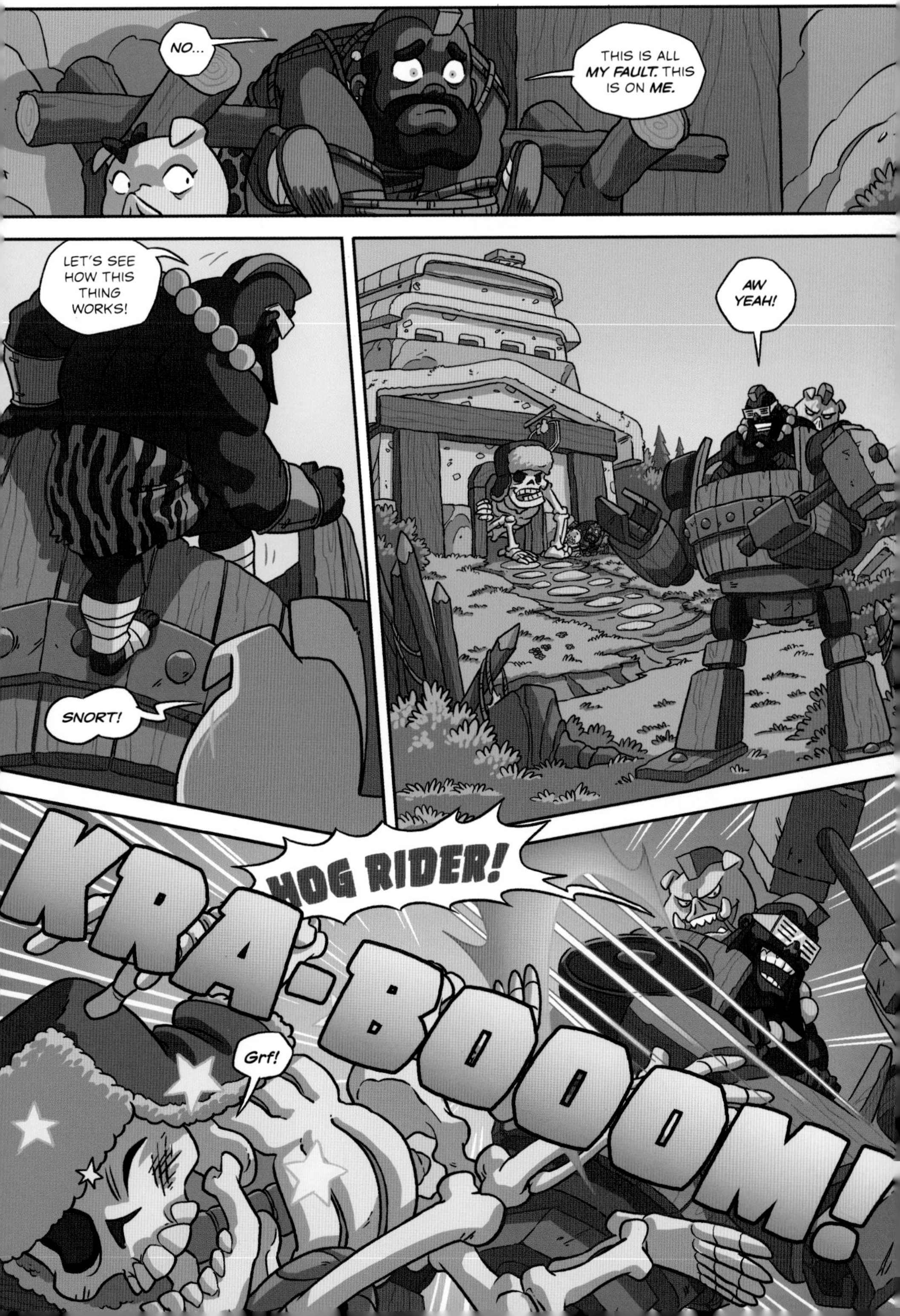
NO...
THIS IS ALL MY FAULT. THIS IS ON ME.
LET'S SEE HOW THIS THING WORKS!
SNORT!
AW YEAH!
HOG RIDER!
KRA-BOOOOM!
Grf!

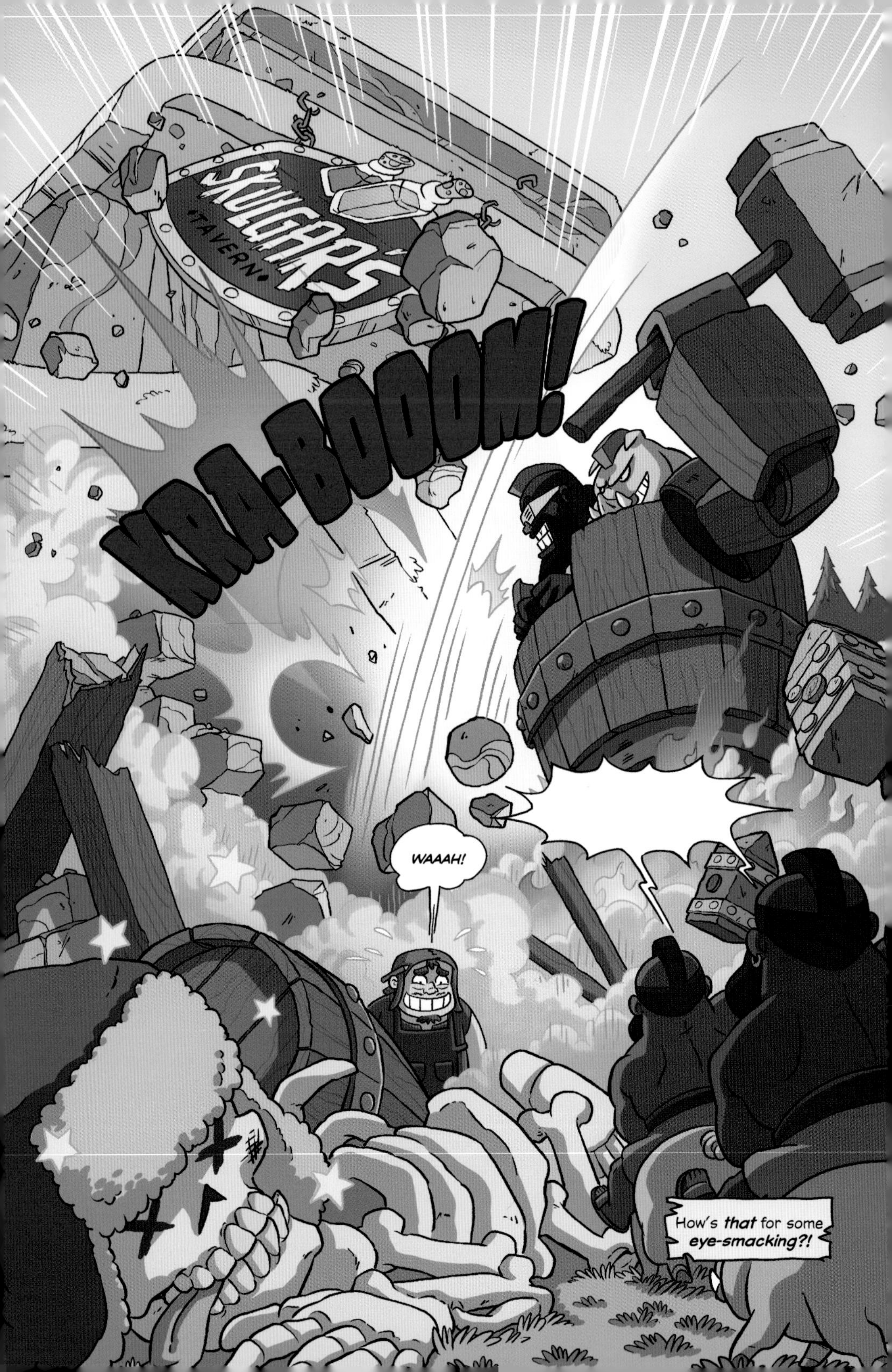
SKULGAR'S
TAVERN
KRA-BOOOM!
WAAAH!
How's *that* for some *eye-smacking?!*

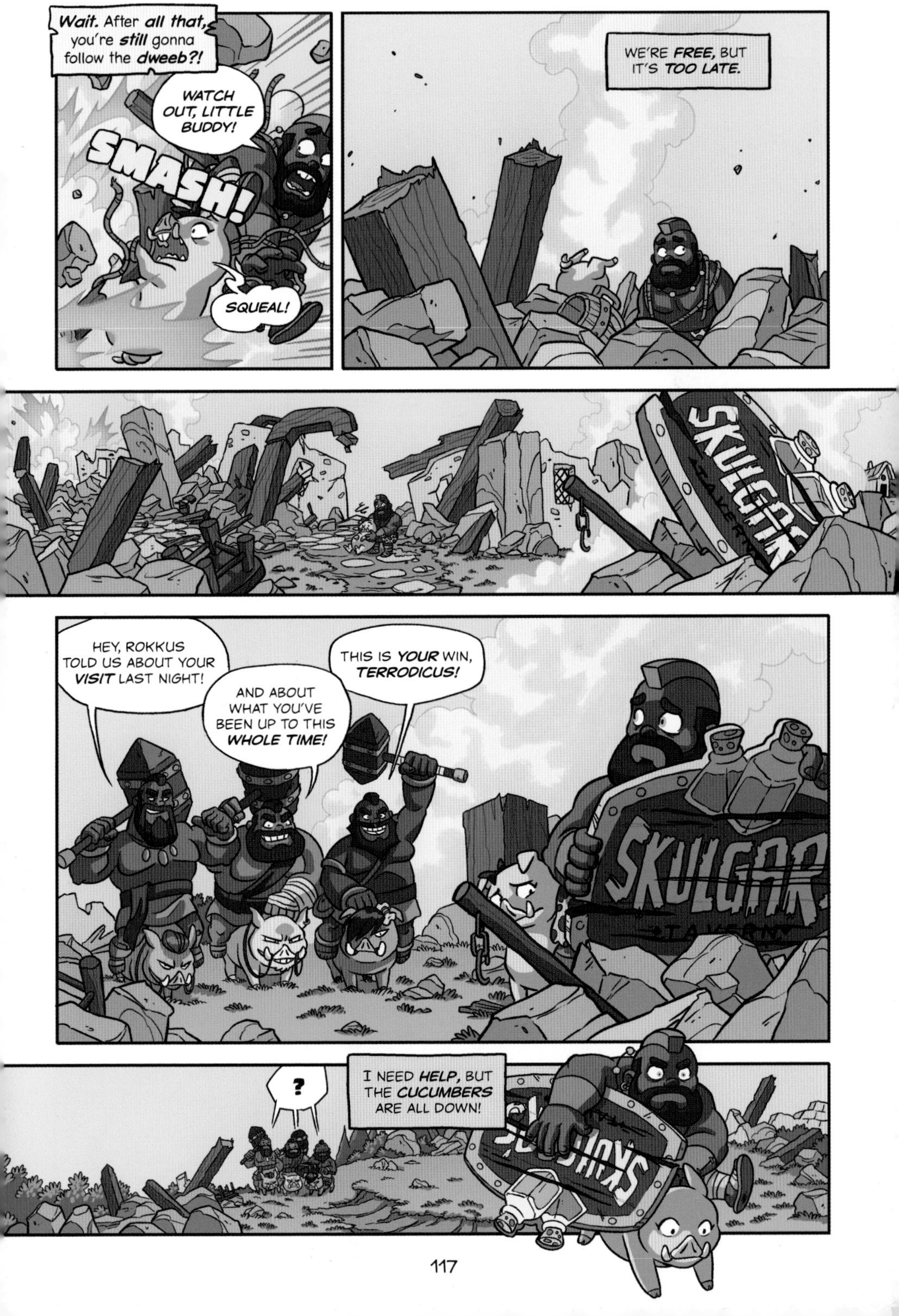

Wait. After all that, you're still gonna follow the dweeb?!
WATCH OUT, LITTLE BUDDY!
SMASH!
SQUEAL!
WE'RE FREE, BUT IT'S TOO LATE.
SKULGAR
HEY, ROKKUS TOLD US ABOUT YOUR VISIT LAST NIGHT!
AND ABOUT WHAT YOU'VE BEEN UP TO THIS WHOLE TIME!
THIS IS YOUR WIN, TERRODICUS!
SKULGAR
?
I NEED HELP, BUT THE CUCUMBERS ARE ALL DOWN!

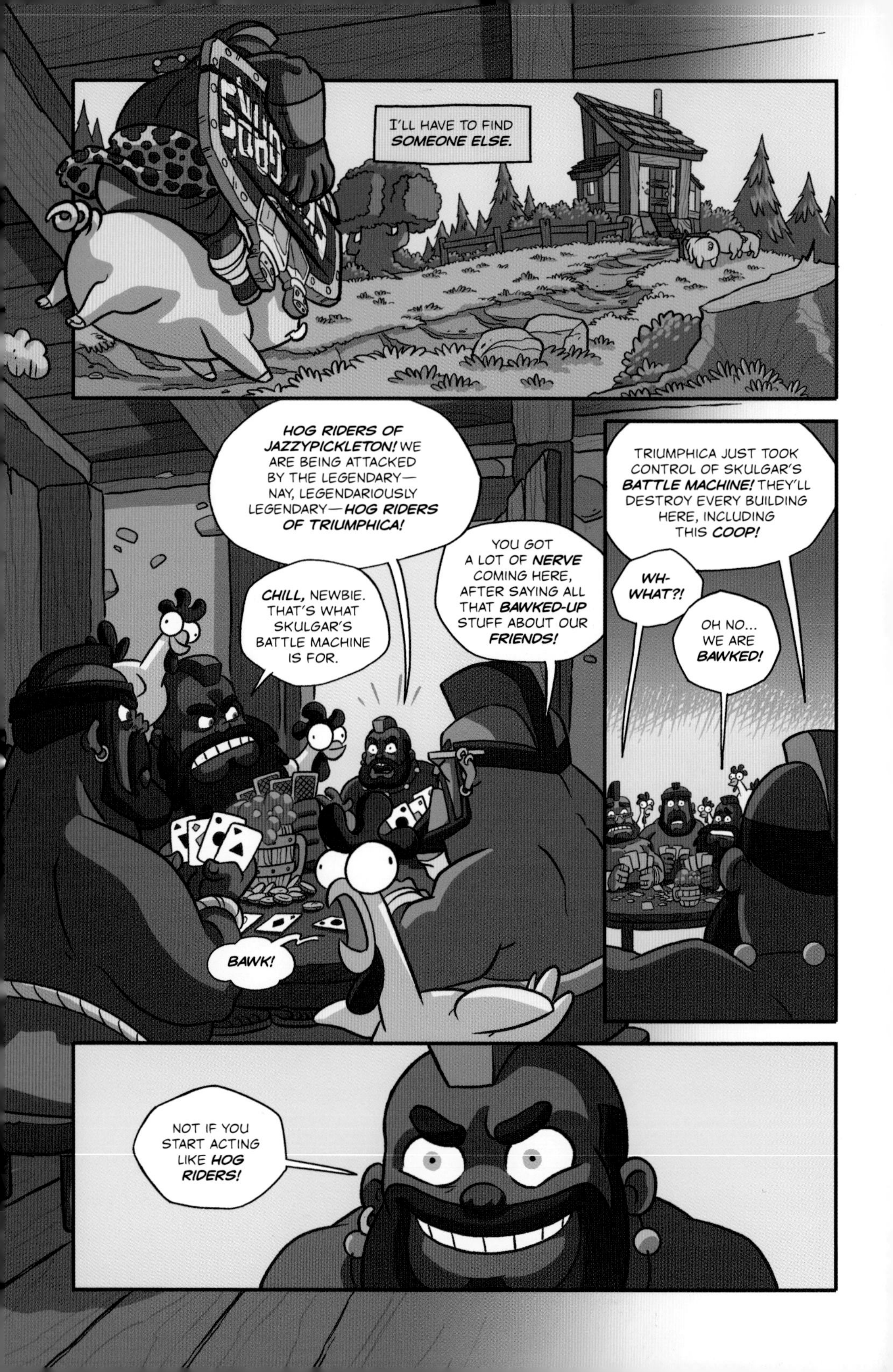

I'LL HAVE TO FIND SOMEONE ELSE.
HOG RIDERS OF JAZZYPICKLETON! WE ARE BEING ATTACKED BY THE LEGENDARY— NAY, LEGENDARIOUSLY LEGENDARY—HOG RIDERS OF TRIUMPHICA!
CHILL, NEWBIE. THAT'S WHAT SKULGAR'S BATTLE MACHINE IS FOR.
YOU GOT A LOT OF NERVE COMING HERE, AFTER SAYING ALL THAT BAWKED-UP STUFF ABOUT OUR FRIENDS!
BAWK!
TRIUMPHICA JUST TOOK CONTROL OF SKULGAR'S BATTLE MACHINE! THEY'LL DESTROY EVERY BUILDING HERE, INCLUDING THIS COOP!
WH-WHAT?!
OH NO... WE ARE BAWKED!
NOT IF YOU START ACTING LIKE HOG RIDERS!

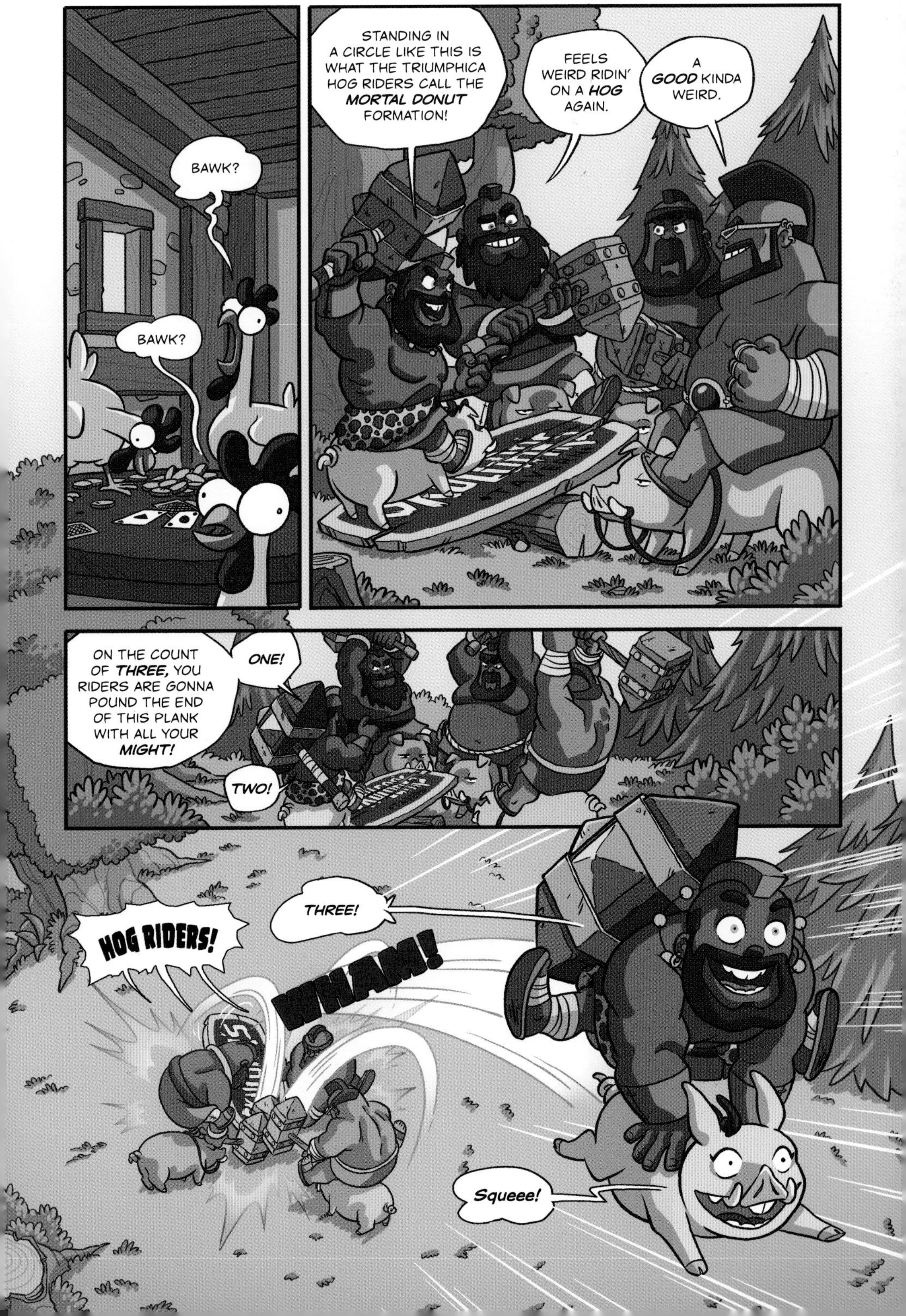
BAWK?
BAWK?
STANDING IN A CIRCLE LIKE THIS IS WHAT THE TRIUMPHICA HOG RIDERS CALL THE **MORTAL DONUT** FORMATION!
FEELS WEIRD RIDIN' ON A **HOG** AGAIN.
A **GOOD** KINDA WEIRD.
ON THE COUNT OF **THREE,** YOU RIDERS ARE GONNA POUND THE END OF THIS PLANK WITH ALL YOUR **MIGHT!**
ONE!
TWO!
HOG RIDERS!
WHAM!
THREE!
Squeee!

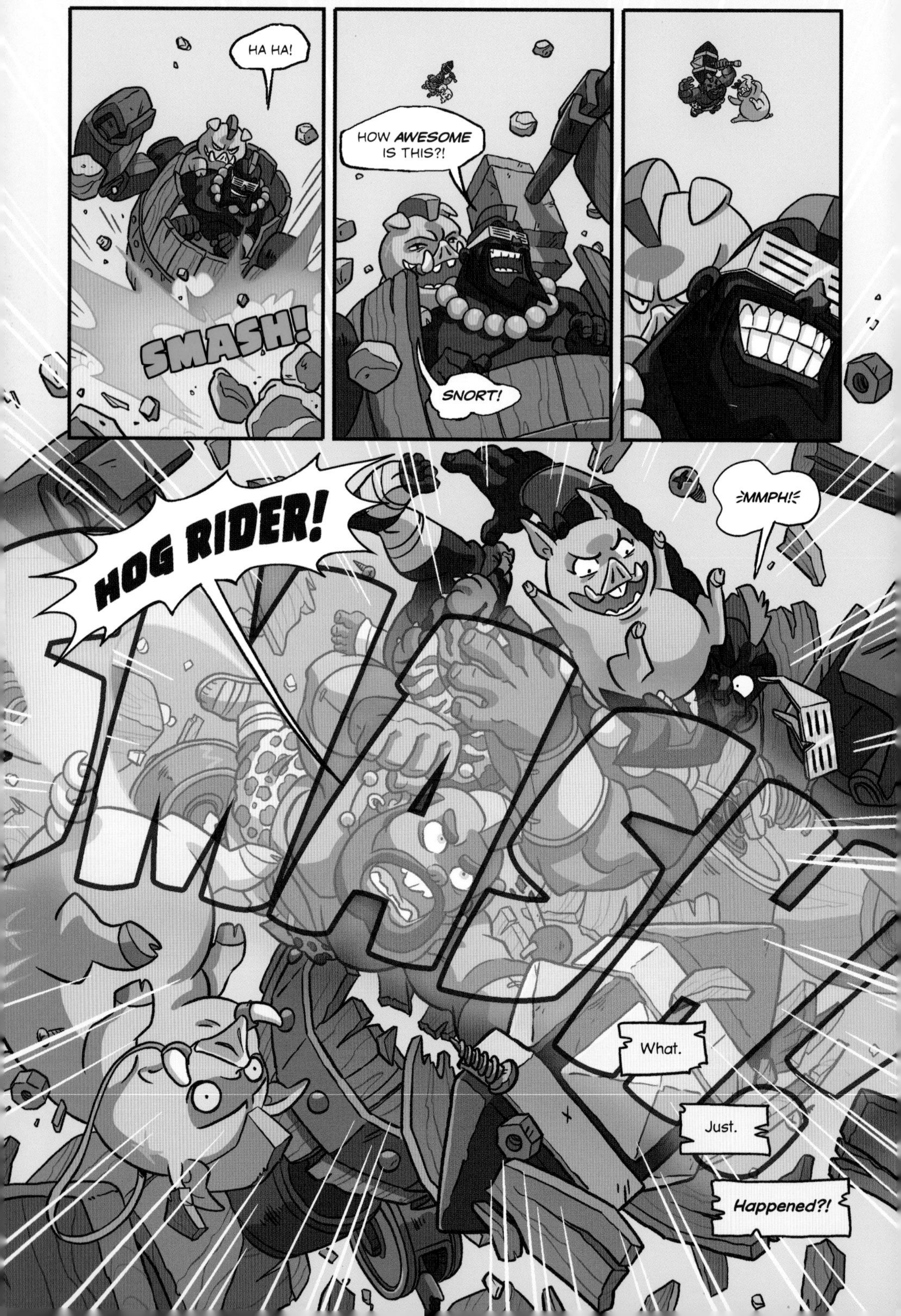
HA HA!
SMASH!
HOW AWESOME IS THIS?!
SNORT!
HOG RIDER!
MMPH!
What.
Just.
Happened?!

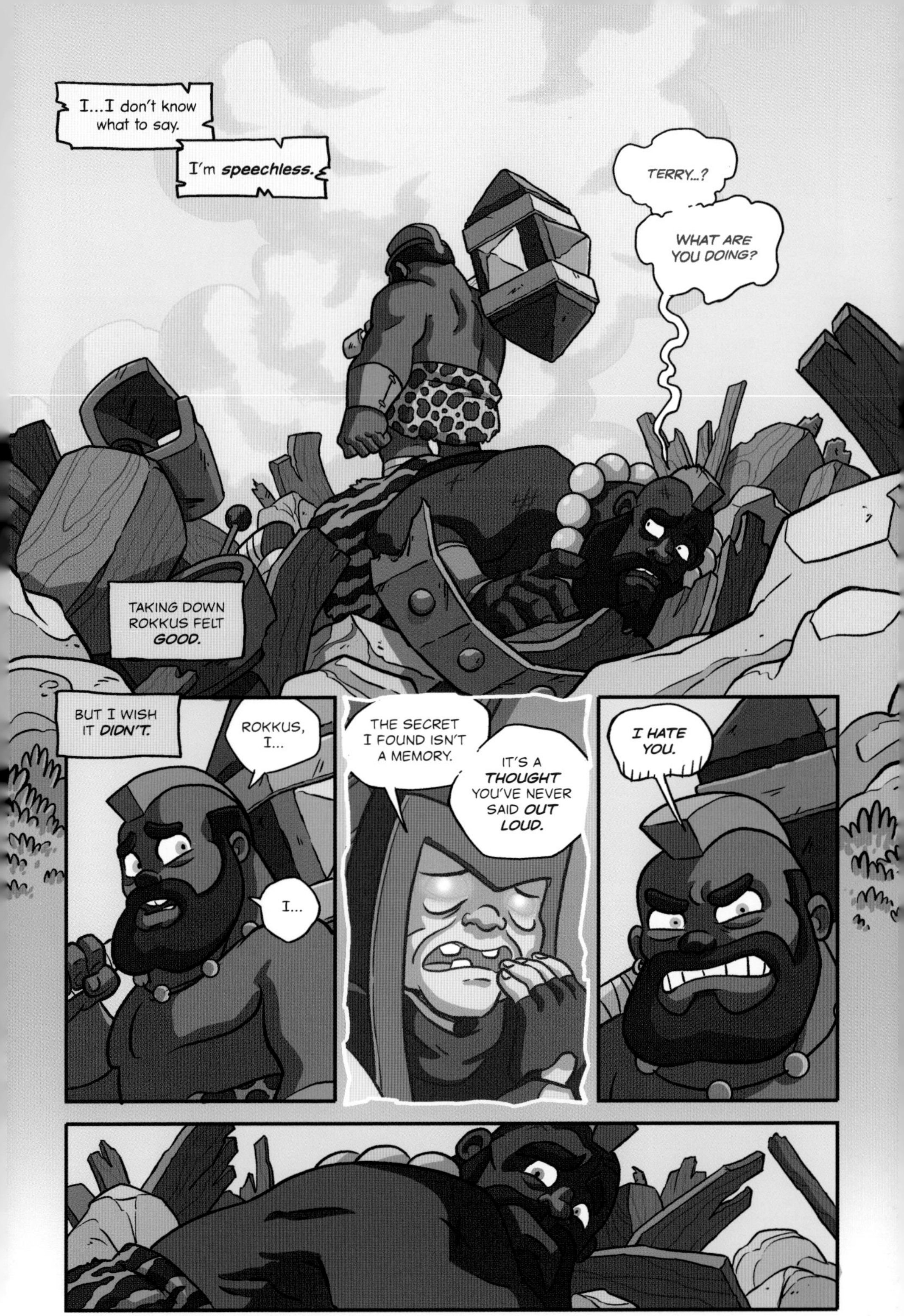

I...I don't know what to say.
I'm speechless.
TERRY...?
WHAT ARE YOU DOING?
TAKING DOWN ROKKUS FELT GOOD.
BUT I WISH IT DIDN'T.
ROKKUS, I...
I...
THE SECRET I FOUND ISN'T A MEMORY.
IT'S A THOUGHT YOU'VE NEVER SAID OUT LOUD.
I HATE YOU.

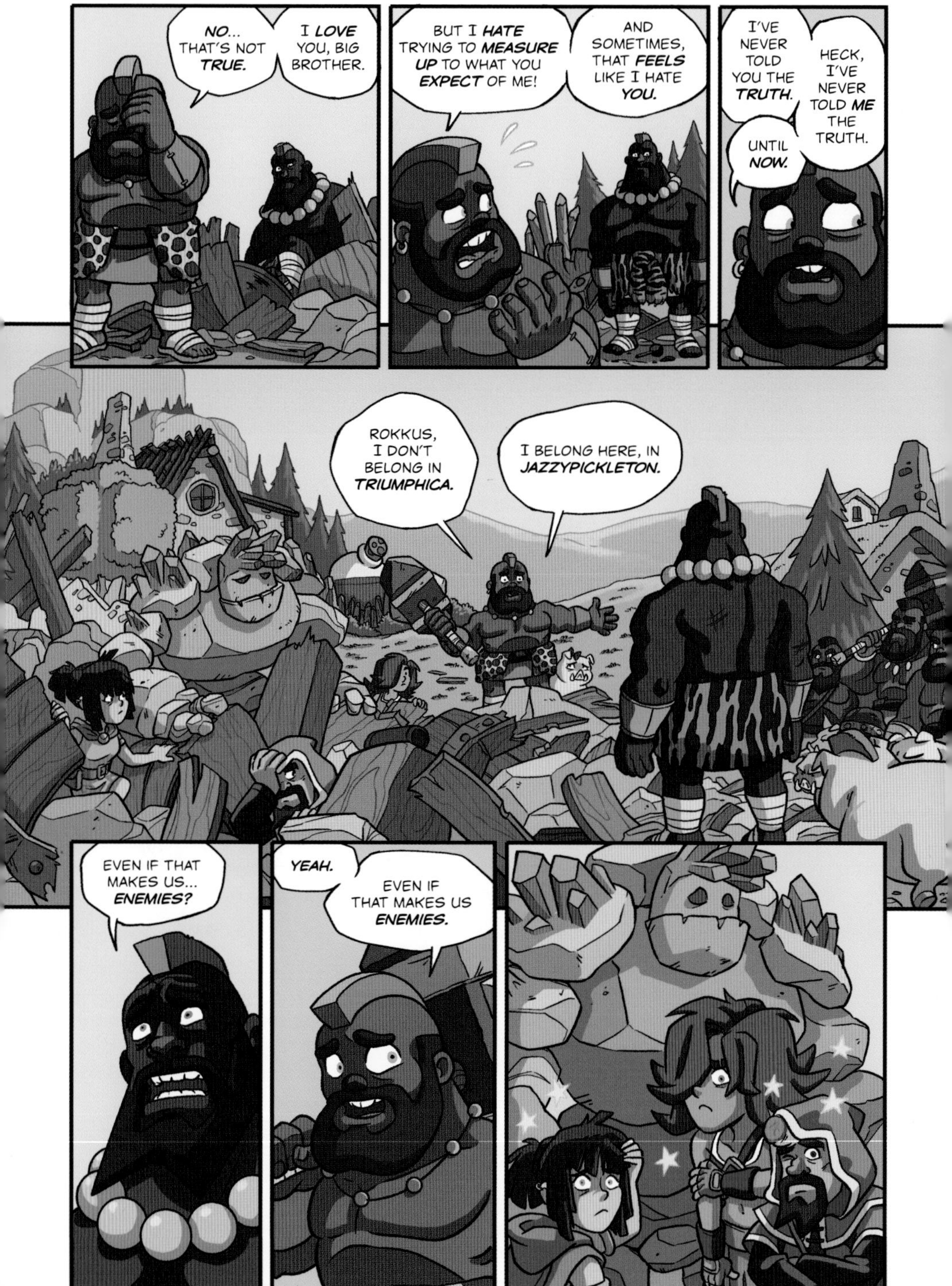

NO... THAT'S NOT TRUE.
I LOVE YOU, BIG BROTHER.
BUT I HATE TRYING TO MEASURE UP TO WHAT YOU EXPECT OF ME!
AND SOMETIMES, THAT FEELS LIKE I HATE YOU.
I'VE NEVER TOLD YOU THE TRUTH.
HECK, I'VE NEVER TOLD ME THE TRUTH.
UNTIL NOW.
ROKKUS, I DON'T BELONG IN TRIUMPHICA.
I BELONG HERE, IN JAZZYPICKLETON.
EVEN IF THAT MAKES US... ENEMIES?
YEAH.
EVEN IF THAT MAKES US ENEMIES.

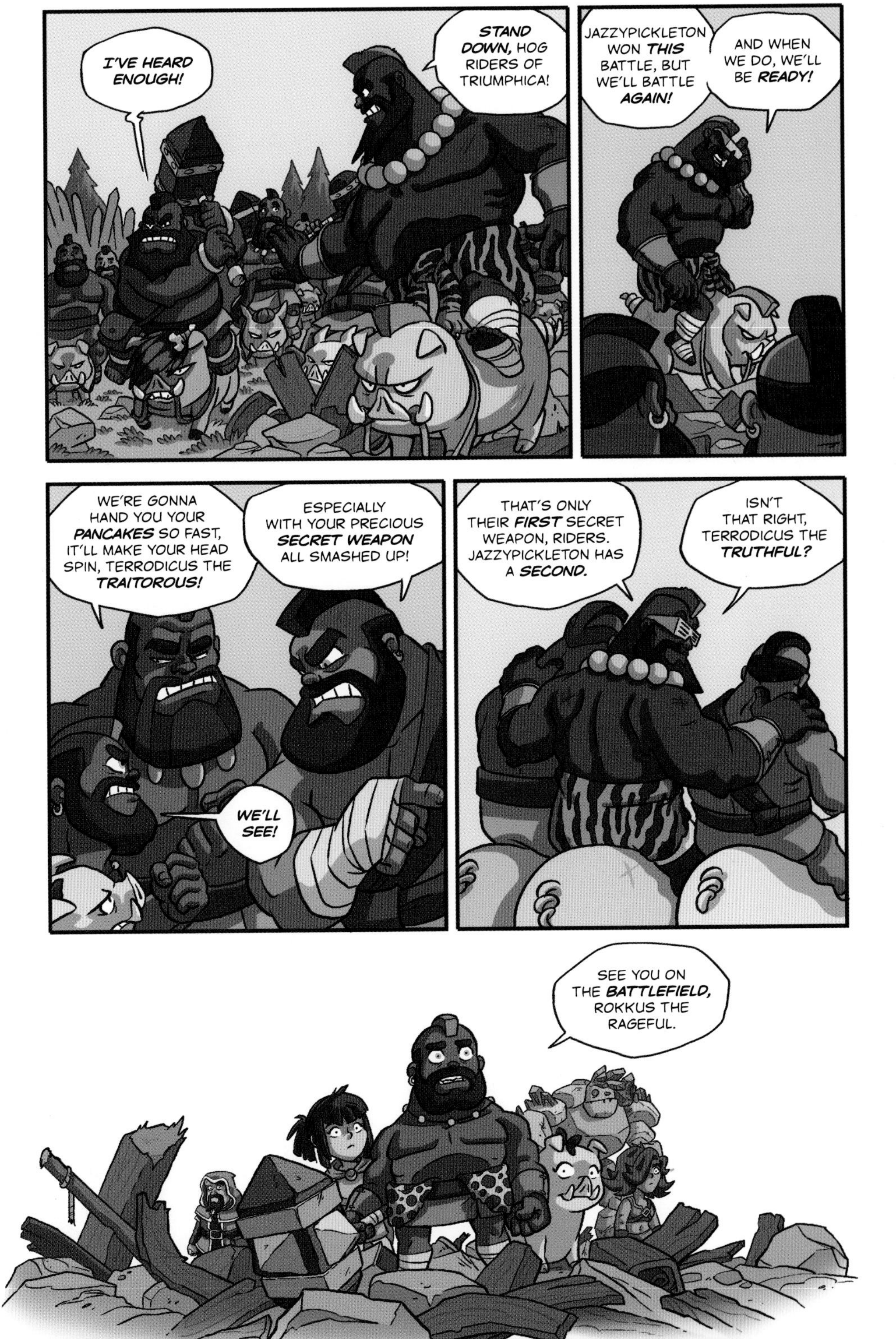

I'VE HEARD ENOUGH!
STAND DOWN, HOG RIDERS OF TRIUMPHICA!
JAZZYPICKLETON WON THIS BATTLE, BUT WE'LL BATTLE AGAIN!
AND WHEN WE DO, WE'LL BE READY!
WE'RE GONNA HAND YOU YOUR PANCAKES SO FAST, IT'LL MAKE YOUR HEAD SPIN, TERRODICUS THE TRAITOROUS!
ESPECIALLY WITH YOUR PRECIOUS SECRET WEAPON ALL SMASHED UP!
WE'LL SEE!
THAT'S ONLY THEIR FIRST SECRET WEAPON, RIDERS. JAZZYPICKLETON HAS A SECOND.
ISN'T THAT RIGHT, TERRODICUS THE TRUTHFUL?
SEE YOU ON THE BATTLEFIELD, ROKKUS THE RAGEFUL.

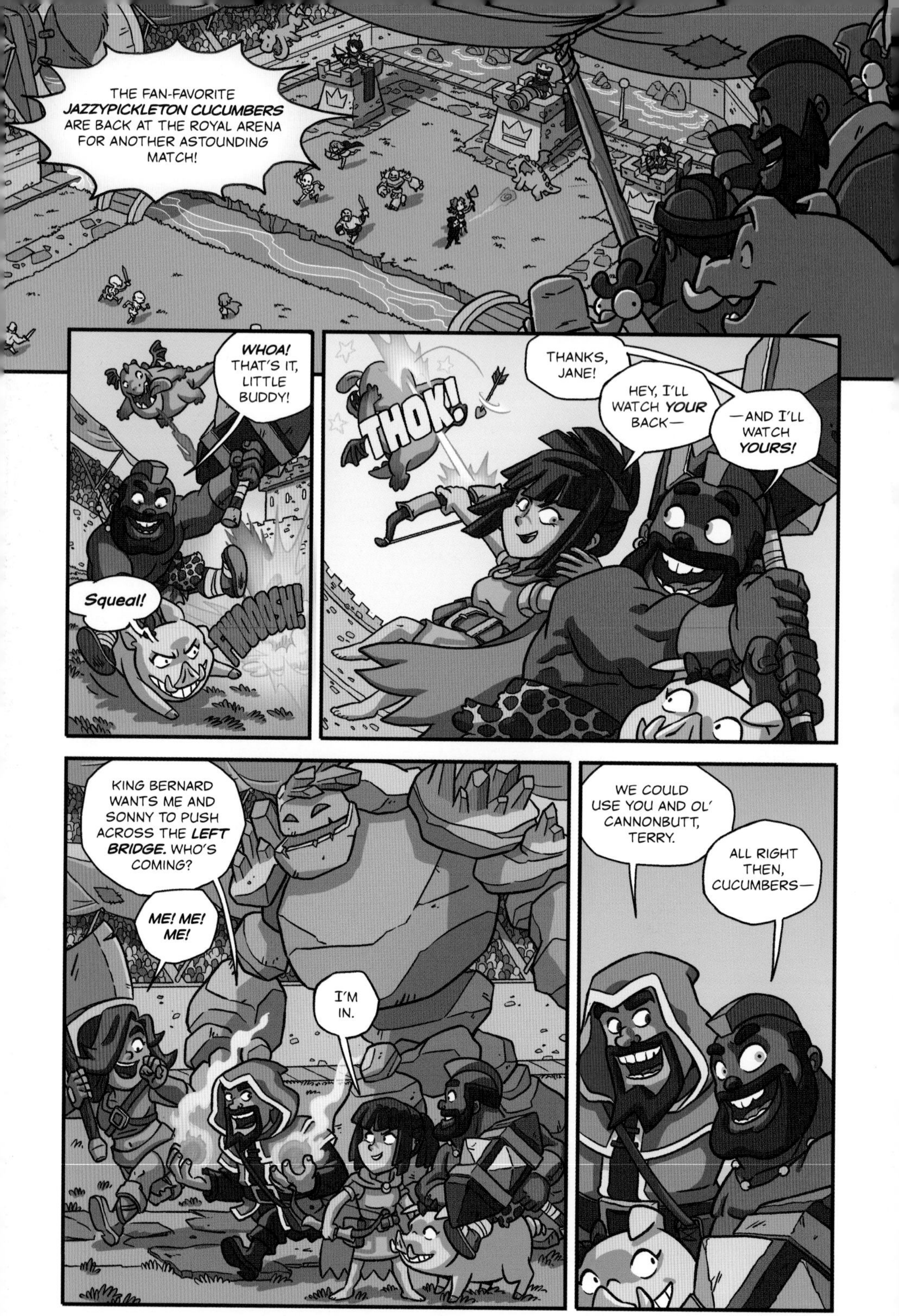
THE FAN-FAVORITE JAZZYPICKLETON CUCUMBERS ARE BACK AT THE ROYAL ARENA FOR ANOTHER ASTOUNDING MATCH!
WHOA! THAT'S IT, LITTLE BUDDY!
Squeal!
THOK!
THANKS, JANE!
HEY, I'LL WATCH YOUR BACK—
—AND I'LL WATCH YOURS!
KING BERNARD WANTS ME AND SONNY TO PUSH ACROSS THE LEFT BRIDGE. WHO'S COMING?
ME! ME! ME!
I'M IN.
WE COULD USE YOU AND OL' CANNONBUTT, TERRY.
ALL RIGHT THEN, CUCUMBERS—

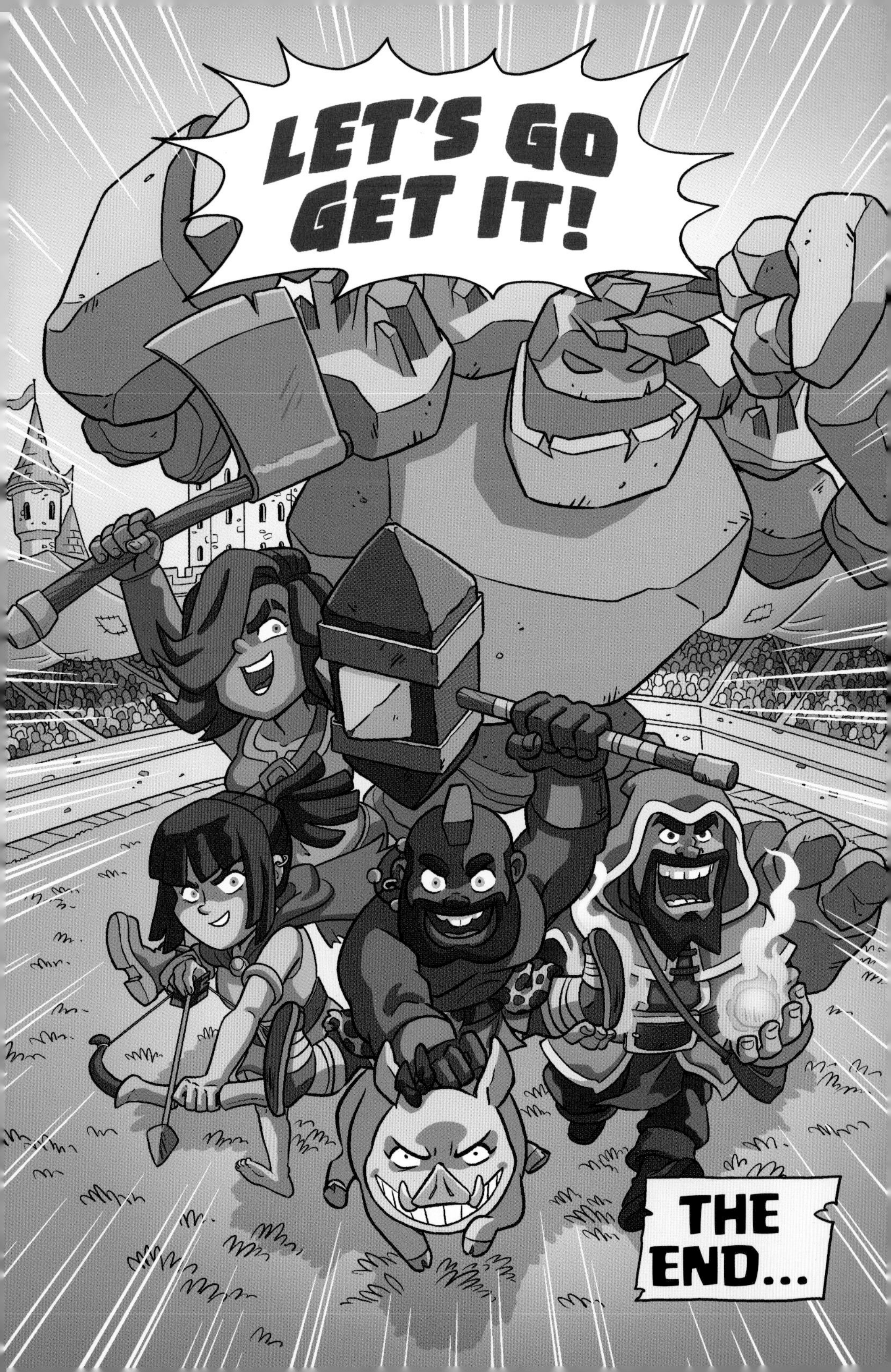
LET'S GO GET IT!
THE END...

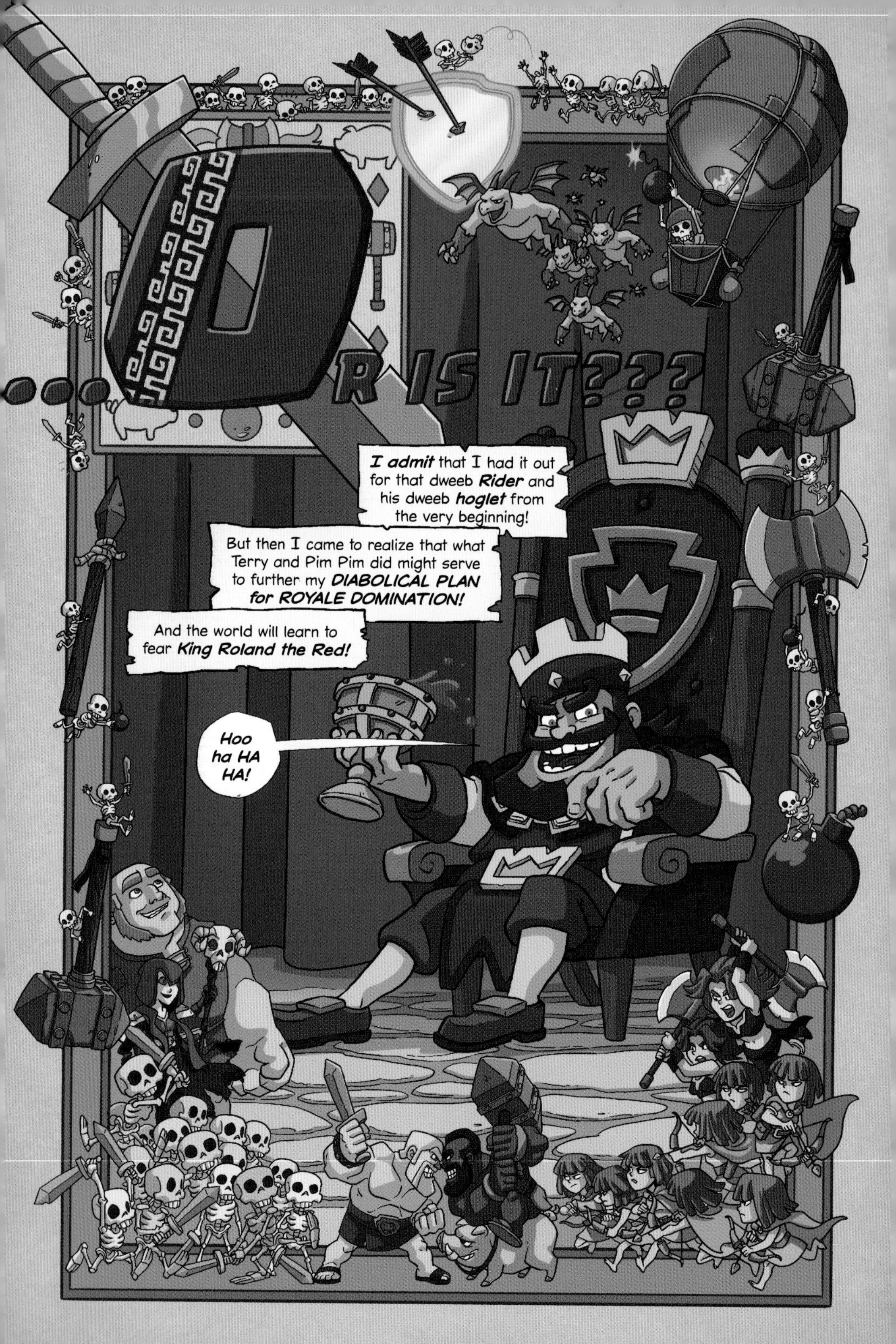
...OR IS IT???
I admit that I had it out for that dweeb Rider and his dweeb hoglet from the very beginning!
But then I came to realize that what Terry and Pim Pim did might serve to further my DIABOLICAL PLAN for ROYALE DOMINATION!
And the world will learn to fear King Roland the Red!
Hoo ha HA HA!

THE END!

THE BOOKS of CLASH

ART GALLERY

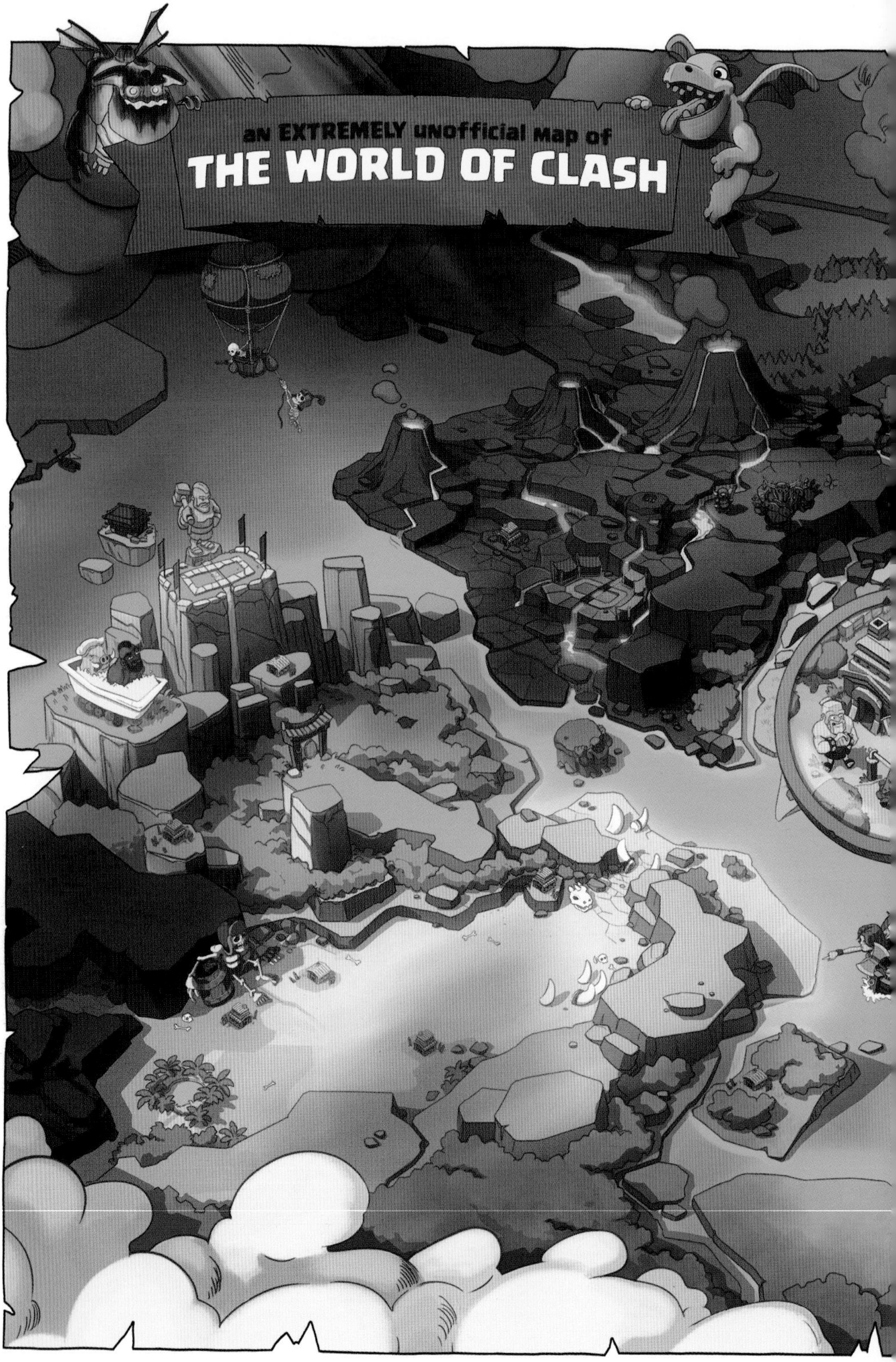
an EXTREMELY unofficial Map of
THE WORLD OF CLASH

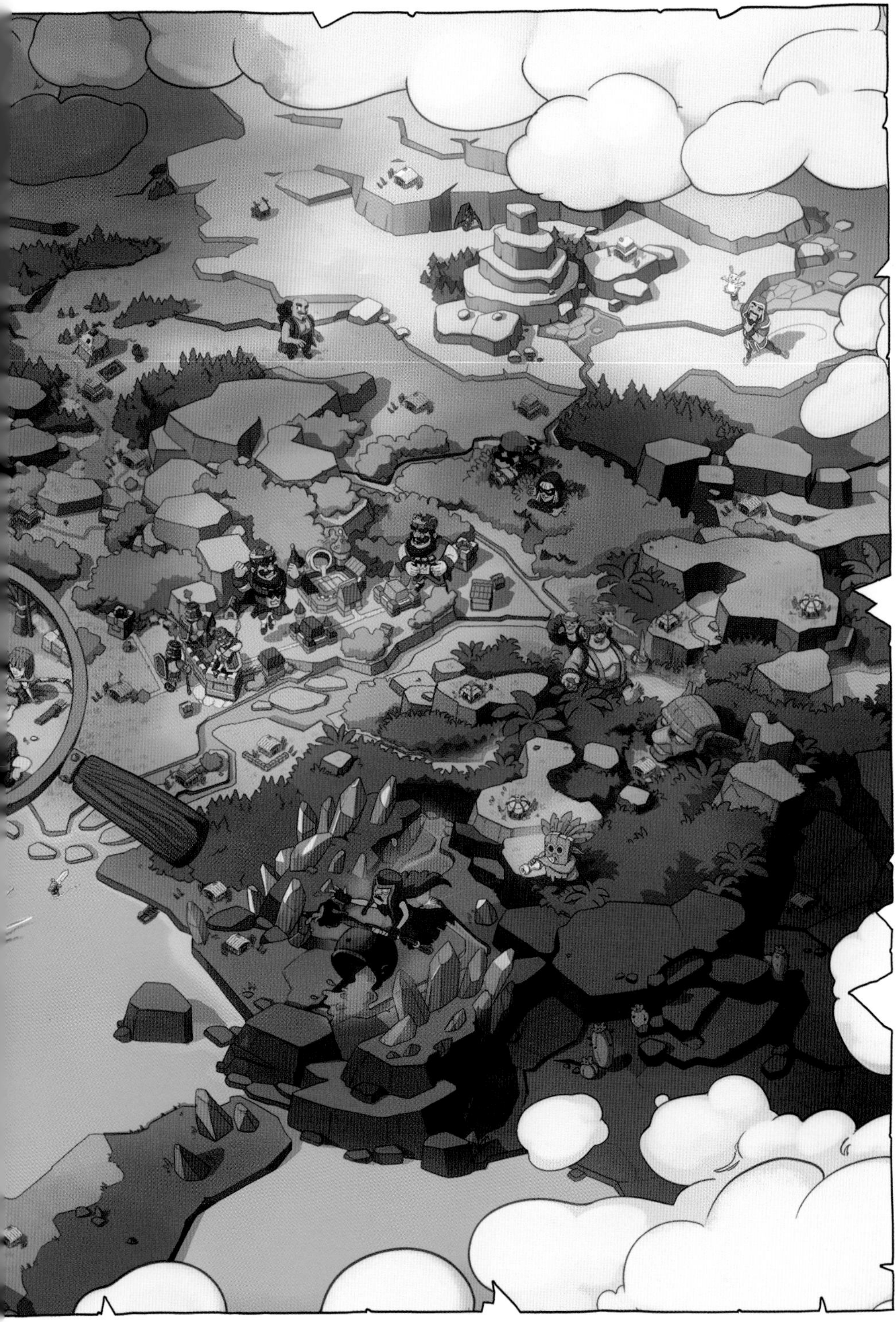

TERRY   PIM PIM

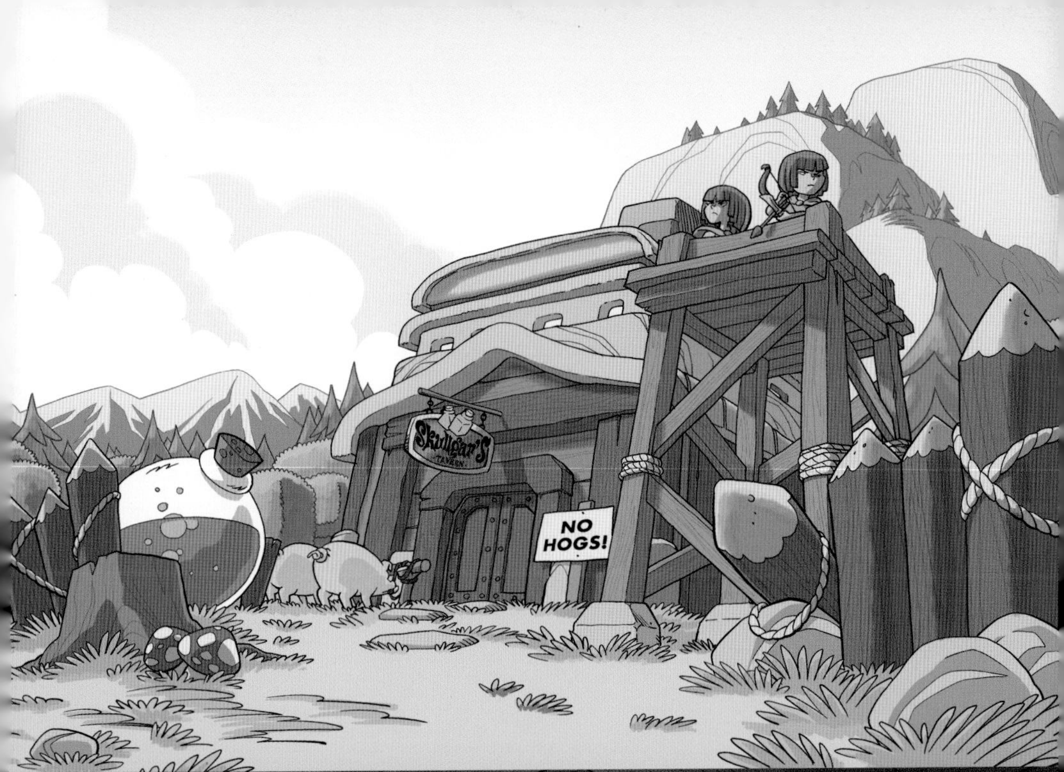
Skullgar's
TAVERN
NO HOGS!

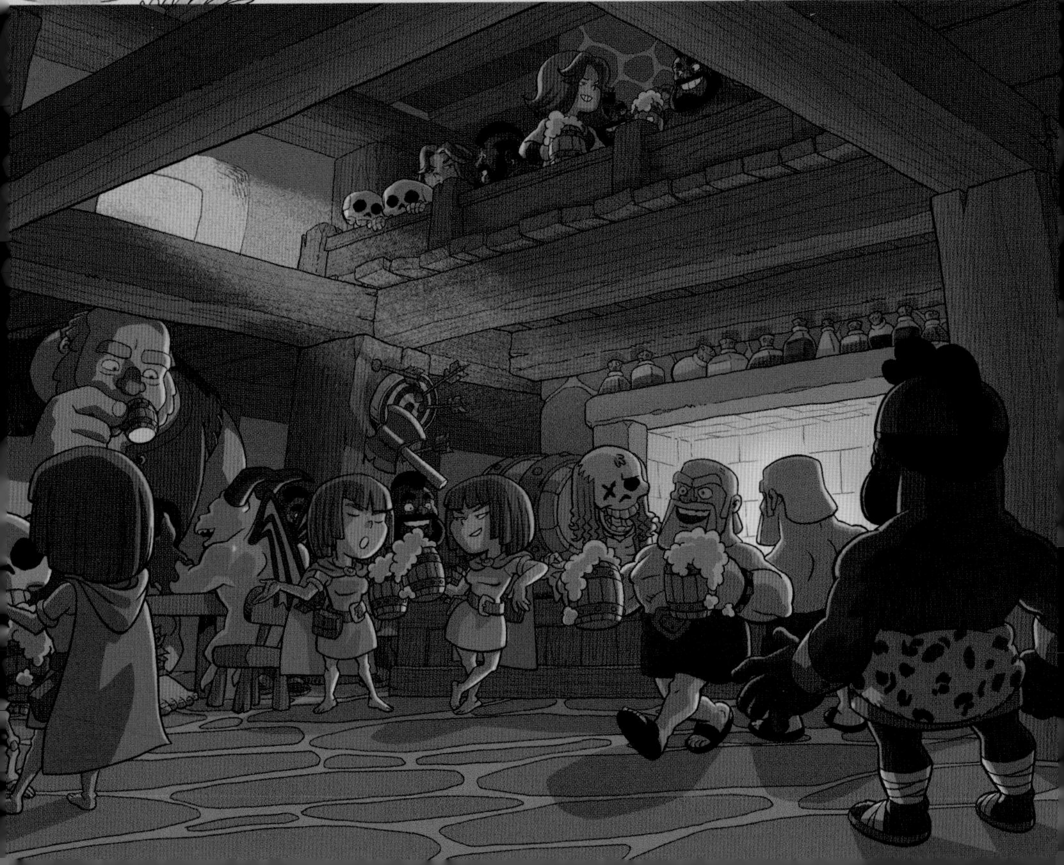

Introducing...

THE JAZZYPICKLETON CUCUMBERS

Jane

Yolanda

Zeke

SONNY

PAM

MASTERS OF CLASH

TIPS & TRICKS FROM CLASH OF CLANS & CLASH ROYALE'S MOST VALUABLE PLAYERS

CREATOR: GALADON

youtube.com/GaladonGaming

Hog Riders will always target *only* defensive structures until all are gone—so plan accordingly! Bring clean-up troops to clear the remaining buildings once your hogs have destroyed the defenses!

Hog Riders *love* Healing Spells! Healing Spells are a great pairing with any Hog Rider army—just remember to place them ahead of your hogs—predicting their path is a key to success!

A single Hog Rider can sometimes be used to activate the defensive Clan Castle as it will target defenses and often reach farther into a base than other troops!

CREATOR: OJ
youtube.com/OrangeJuiceGaming

THE ETERNAL FORMATION

The 2.6 hog cycle is one of the most versatile decks in Clash Royale history, which focuses on the Hog Rider being the main win condition while defending against opponents with low elixir cards. Knowing when to attack and when to defend is the key when trying to master the 2.6 hog cycle. Precise placement of units allows the user to defend against a wide variety of decks. The popularity of the 2.6 hog cycle has created an entire range of decks that use the same premise with one main win condition, while being able to defend various decks with low elixir cards.

THE LEGEND OF THE PIG PUSH

The hog hop is a technique that allows Hog Riders to ignore any buildings that would normally pull the hogs to the center of the map. To counteract this, if you plant a Hog Rider on the farthest tile of the bridge, the Hog Rider will hop the bridge so that buildings in the center are out of its field of vision.

THE PERFECT STORM

Activation of a king tower increases defensive power of the opponent immensely and should be avoided at all costs. Since Hog Riders only attack buildings, you can use a tornado to pull the Hog Rider to activate the king tower. If timed correctly, you can pull a Hog Rider so it completely ignores the Princess Towers.

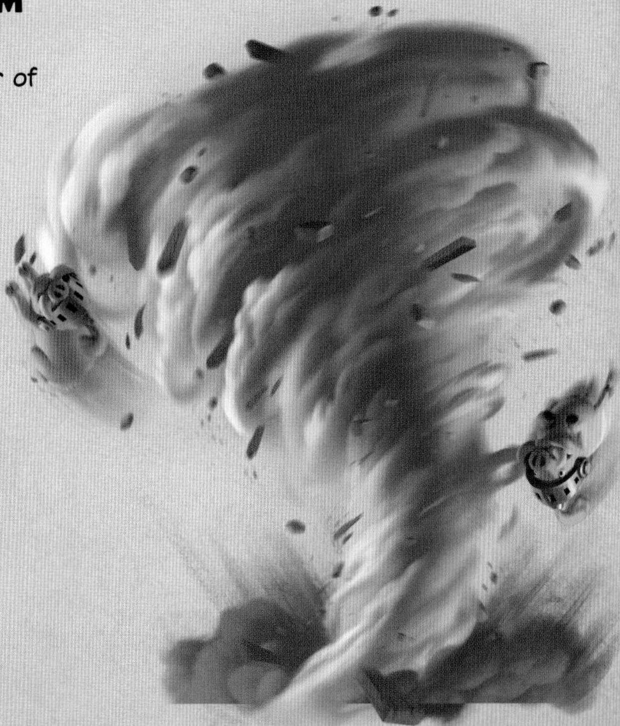

Gene Luen Yang writes, and sometimes draws, comic books and graphic novels. He was named a National Ambassador for Young People's Literature by the Library of Congress in 2016, and advocates for the importance of reading, especially reading diversely. *American Born Chinese*, his first graphic novel from First Second, was a winner of the Printz Award and an Eisner Award. His two-volume graphic novel, *Boxers & Saints*, won the LA Times Book Prize and was a National Book Award finalist. His nonfiction graphic novel, *Dragon Hoops*, received an Eisner Award and a Printz honor. His other comics work includes *Secret Coders* (with Mike Holmes), *The Shadow Hero* (with Sonny Liew), as well as *Superman Smashes the Klan* and the Avatar: The Last Airbender series (both with Gurihiru). In 2016, he was named a MacArthur Foundation Fellow.

Les McClaine is the Eisner Award–nominated author of *Jonny Crossbones*, *Life with Leslie*, *Repeat Until Death*, and *Highway 13*. He has also illustrated numerous comics including The Tick and The Middleman. His other illustration credits include *Tune: Still Life*, *Head Games: The Graphic Novel*, *Old Souls*, and *Maker Comics: Live Sustainably!*, all from First Second.

Alison Acton is a Canadian artist with a background in comics and traditional animation. She's worked for studios like Spumco, Pocket Gems, and Big Jump, and publishers like HarperCollins, Tokyopop, and First Second. She loves creating expressive characters, writing snarky dialogue, teaching jiu-jitsu, and taking long dog walks away from her three boys who always invade the office and shed Legos EVERYWHERE.

:01

Fi̶r̶st̶ S̶e̶con̶d̶

Published by First Second
First Second is an imprint of Roaring Brook Press,
a division of Holtzbrinck Publishing Holdings Limited Partnership
120 Broadway, New York, NY 10271
firstsecondbooks.com
mackids.com

Library of Congress Cataloging-in-Publication Data is available.

Our books may be purchased in bulk for promotional, educational, or business use.
Please contact your local bookseller or the Macmillan Corporate and
Premium Sales Department at (800) 221-7945 ext. 5442
or by email at MacmillanSpecialMarkets@macmillan.com.

FIRST
EDITION

First edition, 2023
Edited by Mark Siegel and Heather Antos
Cover design by Kirk Benshoff
Interior book design by Angela Boyle and Molly Johanson
Pencils by Les McClaine
Inks by Alison Acton
Color by Karina Edwards and Alex Campbell
Production editing by Dawn Ryan and Avia Perez

Thumbnailed on an iPad Pro with an Apple Pencil. Penciled in
Clip Studio Paint EX using a Cintiq 27QHD with a Mac Mini. Inked digitally in
Photoshop on a Cintiq. Colored digitally in Adobe Photoshop. Lettered with the
Dave Gibbons Lower font from Comicraft

China by 1010 Printing International Ltd., North Point, Hong Kong

ISBN 978-1-250-81626-9 (paperback)
1 3 5 7 9 10 8 6 4 2

ISBN 978-1-250-81625-2 (hardcover)
1 3 5 7 9 10 8 6 4 2

Don't miss your next favorite book from First Second!
For the latest updates go to firstsecondnewsletter.com and sign up for our
enewsletter.

BY ART
WE LIVE

Meanwhile...

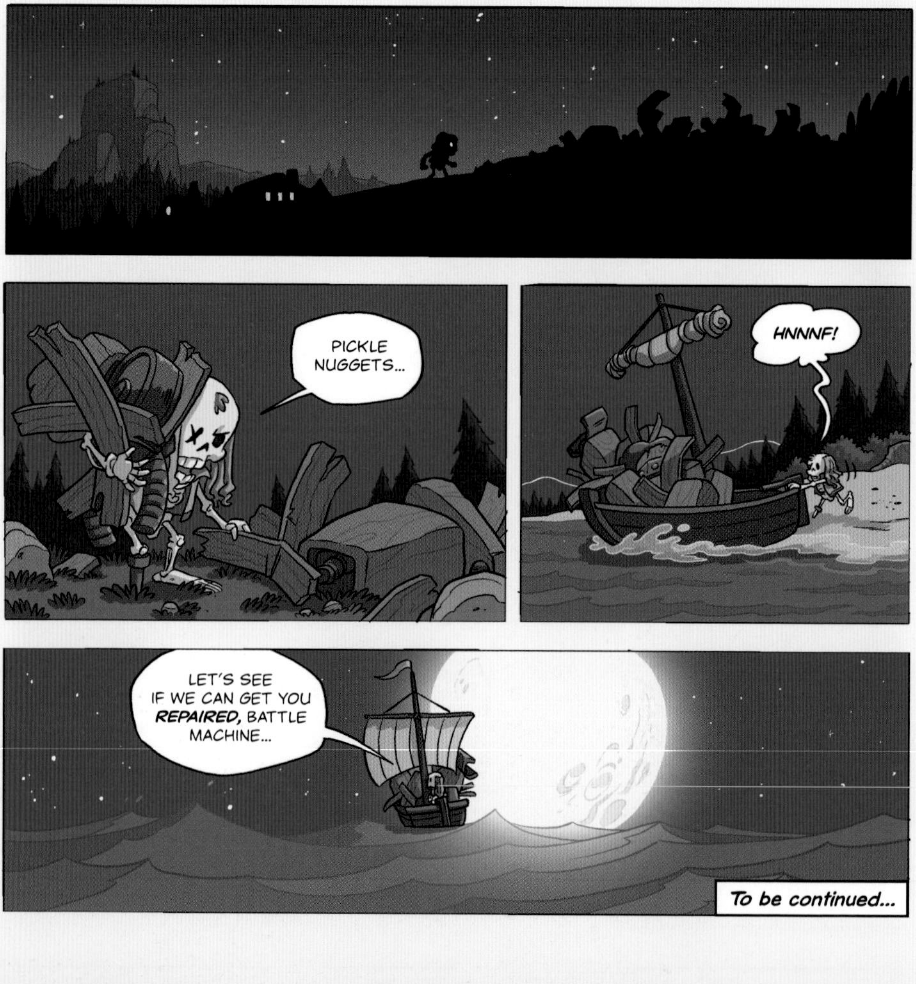
PICKLE NUGGETS...
HNNNF!
LET'S SEE IF WE CAN GET YOU ***REPAIRED,*** BATTLE MACHINE...
To be continued...